A QUEEN

by Sam Burnell

First published in eBook and paperback 2017
Second Edition 2019

•

© Sam Burnell 2017

•

The right of Sam Burnell to be identified as the author of this work has been asserted by her in accordance with the Copyright, Designs and Patents Act 1988.

All rights reserved. No part of this publication may be reproduced, stored in or introduced into a retrieval system, or transmitted, in any form, or by any means (electronic, mechanical, photocopying, recording or otherwise) without the prior written permission of the writer. Any person who does any unauthorised act in relation to this publication may be liable to criminal prosecution and civil claims for damages.

Thank you for respecting the hard work of this author.

Please note, this book is written in British English, so some spellings will vary from US English.

The Mercenary For Hire Series

A Queen's Spy
A Queen's Traitor
A Queen's Mercenary
A Queen's Knight
A Queen's Assassin
A Queen's Executioner
A Queen's Champion
A Queen's Conspirator
Audio Books

For All My Children

Jules
Saffron
Savannah
Spyke

Character List

The English Court

John Dudley - Duke of Northumberland
Jane Grey - Earl of Suffolk's daughter married to Guildford Dudley
Henry Sidney - Northumberland's son-in-law and friend of Edward VI
Duke of Suffolk - Henry Grey - Jane's father
Thomas Seymour - husband of Catherine Parr, Henry VIII's last wife
Sir Thomas Wyatt - Conspirator against Mary I
Edward Courtenay - Plantagenet descendent with a tenuous claim to the throne
Earl of Derby - Mary's supporter
Lord Effingham - Mary's councillor
Kate Ashley - Elizabeth's governess
Renard - Spanish Ambassador
Henry Walgrave - Renard's man
Thomas Pierce - Renard's man
Somer - Crown Servant

The Byrne Household

Edward Byrne - One of Northumberland's conspirators
Judith Byrne - His wife
Geoffrey Byrne - His son
Whickham - One of Northumberland's conspirators

The de Bernay Household

Peter de Bernay – A supporter of Mary, and owner of Assingham
Anne de Bernay – his wife
Catherine de Bernay – his daughter
Martha – servant
John – servant

Richard's Mercenary Band

Dan – Also a family servant
Mat
Marc
Froggy Tate
Alan
Robby
Pierre
Martin
Gavin

Harry's Men

Peter Hardwood
Willy
Gad
Hal
Nancy – Hal's sister in law
Spratty

Other Characters

Jamie – A priest at Burton Village

Mya - A London Pawn broker
Robert Hastley - Northumberland's supporter, owner of
Burton
Guy - Hastley's servant
Knoll - Miller at Burton
Carew - One of Wyatt's conspirators
Hanwyn - Carew's servant
Sir Ayscough - Lincoln Sheriff

Edward VI Devise for the Succession

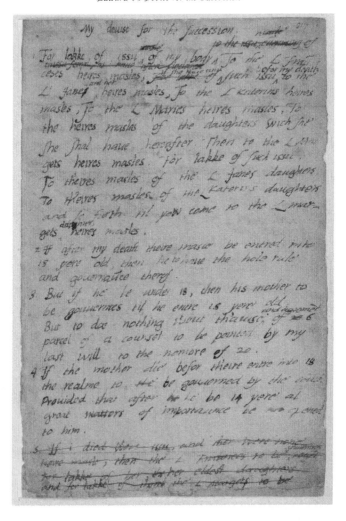

Introduction

"*Richard Fitzwarren is* joining the hunt."

The news passed quickly amongst those gathering for the morning expedition, spreading with it a palpable tension. When Robert Fitzwarren uttered his brother's name, it was with scornful contempt. His servants exchanged expectant glances; they knew of the enmity between the two, although not the cause. When they spoke, it was quietly, in low voices, asking each other, 'Would he dare to come?' and 'Would Robert kill him if he did?'

The mist still clung to the fields, stealing the colour from the trees as the group of men readied themselves for the chase through fog-riddled moor and boggy marshland. A mounted man at the top of a hill cast a watchful gaze upon them. Although a mile distant, the muffled conversations, the laughter and the barking of the dogs still reached his ears. It might have been a pleasant scene had they not been hunting for him. Automatically Richard's hand went to his doublet, and he felt beneath the material the hard square outline of the folded parchment. This was the confrontation that he had waited for. Robert would not be able to escape from the facts he carried with him. Holding his own horse still, Richard Fitzwarren waited.

The pack broke and a group of riders headed up the hill towards him. Richard glared at the man at their head. This time, Robert... He was ready for the confrontation and was surprised when the group of riders slowed and stopped a good distance away. Too late, he realised their intention. Hauling hard on the reins, the horse's serpentine neck twisted towards the trees, his heels hard on her sides, pressing her to flight.

Steel tipped, the wooden shaft loosed from the bow, flew with deadly accuracy and tore into her neck as the mare turned her proud head towards the sanctuary of the trees.

Taking only three more trembling steps, the dying horse collapsed beneath him, throwing him to the ground. Instinctively, Richard slipped his feet from the stirrups as he fell, pushing away from her crushing body. The fall was awkward, the mare's last convulsive shake pitching him hard against a fallen bough. The snap was sickening as his left arm broke.

The mare's faltering final steps had brought him closer to the safety of the trees. Dizzy, breathing heavily, and with his stomach threatening to betray him, Richard scrambled into the leafy refuge. Behind him, the hooves of his pursuers' horses pounded up the hill.

Leaning heavily against a tree, eyes closed, he fought to stay conscious. Sweat beaded on his forehead, his body shook, and his stomach convulsed. Retching made the splintered bone grate. Richard realised his vision was darkening.

No, no, not now. Please God, not now.

He wiped the back of his hand across his mouth, forcing himself to take even breaths.

He had been stupid, so damned stupid. What had possessed him to think his brother would do no more than confront him? He knew Robert better than that. Now they would run him to ground and he couldn't even give himself the satisfaction of a fighting end.

Biting back a cry he pushed the broken arm inside his jacket. Damn Robert to Hell! Could this day get any worse?

With the arm supported, the pain lessened. The trunk behind him was taking his weight, and Richard was grateful for the respite. With care, he drew his sword and was thankful to feel, for the last time, the familiar weight in his hand of the finely-edged Toledo blade. The hand-and-a-half bastard sword was a heavy weapon. Richard knew he would have difficulty wielding it with just one hand. The motto on the quillons beneath the hilt mocked him: *Let them hate so long as they fear.* Robert might hate him but he doubted at this moment if he could instil fear in anyone.

Robert's men were closing in, thrashing their way through the small wood, shouting to each other as they searched for him. It wasn't going to be long before someone found him. Instinct tightened his grip on the leather hilt, whitening his knuckles.

As he waited, one of Robert's men tethered their horse at the forest's edge, near the dead mare, and began to walk towards him. Richard's eyes were fastened on his face; he knew the man would not see him where he leaned heavily against the tree.

Don't turn around...keep walking. Richard's gaze switched to the horse. Could he make it?

But turn around the man did and only feet from Richard whose blade he found levelled at his chest. In a straight fight, on a good day, Richard would not have waited but with a broken arm, he didn't weigh his chances of success that highly. In fustian and old leather, Richard guessed the man was a servant, not one of his brother's companions.

"Hold! This is not our argument." Richard's voice was taut with pain as he delivered the words.

His steel-grey eyes held the other's blue ones. The servant raised his hands in a gesture of supplication and took a measured step backward. About to push himself from the tree and make his unsteady way towards the horse, Richard stopped when another mount came crashing through the undergrowth. It was Harry, his cousin, his brother's lapdog and most ardent admirer.

Jesus. Harry! I was wrong. Today could indeed get worse.

"Jack, have you seen him?" the rider yelled at the servant. "Robert has placed a purse on his head."

Then the unexpected happened.

Jack stepped towards Harry, took hold of his boot with both hands, rived it from the stirrup and thrust him over the horse's back. Harry, wailing, landed on his back on the forest floor.

Richard needed no further invitation. He caught the reins Jack threw at him and hauled himself into the saddle. Turning the horse, he joined his rescuer, and the pair pushed the horses into a gallop down the hillside.

Chapter One

London - February 1553

John Dudley, Duke of Northumberland, the most powerful man in England, was nervous. He found himself pacing outside the bedchamber of his young king. Henry Grey, Duke of Suffolk, watched him from where he sat near one of the windows and shook his head.

Grey was a man of ambition and determination. In Henry's court he had been the old king's sword bearer, held offices of state, and even been part of the glut of youthful courtiers the King had surrounded himself with. Grey had been among those leading the troops that captured Bologna, an able soldier and capable political animal whose personal aspirations were limitless. He had found himself ousted from Edward's court by Somerset, England's protector, who recognised all too well the threat Grey posed, for his marriage to Frances Brandon had connected his family to the throne. Somerset's desire to hold the power alone led to his downfall; he had been cleared from Grey's path when the young king had signed the warrant for the protector's execution.

"For God's sake, man, sit down!" Suffolk sounded exasperated.

Northumberland paused in his traverse of the room and turned towards the speaker. "I can't just sit in here while those fools in there continue to mistreat him, can I?"

"John, there's not a lot else you can do, is there?" Suffolk spoke bluntly, his words lacking in concern.

Northumberland crossed the room and took a seat opposite. If Edward died, then it would be Suffolk who would hold the balance of power. The Duke knew it, and his patience with Grey's ambition was wearing thin. "It seems I am thwarted at every turn."

Suffolk sighed. "He will be well again. You need to have faith in that. He has been ill before. Remember how unwell he was before Christmas and he recovered, didn't he?"

Northumberland nodded, for Suffolk was indeed right. He was now, in February, no worse than he had been then and the lad had recovered. "We are finally steering the country to a smoother path. Edward ill is the last thing I need."

"You have Edward's ear. Now that Somerset is gone, you are regent in all but name. Look at the success of Parliament's measures to quell unrest. You've secured peace, and that is an achievement," Suffolk said.

"It's an uneasy one though, Henry, and you know it," Northumberland replied.

"It was always going to be difficult. England has suffered such a run of bad harvests for the last three years, the sweating sickness has reduced her labourers and prices are spiralling ever higher. What else could you do? Somerset pressed Edward twice to debase the coinage and look where that got us?" Suffolk grumbled. Somerset's fiscal measures had persuaded Parliament to debase the coinage twice, once in '49 and then again in '51, destroying faith in the currency.

"It's left us with high prices and unrest, but these are minor troughs. They have to be. With a steady hand guiding England, it can develop and grow. I know it can. But we need Edward to be strong and well," Northumberland said. He knew he should have been happier. He had all he could want. The power was his; he had outwardly succeeded. However, the pivotal point of his power, the keystone upon which it relied, was crumbling. Edward VI, King of England, was dying, and despite Suffolk's reassurances, he knew in his heart this was the truth. To be cheated of it all by death seemed such a cruel turn of fate. Northumberland needed Edward; without him, his fall was sure. He had made too many enemies by his own hand as he rose toward his supreme goal.

The door opened quietly and Northumberland was joined by Henry Sidney, his son-in-law and the King's close friend. Edward feared the doctors, who had yet again forced their ministrations on his shattered body and had wanted the comfort of his friend's company.

"Well, Henry, what news?" Northumberland asked.

Henry Sidney shook his head. He did not meet the Duke's enquiring gaze. Tired himself, he dropped into a chair by the fire, any propriety forgotten.

"Henry, tell me!" Northumberland demanded.

"He is dying." Henry quietly supplied the information the Duke desperately wanted but feared to hear.

"By God, they don't know what they are talking about," Northumberland boomed.

Henry tried to grasp the Northumberland's sleeve, but the other had launched himself so rapidly at the door that he missed, catching instead a handful of the ermine-trimmed cloak. He pulled on it sharply. "No, no, you can't." Henry was drawn from his seat by the effort required to stop Northumberland.

"Why?" Northumberland turned angrily on him, hauling the fabric from Henry's hand.

"He doesn't know. He doesn't know! To tell him may... Please, spare him this. Wait until they emerge, but please..." Henry pleaded; he had a genuine love for Edward.

"Yes, yes... Sit down." Northumberland moved to seat himself opposite Henry Sidney. "You are right, the boy is ill. There is no need to add to it with the lunatic ravings of these so-called medics. He needs peace and rest. This has always served him well before. The lad is exhausted. I have told them he needs to be left alone. Time and the Lord will see him well." Northumberland spoke to himself, uttering the reassurances he needed to hear. Perhaps their vocalisation would lead to their reality, the worry for his own fortunes written plainly on his face.

For the first time, Henry experienced a bitter dislike of his father-in-law.

Since February, Edward had worsened and Northumberland finally acknowledged what the doctors had told him. Edward, though, variously accepted and denied it. He had been ill so often during his life that he had come to expect recovery. As Edward's life-force ebbed, all the power -all Northumberland had worked for–was slipping through his fingers. To Northumberland, his own loss felt physical. Worse than that, he was being forced to bend to the will of Henry VIII. Every time he walked under the portraits of England's largest monarch, he was sure they were laughing at him.

Northumberland was desperate. And what he was doing bore this out. Under the Succession Act of 1544, Henry VIII had left a son as his heir. If Edward died childless, the throne would pass to Mary and then to Elizabeth. If this failed, the crown would go to the male descendants of Henry's younger sister, Lady Frances Grey. This was Northumberland's key, and his plan was both simple and crude: Lady Frances was blessed with daughters only and as such, there were no eligible male heirs. So, to generate one in whom the succession could be lodged, he married his son, Guildford Dudley, to the eldest daughter, Jane Grey. If Guildford could get the girl with child quickly, then he had another heir.

In May he held a 'Devise for the succession', signed by Edward, leaving his crown to the male heirs of Lady Frances Grey. Hopefully, the brat, Jane, could be brought to bed of one before Edward died. He closed his ears to the legality of the document. For him, the signature and seal of Edward were enough to carry its weight. Legally, the document could not stand flouting as it did the Succession Act of 1544, and also because it named non-existent persons as heirs. He relied on time: time for Jane to produce him an heir and then the document could be safely amended to name the child, and time hopefully for Edward VI to see it born.

Chapter Two

France – March 1553

The sea was stormy, which was bad, both for those who earned their living from its depths and those who wished to travel over its surface. Jack was in the latter category.

A storm, lasting three days so far, had kept the boat he was to take to England tied securely in the harbour, leaving Jack to loiter in the alehouses of Dieppe, trying to amuse himself with his scant supply of coins. Lodging at the Firkin, an English-owned inn, he waited with other travellers for the winds to die and the white-topped waves to lessen their furious pounding of the sea defences.

Thunder clouded the sky, making it prematurely dark. Jack stared out to sea; somewhere out there was England, and between him and his home, the sea boiled. Jack got the distinct feeling that England didn't want him back.

Opening the door, the inn welcomed him with smoky air bearing a heavy odour of dampened wool, stale food, and the sea coal that crackled in the fire. The room, with its low ceiling and haphazard arrangement of benches and tables, was warm and friendly; the contrast with the inhospitable evening outside was stark. Most customers sat in small groups, the benches pulled in a semi-circle around the fire. The seats that were vacant were those against the shadowed walls.

Jack, uncomfortably aware of the damp eking its way through his rain-sodden cloak, pulled it from his shoulders, shaking the water from it. Shabby from the years of being slept in, ridden in, and fought in, the splotched mud could detract little from it that time and use had not already claimed.

"Hey! Watch what you are doing," complained a voice loudly in English with an accent from the Fens.

Lowering the cloak, he found the source of the words; a red-faced priest he had splashed with mud and water.

Mumbling an automatic apology, sodden drapery over his arm, Jack made to leave.

"And what sort of apology do you call that?" The little man caught Jack's sleeve in a wiry grasp.

"I said I was sorry," Jack growled, his words not at all in accordance with his tone.

"Well, you don't sound as if you mean it! Words spoken without conviction are, as Saul taught us, a sin against the ears."

"What do you want me to do?" Jack wrenched his arm free.

The priest observed him closely from under bushy eyebrows and an expansive forehead wrinkled like the leather of an ill-cured hide. Small black eyes narrowed as a thought seemed to occur to him. "Sit." The priest's voice was used to commanding from the pulpit.

"What for?" Jack snapped.

"Because I asked you to. Now, sit down." A naked leg protruded from his robes, pushing a stool towards Jack.

Jack, grunting, took the offered seat, depositing his saturated cloak over the end of the bench.

"I'm guessing you weren't off anywhere in particular?" the priest enquired further.

Jack shook his head in reply.

"Well, you don't look much like good company, do you?"

"Should I be?" Jack's annoyance had not completely subsided. A sinew toughened hand reached again for his cloak. Jack had no intention of being berated by an old cleric in dirty vestments with an attitude that matched the weather.

"Just hold your tongue, will you?" A look of long-suffering creased the priest's face. "I'll make a deal with you. Match that and we'll spend a pleasant evening together. That is the least you can do for soaking a poor old man." Three coins appeared on the table.

"Poor old man? There's an ox beneath that robe. You'll get no sympathy from me," Jack scoffed, though he couldn't keep an amused look from his face.

"I'm not asking you for sympathy, just to match that." A bony forefinger, almost skeletal beneath papered skin, prodded the largest of the three coins.

Jack recognised them for what they were, enough to pay for half a pitcher of ale. He wondered if the priest habitually passed his evenings at the expense of others. He was well enough acquainted with the game to know that holy orders would not bar the cleric from guzzling his ale at twice his own rate. But then, he had little money left, and it was an option preferable to returning to his room to wait and see if morning brought pleasant weather.

"I don't know why, old man, but I'll match you," Jack conceded.

"Call me Jamie, my son." The priest grinned, a little too triumphantly for Jack's liking.

Jack scooped up the coins, added his own, and busied himself with ordering ale. His appearance marked him out, and he easily secured the attention of the serving staff. Jack's blond hair, darkened by water, was as lustrous as a May dance maidens when dry. Anyone casting a glance towards him would see the brown leather jerkin, its stitching slightly frayed at one shoulder, the elbows and front smoothed and darkened with the dirt of wear. The only evidence of care was on the wide, polished sword belt and shining quillons below the hilt. Possibly once a soldier, they would conclude, and now probably for hire; recent times did not look as if they had been too kind.

Jack was surprised to find how easy a companion Jamie was, and he talked freely as they shared the pitcher of warm ale. He was further surprised, and a little ashamed, when the jug was emptied and Jamie insisted on paying in full for a fresh one. The discourse so far had covered such general topics as the ill-health of the English monarch, the continued strings of power gathered in fistfuls by Northumberland, the price wars that had starved some of those lucky enough to survive the sweating sickness, plus the inevitable conversation about the ferocity of the storm that continued to rage outside.

"There you go, my son." Jamie filled Jack's cup and then his own.

"Please, don't say that. No one has ever called me son and I would rather you didn't change that now." Jack avoided his gaze.

Jamie, under white-flecked eyebrows, continued to observe his companion closely for a moment. But he ignored the black look that Jack had cast over him, and to Jack's further annoyance, he said, "Ah, so that's your curse, is it? There was no harm meant, lad." From a lifetime of confessions, it appeared that the priest saw no barriers to his curiosity, brushing aside Jack's warning words.

"No, the harm was done years ago," Jack muttered to himself, draining his cup and attempting to cover his discomfort.

"Troubles you, does it?" Jamie asked bluntly.

"Wouldn't it bother you?" Jack threw back the response automatic.

"Well, that does depend, doesn't it? I know nothing about you. Tell me something and I'll think about it. If sympathy is the medicine you are looking for, though, you'll not get it from me." Jamie refilled Jack's emptied cup. "Now, don't you look at me like that? There is nothing here to be wary of, only an old man who tries to serve God as best he can. Come on, lad, tell me something of yourself."

Jack opened with a barb sharpened by bitterness and loaded with resentment. "My mother lives in St Agnes' Abbey." He watched with some satisfaction as Jamie's eyebrows rose towards his reduced hairline. He had used the words often enough to know the reaction they produced. Jamie's, although mild, was as he had come to expect. "Not then, of course, not when she bore me. Before that, she was a lady-in-waiting." Jack paused. "Fitzwarren's lady found out, and she went to St Agnes' after I was born."

Jamie interjected, "Ah, so you're a Lord's bastard, are you?"

Jack cast icy-blue eyes on him as he bestowed upon Jack the title he so resented. The priest did not avoid his glowering look.

"Makes no difference," Jack growled. "Fitzwarren had four sons; there was never a shortage of heirs. I was, shall we say, an unwelcome sight to his lady. Fitzwarren would have had me in the house, but not his wife. So he placed me in his brother's household, where I was brought up waiting on his sons." Jack stopped; this was as far as he usually went. There was bitterness in his voice. Jack knew his story was not an uncommon one. During his life, as well-travelled as he was, he had heard it from others. Some bore the brand openly and cursed humanity for it, seemingly uncaring; some carried it secretly and silently, ever afraid of discovery. A few laid it to rest and were not burdened by the faults of their fathers. Jack, however, knew he did not fall into the latter category.

"Not a happy life, eh?" Jamie asked, prompting Jack to continue.

"I did better than most, I suppose. What my cousins learnt, I learnt; what they did, I did but..." Jack paused, smiling widely at the memory of it, "... better."

"An arrogant claim," Jamie reprimanded, then smiling he added, "I'll allow you it. So you made no friends with them then?"

"Something like that. The youngest of my cousins, Harry, went to London and I followed. I had no wish to stay," Jack explained.

Jamie's expression was still curious. "I'm sure there's more to your story than just that. Come on then, tell me," then when Jack did not reply, he asked, "Did you get on with Harry, then?"

Jack's expression remained blank, but he answered the question with a shake of his blond head.

Undeterred, the priest persisted. "Did you meet your brothers again?"

This time, Jamie did get a reaction. One corner of Jack's mouth twisted in a wry grin. "Oh yes."

Jamie leaned close, his eyes fastened on Jack's. "Go on. You told me there were four sons."

"Yes," Jack confirmed. "Peter, Robert, William, and Richard."

"You know them all, then?" Jamie asked.

"Peter was heir, but died young. Broke his neck in a fall from a horse. I never knew him." A voice devoid of emotion gave a factual account. "William joined the church young, but the other two..." Jack's voice trailed off.

"So, which of the other two, Richard or Robin, did you meet first?" Jamie queried.

"Robert," Jack corrected.

"Richard or Robert then. Which first?"

There was a pause. "Robert," Jack said. "Harry went to London, and I went with him. Harry used to hunt with one of his cousins. A right arrogant bastard he is, Robert Fitzwarren." He pronounced his brother's name with malicious precision, it was obvious to his companion that he bore no love for the man.

"Ah, your brother."

"Yes, but he didn't know it, and I wasn't about to enlighten him. He'd have had me whipped to death."

Jack stopped again. "I was no more than Harry's servant."

"I understand the situation. But there's a story here, am I right? Go on, lad, tell it."

Jack turned serious eyes on the priest. "You're not interested."

"I am, lad." Jamie's tone was sincere.

Jack didn't know why he had continued. Maybe it was the priest's insistent questions and his authoritative manner, or maybe Jack just wanted to talk to someone. "You are right about that. There is a story." Stretching his shoulders, he settled himself back at the table. "There was a hunt. Harry told us we'd join Robert that Saturday. There was nothing unusual in that, but," Jack paused for effect, "he said Richard Fitzwarren would be there."

"Ah, your other brother," Jamie said, and then asked, "Younger or older than Robert?"

"Robert became heir when Peter died. Richard is... You know, I'm not sure if he's the youngest of the four or not." Jack's brow furrowed as Jamie's explorations led to the discovery that his knowledge of his brother remained incomplete. "Anyway, that's beside the point. Harry knew there was some feud between the pair. I had heard as much, but I didn't know why. I still don't know what the crux of it was. Harry told me that the previous time they met, Robert left with half of his ear missing. Needless to say, Harry was looking forward to a fight between the two."

"You don't like Harry?" It was more an observation than a question.

Jack paused, recollecting his former master. "No. He is an idiot. Robert has him following like a puppy. He borrows money from him, abuses him and still Harry goes back for more." Jack stopped suddenly. His eyes returned from the past to focus on Jamie's face.

"Go on, lad, you can't leave me there," Jamie prompted.

Jack looked at his listener's eager face and continued with his story. "I'd never seen Richard before.

I was looking for someone who looked like me. Or Robert." Robert was added as an afterthought. "So when we arrived, I was holding Harry's horse, and I recognised Robert surrounded by his usual retinue, including Harry. There was no one else there who looked like he could be Richard. Then the horn blew and Harry summoned me to bring his horse. I asked him where Richard was. He laughed and told me that he hadn't dared to join them. It was obvious that this had been what Robert's flock had been laughing about. I suppose I was disappointed, but not for long." Jack took a drink, grinning. "You see, he was already there, on the moor."

"How did you know it was him?" Jamie asked.

"I knew it must be him when Robert saw him and held up his hand for his rabble to stop. He looked nothing like Robert, believe me." Jack leant towards Jamie in a confidential manner and said, "Robert looks like the scraps from a bantam fight. You know what I mean, all colour and baubles?"

Jamie laughed. "I know the type, all piss an' wind."

"Exactly. Richard, he was in the distance, was dressed in black: cloak, boots, jacket, hair, horse, the lot. He sat up there on the moor, leaning slightly forward in the saddle, watching Robert. Harry rode up to join Robert, and I followed. More than a little curious by now, I can tell you. Robert yelled at the top of his voice, 'We have our quarry!'" Jack paused, looking closely at Jamie to see if he comprehended the implication of Robert's intent all those years ago. Not convinced, he added, "meaning Richard."

"Yes, lad, I'm with you. Get on with it," Jamie said briskly.

Satisfied with his listener's understanding, Jack continued. "The group, on Robert's command, went bellowing up the hill after him. There were trees as you crested the top of the moor about a quarter mile ahead, and Richard was riding towards them. Not quickly, though. Robert demanded a bow. Now I'll give him this; he is a fine shot. Richard saw what he meant to do and turned his horse to the trees, but he was too late. I saw the animal later, straight through the neck, clean as you like." Jack sat shaking his head at the memory of it. He reached for the jug to fill the cups.

Jamie moved quicker. "I'll do that, lad. Did he get to the trees then?" The story paused in the wake of a fresh assault of white lightning, followed by a seemingly cataclysmic boom.

The thunder subsided and Jack took up the tale once more. "The horse fell. I saw it go down, and the rider seemed to go under it. Robert rode like hell across the moor. I was at his side when he got there, and I expected to see a man pinned beneath the beast. Anyway, he wasn't. He must have stayed low so we couldn't see him and made it into the cover of the trees. Robert was as mad as the devil. He was sure he had trapped his brother." Jack stopped, laughing at the memory of Robert's blustering, wide-eyed disbelief. "Robert ordered his men to flush him out; there wasn't much cover, maybe half an acre or so of wood in a hollow. They rode off round the back of the trees to try to drive him towards Robert. I couldn't believe it. I knew for sure he meant to take the man's life."

Jack stopped, the story running on before his eyes, denying Jamie a narrative.

"So you did something, eh?" Jamie prompted him again.

"Aye, I did. They went off to my left and right, but I knew he must have gone straight into the trees from the horse; it made sense because it was the closest path to safety. So I sought to follow him. Maybe, I thought, I could find him first."

"Did you?"

"If you'll let me, I'll tell you," Jack snapped. "No, he found me. I wasn't dressed well enough to be taken for one of Robert's followers and he took me for a servant or a stable hand or such like. He was behind me; I must have walked straight past him." There was still a measure of disbelief in Jack's voice as he recalled how he had missed the man. "He said, 'Hold! This is not our argument.' I turned and Richard was leaning against a tree. He had a goodly cut on his forehead and his left arm was tucked into his jacket–I found out later that he broke it in the fall–but he still had a sword in his right hand, levelled at my chest. I can tell you, my heart stopped."

"What did you say? Surely you said something," Jamie interjected eagerly.

"I did what all men should do when faced with Richard Fitzwarren and three feet of drawn steel, or woe betide them. I backed away."

"Aye, lad, that's what you know now, but what about back then?" Jamie directed Jack's mind back to the time in the woods on Harlsey Moor.

"I knew if he was anything like Robert, he would have been taught well. I was going to invite him to take my horse when Harry came crashing through the undergrowth, yelling, asking me had I seen Richard. I raised my hand to signal Richard to be still where he was. Harry, the sop, rides up to me. I'm standing at his stirrup, looking up at his child's face. He had no idea what game he played for Robert." Jack paused, shaking his head.

Jamie didn't interrupt, sitting patiently and waiting for Jack to continue.

"I grabbed his leg; I'll never forget the surprise on his face as I threw him out of the saddle. He lay on the floor, wailing like a babe." Jack was smiling broadly again. "Richard still stood there watching. He hadn't moved and there was an odd look on his face. I threw the reins at him and we rode out of the woods like the devil was on our tails, and I suppose it was." Jack chuckled as he dwelt on Harry's downfall.

"So, did you tell him who you were?" Jamie drew Jack's attention back.

"I didn't, not then. We finally pulled up outside the village..." Jack's mind drifted back to the misty road again, two horses sweating and steaming in the morning air, stamping and pulling at their bits as their riders forced them to a halt.

Richard pulled his mount in front of Jack's. "I am Richard Fitzwarren, as you might have guessed, and I believe I owe you my thanks for the horse." The horse below him wheeled and pulled, turning to its other flank. With difficulty, Richard pulled the agitated animal back to square it with Jack's mount. "You have sacrificed your position for me. Your master will not welcome you back."

Jack thought Richard was reaching for money. "No, you are not indebted to me."

"Here, it's all I have." Richard held in his hand the sword he had previously levelled at Jack. He threw it horizontally over the short distance between the horses and Jack intercepted the scabbard. Richard's horse wheeled round again, pushing itself against Jack's, which took fright at the collision. It was only with extreme effort that he stopped the excited animal from taking flight.

"Make sure they give you a good price for it. Adieu." With that, Richard released the reins on the animal and horse and rider, disappeared from view.

"Surely you followed him, though?" Jamie asked.

Jack looked up, drawn back from the past. "No." He shook his head. "I don't know why. God, I didn't know him, it seemed so..." Jack couldn't find the words and was saved from having to by a whip crack and tumultuous roar from the elements.

"Ah, so that's where you got it from. I was wondering." Jamie pointed at the sword. Turning his head sideways, he tried to read the etched inscription that ran along the quillons.

"Oderint dum metuant," Jack read out the Latin inscription.

Jamie stopped him from supplying the translation. "I know, lad, I'm not as stupid as I look, and I'd lay a wager than my Latin is better than yours. Let them hate, so long as they fear. Am I right?" The look on Jack's face told him he was and Jamie beamed happily. "Anyway, did you catch up with him again?"

"I did. I spent a year in London or thereabouts keeping out of Harry's way. It wasn't easy; he wanted my blood." Jack grinned. "Eventually I went to France. There was a small village near Paris called... I can't think of the name of it."

"Never mind the name, my son." Jamie smiled weakly at his slip. "Sorry, lad."

"Huh." Jack had missed Jamie's closing words. He continued, "Anyway, there was a festival with a local champion swinging a sword around. I was short of money and I won myself a fair purse. I didn't know Richard was there. He told me later he recognised the sword and set out to get it back. He bloody well challenged me!" The indignation in Jack's voice was still fresh as he recalled it. "I couldn't fight him. After some minutes, he stopped and walked towards me..."

Jack had watched the competition for half an hour before he decided that he had little choice but to join in. He was out of money and out of luck.

Inside the circle of men, the game was a dangerous one. The blades were real, and the blows aimed by the combatants were deadly. The current victor had a shield and a cuirass to protect him. Jack had nothing. The last challenger had taken a bad cut to his forearm and had wisely conceded.

Jack had watched the victor closely, and he was confident that the man's skill was lacking deftness and he was drinking heavily between matches.

Draping his cloak over the fence and drawing his own sword, Jack declared himself as the next challenger.

He had two advantages: his opponent had already fought two rounds, and Jack was well trained. Estienne was the name the crowd shouted. Jack waited, ready, while the other downed a jug of proffered ale.

You drink as much as you want, mate. Jack, sober, knew better than to enter a fight with clouded judgement.

Estienne finished the jug and wiped the back of his hand across his mouth.

"Your name?" Estienne demanded in his native language.

"Does that matter?" Jack replied, also in French.

"Ah, so you're an English dog. This is a fight I would take for no wager!" Estienne spat back. Jack's French was fluent, but not good enough to disguise his origins.

The crowd was encouraging Estienne, slapping him on the shoulders and pushing him towards Jack. Another full jug was produced for their champion; from the jeers, they too shared his dislike of the English.

This is not going well, thought Jack. The way they were looking at him, he was going to have to fight Estienne and then take on the crowd.

"I'm not English, you idiot, I'm Scots," Jack lied quickly, a hurt expression on his face.

"Ah, Scotland, the true ally of France," Estienne replied gravely, raising the jug in a toast to his homeland.

Go on, get another jug-full inside you.

"Drink to France and to her valiant ally against the English, Scotland," encouraged Jack cheerfully.

Estienne, belching loudly, thrust the jug into the hands of the spectators and drew his sword. "So we shall see who is the victor then," he announced. "Will it be Scotland, or will it be France?" A cheer went up around him. Estienne, his own hands in the air and sword held aloft, bellowed with them.

Then, without warning, he ran, howling, sword outstretched towards Jack.

You don't run in a sword fight, you bloody idiot. Jack neatly sidestepped his advance, smacking the flat of his sword against the retreating backside, much to the delight of the onlookers.

Angry, Estienne glared back at Jack, who maddened him even further by joining the laughing crowd.

The next blow was meant to kill. Jack sent the blade away from him with more force than it had been delivered with. The look on Estienne's face told of the pain in his arm as the energy from the blow charged into him.

Jack needed to wrong foot him and get him on the ground, but he didn't want to injure Estienne. If he did, the spectators would have him for sure. He got in two loud strikes to the cuirass, both of them leaving impressions on the steel. Estienne was laughing, but the blows had sent him backward. There was a fallen post two steps further back; Jack had every intention of forcing him onto it.

He took the next two blows and parried both. Then a return swing brought his own blade screeching down Estienne's until the hilts clashed together. Jack, faster, got the punch in first, sending Estienne staggering backwards to snare his feet in the wood and land heavily on his backside with Jack's sword resting on his shoulder. The blade, inches from the exposed flesh of his neck, made a clear threat.

Estienne conceded.

Jack offered an outstretched hand to pull him back to his feet.

The crowd applauded their fallen champion, who, arms raised, was acting as if he was still the victor.

Jack cared little, he just wanted his money. He advanced on a small man sat on the floor at edge of the ring, a wooden board on his knees set with neatly placed lines of coins.

Jack held his hand for his winnings.

The little man met his eyes for a moment and then, bending to his left, looked past him. "You have a challenger. The money stays in."

That's all I need. Grumbling under his breath, he turned to see the new entrant to the ring. The low sun was facing him, so his eyes picked out only an outline of a man with a drawn sword.

Jack took three quick paces to his left to get the sun from his eyes. The newcomer was dressed like Jack, without protection, and was relying on his skill for a victory.

Jack, still struck by surprise, hadn't even raised his blade in defence, the point still resting on the grass, his grip loose. When the attack came, it was one meant to rip the blade from his hand. He nearly lost his sword, retaining it only by spinning quickly along the line of the blow. The impact on the blade came just beneath the hilt, making his fingers jar painfully.

Wrong footed, exposing an undefended side to his opponent, Jack swore.

Turning rapidly back to face the other man, his raised blade screamed as it brought the other's to a halt. The crowd roared.

Sun glinted down the sharpened steel as he easily parried another attack, his blade quickly blocking and deflecting the lethal steel. Clearly on the defensive, Jack watched for each new attack and met them with practiced ease.

"Why?" Richard lowered his blade. "I've seen your skill. Why won't you exercise it on me?" Then his eyes widened in recognition. "Harlsey Moor! Thank you again for the horse. I see you put that to good use." He tapped the steel in Jack's hand with his own blade.

"You remember?" Jack found himself struck partially dumb in the presence of his brother.

"Of course." Richard turned to the crowd and yelled, "All bets are off!" He threw an arm around Jack's shoulders. "Come, let me repay you properly."

Late into the night, with alcoholic courage, Jack had told Richard his secret. He had shown him the cross he wore around his neck that bore the Fitzwarren crest. Richard had risen from the table and stood to look at Jack. "You have my commiserations," he had finally pronounced.

"Well, what did you expect?" Jamie asked, looking at Jack as he spilt ale over the table in an effort to blindly fill the cups. "You were in awe of the man. I bet you were making a Harry of yourself all night, eh? So what's he like then, this brother of yours?"

A sardonic grin crept onto Jack's face. "Ah, well, that is the question. I don't know. He keeps his own counsel; what he thinks and what he does are for his own ends. I just try to keep off the sharp side of his temper, mostly."

"Are you still with him, then?"

Jack grunted an affirmation.

"And how do you get on?"

"Not well, not as brothers," Jack complained moodily.

"Not as equals is what you mean, isn't it?" Jamie observed shrewdly.

Jack didn't reply but looked closely at Jamie, wondering at his words.

"Who carried the curse, eh? Do you treat him as equal, eh? From what you said, you don't. You had a picture of him in your mind from when you met him in the woods, didn't you? You lived with the memory of that meeting for two years, and in that time, knowing nothing about him, you made him the brother you never had. Cast a mould that the man wouldn't fit into..."

"Silence!" Jack hissed, outraged.

"I only speak the truth," Jamie said gently. "Takes an odd one like me to see it sometimes. The one you met in the woods doesn't exist, only here." Jamie tapped his head with a bony finger.

"I don't have to listen to this." Jack's blue eyes blazed angrily, his hands tight on the table's edge as he started to stand.

Jamie laid his hand soothingly on Jack's arm, smiling. "Too late, lad, I said it."

The old man's manner drained the anger from Jack and he lowered himself back onto the seat, his head dropping into his hands. It was something he had never considered. Jack took a long drink. He didn't want to consider it either and stared at the table top, brooding, immersed in the thoughts the priest had provoked, struggling with the possibilities. Jack's was a melancholy not overly helped by the alcohol.

Jamie changed the subject. "So, are you bound for England? Everyone here is waiting for the weather to improve." It was a fair assumption, there being many travellers congregated at the inn waiting for the storm to break.

"Aye. Richard has a group of men with him that he hopes to hire, and I can tell you, the prospect of money would be pleasing." Jack allowed the discourse to change path, turning the cup slowly in his hand, his eyes fastened upon it.

"What have you been doing in France, then?" Jamie enquired.

"Since I joined him, same thing," Jack replied bleakly, still not meeting the priest's stare.

"Why leave France then?" Jamie asked.

"We outstayed our welcome." Jack looked up and met Jamie's enquiring gaze. The look on the priest's face told him that he wanted all the details, and he saw no harm in providing them. "We were hired last to protect a mill. Comte Riberac had five mills, two had been burnt to the ground, and he had a mind to keep the last three standing. Turns out the mills belonged to the villages, not to the Comte. He was trying to levy a tax on the villages for all sacks ground, to claim them as his by right."

"And?" Jamie prompted.

"Well, let's put it like this: we didn't get paid. Richard had all the carts with the Comte's ground corn in them driven into the middle of the village market. Those carts were picked over and emptied in a trice," Jack lamented.

"A Godly thing to do," Jamie spoke approvingly.

"That might be the case, but it's left me with no money to my name and what I did have has been hocked," Jack complained moodily, he'd still not forgiven Richard for relieving him of the jewelled cross he'd worn his whole life. Richard had exchanged it for coins and, despite promising to redeem it, Jack was fairly sure he would never see it again.

Neither saw the man Jack had provided with a horse on Harlsey Moor approach and stand quietly at the end of the table. Richard Fitzwarren had been listening to the conversation for a few minutes before he decided to speak.

"Is this a private moment? I would hate to interrupt." The silken voice, cool with indifference, brought both heads up from the table.

"No, sit if you will." Jack's voice bore a weight of resignation.

Jamie grinned. Jack saw the priest looking at his brother and scowled. He knew that the man who had arrived bore no resemblance to himself at all. Dark hair, immaculately dressed, the expression bored, and the eyes telling of a quick intellect. Reservation, confidence bordering on arrogance, Richard was opposite in many ways to his fairer sibling. Richard, with his fine-boned face, dark skin, almost black hair and steel-grey eyes bore no physical similarity to Jack. Richard was shorter and of much slighter build than his stockier brother, and the look in his eyes in particular contrasted sharply with Jack's friendly blue ones. Jack, dressed in fustian and old leather knew he

A Queen's Spy

made a stark contrast to the man now sitting next to him.

No one spoke. Heaven's forces regrouped and surged forward with a charged assault of turbulence. The rolling cannonade drowned all noise in the inn.

Jack flinched.

Richard reached for the pitcher, tipping it to inspect the contents. He looked at the priest. Hard steel eyes told of an inquisitiveness not quite matched by his manner; the corner of his mouth twitched into a smile that carried no humour with it. "Well, it looks as if I shall have to supply the ale if you want to continue with the spiritual guidance of the fair Polynices."

Jack watched Richard summon a serving girl for a fresh pitcher of ale. There was an expensive crested ring on Richard's hand, and Jack saw the priest's eyes linger upon it.

His brother had turned away, employed in the task of obtaining more ale, meeting Jamie's eyes Jack said, "Meet my brother."

"I'd guessed," Jamie said quietly.

Their brief exchange had not, however, been missed by the newcomer who, turning back, addressed Jamie, smiling. "Half-brother to be precise."

The ale arrived and Jamie took the task of filling the cups. Richard, accepting his, addressed Jack. "So, have you been regaling..." pausing, he turned to the priest who supplied him with his name. "... Jamie with tales of our family heritage then?"

Jack, about to speak, was stopped by Jamie who broke in first. "Jack was telling me how you met, an interesting tale."

"A most interesting afternoon if I recall, and an expensive one," Richard replied lightly, his tone still that of the disinterested.

"Expensive?" Jamie queried.

"I lost a horse, a sword, and gained a dependent... eventually." Richard, smiling, clapped Jack on the back.

It was too much for Jack. A black expression settling on his usually lightly humoured features, he rose from the table, glowered at Richard and without a word turned on his heel and left.

"You're a cruel one, aren't you?" Jamie exclaimed, slamming his cup back on the table with some violence, watching his evening's entertainment mount the stairs leading to the rooms above.

Richard looked up, all humour gone from his face. "Am I?"

"It's not Jack's fault." Jamie's words were gauged to produce a reaction.

Richard cast an assessing gaze over Jamie before replying. "Not Jack's fault for being a bastard, or not his fault that he cannot accept me? I will accept that Jack cannot possibly be held to account for the former."

"Both." Jamie had not expected such an accurate response from Richard. "You want him to leave you?"

"It had crossed my mind." Richard's fingers idly turned the cup in his hand.

"That's why you're so cruel to him?" Jamie was back in his stride again. Leaning across the table he continued his friendly interrogation of this family. "That and you don't want him on your conscience. You've walled yourself up in here." Jamie tapped his head for the second time that evening. "No space for another in your life, is there?"

"Do you normally make such rapid judgement on meeting people?"

"Sometimes," Jamie admitted. "I have only what Jack tells me to go on, unless..."

"No, I am in no need of confession. Trust me, my soul is well beyond redemption," Richard replied lightly.

"Dark words. A man who believes he is beyond salvation must feel well-damned indeed. So you'd prefer to meet the devil alone, is that it?" Jamie asked, drawing on his power of office to deliver a rebuke to a man who spoke so blasphemously of his own salvation.

"We are all damned, I believe, and require salvation to save our souls. Don't lecture me. I have Jack to counsel me in the error of my ways, which are, as I am sure you will have heard, not inconsiderable." Richard's voice was still calm, the tone not matching the words. "It was probably you who sent Jack to his bed in a bad mood, rather than me. What exactly did you say to him?"

"Just told the lad a few truths. Nothing he probably didn't know already." Jamie was watching the man before him carefully.

"You don't miss much, do you?"

"It's a talent." Jamie replied, smiling. "Age and experience and a love of God." He leant towards Richard. "Who tells us that..."

Richard cut him off. "I know: love thy brother."

"Precisely," Jamie replied, as if that was the answer they had been seeking all night.

"It's not that easy." Richard's voice was no longer detached.

Jamie looked up quickly at the first hint of confession. "I can see that. He has you cast as something you are not. Well, you might be, I don't know much about you, but I doubt it. Jack can't help it. Give him time, don't force him away because he begs to be a part of your life," Jamie concluded before promptly draining his cup. "Matthew tells us that everyone who is angry with his brother will be liable to make a hasty judgement. Don't let that be you."

"I force him away for his own safety. He does not beg to be a part of my life, he cannot be. He will remain as he is, displaced, and he will stay so while he has me to remind him of his inferiority." Richard's voice was weary, and he sounded as if he was reciting an often-stated fact.

"Why make him feel inferior then?" Jamie asked bluntly.

"By the saints you know so well, I do not; he does it himself," Richard replied, exasperated.

"That's the fault of how he was raised. Sees you as someone to obey, to follow. He can't help that." Then adopting a serious voice he declared, "Love one another with brotherly affection."

"And outdo one another in showing honour," Richard finished the quote and drained his own cup. "Here, I'll leave this. I am sure you will empty it." He rose and, without another word or so much as a backward glance, departed.

Jamie pulled the pitcher towards him and settled down to empty it and muse on an interesting evening.

Richard pushed open the door to his own room. His servant, who was sitting by the fire, looked up at his entry.

"A good night?" Dan asked.

"No." Richard dropped his cloak over the back of a chair and, sitting on the edge of the bed, began pulling boots from his feet. Dan sensed his mood and kept his counsel, busying himself in collecting the discarded clothes as the other flung himself face down on the bed and spoke no more.

Chapter Three

London – March 1553

Nothing but a shadow in a darkened doorway, Jack had watched as Richard Fitzwarren ducked through the low inn entrance. That had been over an hour ago, as dusk filled the gap between day and night.

He wondered at the night's outcome. It was, after all, this meeting alone that had brought Richard, Jack and twenty-one hired men back across the narrow waste of sea between France and England to London. Jack harboured the fervent hope that it would lead to their hire, and soon. His back ached: the chill night air carried with it a cold damp that had begun to penetrate his body.

A taper in a first-floor window flickered and Jack returned his attention to the room and his task of observing those within the inn, and those who may be outside watching. Three others of a likely look had entered shortly after Richard arrived. Too well dressed, they walked with swift purpose, without camaraderie or companionable banter, setting themselves apart from the other patrons who ambled to the door. Illuminated by steady flame, men's faces, lurid in the candlelight, could be seen as they passed the open window.

Jack concluded, correctly, that in this room, a meeting was being conducted, with his brother among the participants. Whatever else he fancied Richard's shortcomings were, a lack of intelligence was not one. He would not provide his lit form as a recognisable portrait framed by the embrasure for any other concealed observer. One man, though had no such qualms. He was elderly and dressed in folds of rich russet, their luxury deepened by the fire's glow. The harshness of age lined his face, the dynamism of youth long since lost, ruddy wine-reddened cheeks heightened by the contrast with the grey shroud of once-brown hair.

Jack turned his eyes to the street again, attentive to detect others, like himself, who spied on the night's work. A drunken sailor, in his inebriated staggering, collided with the inn wall opposite and spent some time sitting in the gutter before he could gather his wits and his balance and clamber back to unsteady feet. The drunk moved unhurriedly from the street, using as support the wall that had caused his original collapse, and which was now so vital in preventing a plummet from the vertical. Jack concluded it could not be a ruse; to act drunk in such a manner would seem too contrived for a sober man.

Three men left the inn. Light from the interior momentarily split the street in half before the door closed once more. Jack guessed they were drinkers from the downstairs room. After a hasty conversation in the fresh air of the night, the group split and two staggered off to Jack's left. The remaining man urinated up the wall before departing.

Jack shifted his weight again, leaning with his other shoulder against the wall. Prepared for a longer wait, he was surprised when Richard emerged from the door. From the preparations and the time of waiting for the meeting, he had expected a long one, not an hour's rapid discussion concluded before the night was late.

Jack watched Richard disappear from sight. He walked without haste, a figure of no particular note in the night. Darkly clothed, as was his style, his obscurity was ensured. Minute inspection was required of the observer to see the finery of the cloth, the expense of tailoring, the high quality of the few jewels, and the arrogance of manner; only then would he concede that this was a man of some significance. Jack glowered at his retreating back. The cuts in expenditure that Richard had forced on Jack, he thought bitterly, he had not turned on himself.

Unable to absent himself until sure all had left, Jack remained. The man with the grizzled fringe emerged, pausing briefly on the threshold of the inn. He looked nervously about him and then ducked back inside. Some minutes later, a carriage drew up in front of the door and Jack's view was blocked as an unknown number boarded. The springs tipped to the weight of the new burden; he suspected three had stepped up from the street.

After a long while, when Jack was wondering if all had departed with the grizzled man, two more emerged from the door. Young, less than Jack's own age, well dressed and extremely in their cups, they staggered in unison, heads together sharing some quiet and slurred conversation, the gist of which Jack could not make out. He judged they were part of the trio who had walked purposefully and soberly to the Inn earlier. Jack saw a servant extinguish the tapers in the room above. It was his signal that his night's work was done, for none now remained. Looking carefully up and down the street, Jack assured himself he was temporarily alone and vacated the doorway, slipping into the dark shadows that clung to the walls and gutters.

He found Richard, as he knew he would, in the rooms they had hired in Aldergate Street, just outside the city walls. He was seated at the desk, writing, a pile of sealed letters sitting neatly in front of him. Richard signed the last and applied the seal to the folded sheet. Jack removed his cloak and cast it absently on the bed from where it slithered to a heap on the floor, Richard noting its careless journey.

"A good night's work?" Jack asked, pulling a chair loudly across the floor.

"Well, that rather depends on who you are." Richard placed the letter with the rest. "If you are the King of England or rank yourself as a contestant in the hierarchical race to claim the succession, then I would say it was not a good night's work." Richard settled back in the chair. "However, if perchance you were out to sell your labours to the highest bidder, then yes, it was a good night's work." Richard paused. "I have completed my sordid tasks."

"Shall I take it then that we are employed? I should hate to have to go back to France penniless." The emphasis on the final word was sufficient for the implication of blame not to go unnoticed. "In fact, come to that, I don't want to go back to France, penniless or not."

Richard ignored the implication. "I thought you enjoyed France?" The guarded grey eyes warned Jack that this was not to be an easy conversation. When he chose, Richard made being difficult an art at which he excelled. Tonight looked set to be another of partial information, half-truths, falsehoods and omission; nothing straightforward or simple.

Jack continued, curiosity being the uneasy victor, "Do we stay in London, or are we to move elsewhere?"

Richard asked, "Why? Do you not want to remain in London, Jack?"

Jack sighed, allowing Richard to change the subject. "Not particularly. My mind would be eased, however, if I knew where Harry was, and your brother, for that matter. London is a dangerous place for both of us."

"If it helps any, Robert is in Kent, hunting, which, as you know, is one of his favourite passions, even if I do not agree on occasion with his choice of quarry. Your master, Harry, plucked temporarily of the finery of my dear older brother, is here in London." Richard watched Jack's face to gauge his reaction.

"Harry is no worry on his own; he'll act only as Robert's message-boy, eager to please as always. You have not been idle then. Can I assume you also wish to avoid the hounds?" Jack asked.

The sarcasm was not lost on Richard. "On the contrary, I am looking forward to meeting Cousin Harry. I admit it has been a while, but I am sure he will remember me."

"What! Are you mad? We're barely back and you want them snapping at our heels?" Jack blurted. The look on his brother's face rang with mischief, but whether it was aimed at himself or Harry, he could not tell.

"I am quite sane," Richard responded coldly.

"Why? We are back in England and on the edge of penury, and you want to start a private war?" There was disbelief on Jack's face.

"That is exactly why I wished to see Cousin Harry. Penury, as you rightly point out, is an unpleasant state. I am going to propose he make us a loan," Richard explained.

"A loan! You are bloody mad!" Jack stood so quickly that the chair toppled and banged on the floor.

"A loan is perhaps the wrong word, loans being generally repaid. However, I think you'll find Harry most agreeable to my terms. Worry not, I won't ask you to deliver my letter to Harry," Richard spoke evenly, still smiling at the reaction he had provoked by his revelations, adding, "Let's just say that there are many who profit from insurrection. However, it is rarely those who directly involve themselves. Harry has ever made bad decisions; one more at my behest will not overly change matters, will it?"

"As you will," Jack retorted grumpily. "You'll do as you please."

"Jack, you are no fun. It's all black and white with you. There are no shades of grey, are there? Settle your temper," Richard said soothingly.

"By the saints, you aimed to anger me! What did you expect me to say?" Jack scooped the chair from the floor. "Go on, tell me more."

"We will be here three days more. Dan has already delivered my invitation to meet with Harry and I don't expect he will want to keep me waiting." Richard had his brother's full and undivided attention.

"Why would Harry wish to meet with you?" Jack asked carefully.

"To keep his head," Richard spoke innocently.

"Give me strength!" Jack uttered the words through clenched teeth. "You'll not leave me like this. What are you up to?"

Richard sighed. "I thought you were about to wash your hands of my intended deeds."

"I was. You drew me back." Jack was not about to be diverted again. "Why will Harry be so keen to meet you?"

"As you so rightly pointed out, I am rapidly running short of coinage, which is a most unhappy state. However, Harry–I believe–still has a good hold on his father's purse strings, would you not agree?" Richard spoke as if explaining the obvious to a child.

"He always had when I was with him. The old man was constantly bailing the bastard out; more to keep him from turning back up at his door, if you ask me." Jack was about to add more, but stopped himself. He was not about to allow Richard to steer him to new conversational pastures.

"As you say, he can raise capital when required, and that is a facility he will have to exercise quite soon," Richard paused. "Poor, unfortunate Harry has allied himself with Northumberland's conspirators."

Jack's eyes narrowed. "It may have escaped your attention, brother, but is that not what we have done?"

"Absolutely not!" Richard was indignant. "We have been merely hired by Lord Byrne to allow him to fulfil his part of this most treasonous bargain. Harry also, it appears, is in the market for men to support Northumberland, and hence marks himself as the Duke's man. He has high hopes of advancement and will not allow me, or the requirement, to hand over a quantity of gold to keep his treasonous intent secret, stand in his way."

"Do I gather from this that Harry does not know who your employer is?" Jack smiled. So Richard would play with poor Harry then. Well, a more deserving recipient for Richard's temper and acid tongue he could not think of, the only sorrow being he was not likely to witness the meeting.

"He is not likely to, at least not in the immediate future. Byrne is a worried man who hedges his bets considerably. We are to leave London in three days and take ourselves to his manor, there to wait for further instructions. He wishes to keep us out of sight until required, so half the men will work as labourers, six will join his household, including us, and the rest will take up residence in the village. He wishes to lend a small help should Northumberland take the day, but should he lose, he needs to be able to cover his tracks and doesn't want an army camped in his fields, drawing the stares of all."

An evil grin settled on Jack's face as he saw now how Harry could be deceived.

Richard continued. "So, we shall be safely hidden from view, and undoubtedly Harry will try to track me down, but unfortunately, he will not be able to find me. Byrne is not likely to admit to my existence and we shall temporarily vanish into England's green fields."

"Whatever you ask for from Harry, add ten extra pieces to it for me." Jack was grinning broadly.

"You will understand now why I ask you to keep yourself out of sight until we leave," Richard was serious again.

"Aye, don't worry; it will be worth a few days of boredom if you can get this over on that bastard," Jack replied a little too quickly. Richard raised his eyebrows slightly as Jack bestowed on Harry his own title for the second time that evening. "How do you know all this? How did you find out where Harry is?"

Richard gave Jack a look that told him instantly that he would not receive an answer to that question. Instead he said, "So, as you can see, I have not been lazing here as you suspected." Richard had a malicious smile on his face.

"Well, you act like it," Jack's words filled the silence, which was uncomfortable for only one of them.

"Possibly. But I am supposed to be idle, rich, careless, carefree, frivolous... Have I missed anything? Ah yes, you think I spend too much as well," Richard added. "Whatever opinion you hold of me, I mind not, but I do mind when you share it so freely."

Jack took the rebuke silently. Richard's voice told him of the danger that lounged before him, a danger that bitter experience had taught him to avoid. "You've made your point," Jack avoided his brother's gaze by studying the frayed stitching on the inside of his left boot.

"Ah well, enough of me." Richard's tone was light again. "So, how did you spend your evening? See anything of any interest?" Richard turned the subject to a fresh track, much to Jack's unconcealed relief.

"The only one I saw clearly was an old man, grey hair at the front." Jack indicated where he meant with his hand. "Looks like a bloody badger; about your height, well fed. He called for a carriage; I didn't see how many boarded. Three others went to the inn soon after you, didn't look the normal type to go to such a place, two left drunk. I don't know where the third went."

"Anyone else watching?" Richard asked.

"Yes, but I didn't see them. The old man stuck his head out of the door and a carriage turned up." Jack's tone was apologetic.

"Would you recognise any of them again?" Richard asked.

"The old man. It was too dark to see the others clearly," Jack was shaking his head.

"The old man was Lord Byrne, if you're interested," Richard supplied.

"Looks a right nervous type," Jack observed.

"He is. Just got himself a young wife. He has no desire to embroil himself too deeply in plots." Richard reached for a book that lay closed on the desk; the conversation was finished.

He did not look up as Jack left.

Richard had come to know of Harry's activities through his recent revival of a network of which he had been a part before he left England. At the age of fourteen, Richard Fitzwarren had been placed by his father in Thomas Seymour's household. Seymour, ever ambitious, would eventually marry Henry VIII's widow. However, long before that, he was involved in all kinds of intrigue, often knowing what the powerful would do before they had even made up their own minds on a course of action. Over the years, he had developed a network of informers and spies the length and breadth of the country: well-paid and reliable sources supplying him with useful information. Richard had worked for him, originally as a scribe, but eventually condensing communications and reporting directly to Seymour on information received. Many of those who wrote to Seymour or visited on a regular basis became well acquainted with Richard Fitzwarren and knew him as Seymour's man. So, when he returned to England's shores, it had taken only a short time to renew some of these links. Seymour was now gone, but his old informants were largely still in place and were delighted by the prospect of increasing their earnings once more. Richard had little else he could use to change his fortune. He would have to use what information he could, where he could, and take what opportunities it offered.

The knock he made on the door of The Angel in Aldergate was answered quickly. It was opened by a burly man, darkly dressed, and with a broad belt containing a wide-bladed knife. His forearms were bare, heavily muscled and darkened with hair, and the knuckles on the hand that held the door open were whitened with scars. His face cracked into a wide grin, showing a mouth of broken and missing teeth.

"Master Fitzwarren, it's good to see you," the man said in welcome, his voice bearing a peculiar whistle leant to it by two missing canines.

Richard returned his smile as he stepped over the threshold of London's most prestigious brothel. "It's good to see you looking to so well, Nathan."

"Mistress Nonny will be pleased to see you," Nathan said as he opened a second door and light from the interior flooded into the small darkened entranceway, where they both stood.

"It will be good to see her as well. Perhaps a game of cards later? I believe you owe me the opportunity of a win?" Richard said pleasantly.

Nathan laughed, "Anytime you like, I shall go easy on you."

"Maybe I have improved," Richard shot back, grinning.

"Not while you've a hole in your arse, Master Fitzwarren," Nathan laughed, "but I shall let you know if you have."

Richard clapped the man on the shoulder and stepped into the welcoming bright and warm embrace of the Angel. In a room to the right were a number of girls, their painted faces belying their profession and their clothing loose and arranged in attractive disarray. All of them had their attention fastened on him and sent him winks and smiles from where they lounged on chairs and cushions, their pale skin lit by the firelight.

They, however, were not the reason for his visit, and his attention was taken by the woman advancing towards him down the corridor. Madame Nonny; large, French, powdered with a heady perfume that surrounded her like an almost tangible presence, had her arms open wide and a genuine smile upon her face.

"Richard! What a pleasure to see you! Where have you been, my pretty?" In a moment she had her arms around him and Richard returned her welcoming embrace.

"I have been, Madam, to many places," Richard pulled her even closer, her scent powerful and delicious and one that turned the pages in his mind back years.

"And without even a goodbye, I should scold you," Nonny said, pulling back in his arms slightly.

"And if you did, I would not mind," Richard said, his eyes smiling. "I have, of course, brought you a gift."

A wide smile appeared on her face and her artfully painted brows arched in delight. "Well then, let us not delay. Come, and tell me everything you have been doing."

Nonny pulled from his arms, exchanged a few brief words with Nathan that he did not hear, and then taking his hand in one of her pale white plump ones led him down the corridor towards her own private quarters.

The rooms were a reflection of their owner. Sumptuous, extravagant and heaped with expensive trappings, from the Turkish rugs on the floor to the hand stitched Breton hangings adorning the walls. Large fat candles burned in holders casting a warm glow around the room and the fireplace added its own dancing orange light to play across the floor.

Seated next to her, Richard took her hand in his and deftly slid his gift into her palm. The brooch he gave her was unmistakably French in design, and her eyes widened at the sight of it. The cornflower blue of the petals was intricately picked out in a shining blue enamel bordered with gold. The centre of the brooch held a sapphire. It was both outrageous and expensive.

A moment later the door opened and glasses, wine, and sweet meats were set before them on the dark rosewood table. Both of them waited patiently until the servant had closed the oak door behind him and the latch clicked securely back into place.

"Oh I have missed you, mon cher." Nonny leant across and planted a slow and deliberate kiss on his cheek.

"Has your life been so boring without me?" Richard replied, taking his glass from the table.

Nonny seemed to consider it for a moment. "Boring perhaps, but fraught no. London is a difficult city to live in at the moment. I have good patronage and many friends, but the price of their support is high."

Richard gestured around the room with the hand that held the glass, noting with mock seriousness, "Madam, it does indeed look as if you are suffering!"

Nonny regarded him with eyes the colour of chestnuts and said in a serious voice, her hand running down the soft material of his sleeve, "I am not the only one who has an appreciation of finery, am I?"

"And long may we both be able to appreciate it," Richard replied, smiling.

It was an hour later when they had traded their news that Richard asked a question, which produced a smile on his hostess's face.

"Does my brother still remain one of your clients?"

"Unfortunately, he does. Only last week, his losses at cards were more than he could afford and he could not settle his debts. Nathan had to intervene, it was... unpleasant." She turned the brooch over in her hand, then lifting her eyes from it, she met Richard's, her expression deadly serious. "I would rather he stopped passing through my doorway. He is a cruel man but, unfortunately, well connected."

Richard nodded. "I understand. I am in London only for a few more days, but when I return, I will dissuade him, I promise."

Nonny's smile brightened immediately. "Good. Our business is concluded, and I am sure you would rather sample the pleasures of the house before you leave?"

Richard lifted her hand from her lap and kissed the back of it. "I thought I was."

Nonny laughed, pulling her hand away as she rose from the seat next to him. "Come with me. I have someone for you to meet."

Richard inclined his head in acceptance and allowed her to lead him from the room, arm linked through his as they walked through the house and up the stairs wrapped in the potent embrace of her perfume. Nonny stopped outside a door. Slipping her arm from his she knocked, smiling at him as she pressed the unlocked door open. "I will leave you. Come and find me before you go."

"Indeed, I will," he said as she turned and departed in a rustle of silks. Raising his hand to the door, he pressed it further open and stepped across the threshold into the dimly lit interior.

There was one occupant, arms folded, leaning against the fire place his profile illuminated by the glow from the flames. "I was wondering if I was to be kept waiting all night," said Thomas Wyatt.

The night was cool and the hour late by the time Richard left The Angel to walk back to the rented rooms above the inn. As he crossed Bank Street, a familiar sight caught his eye, and he realised that his mind had been so preoccupied he had been walking with no real sense of direction. His steps had taken him to the street in London where his father's house was. Light glittered through the diamond glass panes in the upper windows. It was likely then that his father was in residence. When he was away, the house ran on a small staff and the candles would not be wasted in lighting the rooms on the upper floors.

Was Robert there?

Richard set his feet in the opposite direction, away from the house. Now was not the time for that confrontation. No matter how much he wanted to settle that score, it was a personal one and there was little to gain from it. Robert could wait.

An hour later, he arrived back at the inn and found Jack walking towards him down the darkened corridor leading to his room.

"You are late back?" Jack said as he approached.

Jack came to stand a few feet in front of him, and Richard saw his expression suddenly change. "What?" Richard said, his brow furrowing.

"Nothing," Jack replied, his nose wrinkling, "you smell like one of the gutter whores in Houndgate."

"Hardly," Richard laughed. "If this is what you think you smell like when you've been there, then you've a nose worse than a tanner's."

Jack scowled at his brother. "Where have you been? I thought we were supposed to be keeping out of sight?"

"We are, and I have been out of sight," Richard replied, making to pass his brother.

Jack stepped sideways to block his exit, placing a hand on Richard's chest to stop him. "It's one rule for you and another for everyone else, isn't it?"

Richard's gaze dropped to the hand Jack had placed on him before returning it to Jack's face. His voice was stony when he spoke. "No Jack. There is just one set of rules, and they are the ones I set. So abide by them."

Jack dropped his hand back to his side and stood still while Richard pushed past him and entered his room, leaving Jack alone with the heady scent of lavender and musk.

That Harry wanted to meet his cousin, and in the near future, was proved correct when a note in the hand of Jack's former master was delivered to Dan where he waited, propping up the wall of the customs house. Jack did not know of the message's arrival. Having promised to keep out of sight, he was doing just that whilst exploring the dubious charms of the landlord's most prized asset, Molly. The girl had a promise from Jack that he was hoping to fulfil with Richard's success. He held little doubt that he would not bend Harry to his will.

Evening air chilled the warm exhaled breath, clouding it in front of the man as he stood leaning against the wall of the customs house on the bank of the Thames. That this was a poor district, lifeless during the night apart from those of nocturnal, villainous tendencies, had not escaped Richard's attention when he had selected the area. During the daylight hours, it thronged with the business of loading and unloading, haggling and arguing, yelling, bartering, and all the commercial activities associated with the ends of seafaring voyages. Now they had all departed from the scene. The area was studded with low-quality ale houses, frequented by the unfortunate, the unwitting, and the lawless, eager to relieve the insensible sailor of more than the cost of his ale. But near the customs house, there were no such establishments; the scene was still, broken only by the occasional bark and angry growl of dogs foraging for the last few scraps that had been ground under foot during the daylight.

Harry left his comrades and most of his self-confidence tethered with his horse. His courage decreasing step-by-step, he walked to meet the man who threatened his liberty.

Richard had used his surname only in the note, and Harry quite reasonably believed he was being summoned by Robert for his sin of ambition. What Richard was unaware of was that, for once, Harry was acting at his father's behest, and not at Robert's; the latter was no part of a plot for the crown. Harry's greatest fear was not a discovery by the opponents of

Northumberland, but by Robert, whose wrath he feared more than anything else that could be brought to bear against him. Harry's overwhelming dread of the meeting was increased by the forlorn and dangerous stage selected by Richard.

Harry saw the man leaning, as the message had told he would be, against the customs house wall, and still, as he approached, he expected to meet and face Robert. The other did not know that Harry's fear was temporarily misplaced.

A cart, the remains of a smashed barrel its only contents, the staves twisted by some careless impact, cast sharp ragged shadows in the moonlight across the wall. Richard stood among the contorted darkened lines, his form broken and difficult to discern in their camouflage. It was not until he was close that Harry began to wonder who stood in front of him. Dark dress was not Robert's style, whose definitive characteristic was flamboyance. In two more steps, he also realised that this man would fit easily within Robert's frame. Now Harry believed he faced a messenger from the man he feared and his confidence took an upturn, the dread of the meeting lifting slightly, such was his fear of Robert Fitzwarren. Richard didn't speak. It had been a while, so he gave the other time for recognition to fully dawn and watched as, in all its revealing colours, it lit and then settled on Harry's puffy, well-fed face.

"You..." was all Harry could say when he finally regained the use of his tongue. Richard chose still not to speak, but smiled malevolently at his proposed benefactor.

"So you're back. Robert will be pleased about that. Is this what you do now, sneak about in darkened corners amongst the slime and filth, eh?" Harry's confidence increased; he had no great fear of Richard.

"If you would so describe your company," Richard's voice was light, his words mocking.

"I know what you want, but I have satisfaction in knowing you'll not live to spend it," Harry spat back.

"So, it may be true," Richard mused. "Who can tell? However, I am proposing a lavish funeral and require funds to provide for it, so…"

"I have your money." Such had been Harry's fear of Richard's brother; he had come prepared. He tossed the sack of coins on the ground in the space between them.

"Such bad grace, Harry. I shall trust your honour and count this at my leisure later."

"I hope to be present when Robert finds you; your head will be severed from your body, have no fear of it," Harry threatened. For Harry, the meeting had gone on long enough already.

"I have little fear of death, Harry, do you?" Richard took a quick step forward to bring him within inches of Harry's face. "Give my brother a message, will you, when you tell him of our…'chance encounter'? Tell him that when we meet, I shall take more than his remaining ear."

Harry kept his eyes on Richard until he judged himself a safe distance from his aggressor, then he turned on his heel and strode from the docks. Richard waited until he was out of sight before walking to the quay, the money disappearing inside his coat. Dropping suddenly to his knees, Richard swung himself easily over the edge, his weight on a hemp rope tied to the mooring bollard above. He dropped down until his feet landed softly in the small rocking boat moored at the rope's end.

"Well, he's right mad now, isn't he, and he'll be back off to your brother, Robert, fair sharp," Dan commented as Richard seated himself.

"I am counting on it, Dan," Richard smiled.

"One of these days, that brain of yours will be spread all over the ground. That's where you're going to end up if you keep trying to play like this," Dan growled. Thick, veined hands grasped the oars and began to propel the boat back down the river.

"You worry too much, Dan. It's inevitable that Harry will tell Robert of our encounter. He hopes already to offset the loss he has made tonight, and more, with the blood that runs through my veins. That's why he was so eager to part with this." Richard tapped the bag of coins inside his jacket. "Knowing his greed and offering the possibility of catching me was part of the bargain I placed. Even now, I have no doubt Harry has men riding to all the escapes he thinks I might take, hoping to waylay me as I run to spend his gold. Dan... I have no intention of being caught."

"Aye, that's as may be tonight, but there'll be other nights, mark it." Dan drove the oars hard into the black, silken surface of the water, exercising his annoyance by moving the boat a pace faster through the current.

Harry sat astride his horse as two men rode back to pull up next to him. The nearest shook his head. "No sign, Sir. From what you say, he could be living in there." The man cast a glance back over his shoulder towards the docklands.

Harry's mind had already cast Richard Fitzwarren in the mould of low life; he could visualise him sneaking amongst the dirt and filth. "Tomorrow, get down here and find out where he is. There's a purse for the man who brings me news of his whereabouts. Make that known amongst the others. I will have him!" Harry barked. Surrounded by his own men, he felt sure of himself once more, and so he turned his horse back in the direction of comforts so alien to the present setting and yet so necessary to Harry: goose feather pillows, malmsey, and raging fires.

The men searched most earnestly the following day, spurred by the promised reward. However, enquiries amongst the lowest levels of London society brought scant information regarding the man whom Harry's men sought.

He stood alone in the long hall, as was his wont of late, hands clasped behind his back. Northumberland stared up at the portrait of the man who had so magnificently changed the rules to marriage, to ruling, to legitimacy. He wondered if the portraits still laughed at him. If they did, he was no longer aware of it.

Time was not to be on his side. In June, John Dudley, Duke of Northumberland, accepted the imminent death of Edward; it was a matter of weeks, if not days, he had been told. There was no way Jane and Guildford could produce the heir he needed. Northumberland needed to get the Devise changed. Edward had to sign the amendment with the Privy Councillors witnessing it. The heir to the throne would then be the Protestant Lady Jane. Dudley began to draw support to his cause. Lady Jane must ascend to the throne of England and Catholic Mary, the chief rival to his scheme, must be secured, when the time came, in the Tower.

The Devise for the success was written in Edward's own hand. A single page whose words would direct the future of England. Naming Jane Grey's male heirs as his successor had placed the event of his death far into the future. Northumberland had been able to assure the young monarch that this was a mere security, an eventuality that he needed to provide against. Now, however, Northumberland needed Edward to change it, and that required that the boy be aware of the immediacy of his death.

Edward, propped up on pillows, his breath rasping noisily from tortured lungs, regarded the Duke with dark-rimmed eyes as he approached the bed.

"Where is Henry? Send him back. I don't want to be alone." Young Sidney, who spent his days at the boy's bedside, now slept in an adjacent room, so he was on hand when he was needed.

"I have a grave task," Northumberland said as he pulled a chair close to the side of the bed and sat down slowly, his eyes never leaving Edward's spent body.

Edward regarded him with a frightened gaze.

"Your country, your Kingdom needs you to safeguard her. Your physicians tell me that God is calling you to his side." Northumberland spoke the words slowly, watching Edward carefully, hoping the boy still had the capacity to understand what he was telling him and that he was not too late.

A gasp caught in the dry throat, and Edward's cracked lips parted, his voice little more than a whisper. "But Henry is giving me one of Brom's pups when they are born next month."

Northumberland ignored the remark and the boy's distress. "I need you to perform for me one last task, a simple one, and I will help."

Edward looked at him, confusion plain on his face. "Did you hear me?"

"We need you to amend the Devise, we will help you. Will you do it? It is a simple matter of a few words," Northumberland pressed, leaning towards the boy.

"I want Henry," Edward said, his voice cracking.

"He shall be returned to you, *after* this is complete," Northumberland's voice was hard.

"Please." Edward protested, trying to raise himself up on the pillows.

"He will be brought back to you as soon as we have this simple matter dealt with."

"Henry, come to me," the boy tried to raise his voice and call for his friend, but the command could not be heard outside of the darkened bedroom. "Bring him back, please," Edward tried again.

"Once this is done. The longer we argue, the longer you will be without him," Northumberland made the threat quite clear.

"I will do it. Bring him back," Edward conceded quietly, desperation in his voice.

"Very well," Northumberland, his hands on the arms of the chair, he began to rise.

"Only if you bring him back now, I'll do it, but I want Henry here, now," Edward managed. The effort of making the demand sent him into a coughing fit, his body falling back against the pillows.

Northumberland did not really want any more witnesses to this event than was necessary, and those that would see it had been carefully chosen. Henry Sidney, though, posed little threat, and he was sure he could control him. "As you wish."

The assembled group had evidently been waiting outside of the door. Privy councillors chosen for their loyalty to Northumberland, they would witness the changes. Entering with them, alarm on his face, was Henry Sidney.

The sheet that required Edward's alteration was placed on his lap on the bed. When it became obvious that the boy was reclined too far to be able to write, it was Northumberland who hoisted him up while another of those in attendance pressed a pillow behind his back to support him. Hunched over, damp hair clinging to his temples, Edward tried to focus on the sheet on the board before him.

"Here, I want you to draw a line through these words," Northumberland indicated with a blunt forefinger where he meant on the sheet.

"I can't see them properly," Edward's whistling voice declared.

Northumberland growled an order and a second sheet of clean parchment was produced, dropping it over the Devise, it covered up the bottom lines exposing only the first line. "The first line at the top, strike it through." A pen was placed in his hand, his fingers coaxed around the quill.

"Leave him be." Henry Sidney pushed between the councillors.

"Henry, sit with me," Edward managed, and the pen they had pressed into his right hand dropped to the covers.

"Damn it, Henry, stand back. This needs to be done," Northumberland growled. Retrieving the pen he slid it back into Edward's hand. "These words, strike them through."

A deadly silence fell as a pale emaciated hand drew a line through the first sentence on the Devise.

For lakke or issue of my body cumming of thissu femal

There was an exclamation from the man to Northumberland's left, and a rapid and heated conversation. Henry Sidney looked in alarm between the dying boy in the bed and the squabbling Privy Councillors.

"We needed that line! It still needs to say 'For lack of issue,'" the man supplied when Northumberland turned on him. "He's erased too much."

"Damn it man, you needed to be clear!" Northumberland swiped the devise from the board in front of Edward and the men in the room peered at the ruined document.

"He can write it in again here," one pointed to the space left between the title and the erased line, "as long as it's between the title and the signature, it will still be binding."

Northumberland, having difficulty containing his temper, turned back to Edward. "I was badly advised, your Majesty, just a few more words from you and we will leave you in peace." Then to the man on the opposite side of the bed, "Give him a pen, hold it for him."

The pen was again in Edward's hand, and slowly he wrote the words one at a time that Northumberland dictated. Each one written above the line he had struck out, and each one in a shaky script.

"For." Six pairs of eyes watched the word appear on the parchment.

"Lack, yes lack. That's right, now write 'of issue'..."

The process took place in silence, the only sound the tiny scratches on the page from the quill's tip and Northumberland's voice directing the writer.

"You've missed male," the man to the left of Northumberland piped up when Edward had finished as he was directed.

"Male!" Northumberland rounded upon him.

"It should read 'lack of issue male of my body,'" the councillor supplied again.

Northumberland's colour had risen again, and before further argument could ensue he had pushed the pen back into Edward's hand, sliding the Devise beneath it, demanding "male, write that one word here."

"No!" The call came from the man holding the board on the opposite side of the bed. "It's the lady's male heirs, not his, you fool."

There followed a frantic and loud argument during which the Devise for the succession was amended five more times, more words that Edward had added were crossed out. The final document witnessed and signed by the King that would direct the succession after his death looked more like a schoolboy's poor work rather than the instrument that would determine who controlled England during this tumultuous time.

Chapter Four

London – May 1553

At Syon House on the Thames, the ready pawn, Jane, waited to be moved one or maybe two paces forward. Northumberland was there too, deep in conversation with Jane's father, Henry Grey, Duke of Suffolk. The subject, as always, was a further assessment of the strengths and likely success of Northumberland's subversion of the succession. Dissecting, county by county, the likely support and evaluating which could be counted on.

"If it comes to it, we can hold London against Mary. Her support is confined to the North. The Protestant cause will pull southern counties to us, cutting her off before she can draw them from the north, and we will take the day," Suffolk summarised the discussion.

"Mary's papacy will bring her no support on that front, I agree. We must be prepared," Northumberland replied thoughtfully.

"Can we count on Cranmer?"

"Has he any choice?" Northumberland sputtered. "He knows his execution awaits him if Mary has her way, and Ridley knows that as well."

Thomas Cranmer, Archbishop of Canterbury, was an ardent supporter of the reformed religion. Ridley, Bishop of London, was an adherent of Cranmer's. Both men held a lot of sway. Ultimately, though, they would do what was best for themselves.

"They are powerful men, John, and they can pull many to our side. We need to nurture their support," Suffolk pointed out.

"I need do no such thing!" Northumberland replied angrily. "Understand this," he said, leaning forward. "Mary will throw the altar cloth over all of England the first day she puts a toe on the steps to the throne. All Protestants will suffocate under its weight. Cranmer and Ridley cannot afford to hesitate. It is Jane, and the reformed religion or a heretic's end. I should say it would not be a difficult choice."

Suffolk was not intimidated by Northumberland's attitude. "Can I take it from this that your policy on publicising the state of Edward's health has changed? I assume that there are still only a few who know how perilously close to death he is."

"Word will spread soon amongst our supporters. They should only need a little time to consider the alternatives. You forget, Henry, times are changing. Here is an opportunity that for many comes rarely in a lifetime. Those who stand with us know where our favours will lie when Mary is in the Tower. I rely on the Protestant cause, yes, but more than that, Henry, I rely on ambition. Ambition is the key."

Suffolk sat back in his seat and considered Northumberland's words. There was not much he could say, for it was his ambition that had led him to marry Jane to his son. He saw two men behind the throne of England: Northumberland, father-in-law of the Queen, and himself, with an even closer tie.

"So, how fares Jane?" Northumberland asked after a lengthy pause.

"Jane is much improved. Some minor ailment, I am told, laid her low last week." Suffolk didn't want to talk about Jane.

"Good, that is progress. We cannot have another in ill health." Suffolk knew that Northumberland's interest in the health of his son's new wife was no idle enquiry.

The answer Suffolk should have given was no. Jane was not faring well and was not a willing participant in their plans. Jane fought with her new husband, verbal battles so severe she now refused to speak to her father. For the last week, she had been shut in her room for fear of her yelling to anyone who would listen to what Suffolk planned to do with her. Jane, it seemed, had no illusions that it was for her father and Northumberland that she was to be made monarch. Recognising that she was nothing more than a piece on a chessboard she had told her father, on the last occasion she had spoken to him, that he should look in a mirror for she was sure he would see the strings on which Northumberland had such a tight hold.

Suffolk tapped his fingers against the chair arm. He was sure Northumberland was losing his political charm. He made assumptions about the support he would receive and did little these days to consolidate it. Suffolk's suspicions that he had allied himself to the wrong camp were always with him. The arrogance of the man with whom he now supped did nothing to help allay his fears.

On the same night on the other side of London, another meeting was taking place at which Northumberland's plans were being discussed.

Thomas Wyatt was a military commander of some note. His prowess on the field had, however, been born of necessity. The estates he had inherited from his father were riddled with debt and it had forced him to pursue a military career, which he did with success. His battlefield endeavours had provided him political status as the member of Parliament for Kent. He had not been at the meeting in London with Byrne. His loyalties lay with Mary's claim to the throne. Northumberland was a man who Wyatt did not like, and his scheme to change the succession shocked him.

Northumberland had petitioned many men, seeking support for his cause, Wyatt amongst them, but his feeble arguments were nothing more than a thin veneer to legitimise a scheme to place himself on the throne, and one Wyatt could not countenance.

Richard had met Wyatt before. His estate in Kent was adjacent to some of his father's land, and they had also met when Richard had worked for Seymour. Wyatt was a man crippled by a flawed inheritance, and he had traded information with Seymour in return for his patronage. With Seymour behind him, he had secured a command of his own and made a name for himself. When he was at Court, he lodged in an elegant town house belonging to his sister near The Strand, and it was here that Richard sought him out.

"You've spoken to Northumberland then?" Richard enquired. Both men sat in high-backed chairs facing a warming fire. Between them was set a low table with glasses and a wine flagon, now half empty.

Thomas Wyatt, shifting in the chair, straightened his legs out, moving his feet closer to the fire. "Who hasn't spoken to him? He's become incautious in the extreme. What started out as quiet enquiry has become his battle cry. He might as well nail a proclamation to every door, stating his intent. He's overstretched himself mightily."

"Overstretched?" queried Richard, reaching over and topping off Wyatt's glass.

"The man begs for support and makes repeated promises, and they are promises he cannot keep. I was talking with Godfrey Mount last week, he's got a large estate near the Welsh borders, and he could raise a fair number of men if he was pressed to do so," Wyatt paused.

"Go on," Richard prompted.

"Northumberland promised to resolve a property dispute in Godfrey's favour if he would pledge his support. It transpires that Northumberland promised the same to Lord Neath as well, the very man whom Godfrey is in dispute with. Now the fool has lost the support of both men. Mount was going to back Northumberland but when he found out about this double dealing, he withdrew from the cause entirely, pledging himself to Mary." Wyatt reached for the glass and eyed Richard over the rim. "So which side are you going to join when the time comes?"

Richard settled back into the chair and regarded Wyatt seriously. "Unlike you, no one is seeking my support with gilded promises."

A smile twitched the corner of Wyatt's mouth. "So, you'll wait and see then?"

Richard shrugged. "Perhaps."

"Well avoid Northumberland, otherwise you'll have tied yourself to another worthless scoundrel who will be bound for the block," Wyatt replied, swilling the wine around the inside of the glass and watching the stain of it drain back towards the bottom.

Richard ignored the reference to Seymour and turned the conversation instead, now in a direction he wanted it to go. "You used to supply Seymour with information, and I know you are still well placed at Court and in Parliament as well."

Wyatt smiled. "So, we get to the point at last. You want my support?"

"I do. It might be that you can help me find my feet on the right side of the path," Richard supplied. "You are no supporter of Northumberland. If you have any news from his camp, I would like to know it."

Thomas Wyatt rubbed a hand over his face thoughtfully. "And why would I want to do that?"

Richard reached inside his doublet and fished out a small red leather purse, the top of it tied closed with cord. He dropped it onto the table between them, where on landing it made an unmistakable chink as the coins inside rattled.

Wyatt, his eyebrows raised, placed his glass on the table and took the purse, deftly pulling the securing string loose so he could observe the contents. Hefting it in his hand, his eyes could see the ten gold coins inside. Wyatt pulled the cord tight again, closing the purse and set it back on the table next to the glass. "That is quite a sum. What is it you want to know?"

"Who his supporters are, what they can lend to him in terms of military strength, and who is against him? I am sure the situation is not a fixed one," Richard said.

Wyatt grunted. "You'd be right. There are many men who make it quite plain that they are in the marketplace for the best deal. Mary is not at court, her faction remains quiet, and at the moment, it is only Northumberland who is seeking to turn everyone to his side."

When Richard left an hour later, the purse remained on the table and he was confident that Wyatt would supply him with news. Wyatt had no liking for Northumberland, and even less liking for the contrived plan he was intending to use to secure the power behind the throne.

The purse that Harry offered did not go unclaimed. In the end, it was the prize of one man. That he did not live to take possession was because of his fatal misjudgement of the ability of his quarry.

At Harry's direction, his men searched alehouses, brothels and all places where men who had slipped from the last rung of the ladder of humanity sought obscurity. One, Peter Hardwood, avoided looking in the dockland. He took himself instead on a tour of the usurers, moneylenders, and pawnbrokers; the *mont-de-piété* of London. Harry had described a man outcast and short of money. Well, maybe he had borrowed, thought Peter, who from times spent as a collector of debts for a previous master knew the marketplace well, and most of those who operated within it.

Mya the Jew was his first call after the bells had struck noon. His customers always thought of him as half a man, so short and spare of frame he was almost a dwarf, and yet he lacked the ill-proportioned limbs of that breed. But whatever lack of physical presence Mya's God had blessed him with, they knew he had been greatly endowed with what lay between his ears.

Items for sale were kept in the front part of the shop under the watchful eyes of a pair of unlikely looking shop attendants. Two stocky men, short blades visible in their belts and with bare muscled forearms, ensured Mya's goods remained secure in the shop.

Here, all manner of chattels crowded the uneven wooden shelves: household pewter of varying quality, pots and pans of all sizes. A lute with two broken strings vied for position with a pile of assorted bridles, candleholders, and two sooty oil lamps. There was a display of ill-matching brown earthenware plates, jugs and bowls and, out of reach of straying fingers, cheap women's jewellery hung from a nail-spiked board next to a long, worn display of boots a cobbler would despair at.

Wheat prices had doubled in 1550, and poor harvests in the two successive years had kept prices high. Mya had fared well from the misfortune of the common man. When times were hard, men needed money. To start with, they took the coins home and fed their families, but then, as life tumbled towards hopelessness, they needed money for the oblivion of the alehouse. As Peter waited to see Mya, his eyes ran over the shelves packed with trinkets. The deaths of their owners had rendered them superfluous; so many lives had been lost in the sweating sickness epidemic the previous year.

Scenting profit, the withered usurer listened hopefully to Peter's questions, head tipped back to defy his lack of height and look into Peter's face. No, he had not seen such a man. Of course, he scoffed back at Peter. He had an excellent memory for all who owed him money, and the one Hardwood sought was, most unfortunately, not among them.

Peter thanked Mya briskly for his time. He turned, his hand about to lift the curtain so he could duck back from Mya's inner sanctum to the shop, when something caught his eye.

Behind the cloth that partitioned the back part of the shop, and where Mya conducted private business, gems and other items of worth were neatly stacked on shelves under the Jew's watchful gaze, the owners and marks loaned against them carefully transcribed in Mya's books. Some would be without owners, redemption time long past, payment not made; for others, the owners would remain hopeful of possessing again the goods they had been forced to leave in return for scant coinage. Peter had now spent three years in Harry's service. He was well aware of his master's worship and fear of Robert Fitzwarren, and had seen the man frequently. He instantly recognised the Fitzwarren crest engraved in the silver work of a sword hilt. The sword lay horizontally along the back of a shelf it shared with a selection of ladie's trinket boxes. Next to the hilt stood four matched silver goblets, not of the current fashion, but all containing a good portion of the valued metal. Their surfaces had been tainted by the acidic touch of fingers, the marks contrasting with the high shine from the weapon. Peter knew it had not been there long.

Peter turned back to Mya. "It appears you might be able to help me after all."

Mya lifted his eyes to Peter's face and smiled. "That would be most fortunate. Please tell me how?" Mya's eyes followed Peter's up to the shelf where the sword lay.

"How long have you had that sword?" Peter asked.

"Mmm... The man you seek is not the one who brought that; he does not fit the description you gave. However, there may be some connection. My records could be checked..." Mya left the sentence unfinished.

"For a price?" Peter grinned.

Everything in Mya's shop had a price, even information. Currency tendered, Mya smiled toothlessly and turned to the half-completed and most current page in the ledger. The blank lines still following the entry told Peter that Mya had not been in possession of the item long. Mya confirmed he had received it less than two days ago. The name entered on the page was, of course, a lie, and the description Mya gave of his customer initially was unlike the one Harry had given Peter.

"Did the man who left this have yellow hair?" Peter asked, his attention riveted on the usurer.

Mya nodded. "Yes, as bright as gold."

"And did he have blue eyes?" Peter asked quickly, a hopeful expression settling on his face.

"Bright blue, like sapphires," Mya supplied.

"Jack," Peter spoke the name slowly. He had served in Harry's household with Jack and knew of the incident on Harlsey moor when Jack, for some unknown reason, had changed sides. Jack was a man marked by his appearance, and one never easily forgotten.

"Is this the man you are looking for?" Mya pressed.

"No, but I think he maybe the servant of the man I am trying to trace. It seems likely that he sent him here to exchange his sword for coin rather than coming himself," Peter concluded, grinning.

"I am pleased I could help," Mya replied.

"This is where men of his type always end up when they are short of money to keep them in the alehouse for a few more nights," Peter replied, an edge of disgust in his voice.

"It's a curse on some men," Mya agreed sadly, "but I just offer a service where I can. What they spend their money on is out of my control."

"And I am pleased you've offered your service to this man. It has been useful to me indeed."

Peter handed Mya his remaining coins to ensure he shared this gem with no one else and, with a promise of more, rapidly retrieved his horse and made his way quickly back to Harry.

Jack's careless disposal of his sword had been borne of physical desperation when Molly finally refused to live on promises anymore. Jack had been forced to find some coin, and that coin had been provided by Mya. As soon as Richard gave Jack the money he had asked for, Jack set off to redeem what was his. But the shop was now being watched. Peter was rewarded sooner than he would have let himself dream when Jack swung down from his horse and ducked through the low door into the dim confines of Mya's shop. Jack emerged after conducting the rapid transaction. Armed once more, he pulled himself back into the saddle, and turned his horse from the pawnshop.

He was not in a hurry and Peter, now with three of Harry's men to help him, had little difficulty following him. Still aware of Richard's words to keep his head down, Jack returned directly to the inn, leading Harry straight to Richard Fitzwarren.

Harry wanted Richard alive; he wished to deliver the ultimate gift to Robert to toy with as he wished. As for Jack, Harry's eyes had clearly conveyed the message to Peter that the demise of the man could not happen soon enough.

"Tonight, Jack, be ready to leave. I want to be at Byrne's tomorrow."

Richard was perched on the window ledge, absently watching the street below.

"I shall be glad to be out of here," Jack mused.

"How will you cope, Jack?" Richard asked, looking carefully at his brother. "We are to spend weeks, perhaps months, quietly in the country. If a few days in an Inn have driven you to distraction, how does that prospect please you?"

Jack shot Richard a dark look. "I shall be again at my own control, not forced to hide away out of sight while you decide our fate."

"Ah, so you see your fate in my poor and inadequate hands. Now that is a worry," Richard's voice was mocking. "Do you think I am equal to the task?"

"I agree it's a worry," Jack's tone was sarcastic.

"The remedy is in your own hands," Richard provided.

"Fate has brought me so far. I shall wait and see where it takes me next," Jack declared.

"Fate!" Richard was finally annoyed. "Fate is the excuse of the uninventive, the unimaginative, and the ignorant. I had no idea you were all three! Fate, in this instance, means, I assume, that you will wait and see what is brought to you by my efforts. I feel much like a bantam with a bet on it. Thank you, however, for the confidence."

"I only meant..." Jack tried, but they were poor words and it was obvious he had never intended to complete the sentence.

"Leave it, Jack, and me. Go. Find some place comfy and contemplate the future and what place, if any, you have in it." Richard was still angry.

"Damn you... I will be ready tonight! I'll not stand and listen to any more of your twisted words."

Richard regarded him with a cool, level gaze. "The solution to that is most certainly in your own hands."

"One of these days I will bloody leave you and you can find someone else to do your bidding!" Jack left, slamming the door hard in its badly fitted frame.

Richard left his room shortly after and set himself towards the stables at the back of the inn where his own horse was kept. Crossing the yard, his attention was caught by a heated argument taking place between a girl and a water carrier. He couldn't quite keep a smile from his face as he listened to the girl berating the man. Slim, brown-haired, and half the water carrier's size, she'd squared herself up to him and clearly had no intention of backing down.

"It's filthy. I'm not paying, I don't care what you say you are going to do to me," the girl blazed, hands on her hips, elbows jutting out sideways.

"There's nothing wrong with it. Now pay up." The water carrier shrugged one of the leather straps from his shoulder.

"I will not. I wouldn't wash my feet in that. It's that bloody filthy." The girl glared at him, her eyes alight with temper.

"I didn't break my back lugging that up here to be talked to like this," he growled as he loosened the second strap and dropped the keg to the ground. The pewter cups tied to the side jangled noisily on the cobbles. A huge paw like hand flew through the air destined to land on the side of the girl's face.

The water carrier yelped in surprise as his wrist was grasped and painfully wrenched downwards.

"Let's see if she's telling the truth, shall we?" Richard said quietly, still gripping the man's wrist,

"What's this got to do with you?" The water carrier's voice was high pitched, and he gasped against the pain.

"I too like clean water, so let's see what you've got in here." Richard, releasing his wrist, pushed him away hard. There was a bung on the side of the keg and he kicked it loose.

"No!" yelled the water carrier as his wares escaped in great big belching glugs from the wooden cask.

Richard dipped a hand into the cool cascade and held up the palm full in front of the water carrier's face. "She's right. I've seen cleaner puddles in the street." Richard cast the filthy dregs into the man's face who flinched as if he had been struck. "Now go."

A moment later, the water carrier pressed the bung home again and, hastily hitching one of the leather straps over his shoulder, hurriedly made his way from the yard. Richard turned to the girl. "Go to Great Conduit Street near Mercers' Chapel, you'll get better water there."

Her eyes were still full of anger. "I've not time, and he knows it."

Richard resisted a smile, instead he said seriously, "Mistress, I am sorry the water carrier tried to dupe you."

"The likes of him won't dupe me. Do I look like I was born last week?"

Richard, amused, kept it from his voice. "No, no, you don't." Then unable to stop himself, he added, "Maybe a week last Tuesday, but certainly not last week."

The girl's eyes widened, and a curse slipped past her lips.

"Here, straighten your face, and try Great Conduit Street." Richard, grinning, flipped a coin towards her through the air.

A filthy hand snatched the coin from the air. Her eyes never leaving his face.

Richard turned to continue his journey to the stables and heard the landlady calling for the girl from inside the inn.

"Lizbet, where the bloody hell are you?"

The Duke of Suffolk was also at that moment being tried by another difficult conversation. Jane was still at Syon House in quiet retreat as befitted a newlywed. Unfortunately, Jane was not acting as a newly wedded daughter should.

"Jane. I hear your argument but, Jane, understand this if nothing else: the act is done; the time is past. You are married to Guildford. Edward will name you as his successor, and your reason, your philosophy, your morals and your bloody ideals matter naught. They cannot change it." Suffolk's head ached with the desperation of his arguments.

Jane didn't reply, but turned in a swirl of rose velvet to gaze moodily from the window.

Suffolk advanced to stand behind his daughter. "Fathers are set to try and gain the best for their children. I admit, as you constantly remind me, that this is an opportunity for me, but why can you not see it as an equal opportunity for yourself?"

Jane still stood staring through the glass panes.

Suffolk saw her lack of words as an improvement on the tirades she had previously thrown at him. He was hopeful the girl was finally seeing sense. He continued, "Jane, you are sensible. Tell me then what you propose to do when the time comes. Admit it; there is little you can do." That concluded Suffolk's case, and he left his daughter staring from the window, not seeing the tears slide with anguished abandon down her young face.

Peter had heard plenty of tales and alehouse gossip about Robert Fitzwarren's feud with his brother, and of the death he had attempted to deliver at Harlsey Moor. The reason for the deep and rancid hatred that lay within Robert had remained the subject of conjecture: some childhood transgression, some woman. Whatever the true reason, it had never come to light.

Conversations on the matter had dwindled steadily after Richard Fitzwarren had left England's shores and Peter had even heard a rumour that Richard had met his death in France. Peter himself had been a part of the pack that had pursued Richard when Jack, for some reason unknown, had changed sides and rescued him from, according to Harry, the certain death he had been about to deliver.

Of Richard, Peter knew little. Most tales from Harry and Robert cast the man he now pursued as a coward and a trickster, one who spent his life skulking in the gutter and would turn tail and run, as he had done at Harlsey Moor, rather than face an adversary. No honour, no courage: a weasel of a man.

Peter Hardwood made his first mistake in believing he had little to fear from Richard Fitzwarren, who he expected to easily capture and return to Harry in exchange for his pension.

Peter had already made discreet enquiries of the landlord and, on a promise of recompensing him for "any damage which might ensue," knew the room his prey occupied. Jack he had seen walking the short distance to the stables. He had kept himself out of sight and the other had not seen him; Jack's ability he did not underestimate having served with him. He had to risk losing him, for Richard was his quarry. Jack was merely something his master would prefer to have stopped from breathing. He could deal with him later.

The third door along the corridor belonged to the man they sought who, by all accounts, for they had watched the inn since their arrival, had not left his room. Peter motioned with his head for the two men to take up positions on either side of the door, flush against the wall. Peter knocked quietly but firmly. There was a muffled reply from within, which he took to mean he should admit himself. Signalling to the others to hold their positions, he unlatched the door, letting it swing open on its hinges. There was only one occupant, seated reading by the fire. Peter smiled, his expression confident.

"Jack, back so..." Richard was on his feet in a moment, his sword drawn.

"Your mistake," Peter said, smiling viciously. "So you're Fitzwarren?"

If the man before him had not met his gaze and silently acknowledged his name, he would have believed he had the wrong room. Expecting the filth of gutter-life, he was instead faced with a vision of tall elegance whose dark eyes showed no fear.

"I'd lay down your blade, for it'll do you no good. Willy, Gad..." The two waiting outside obeyed the command. Richard heard the whistle of steel as swords were drawn and they entered behind their leader.

"Now, put up your blade or you'll be regretting it." Peter's level weapon underlined his point.

"The odds seem in my favour. I shall take them, I think," Richard replied.

"I'll give you one more chance." Peter was no longer smiling, hoping now that the man would not take it. Then he made his second mistake. Armed only with a short blade, he did not have the advantage that his opponent had. With a jarring crash of silvered steel, Richard brought his longer sword quickly up under Peter's, making his aggressor's arm flail wildly in the air. Peter's face displayed desperation as he fought to regain control of his sword arm and bring his steel back in front of him to protect his torso before it was too late.

It was too late.

Richard slid a steel point easily through a leather jerkin and then neatly on, through ribs to pierce the beating heart of Peter Hardwood. In the second it took for Richard to withdraw his sword from the dead man and for the corpse to hit the floor, Peter's men set on him. The attacker to the left had the advantage of a shorter distance and his fist, tight around the hilt of a dagger, was arcing it towards Richard's head. The technique was clumsy, relying on power for its deadliness. Richard stepped nimbly back, kicked a chair into the man's path, giving him time to withdraw his sword from the dead man and avoid the lethal sweep of the dagger. His sword, running with the crimson of Peter's blood, deflected the first thrust from the third man.

The room was small and forced them close together. As the other's blade hit the hilt, Richard threw the force of his body round and heard the steel snap. The move was perfect but its execution was flawed, for as he spun to break it he brought himself to face the man whose ill-aimed death sweep with the dagger he had easily evaded. In the second before the blade broke and his sword was employed and locked, tempered steel sliced into the flesh of his right shoulder. The man leered, exposing a row of glistening black stumped teeth, but believing the game was his proved fatal. Richard's jacket took the brunt of the force, but the wound was still deep.

Dropping his sword from the weakening right grasp into his left hand, he brought the blade heavily into the man's left arm. It was not a killing blow, but he reeled from it, his body bending to its force. Richard levelled the blade a second time and forced its point into gut and intestine. The man doubled over, then sagged to the floor, hands clasped to the gashed wound in his midsection. Richard turned instinctively to protect his right side from the assailant whose blade he had severed. He had no need; the man's body slithered from the short knife Dan had pulled across his throat.

"I told you, but do you bloody listen?" Dan moved to the man, kneeling with both hands clenched to his guts and moaning loudly. He drew the knife blade quickly across his neck.

Jack fell through the doorway in time to see Dan dispatch the kneeling man and knew that the fight was done. "Bloody hell!" Jack took the sword from his brother and dropped it heavily on the floor. "Are you alright?"

Richard pulled away from Jack's helping hands. "Do you know how much good steel costs?"

"I'm sure you are going to... God's bones! It's Pete– he's Harry's man! He was with Harry before I left. How did he track us here?" Jack demanded. "This is terrible! I told you what would bloody happen, and you didn't listen. Is someone going to have to die before you learn?

Richard sat on the bed as Dan examined the wound. "Jack has..." He pulled the sleeve away none too gently. "... got a point."

"Yes." Richard flinched from Dan's ministrations. "So you get to be right for once," he finished through gritted teeth.

"It's a clean cut," Dan pronounced bluntly.

"I'm so pleased." Richard retorted.

"What are we going to do now?" Jack asked. "We need to get out of here. Now."

"Take the men to Carney Bridge." Richard stopped as Dan yanked a makeshift bandage onto his arm. "Damn you! Could you be a bit more careful?"

Dan just grunted.

"Collect the men and go to Carney Bridge." Richard said through clenched teeth.

There was another rough tug on his arm. "Dan, you've made your point! I'll send word to you, Jack. Now go before anyone else turns up."

Chapter Five

Bedfordshire – May 1553

Jack worried all the way to Carney Bridge, and once there, he continued to torment himself. Richard's men had been split into three groups while residing in the city; six were with Richard, eight were billeted at the Fox, and the remaining seven awaited their arrival at Carney Bridge. Joined once more, they would move swiftly to Lord Byrne's Manor; or at least, that was the plan. Now Jack was not so sure. Riding with twelve men at his back, he was uncertain what they would do when they arrived. Jack felt strangely exposed, the feeling prickling up and down his spine; never before had he found himself alone with the solitary role of command. He was plagued with the knowledge that there was no longer a certain course of action. And worse, he was dubious about his own ability now that he was faced with the need to assess it.

He refused to comment to those who rode beside him; there were only three people who knew of the day's events and Jack had no intention of sharing the news. They would feel leaderless; without their master, the thread that held them would break and they would disintegrate back into their component parts, becoming again the rabble they once were. And within that rabble, there were plenty of factions.

There was Alan, a hard and cruel man, and it was well known that to keep on his good side was a sound idea. He had held some post in the King's army but, for some reason, he didn't care to share. He had deserted, yet he still craved the rank and power he had once held. Robby was one of Alan's men. A petty thief, he'd been in and out of gaol most of his life in between a sporadic mercenary career. He kept close to Alan, thinking that would ensure an easier life. There were others loyal to Richard, if not particularly keen on Jack. There was Dan who had been with Richard since boyhood, and others who owed him their life or liberty such as Marc and Froggy Tate. Jack knew he could rely on them to follow his brother's instructions.

He knew he lacked the physical energy and force of will his brother exercised, along with the natural obedience due to him as a Lord's son, and Jack doubted the men would follow his command. Richard had negotiated their hire with Lord Byrne and it was unlikely that a Lord would accept a man with no name and no standing in Richard's place. Jack damned fate, and anything else that got within vocal reach on the journey.

Harry's thoughts that day also turned to Richard; they were not tinged with concern but coloured crimson with hatred. The assault at the Inn was swiftly reported back, although the details were vague. There had been a fight; Harry's messenger had seen a commotion as he waited for the return of his fellows, but neither they nor the man his master wanted had appeared. Harry yelled, but his temper was ineffectual. The man knew only that the men Harry had sent were missing, and the landlord had left the yard of the inn, calling for the watch. Having no wish to be implicated, the messenger had made a judicious exit at this point. Clothed in the righteous indignation of the wronged, Harry rode with a not inconsiderable escort to the inn to find out what had occurred, eager still to make of Richard a prize he could present to Robert.

The sight that met his greedy eyes was not the one he had anticipated. Three men, good men at that, had been piled in a bloody mess on the back of a market barrow in the inn's courtyard. On the top of the pile of lifeless, tangled limbs lay Peter on his back, arms flung akimbo, head tipped back, mouth open in a silent exclamation of surprise as he stared up at his master for the last time. Harry, still on his horse, could not take his eyes from the twisted wreckage of his servants. A dog stood patiently licking Peter's paled hand that hung over the cart's low wooden side, its grubby fur streaked with crimson from the thick globules that had leaked through the barrow.

"You..." Harry recovered himself and shouted at the two men deep in conversation behind the barrow. One, dressed simply, was talking rapidly, his arms thrown wide in an expression of helplessness. The other, in military garb, was listening intently, his arms folded. Both looked up at the sound of Harry's voice. Annoyance plainly showed on the soldier's face.

"You, come here," Harry addressed the one of rank, pointing arrogantly with his whip. The soldier exchanged another brief and quiet word with the man he had been quizzing and walked past the corpse-laden barrow to stand in front of Harry's horse. He eyed the man's finery and cost of his clothes but seemed to have decided to wait for the next address rather than speak himself.

Harry waved his whip expansively over the barrow. The words would not easily form. "These..." He paused, his eyes had been drawn back to Peter's unseeing gaze, and it took a moment for him to break away from the dead stare. "These are my men. What happened? Where is the culprit?" Harry's voice was loud, with an edge generated by the unsettling scene and a temper about to break.

"That, Sir, is what I have been attempting to find out. If these were your men, maybe you can provide an explanation."

The soldier's interest in Harry kindled as he looked up into the puffy, emotionally confused visage. Harry's eyes could not prevent themselves from flicking back to Peter's face. Tearing himself from it, he stared instead at the white trembling fingers grasping his whip. He seemed not to have heard the soldier's words.

"These are all your men?" the soldier tried again.

"Yes." The answer was reaction only; Harry's composure was still not fully recovered.

"What were they at here?" the soldier persisted.

"Trying... to find... a criminal..." Harry stammered, "A man who appears now also to be a murderer. Do you have him?" Harry leant forward in the saddle, suddenly eager. His mind had conjured up a picture of a fourth corpse. A pleasing image of a partially dismembered, disfigured, and bleeding body, one that replaced the horror in the cart, and this vision disturbed him not at all.

"That, Sir, was what I was trying to find out from the landlord," the soldier replied patiently, gesturing back at the man who had been helplessly waving his arms about. "He let the room where this deed took place, but to a man he has no name for, and that person is no longer here. The man can describe him; perhaps the description could help you to put a name..."

"You fool!" Harry yelled, a nasty sneer sliding across his features. "I know well who is responsible." Any intention Harry had of wanting to keep the identity of the man he sought to himself was lost to him as his temper flared. "Richard Fitzwarren is who you seek for this day's work, and let that be known."

He roughly yanked the reins in his hands and the leather straps tightened as the startled horse was hauled away from the courtyard. More questions would follow, but Harry was not prepared to be grilled by some underling in a common yard in front of his both living and dead retinue.

Away from the inn, his path was blocked by a glut of street children fighting boisterously over fruit fallen from a market cart. The owner had abandoned his seat on the cart and was bobbing up and down among them. Eventually retrieved, unspoilt fruit clasped to his chest, a free arm aimed ineffectual blows at any ragged urchins who came too near. Harry took in the scene in a second. None of the children had heard his approach. The ugly sneer he had turned on the soldier spread once more across his lips. Cruelly, he spurred the horse forwards, flesh squashing as easily as ripened fruit below the iron-shod hooves. The stallholder fled, his wares falling forgotten from his arms as he threw himself from the advancing horses.

Dan had served Richard since he was a child. Mat, although he had only been with Richard some two years, had been saved from a sword point by the master and was equally loyal. They had half-carried Richard from the inn in London and made good their escape before the soldiers turned up, relocating to another inn some five miles distant. Although Richard's injury was not severe, he had lost a fair amount of blood and was certainly not fit for a long ride. Mat, at Richard's direction, had returned to the original inn, spending two hours all eyes and ears. After Harry had left, two of his men had remained drawn to the scent of ale. Mat had joined them. A curious observer with enough coin to buy ale, he had been welcomed.

Dan met Mat in the inn downstairs. It was a quiet place frequented by local folk. Patrons scattered in small clustered groups of twos and threes amongst the tables, filling the inn with the low undertone of conversation, the words indiscernible. The blacksmith's huge hands dwarfed the cup he held as he used it to gesture to the wheelwright who had joined him in friendly conversation. Farm workers, knees browned with soil, hands tinted with ochre, spoke in tired voices. The landlord finally brought cups and a jug of ale drawn from the barrel in the corner.

"Well?" Dan asked.

"Harry's men alright; the place was crawling with them. Bastard turned up himself while I was there," Mat replied.

"Are you sure no one saw you, did not connect you?" Dan leant closer to his companion.

"It isn't me you should worry about," Mat said grimly.

Dan cast an enquiring look over his companion. "Go on?"

"Ah well now, who do you think, eh?" Mat paused for effect; he could already see the suspicion forming on the other's face. "Aye, you're right. Put his sword in hock, and got himself followed, stupid bastard."

"For Christ's sake!" Dan bowed his head and covered his face with his hands. "Has Jack got no bloody sense?"

"Apparently not." Mat lifted his drink. "And the master?"

"A fouler temper I have never seen him in, which is why I am down here and he's..." Dan looked at the ceiling.

"He has some of the devil in him, that's a fact." Mat took a lengthy draught. Belching, he continued. "You going to tell the Master how Harry found him, then? I bloody would. Jack doesn't use this." Mat tapped his head with a thick, hairy forefinger.

Dan seemed to be in agreement. "I'll tell him if he asks. Jack's no fool, but put him in the same room as the Master and he doesn't know whether to run round yapping like a pup or bite."

"Well, I wonder what he's at sometimes." Mat pointed a finger sternly at Dan to underline his words. "He's no pup. He's a bastard, and it's in his bloody nature to want what he hasn't got. The Master knows that as well. It vexes me though why he puts up with him sometimes."

"However, it's been mixed, they've got the same blood in them, and that counts for something," Dan spoke firmly. There was more he could have said, more he knew, but he couldn't share it.

"Not bloody much, judging by the fact that Robert wants to bleed every last drop from them both, blood kin or no," Mat scoffed.

"Well, that's it, isn't it?" Dan leaned forward. "Perhaps the Master doesn't want another brother itching to put a blade through him. It'll go one way or the other. I hope for their sakes and ours they'll stand together."

"If Jack acts like this again, he'll be standing alone," Mat said bluntly.

Dan sighed. "There was no intention in what he did. It's as you said, he didn't think."

"I'm sure you'd not be so quick to defend me." Mat sounded angry that Dan did not share his disgust at Jack's foolishness.

"I don't defend him, Mat. Jack's here because the master wants him here and while that's the case, I'll follow his wishes." Dan gestured with the jug for Mat to present his cup for a refill. "Now, let's see if a little more of this will lessen some of that temper of yours."

Mat sighed and pushed his cup forward. "Well, it's the way I feel. The Master would have either of our hides for an act such as that."

"That's as may be." Dan used a quiet voice, aimed at calming the other's ire before it flared again, fuelled by ale. "But let's drink to the fact that as yet we have avoided it." Dan paused and placed the jug carefully back on the table. "Although, if I do recall, there was a moment when you almost managed it." Dan looked at the furrows on Mat's brow and his grin widened. "How did it go again? Ah yes, I remember... One wench, one husband, three brothers, and more kinfolk than can gather at a market. You did try to start your own war that day, didn't you?"

A smile spread across Mat's face. "I do remember how a tumble in a hayfield in France had brought the whole village out. Armed with forks, sticks, rolling pins and anything they could find to thrash the Englishmen who they thought were set to despoil all their womenfolk. No sense of humour, that was their problem," Mat chortled. "Mind you, she was worth it. If I had the chance again, I'd take the lot of them on for her."

"As I recall, your wenching cost me a right good stab in the arse with a hay fork trying to keep you in possession of your manhood," Dan said with mock seriousness.

While Dan and Mat shared the evening, Jack sat alone, staring at the meal set before him. A sludge of unidentifiable vegetables hid at the bottom of the bowl below a thin layer of lukewarm broth purporting to be rabbit stew. Jack stared at the greasy surface as it cooled, the dark wheaten bread in his right hand forgotten, as now was the desire to eat.

What was he going to do? It was the only thought he found himself capable of; he could not move beyond it. Breathing deeply, he pushed his hair back out of his eyes and looked around him for the first time since the light had disappeared from the sky. In the shadows, he recognised the faces of the men he had ridden with, waiting and sitting in groups. He saw some glance over at him surreptitiously. If they caught his eye, they quickly looked back at their companions. He didn't know what to do. The questions from the men he had ignored or, when pressed, spat back at them contemptuous answers until they had stopped asking, for which he was thankful.

Well, you've ruined everything now, Richard, haven't you? Jack thought. Pete was Harry's man, all right. He was there because you thought you could best Harry. I told you that it was bloody mad, but oh no, you wouldn't take heed, would you? And now what do you expect me to do? Jack silently cursed his absent brother. It didn't help. He still did not know what he was going to do.

"Do you want that, eh?" The voice from above him filtered through his angered thoughts. "You'll still have to pay, whether you eat it or not." The woman's voice above him increased in intensity. "I said, do you want it or not?"

Jack looked up at the pock-marked face. Grey, grease-matted hair snaked from beneath the once white cap. A lace edge, frayed away, hung over the wrinkled, dirty forehead in a curtain of straggling threads. Jack said nothing, but he matched the crone's stare. Pulling a coin from his belt, he sent it skittering across the table. A bony-knuckled hand snatched it, ending the spinning dance. She muttered something, tucked the coin from sight and turned, leaving Jack alone once more. Straightening his back from the slump his body had been drawn into by the weight of his thoughts, he pushed his bowl away. Some of the partially congealed contents slid over the rim to join the thick veneer of dried food and spilt ale already on the table.

Jack resolved to do something but characteristically decided to put off the decision until the following morning. He turned his thoughts to whether he should rent a room for himself above the Inn or share the communal quarters with the rest of the men. Though he badly wanted to divorce himself from his questioning companions, it was not possible. Jack, as usual, had few coins in his pocket. He was forced to try to find sleep in the room that doubled as a store with twelve other men, several empty barrels, a broken plough and jumbles of household debris the owner thought was still of some use. But the room was dry, and well heated by the number of slumbering bodies.

The other sleeping men grunted as they pulled covers tight to fend off the cold blast of air that heralded Mat's entrance. It was only Jack, unable to sleep, who saw Mat in the doorway. Alarmed that something had happened, he was on his feet in a moment, but Mat had already retreated from the fetid quarters. Stooping, he retrieved his fallen cloak and, wrapping the folds tightly around himself, stepped over the sleeping men and followed Mat.

"You stand there and look innocent, don't you, eh?" Mat challenged.

Jack said nothing, his confusion growing as his mind groped for some fact to allow him to understand Mat's aggressive tone.

Mat did not leave Jack ignorant for long. Jack soon knew how eager Mat was to let him know of the mistake he had made and that there was no doubt as to where the blame lay.

"Why the Master trusts you with anything I have no idea! You're a bloody fool, Jack, and a dangerous one at that." Mat remained furious. "I hope you know what you've done, and I hope the Master makes you suffer for it."

Mat also carried with him Richard's instructions for Jack, and the means, in the form of a weighty silver purse, to carry them out. The aim was to divide again what Jack had reunited, to break down the band into smaller groups, none of which knew where the others resided, the only link between them being Jack who directed them, and Richard who instructed him. The division was simple enough. Small groups were dispatched during the day to locations specified by Richard and given custody of a portion of the money they were due: enough for lodgings, enough for wine and women, enough to keep them until they were contacted again.

Two groups were dispatched as journeying labourers who came every year from the villages to work in the fields. A few more unfamiliar faces would not be commented on. There was some general complaint. No one fancied weeks of toil over the plough for labourer's wages. However, as he pointed out, Jack's portion of the coins made them the best paid farm workers in all of England, something none could disagree with. They walked; soil turners didn't own horses. A third party went, under the guise of traders, to a village where annually a horse fair took place. For a few weeks, they gathered and variously drank, wenched, and insulted each other boisterously in the haggle over horseflesh; the horses from those who had left on foot went with them. Jack had thought Richard had been idle when he had been in London, now he knew a little of what had occupied his time.

Mat passed on the detail verbally to Jack after he returned to the inn. Jack's face was grimly set, his back straight, the strain of the initial shock gone from him. The morning's work had made a considerable dent in the money Mat had passed to Jack, who guessed it comprised almost Richard's entire stock of coins. Jack calculated Richard must have scant means for his own support, having passed on almost all of what he had.

Jack eyed Mat, who had remained with him as he had executed the plans during the morning. "Has he enough?" It was the first reference to his brother that had been made since Mat had spoken harshly to him before daybreak.

"Aye, Dan's with the Master, don't worry about that," Mat said, and then added, "Jack, you've done well this morning. If you wanted to make recompense for what you did, you have set out on the right path."

Jack accepted Mat's words in silence. The instructions that he passed on had been executed without fault. Jack brooked no argument that day from anyone and by midmorning they were all departed separately from the Inn at Carney Bridge.

There were only the two of them left now. Following Richard's directions, they remained at the Inn for two more nights, and then they made the short and uneventful journey to Lord Byrne's.

Jack judged the Manor when it came into view to be an affluent enough place. Hazeldene's walls were in good repair, fences stood sturdily, and the land around was ordered and well controlled. Hazeldene had grown from an original Norman stronghold to more of a country residence. Wings had been added in an unplanned manner. The outline in the last light of the afternoon showed rooflines at a dozen differing levels. In one wing the low sun glinted in the diamond glass panelled window, its uneven facets reflecting the light like the rippled surface of a pond. Byrne, Jack assessed, was not short of money. His nerves had returned again as they rode up the final stretch towards the gate, unsure of the reception he would receive. Their horses moved at a slow amble. Jack saw that the gates to the enclosed courtyard stood open, but he was denied a view of the interior by a slight bend in the path ahead.

"Looks like a pleasant enough place to spend a few weeks, doesn't it?" Mat said, inclining his head towards Jack.

Jack didn't reply–his thoughts were elsewhere–and he was not looking forward to the encounter with Byrne. It was only four days since they had left London and there was a good possibility that the communication Richard was supposed to have sent to Byrne to advise of their arrival had not preceded him. The moment would not be one to relish if he had to inform their employer that, albeit temporarily, the mercenary leader he had hired was indisposed. The even more unpleasant knowledge that this was his fault dogged Jack's every waking hour. The agony of it was worse because, whichever way he looked at it, he could see no way that he would have acted differently. Richard had warned him and he had casually ignored his words and left the inn. If the warning had been couched in stronger terms, or even if he had been aware that Peter was trying to find their lodgings, Jack would still, he was sure, have decided he could outwit Harry's lackeys and exchange his sword for silver. It was a hard and bloody lesson indeed.

The two horses, side by side, turned the bend in the path. Jack's view of the courtyard was still incomplete, but Mat, who had ridden round the outside, was the first to see fully into the confines of Hazeldene.

"There, Jack, near the stable door! It's the Master's horse," Mat said quickly.

"Dan could have ridden it here," Jack replied, his eyes intent on finding a further sign of his brother.

"Maybe," Mat agreed.

Jack's mind ran through the possibilities; the most favoured one that his brother had preceded him. He did not want to hope for.

Their horses drew level with the gate and passed on beneath the Norman arch. Jack was loosening a foot from its stirrup as his mount drew to a stand when the evidence came to him of Richard's presence. From behind him came his brother's level voice in pleasant conversation with another. The words he could not catch, but the sound of it was unmistakable.

Jack dropped from the saddle and turned a little uneasily towards the brother he had almost killed with carelessness. Richard was descending the stairs from what was probably the main hall. His partner in conversation, a young woman, was standing smiling in the doorway. Richard had evidently been taking his leave of her.

Jack was not prepared for this encounter. Did Richard know how Harry's men had found him? If he did, the pleasant expression on his face as he approached did not tell him so.

"I trust the journey was a pleasant one?" Richard dropped down the last two steps. Jack, temporarily at a loss for adequate words, said nothing. "Dan," Richard continued, "will show you where to go." Jack turned to see the big man lumbering towards them. "I will no doubt see you later."

"Where are you going?" Jack said, recovering himself.

Richard stopped. His grey eyes met Jack's for the first time. "To while away some pleasant hours in the company of a lady," he said. His face lost its pleasant expression, and he added, "The cost, however, is extremely cheap: a few lessons of chess."

Oh God, he knew!

The thought avalanched through Jack's brain as he watched his brother turn his back and ascend the stairs once more towards the hall door.

Chapter Six

Bedfordshire – May 1553

After some enquiry, Jack discovered Richard had been allocated quarters within the main house. He found the general area and, in the process of trying to locate the precise room, met Dan as he rounded a corner. The big man came towards him, blocking his path. Behind Dan was a short corridor containing two doors, one on either side of the passage, which then came to an abrupt end.

"I want to see him," Jack whispered.

"You can't," Dan growled firmly but equally quietly.

"Why not?" Jack retreated a step down the corridor as Dan continued to come towards him.

"Why do you think?" Dan retorted.

"He seemed…"

Dan did not let him finish. "Seemed all right this afternoon? Is that what you were going to say?" Dan brought his face close to Jack's. "And if he's all right you can set yourself on a journey to heal your own soul. No point in Jack suffering if the rest of the world's back to rights, is there now? Well, you don't look too closely do you?"

Jack didn't wait for Dan to conclude his lecture, but ducked under his right arm and spun quickly past him to the nearest door. The expression on Dan's face told him he had the right room. It took only a moment for him to turn the ringed handle, lifting the latch on the inside, and slide through the opening, closing the panel behind him. Dan stood alone in the corridor. His hand hovered near the door for only a moment before dropping back to his side.

A single candle lit the room, its flicker in the draught of air the only movement. Stationary on the threshold, Jack watched the sleeping man. Richard was obviously not immobile in slumber, for the sheets were in disarray. Though grasped in a sleep-clenched hand, they had slithered from his naked body. So, Jack gained his first knowledge of something his brother must have taken pains to conceal.

The brand from the lash, long since healed, spoke to him in parallel scars from the exposed back. Sweat pooled, then ran in minute rivulets down the tracks of the whip marks, further dampening the already sodden sheets. Jack stared, comprehension dawning of another gap in his knowledge of his brother's life.

Drawing his eyes at last from the signs of punishment, he looked at the bandages that covered the fresh wound. Even in the dim candlelight, the skin's pale hue still showed. Hair, darkened to raven-black with perspiration, clung to a cheekbone, its dark veil hiding the expression of the sleeper.

Richard breathed out and Jack held his own breath as he watched the other's body rise and fall with the exercise of his lungs. Jack no longer wished to wake him. The picture was one of total exhaustion; his bodily torment could only increase in consciousness. Subdued, Jack turned and left, quieter than he had entered, the candle flame hardly recording the closing of the door.

The dark angry eyes of Dan were waiting for him. But as Jack took care to soundlessly drop the latch back, Dan knew his charge remained undisturbed.

"You're employed as a stable hand, Jack. Find Mat and act like one." Dan spoke quietly, a kinder tone in his voice.

"I'm sorry," Jack said, shaking his head.

"No need, lad," Dan replied. "You didn't drive him to make this journey. What you may have started by accident, Jack, Master's trying to finish with intent. I've given him laudanum, and he'll not wake before dawn."

Jack did not look up as he spoke. "It was no accident, Dan; it was foolish carelessness. I've no excuse. I just wanted to..." his words drifted away.

"I'm sure you'll have the chance to apologise. But remember, when you do, duck. He's got the temper of the devil in him still, even if he's got a little less blood to fire it with," Dan said.

"What did he say when he found out it was my fault?" Jack asked.

"Like I said, keep yourself at arm's length. Let's just say he wasn't best pleased," Dan warned.

When they reached the top of the darkened stairs, Dan laid a hand briefly on Jack's shoulder, saying nothing, and then watched as he descended the spiral, edging out of sight.

Jack did as Dan had bidden and found Mat. Together, although solitary in their thoughts, they got inconspicuously but thoroughly drunk amongst the straw and feed in an unoccupied stall in the stables.

Harry's anger had lost its volatile edge and was now simmering, waiting to be resurrected to its full passion. The deception had been one thing, but the death of his men had fuelled the vigour he put into locating the man he now wanted to personally tear limb from limb. Robert could have the pieces once Harry's vengeance was complete. To this end, he had not told Robert but, with difficulty, kept the information to himself. Among his men, he tripled the value of the purse, ensuring that discreet and constant enquiries continued in an effort to locate the brother of Robert Fitzwarren.

Betsy remembered the blood; it had been on his shoulder. "Told me he'd been skinning rabbits, but I didn't believe him. He was in a right hurry. I said to Nev, didn't I, Nev, that I didn't believe him, skinning rabbits and with a gentleman's sword on his belt. Most like been skinning the owner of it if you ask me. That's what I said, wasn't it, Nev?"

Nev, the beleaguered landlord of the Swan, smiled weakly at his wife.

"Did you say where they were going?" One of Harry's men asked hopefully.

"They asked which road to take for Hazeldene. I'm guessing that's where they were heading. Well now, what'll you be having, lads? This is an establishment, after all," Betsy said, smiling as one man dug his hand in his pocket for a coin.

The two men grinned at each other as Betsy filled a jug. This would be news that would indeed please their master.

Byrne had taken to Richard in a way the younger man found nothing short of annoying. At Hazeldene, there was a distinct lack of male company. The sons of his first marriage were now gone, along with many of the male servants. He had a new wife, young and little more than a child, and she had added only women to the household and Byrne was now feeling more than a little outnumbered. Richard and the men he had brought to the Manor brought a male vigour back to the house, something that had been too long absent for Edward Byrne's liking. The ruse he played with his new wife, Judith, helped. Passing Richard off as his cousin meant Byrne could indulge himself with the man's company as an equal and not have to play Master, as he knew he should.

When Edward looked at Richard, he could not help but feel sorrow at his own lost youth. His once athletic frame had sagged, and the sharp and agile mind he had taken such pride in had begun to desert him. The effect Richard had on Byrne was to force his sluggish brain to think once again. He spent hours now, seeking out ideas and running them to their various conclusions in his mind. And this was where his current problem now lay. More and more did his thoughts dwell on Northumberland, and no longer as the inevitable victor in a race for control of the crown. Richard had forced his lazy mind to consider the outcome. Mary he had always perceived as old, Catholic, unpopular, and merely a reminder of a bygone era, lacking support or the authority to direct anyone.

Northumberland, on the other hand, was already in favour: beloved of the dying monarch, Edward, and influential with the powerful. That he should champion Edward's choice for his successor had seemed natural. Until now, the only issue for Byrne and his confidants was how to help. And, more importantly, how to ensure that as the Duke rose, they too would rise as well. They saw Northumberland for what he was: a self-seeking nobleman with a lust for more power than was his right. But they allowed him his greed, as long as they too could all scramble aboard the royal train and take a controlling role in the nation's affairs.

But Byrne had been listening to Richard and had begun to credit Henry's eldest daughter with more intelligence than he had previously given her. He had been surprised to find out that Mary, her loyalist supporters around her, had gone into retreat. He wondered if she knew how mortally ill Edward was. Richard was sure she did and thought she was more aware and better informed than the Duke believed. It was known that Mary and Edward got on passably well. Byrne had heard this and had, in his ignorance, attributed it to an old lady's desire to keep her pension. Richard had raised his eyebrows when Byrne had said this and then laughed uproariously. Mary might,

Richard pointed out when he had stopped laughing, be playing just as critical a political game as Northumberland, albeit in skirts. The more Byrne considered it, the more he had to admit that the woman might be more of a threat than he had ever thought her to be.

Byrne had met with Lord Whickham, who had the role of coordinating some of the conspirators. "Communication," he had emphasised to Edward Byrne, "is essential. We must all be aware of the time when it nears. Your Manor lies in a line," Whickham had prodded the map, "with Percy here, London here, myself here, and..." His finger had hovered for a second over the map as his geography temporarily eluded him. "Ah yes, and Darcy here."

Byrne's face had fallen as Whickham informed him they proposed to use Hazeldene as a central point where they could have meetings and from where news could be circulated amongst them. Hazeldene would be used to pass on the direct news of any move Northumberland himself made. Byrne had quickly realised that this would link him too closely with the plot; should any of this become known, he would easily be identified as a ringleader. He guessed correctly that none of the others wanted to take this risk and that he had been nominated at some previous meeting in his absence. He had protested; his Manor was not that convenient, arguing that surely Percy was best placed for this task? But they overruled him.

"We'll need a network, Byrne, and I think you're just the man to set it up," Whickham had said.

Byrne had smiled bitterly at that. Whickham gave him names of men, members of the conspirator's households who could, he hoped, be trusted, and would transport the information. Byrne had ridden back from the meeting with a heavy heart and a sense of dread. However, the journey gave him the time he needed to think, and when his horse breasted the opened gates at Hazeldene, he had found a solution. Now all he needed to do was find the man to carry it out.

Edward found Richard perched on the low wall at the back of the stables, the last rays of the afternoon sun still warming him. "Your man said I could find you here." He sat next to Richard. "I'm just back from Whickham and I have work for you."

Richard's face showed mild interest as Edward handed the paper Whickham had given him along with the instructions, the very ones which were to have been his to carry out. He added his own twist, telling Richard he wanted him to organise the meetings and transfer information from Assingham, a neighbouring house, hoping to draw attention away from his own involvement.

"You'll have seen the place, about a mile and a half distant," Edward said.

"He's not on your list." Richard was still scanning the paper.

"Who's not?" asked Edward, confused.

"The owner of Assingham," Richard replied, "Peter de Bernay, I believe."

"Of course he's not," Edward said condescendingly. "He's Mary's man. But he's been away for months and not likely to return. His lady is there and a few servants."

"I fail to see why we risk sneaking to an unfriendly Manor to pass information. We risk being seen and followed," Richard commented, refolding the paper.

"Damn it man, no one will suspect that information is being passed from the Duke through one of Mary's supporters! Anyway, I leave it in your hands." Edward rose: the other man's tempered gaze unnerved him. "You have your instructions." He took his leave of Richard, eager to wash his hands of the matter. If all went well, everything that Whickham requested he do would be completed with nary a sign pointing to his involvement.

Richard watched him leave. Poor simple Edward, did he really think he could throw the scent of insurrection away from his own house by such a poor plan as this?

Standing and stretching, he set off to find Dan. He had taken a fancy for a ride in the late afternoon sun. Assingham came into view. Not that it provided a pleasant sight for the eyes, the poor mean structure that it was. Its origins were probably Saxon, and it had not been treated to the Norman building scheme visited on Hazeldene's past. A wooden-roofed stone hall towered over the ramshackle huts and walls of the Manor that ran from its flanks. All parts of the main stone building had been used as lean-to walls, saving materials and lending to the extensions some rigidity. Richard's horse had drawn itself to a voluntary stand, and he leant forward, arms crossed, elbows on the saddle, picking out the tiny movements in the distance which comprised the life at Assingham.

Richard had taken the signet ring from his hand and pressed it into the soft wax. Holding it between thumb and forefinger, he laid cool eyes on the crest that stared back at him. It wasn't the Fitzwarren crest, that ring sat still on his right hand. This one he had commissioned himself and the impression it left was unique, recognisable only to those within his network. The image it left was one depicting a double-headed eagle, an ancient Byzantine symbol for empire. To Richard, though, the eagle's heads looking away from each other were a clear signifier of duplicity. It had been a device used by Seymour and reviving it leant credibility to his communications.

Many who saw it would remember Seymour, and even though that man had fallen from grace, his network had been so far-reaching and so thoroughly entwined throughout the court that there was little he did not know about. Very few had ever really known who had coordinated Seymour's network. Richard knew it had been Thomas Archant, dead now, and not likely to be sending messages anytime soon, and it was Archant's role he took and emulated.

There was a light tap at the door.

Richard quickly stowed the sealed letter inside his doublet, pressing himself up from the desk as the knock came again, this time slightly louder and even more rapidly made.

Opening the door, he was forced to take a rapid step backward as Judith stumbled into the room, one hand holding a lit candle. She was wearing a bed robe that fell to the floor, her hair, normally tightly bound and coifed, coiled over her shoulders in long wavy locks.

Richard's eyes took in the situation in an instant and he forced himself to bury the comment that would have been his first choice.

"Judith, what a surprise? Is something wrong? Can I help?" Richard said, managing to put the sound of real concern in his voice.

"The door, please, you must close the door," Judith said quickly.

Reaching past her, Richard pressed it closed, and as he did, the girl dropped the candle holder onto the top of a coffer and flung her arms around his neck. Her head against his chest, she missed the expression of pure annoyance that settled on his face. Dealing with a moonstruck girl was not part of his plans.

"I knew you'd feel the same as I do." Judith wrapped her arms tighter around him.

Resisting the urge to press her from him, Richard instead returned her embrace. "My love, how could I not have fallen for your beauty and your charm? How cruel is Fate to have married you to my cousin?"

"I know, I know." Judith tipped her head back and shifted one of her arms until it was round his neck, clearly intent upon kissing him.

Richard lowered his head. He was close enough to feel her breath on his face when he stopped. In a sudden movement, he planted a finger firmly across her lips. "Shhhh, not a sound," he whispered. "There's someone outside the door."

Judith's eyes widened in horror.

Richard pulled her arms from around him and pushed her to the other side of the door. "Wait here."

A moment later, he had disappeared into the corridor outside, leaving Judith alone in his room. Richard walked up the corridor half a dozen paces, his footsteps overly noisy, and then returned to the room, letting himself back in quickly.

"It's Jane, your maid looking for you," Richard said, his voice sounding worried. "She's gone down to the kitchen. If you are quick, you'll be able to get back to your rooms before she returns. My love, another night will be ours." He pulled her close, bestowed a kiss on her forehead, and before she could say another word, he had returned the candle holder to her and propelled her back into the corridor.

Jack resided at Hazeldene following a subdued routine for four weeks before he was admitted once more to the company of his brother. He knew from Dan that Richard had recovered from the wound he had received in London.

Jack drove his fork, without much enthusiasm or vigour, into the hay, lifted the fodder shoulder high and dropped it into the cart, where it was raked into some order by Marc. Shaking the fork free from the twisted grass stems, he found Richard walking towards him across the yard. Immaculately dressed as usual, he was in stark contrast to Jack, who sported soiled knees and a crown of hay sprigs.

Richard leant against the partly loaded cart and watched as Jack stabbed another forkful of hay to death before loading it into the cart. More twisted stems of summer grass fell from the bundle and snared themselves in Jack's fair hair.

"You do know you look more like a scarecrow," Richard sounded amused.

Jack angrily brushed the hay from his hair and glowered at Richard.

Marc was one of Richard's men and his eyes brightened at the prospect of the coming conversation. It was well known that the Master treated his bastard sibling with little more than contempt, and Jack had no doubt there would be a good audience for any argument.

"I have a mind to ride to the village. Dan presses me to take you with me," Richard said casually.

"Why?" Jack asked, embedding the fork deep in the hay.

"Is that, 'Why am I going to the village?' Or 'Why should I take you with me?'" Richard asked.

"Either would be a start," Jack grunted.

"Why I want to go out is my business. Why you're going is because Dan feels it would be good for your soul," Richard replied.

Richard delivered instructions to ready two horses, and then he turned away, leaving Jack watching his retreating back.

"Well, you'll be having a nice afternoon." Marc chuckled, receiving a withering look from Jack.

A thin line of white clouds were rolling over the hills behind Hazeldene, breaking over them like a slow and silent wave. Behind the white lay a darkened sky and the air, stirred by the wind, held the scent of rain.

The horses were ready, standing side by side: groomed, saddled, eager for some exercise, their ears twitching and eyes darting with equine curiosity. Jack was inspecting some frayed stitching in the loop of the harness on Richard's horse when his brother arrived. The Arab, named Corracha for his fiery spirit, tugged against Jack's hold.

"Such attention to detail! I didn't think you would take to your role so well."

His brother's words, spoken so close, so quietly, almost made him jump. Suppressing the reaction, Jack took a long slow breath, giving himself time to bury the angry reply which threatened to burst forth. Rebuckling the strap with care before untying Richard's horse, he turned and handed the reins to his brother, knuckles white on the leather.

Richard took the offered horse and led it clip-clopping over the cobbles to the middle of the courtyard before he mounted. "Are you coming then?" Richard called down as he moved Corracha expertly sideways, crossing the gap between them. Then, turning to the gateway, shortening the reins, he set him towards the opening.

"Damn!" Jack's horse was still tethered. Dragging the reins free, he vaulted into the saddle. The slender neck twisted to face the gate and follow the direction Richard had gone. Before his feet were secured in the stirrups, he had forced the mare to a brutal gallop.

Jack caught up only when Richard slowed the pace, a mile or so distant from Hazeldene. He pulled his horse to a jolting halt next to Richard's. Corracha had enjoyed the scant exercise. He wanted more, throwing his head up, threatening to snap the reins from his rider's hands. The short journey had taken its toll on Richard; sweat beaded on his forehead and lank strands of raven hair clung wetly to one cheek. In the four weeks he had been at Hazeldene, Richard had given his body as much chance to recover as possible and had ridden little.

"Well, despite Dan's fears, I haven't fallen off yet," Richard said, breathing heavily.

"Only by bloody luck," Jack countered.

"Oh, you think so?" Richard said, setting his heels to the horse again.

This time, though, Jack was in the lead, his horse pounding over the soft earth, clods flying from her hooves as her legs moved easily beneath her in agile flight. Feeling the first break in her stride, Jack finally slowed, lessening her pace gradually until she bore him at an ambling walk.

A snort from velvet nostrils behind him met his ears. His brother must have caught up to him. His horse, Ebony, set a pheasant from its concealed retreat in the dried grass and thicket of the previous summer. She raised her head at the sudden squawking explosion. A loud neigh and sudden stamping of hooves came from the nervy and considerably more highly strung Arab behind him.

Looking round at the horse's exclamation, he found Corracha without his rider. A glance behind told him that Richard had taken no immediate fall. The Arab must have followed his own animal after its rider had departed from the saddle. Jack moved with practiced calm and caught the reins of the spooked horse, then began to retrace his journey.

Glancing back up the gentle slope he had descended, he quickly found what he sought. An untidy black heap some way distant on the grassy hill could be nothing else but his brother. Tightening his grip on the Arab's reins and forcing his own tired horse back to a gallop, Jack made his way to the tangle of cloth that was now propped up on one good elbow, looking up at him. Jack supposed the delay in his arrival had allowed Richard to recover from the pain of his fall.

"Hello, nursemaid," Richard called up cheerfully, his nonchalance feigned.

Jack remained on his horse. "Would you like a hand up?"

"No, I think I would prefer to remain here a while, if that's all right. The pretence will be that this spot provides a most excellent view. The reality is that I think I've broken my arm." Richard's words drew Jack's eyes to the arm laying behind his back, the palm of the hand facing in entirely the wrong direction.

Jack dropped from the saddle, looping the Arab's reins over the pommel of his own horse, relying on Ebony's obedience to keep them on the hillside. Crouching down in front of Richard, Jack found he couldn't view the extent of the injury. In the fall, the cloak had wrapped around him and Richard now lay on the edges, his body trapped within the folds.

"You want me to help?" Jack said, rocking back on his haunches.

"Looks like I have little choice," Richard said, a weak smile on his strained face.

Jack took hold of the front of Richard's doublet and shirt, lifting him far enough to pull the tangled folds of the cloak free. Richard's head was near his ear, and he heard the pained gasp as he extracted the cloth. Instead of laying him back, he held him there, half sitting, propped against his own body.

"Well, it is both good and bad," Jack said, giving his brother time to recover from the recent pain.

"Go on," Richard said weakly, his breath still ragged.

"It's not broken, which is good," Jack said, running his hands over the unresponsive limb. "But the bad news is..."

Richard screamed, even though Jack attempted to make the replacement of the shoulder swift and clean, giving Richard no time to protest or struggle in apprehension. The shoulder back in place, Jack waited, supporting the lighter form of his brother against his right shoulder. Richard's breathing was harsh and painfully uneven. After a time he tried to push himself away, but the strength he needed had drained from his remaining good arm, and he slumped back, his face again pressed to Jack's shoulder. Jack smiled, knowing his brother was not enjoying his moment of helplessness. Levering him forward, he sat back. Richard knelt, swaying a little in front of him, his skin ashen.

"If I didn't know better, I would say you had just made another attempt to get rid of me." The words were meant with humour, but the effort of speaking them took away any lightness there might have been.

"Do I take it that was meant as thanks?" Jack asked.

"Thanks? No... I do not think... thanks is a word that readily springs to mind... I would give thanks only at this moment for one thing..." Richard swallowed hard, taking a shaking breath to settle his body's rhythm back towards normality.

"What's that then?" Jack enquired.

"Unconsciousness," Richard replied. "Where did you learn to do that?"

"Calves are often born with their legs like that," Jack said cheerfully.

"God, you practised on animals! I am so pleased you shared that knowledge with me after the event," Richard said. With his good arm he lowered himself shakily back to the grass and lay looking up at the clouds, they twisted, grey and confused, across an uncertain sky.

"How do you feel?" Jack asked.

"Terrible," Richard replied with honesty. "For my sins on earth, which are many as you keep reminding me, it appears I have been delivered to the depths of Hell early."

"That's probably where you deserve to be."

"Half dead." Richard stiffly pushed himself to sit up. "I know, before you say it, I have no one to blame for this but myself. Don't I know it!"

"I was going to say no such thing," Jack replied with satisfaction. "It was obvious; I didn't think I needed to tell you." With exaggerated ease, Jack stood and brushed the remnants of the meadow grass from his doublet. "Are you stopping there all day?"

"I am not sure I have a choice," Richard replied, still sitting, his weight taken on his remaining good arm.

He didn't look comfortable, Jack thought. "Here..." He extended a hand. Richard grasped his wrist and Jack pulled him smoothly back to the vertical. "To the village another day, then?" Jack said, standing back while Richard straightened his aching, complaining muscles.

Richard rubbed his face with one hand and pushed the tangled hair back from his eyes.

"Come on, nursemaid, I still want to go to the village." There was a slight smile on his face as he turned towards his horse, which had obediently remained standing next to its companion. "Here's your chance to redeem yourself." Richard stood near Corracha. Turning his head slightly, he looked back at Jack. "There is no way I can get up on my own. Come on, I'm not often helpless. Enjoy your moment."

"I am not enjoying it, but you are starting to tempt me to leave you here."

"Ah well, at least we are back on the same easy terms as usual," Richard said, exasperated. "Jack! Stop being so bloody prickly."

Jack, feeling a little guilty at the accuracy of the observation, moved to lift Richard into his saddle. "Come on, let's get you to the village so you can make someone else's life a misery." Jack lifted himself smoothly onto his own horse. Suddenly, he blurted the words that had been burning inside him all day. "I regret what happened; if you cannot forgive me I shall leave." He looked across to make sure Richard was listening. "But do not keep me here to torment."

"Have I been tormenting you? I think you've been doing a fine job of that yourself; you needed no help from me." Richard turned his horse to draw level with Jack's, the reins held in his good hand. "I'm confident, even if you aren't, that it won't happen again. Please spare me and the rest of the world the penitent man. There is little of value or use to be gained from it, for either of us; the competent man is much preferred."

Jack took his words in silence, a response beyond him.

"God, Jack, can I not say it plain enough? Bloody well forget it. It's in the past in my mind. Let it be the same in yours."

"Sorry," Jack managed, his voice stilted.

"I was just being..."

Jack cut him off, a weary smile on his face. "Your usual self. Yes, I know. Come on. Let's get to the village before people start to believe I have tried to rid the earth of you."

"I would view it as an improvement if I could remain in the saddle, if I didn't have to rely on your calving talents, and if you would ride with a slightly easier conscience. You make for poor company sitting there glum and silent. Despite what you think, I prefer you as a rash fool rather than a repentant sinner. The halo does not sit well," Richard said drily.

"And I thought I was on my best behaviour," Jack said innocently.

"Spare me it, please," Richard said, his voice sounded weary.

Whether the day had eased the tension that Jack felt was between them remained to be seen. Jack still struggled with what he had done. He could not forget it, but at least the subject was buried in a shallow grave. Time would place further layers of dirt over the insubstantial scattering of platitudes until it was well sunk within their minds.

Midday found them in the village and Richard leading them to an inn. In the recent past, unless he had ridden abroad alone before, Jack could think of no time his brother could have been there. Richard bade Jack remain in the yard with the horses and there was a little less officiousness in his tone.

Jack amused himself by watching the rounded behind of a tavern wench bob up and down as its owner busied herself washing what appeared to be furs in the horse trough. Such was her vigour that much of the ground around the trough stood deep in water. Beyond the pond, glittering tracks ran across the yard to find new cracks and dips to explore; Jack stepped sideways to preserve the dryness of his feet as one such minor river branched from the delta at the trough's source and set a course towards him. The move, when he looked past the hessian-clad backside, gave him a view into the inn, where he saw Richard in close conversation. He did not recognise the short man, clothed in ragged poverty, that he was talking to. Jack looked back at the maid of the large behind to avoid any accusation of spying; Richard had already told him bitingly that his reasons for coming here were private.

Richard quickly found the man he had ridden to the village to meet, waiting for him.

"I thought you weren't coming. It's been a long time since I saw your face," the short man said, shifting his weight and leaning heavily on the stick he carried.

"A while," agreed Richard. Smiling, he gestured for the man to seat himself.

"I'll not stop. I have what you want, but I can't understand why you want it." The man dug beneath the layers of dirty fabric and retrieved a packet wrapped in pigskin and tied tightly with cord.

"Steven, my thanks." Richard deftly exchanged the bundle for coins.

"Ah, I wish I could say no to you." The old face was sad, the eyes that looked into Richard's were watery with age.

Richard clapped the man on the arm. "The world is, as you and I have found out, most wholly unfair."

Steven looked up at that, but Richard was glancing through the window. "Why do you want it? It'll do you no good. I can't see the use of it. It'll do you no good against Robert either; if he knew you'd got that, he'd not rest till he's killed you. You be careful."

A slight smile wandered onto the younger face. "And do you think he'll manage to put a knife between my ribs?"

Steven's face cracked into a toothless grin. "Ah God, lad, no, I suppose not. Never could, never will."

"Well, your confidence cheers me." Richard smiled.

Jack did not have long to wait before Richard returned to the yard, squinting as he emerged into the light, and summoned Jack to join him. Jack did not ask about the man Richard had met. The day was going well. Why make it take a turn for the worse?

Ale arrived, and Jack filled the cups from the pitcher. "So, back to Hazeldene next?" he enquired, attempting to start the conversation off on a safe and neutral line.

Richard was swirling his drink around the cup, his thoughts seemingly elsewhere. Jack did not press his question, but waited. At last Richard sat back, careful not to place any weight on his injured shoulder, and observed his brother. "Tell me something, Jack. Why do you stay? For let us not lie, it's not for love of myself, is it?"

Jack was caught off guard. He didn't know what to say. The response that came to mind would sound stupid in the face of what Richard had just said.

Richard continued. "No reason at all, then?"

"I haven't got a lot of choice at the moment; Harry will be after both of our hides. Why do you ask?"

"Idle curiosity, nothing else. There must be some reason." Richard leant across the table. "Do you not feel sometimes that you would like to make the world a fairer place? It has treated you badly, hasn't it? Would it not be just to take what should have been yours? Would it not be easy to take what I have?"

"What do you mean? You have nothing anyway," Jack said, confused.

Richard laughed. "I have quite a lot: a name, money, power."

"Where exactly?" Jack laughed. "You're the third son of a family that'll have nothing to do with you. I would say that makes your position in this world little better than mine."

"I am pleased to see you hold me in such high esteem," Richard said.

Jack sensed that the previous conversation, whatever it had been, had been closed by Richard. He was still confused, but caution told him not to pursue it. Instead, he said, "We've been here for weeks now. Any signs yet of some plans to move?"

"Death is not as timely as you would like?" Richard asked.

"I wish it on no one: do not imply that I do. I just wanted to know if we are to be called to act."

"Byrne returns from London today. I shall know more then. There is a message network to which I am not privy. Yet," Richard's face showed a slight smile, "worry not, Jack, as soon as I know I will run to find you. Either way, we get paid, and that is, after all, the crux of the matter. I would have thought you would have preferred the opportunity to take the money without having to wield steel to earn it."

"That would suit me fine." Jack drained his cup and reached for the pitcher once more. "I just like to know what's happening. This place is so far removed, no news passes here."

"Which, as it happens, is a good thing, don't you agree? No one is going to track us easily to Hazeldene. I have a task for you. Here..." Richard pulled from his loosened jacket a purse and passed it to Jack, who accepted the coins with a puzzled look. "It will take you a couple of days. You know where all the men are. Go and make sure they have not squandered what you gave them and are languishing in penury."

"When?" Jack pocketed the coins quickly, out of sight.

"Well, now would seem as good a time as any, wouldn't it? This village is well on the road you need to take," Richard said. He took out the bundle of letters, which he had been planning to deliver himself, but something made him change his mind. "These," he slid the package across the table to Jack, "need to be delivered in two days. You will meet a man here by the name of Ashley who'll have letters for me. Please, Jack, don't lose these; our future depends on them."

"Don't worry. Two days' time you say? I'll be here," Jack said, accepting the bundle.

Richard told him what the messenger looked like, hoping that Jack wouldn't let him down. The letters Jack would collect were coming from London, from some of Seymour's old contacts. One in particular was well placed in Northumberland's household, and any news from that quarter was not only interesting, but could be valuable as well.

Chapter Seven

Bedfordshire – June 1553

The main doors to Hazeldene's hall stood open with sweet, fresh air being drawn into the house's welcome embrace. Richard leant on the cool stone frame, arms crossed in front of him, and looked out across the yard. He was watching Byrne's wife, Judith. Colourful, careless, and expensive, she skipped across the yard to a horse being held by Dan. A second woman descended from it, a little unsteadily.

The new arrival was Catherine de Bernay, aged thirteen, daughter to Peter de Bernay, owner of the manor at Assingham just two miles away. The girl still lacked the proportions of a woman's figure and was all elbows, knees, and knuckles, with not a spare scrap of flesh on her. Dresses hung from two bony boy's shoulders and seemed to hardly touch the body again except to expose a jutting hip. The whole unhappy appearance was worsened by her unnatural height, and there was little in the way of pleasant features to alleviate it.

The two women, arms linked, made their way across the yard to the steps. Richard stepped back into the shadow of the arch, and neither of the approaching women saw him as they ascended the stairs.

"You must come..." Judith was pleading, her attention on her companion and not on the man she was about to walk into. "Oh! You gave me such a fright!" Judith's eyes devoured Richard's face, her manners temporarily forgotten. "Catherine, forgive me. This is Edward's cousin, Richard." Judith placed upon him what she hoped was her most charming and winning smile. Catherine smiled politely into the unsmiling face and found herself turning quite red under the unfriendly gaze he turned on her.

"Ladies." Richard bowed most flamboyantly before descending the steps from the hall. A mild look of disappointment crossed Judith's childish face at his departure. When she returned her attention to her companion, her face and voice had lost its animation. The slight smile Richard had fixed on Judith dropped forgotten from his face as he walked down the steps.

While the lady of the house entertained her friend, one of Richard's men slipped unobserved into the Byrne family chapel. Robby had been there before, and although he had taken nothing the first time, the pull of the silver plate was more than he could bear. He took only one item, stowing it away beneath his jacket. There were another eight on the shelf above the altar. No one would notice that once there had been nine.

Harry leant forward across the table, eyes pig-like in their intensity and sparkling with anticipation. A podgy fat-slicked hand held a partially consumed chicken leg.

"You found him! By God, tell me where."

The master's enthusiasm was marked by both of the men who stood before him.

It was Hal who spoke, his voice holding a ring of pride in their success. "I told Spratty here we'd find him, and we did. Wasn't easy like, Sir, and we've had a right run around I can tell you, but we did find him for you."

Harry's impatience burst from his greased lips. "Tell me, man! You'll be paid, have no fear. Now tell me where!"

Hal cast a glance at Spratty, who was examining his boots and looked unlikely to supply his master with the information in the face of Harry's temper. Hal was forced to continue relating what Betsy, the erstwhile landlady of the White Horse, had told them.

Harry looked perplexed, his small eyes narrowing further. "Where is he now, then?" his fat jowls wagged as he demanded. "Did he live?"

"Yes, Sir. He stopped at the White Horse two days and then went north. We tracked him though, me and Spratty did, and he's with Lord Byrne at his Manor Hazeldene near..."

Harry cut off the stumbling Hal. "Byrne... Byrne..." Harry seemed to be considering the name, rolling it maliciously off his tongue. Hal and Spratty were temporarily forgotten.

Deliberately, and with care, the wrappings were removed from the paper. Dry and cracked with age, it had survived so long; to wreak its destruction now with carelessness was not the reader's intention. The document inside, entrusted to a priest so long ago, refused to be pressed flat, and the reader had to review the words along each angled section of the paper. It was a deposition, forced from William Fitzwarren by his conscience and a well-meaning little priest, documentary evidence that he vowed to set right the wrong he had perpetrated on himself, his wife, and his son.

You never quite got up the courage though, did you? Richard mused. His father's signature was unmistakable, the last letters snaking their way under the seal, which almost, but not quite, obscured the all-important date. He had known of its existence, known what it spoke of, but proof of that act had been beyond him until now. Richard's smile broadened at the irony of it. To him, it was worthless; only pain could be wrought from its revelations. Was that his purpose? He wondered. Did he simply dress it up in some other guise simply to salve his own conscience? Maybe.

Richard threw himself on the bed and stared unseeing at the canopy. Was this how Jack felt? Was he falling prey to what he so despised in his brother? No! A hand balled into a fist, paper cracked. No! Your sin will not damn me.

It was not until spring changed to early summer that two letters arrived from Peter de Bernay: one for Gavin, the keeper of Assingham in its master's absence, and another for Anne, its lady. Her daughter came in hard on the heels of the messenger.

"Mama, it's from Father. Is there a letter for us?" Catherine asked.

"Yes," Anne said, turning away from her daughter as she tried to read the words over her arm. "A minute, child, let me read." She walked away, leaving Catherine with the messenger, pacing as she read the brief words. Peter hoped she and their daughter were in good health and that all was well at Assingham. Several badly formed halting sentences spoke of his wish to return. However, he stressed that his duty was owed to the Lady Mary and so he was unable to predict his return. He promised to write soon and closed with "your husband."

Anne whipped the hardly used sheet over, hoping perhaps for more on the back and found nothing save her name. Reversing it again, she reread the brief correspondence.

"Mama, can I see? When is he coming home?" Catherine said, coming close and trying again to view the letter.

"Here child." Anne passed the page to Catherine, who devoured the few lines.

"Oh mama, why doesn't he come home? It's been months! He promised me a new pony. You know I have outgrown Clover. He promised," Catherine complained.

"I think your father has more on his mind than ponies, Catherine," Anne scolded.

Catherine stomped from the hall. To cheer her melancholy spirits, Catherine took her mare, Clover, and the pair trotted out in the bright June sun.

"My Lady Catherine, good day to you."

Catherine recognised the approaching rider, Edward's cousin. Last time they had met, his unfriendly gaze had made her face burn; and her skin flushed red again at the memory of it.

"What a pleasant surprise." Catherine's response was automatic, though she sounded far from pleasantly surprised. "And what brings you to Assingham?" Catherine was in no mood for company and hoped he didn't stop long.

"A pleasant day, nothing else. It seemed a pity to waste it inside, so I decided a ride abroad was in order. You were of the same mind?" Richard enquired conversationally.

Catherine almost told him of the unwanted news but thought the better of it; the man was a stranger, and not one she was sure she liked. "Yes, I was, and Clover," she patted the neck of the pony affectionately, "needed the exercise." The height of Richard's Arab dwarfed her own pony, and she found she had to look up a long way to meet those unfriendly eyes.

Their mounts came to a slow and mutual halt, busying themselves, catching mouthfuls of lush summer grass from the rich green line of foliage that attended the stream.

"Shall you have time to visit Hazeldene again while I am there? Judith bid me to ask you if I should see you," Richard enquired, sounding distracted.

"I'm sure I will. Judith is teaching me needlepoint," Catherine remarked absently. *He'll go in a minute*, she thought. He has as much interest in me and Assingham as I have in him. "If you will excuse me..." Catherine tugged none too gently on Clover's reins, but the animal would have none of it and stood solid, straining its head towards the unfinished meal. "Clover, move!" she said sharply. When the horse still ignored her, she resorted to jerking on the reins and pleading with it. "Clover! Please, Clover, please..."

Richard's grey eyes were alive with amusement. Catherine tried again, but the stubborn animal refused to obey. Embarrassment and frustration finally got the upper hand and tears welled up unwanted in her eyes, threatening at the slightest sharp movement to spill forth in telltale tracks down her cheeks.

"Catherine, I think..." Richard ventured.

"I care not what you think, Sir! I wish you to leave my father's land." She stared him full in the face, and cursed herself silently, for now, he could plainly see her wet lashes and the rosy bloom of embarrassment and anger upon her face.

"Good day to you, Lady Catherine." With exaggerated ease, he turned his horse away from the grass. Bringing it to a halt again, he regarded her silently for a moment before adding, in a deceptively casual manner, "Do not turn your child's temper on me, Catherine, for it's not my fault you cannot control your horse." With that final remark, he spurred his mount on and disappeared into the trees on the far side of the stream.

Catherine waited until the horse's haunches had disappeared into the wood before rubbing a sleeve across her dripping nose and cheeks. Clover, unmoved by the encounter, continued to tug vivid green clumps from the stream bank. "You, my dear animal, have a lot to answer for." Dropping from the saddle, she stared into one liquid brown eye. "You could at least look sorry for what you've done."

Jack made his return the following day. Richard was away, and he found Dan eating with Robby and Marc.

"Shift over, Robby," Jack said.

Robby obliged, joining Marc on another bench. Before Jack could sit down, a cat jumped up next to Dan. Jack scooped a hand under the belly of the tabby mouser and deposited him on the floor. The cat, deprived of the hope of tidbits from Dan, switched its attention instead to the newcomer. Jack, a scrap in his hand, threw it towards the cat.

Dan informed him that the Master was out, and that he didn't know where he was. Jack settled for passing what meagre news he had collected from the men to Dan. On the whole, he was happy they would all stay where they were for a few more weeks, but after that, they would grow restless. The only problem he had come across was that Alan had duped Froggy into allowing him to use all the group's money on a dice game. Froggy was ready to leave; he was so terrified of the Master's wrath. Jack had managed to replace some of the lost silver, and informed them curtly that they were farm labourers, so they knew where the remainder would come from.

Alan, however, Jack had spoken to alone. He had ignored Jack's rebuke, telling Jack that he was no worse than him. Jack was renowned for being a willing participant in any game where coins swapped hands, and it was also known that he often lost heavily. Alan had no way of knowing that Jack's most recent losses had led him to enter a deal with a pawnbroker, and to Richard almost losing his life on Peter Hardwood's sword. Faced with his own error in another, Jack had felt his temper rise. Alan had turned away; he held the bastard brother in no great esteem. Rational thought had become lost to Jack's mind. Wheeling the heavier man round with a brutal grip on his shoulder, he had delivered an accurate and teeth-cracking punch. Alan had no chance to deflect the blow or lessen its impact and had been sent staggering backwards, footing lost, ending in a heap at Jack's feet.

"Must have been a bit of a shock to Alan then," Dan observed. He had no particular liking for the man. While he respected his skill with a knife, trouble started too easily around him. He had set himself up as a minor leader who regarded himself as below the Master, but somewhere definitely above Jack, for whom he harboured a dislike he did not bother to hide. That was probably a mistake, Dan reflected, for while the Master nursed his temper and used it harshly but sparingly, Jack's ruled his head all too often. Alan would bear a grudge; it would remain to be seen how he exercised it.

"I'm sure it was, but the bugger deserved it. Anything of interest happen here while I've been away?" Jack said, accepting a lump of fresh, warm, dark bread from the loaf Dan held.

"Ah well, let me see. Master's horse threw a shoe." He eyed Jack, a slight smile on his face. "But not his rider again." Jack looked innocently back at Dan. "Mat's down at the blacksmith's now." He paused. "Then there was Byrne, back yesterday. Nothing's happening yet, by the looks of it." Dan stopped when he heard the voice in the doorway.

"Robby!" Richard said. It was only one word, but it was enough to make Robby stand, his meal forgotten in front of him.

Insolence and anger in the form of Richard leant dangerously against the doorframe, darkening the room. Robby said nothing; his jaw moved as if trying to form a forgotten word, hands clasping and unclasping before him.

"Struck dumb?" the hard voice asked. "That's a shame. For now, you will be unable to offer me a defence."

Robby's eyes widened. "I..."

Richard moved from the doorway to face Robby across the table.

"I will give you a chance." The cross of the knife's hilt rose between them. Cool fingers released their slender hold, and the point embedded itself in the table with a soft thud. "Take the knife before me and I shall judge you innocent."

"And... and if I don't?" Robby stepped back, but his way was blocked by Marc.

The smile Robby received in reply had no humour in it. The Master simply placed both of his hands palms down on the table, waiting.

Licking his lips, Robby wiped his sweating hands on the front of his jacket, then moved ·to match the Master's stance.

Jack stopped breathing, eyes not leaving his brother's impassive face.

"Whenever you like," the Master invited.

Robby breathed heavily, his eyes dropped to the knife.

There was a flash of movement and a second soft, sinister thud. Even Jack found he winced at it. The knife was in Robby's hand, pinning it through flesh and bone to the table.

The latch lifted. Dan shouldered the door hard, forcing the chair behind it to squeal across the boards. He found Richard flat on the floor, his face within folded arms, a wine pitcher next to him.

"Go away," Richard said quietly.

"Get up." Dan kicked the wine jug, sending a fuming spray of liquid over the prone man. "I knew you were drunk when you took Robby on, and I see you've come here to finish."

"I said go away."

Dan grunted. A huge hand scooped an arm from the floor and began to pull Richard to his feet. He was not as drunk as he had assumed. The lithe form twisted free, moving quickly to stand a pace away. "Ha! I don't need your help."

Dan dropped back and fell into the chair. He spoke sadly. "You have a lot left to learn."

"You wish to teach me a lesson?" Richard laughed. "What in? Humility, yet that is not for me. Perhaps honour? No, that was beaten from me long since. Surely you could not think morality? Too late, the corrupt cannot become pure. Or maybe faith, possibly faith, for I confess I have none. Could it be charity, could it? No, I have had enough of charity's acid kisses. Then it must be hope, oh no..." He faltered and laughed harshly. "Hope then, that inspires the spirit, holding the promise of trust, belief, confidence..." An arm outstretched caught the fireplace. He sagged against it, and from there he dropped to his knees. "Am I such a despairing, desperate, lamenting fool? Ruined and undone? For hope is most surely dead."

Dan sighed. "You're drunk."

"Very." The voice was weary and resigned. "You came to find out why Robby ended up with a knife through his hand?"

"I did." Dan's voice was cold.

"Ask Marc and leave me alone."

"I will ask him, but I've a mind to sit here a while." Dan settled back easily into the only chair in the room.

"Please, please, leave me to my own torment, for pity's sake," Richard begged.

Dan sighed, but stayed where he was until Richard succumbed to a drunken, uneasy slumber. Throwing a cover over the younger man, he retrieved the paper he had waited patiently for.

"God no..." He spoke on a breath to the quiet room. Folding the confession, he took it into his care. No wonder the lad was blind drunk.

"Robby, will you hold your bloody hand still!" Jack grasped Robby's wrist firmly and pulled it towards him.

Robby yelped. "Be careful, will you!"

Blood had seeped through the rag wrapped around the hand that was balled in a tight fist around the wound.

"It's you own fault. The eighth commandment might be thou shalt not steal, but you know what the eleventh is, don't you?" Jack roughly pulled the filthy material from Robby's hand.

"No, what is it?" Robby said through gritted teeth.

"Don't get caught. How did he find out, anyway?" Jack asked, examining the hole in Robby's hand with a critical eye. Blood was still trickling from the wound, but luckily the blade had been a slender one, sliding between bone and sinew and the flesh was not badly cut.

"I tried to sell it," Robby confessed.

"Oh, for God's sake, that's a breach of the twelfth then as well–thou shalt not be bloody stupid. Turn your hand over, there, that's right." Jack pressed the hand flat, and Robby winced.

"At least it's your left hand," Jack observed.

"Well, the Master would hardly make it my right, would he? I'd be no bloody use to him then, would I?" Robby observed morosely

"You're lucky he didn't turn you off," Jack replied as he began to rebind the wound after plugging the holes with a greasy cream held in place with wild garlic leaves.

"We could do without him. We don't need him, none of the lads like him. Why don't you take over?" Robby said, watching Jack.

"I would have turned you off," Jack replied, his eyes on the task before him.

"Well, maybe I wouldn't have been forced to steal in the first place if you'd been in charge," Robby whined. "If he'd pay me what I'm worth, then I wouldn't have had to steal, would I?"

"Robby, he pays you enough. It's not his fault you lost half your wages to Mat at cards, is it?" Jack replied.

"Mat cheats. It wasn't my fault," Robby spat back.

"No, he doesn't. Dan told me you were drunk. Mat's good, learn your lesson and don't try to beat him unless you are sober." Jack tied a final wrap of reed mace round the injured hand to keep everything in place, securing it with a knot under Robby's thumb.

"God, that stinks!" Robby commented, his nose wrinkling.

"No more than you do," Jack observed as he finished his task and pushed Robby's hand back towards him.

Dan returned to Richard's room early the next morning. Richard lay, head pillowed on his arm where he had slept, beneath crumpled covers in front of the now dead fire.

"You know about Robert, then?" Dan asked.

"I knew. Surely you cannot be so naïve as to believe Robert's pure hatred springs from some childhood incident?"

"No..." Dan considered his answer. "I thought it was because of Lady Elizabeth."

"Oh no, Robert's hatred is for selfish reasons. He would not trouble himself over things that affected him so little, although I admit it didn't help." Richard rubbed hands over his face. "There is some humour, is there not?"

"Is there?" Dan asked sarcastically. "Go on, tell me what happened and then I'll share what I know."

Richard looked for a moment as if he would resist, but then began surprising Dan. "I went back home, penitent and most humble. My father knew I was not guilty of assaulting Elizabeth. It was well known by then that I was Seymour's scapegoat. It was Seymour who laid his filthy hands on her—not me—but accusations like that don't bury themselves easily and I am sure there were plenty who chose to believe it. Anyway, my father uneasily accepted me until he could find some way of disposing of me. Robert... well, Robert set out to encourage me to leave sooner, and lost half of his ear for the trouble." There was a bitter smile on his face. "I suffered a good beating as well. Steven was the family priest, Lord bless the fool. He told me then that it pained him to see Robert, base born bastard that he is, heir—and a poor one at that. Simple fool! He thought the truth would triumph and took his case to my father, told him that he knew his wrong and that he should put the world to rights before he left it. He gave me his account in writing, but the final proof of it I did not have until recently."

Dan waited for the Richard to continue.

"As it transpires, that great man, William Fitzwarren, my father, decided to conveniently forget my innocence. I rode out with him and Robert, the pretext I cannot remember. Robert knocked me to the ground and tied me to a tree. My father whipped me until he thought I was dead. He told me it was for the shame I had brought on his name, but that was not the reason. Steven helped me and I left." The tale was told without emotion, a recitation of facts now years old. "And you followed me to London."

"I thought your father banished you for what they accused you of with Elizabeth. Robert let it be known that Seymour had whipped you for trying to take her honour. I did not know it was your own father. Sweet Mary!" Dan was shaking his head.

"Oh, Seymour did, but that was nothing compared to what I received at my father's hand. I don't want pity. We had a bargain; I've traded my cold bloody facts, now give me yours."

Dan was shocked by the icy expression that Richard had levelled on him. "I found out from the priest, years before, when he thought your father was about to put right the wrong. As you know—he didn't. It was too bloody late by then. Robert was about twelve and everyone believed him to be William's son. There was no way it could be changed; he had well and truly saddled his bastard on his wife. The priest told Robert as well. He believed the boy could not carry it on his conscience and would persuade his father to set right what had happened. Robert's mother had been well placed with the Abbey, and a substantial donation made by William would make sure she'd not be leaving. He banished the priest, and then your father supposed that the only ones who knew were himself and Robert, but I knew, and so did Steven, and then you, too. No wonder he tried to kill you."

"Why didn't you tell me you knew, even after we left?" Richard asked.

"Why? It was an old crime. There was no way it could be set to rights, and not on the word of a priest long since gone. There is no proof; it could have only caused..."

Dan was cut off by Richard's bitter laughter. "There is nowhere left within my soul for more pain; it could have been no worse." He paused, steadying his thoughts. "There is proof now though, or was. I suppose you've got it."

"Here..." Dan threw the paper across to him. "I didn't think you would want just anyone reading it. What do you propose to do with it?"

Richard laughed. "Fate has dealt me a neat hand, has it not? I wait until dear father dies and lay claim to what Robert has."

"No, you won't," Dan said.

"Why not?" came the sharp reply.

"Because it doesn't belong to you. Despite what you said, you have a conscience."

Richard smiled malevolently. "I want Robert to believe I will do that, and he will. He will find out soon enough from Harry if he doesn't know already that I am back, and he will track me down."

"That's a fair bet after what you did in London to Harry," Dan pointed out unnecessarily.

"I meant that to be the general outcome." Richard was folding the paper carefully back up. "I don't want this at all, but it seems to want me. I almost fed it to the flames. Be damned with them all. I can make my own way, my own fate and my own future. I have no need of the curse this will surely bring." He smiled. "But it seems the curse is as much mine as anyone's." Richard looked away from Dan's face; he had seen the other's expression harden. "Please, allow me a little indulgence in self-pity."

"He will not let you live because of what you know," Dan stated the obvious.

"What Robert doesn't know is that I can prove that he is William's bastard son, and that I have also found his legitimate one. For some reason, William kept that piece of information close to his own heart. Only four people know who his real heir is. Two of us are in this room."

"He had more than one bastard, but the one he placed in his brother's household is the child of his wife," Dan supplied.

"That I was a little unsure of until recently," Richard said quietly. His eyes had wandered back to his hands. "For which I can be forgiven. There is little family resemblance, is there, between myself and Jack?"

Dan knew that was not true. He had known Eleanor, William's wife, dead some fifteen years now. Richard must barely be able to remember the woman. "Jack is made in the image of Eleanor."

"If Jack finds out the truth; that he was born on the right side of the sheets, he will try to take what should have been his. He is fertile ground for jealousy and hate to easily grow."

"God, I know he's not perfect, but why don't you tell him?" Dan concluded.

"Are you mad? He has difficulty accepting me as his brother. How can you expect him to accept that? Then he will be killed, believe me," Richard said bluntly. "On the sword of one of his kinfolk, be it Robert, or even by our father's hand."

"He'll find out sooner or later, believe me, and it would be better if you told him. Explain to him about your father, help him," Dan pleaded.

"In time I will. Just give me time. When Jack finds out the truth, he's not likely to sit around and consider the alternatives. He'll be out of that gate and on a journey to see his father. That will not end well," Richard said wearily. "Let me gather some coin and establish a place for us, then we will be in a better position to..."

"And when's that likely to be? You are not being fair. He is your brother, and you are running short on blood kin who don't wish to kill you. If you don't tell him sooner rather than later, then I will," Dan pressed.

"All right, I will. In time, I will," Richard repeated, lying back on the floor, his eyes unfocused.

"Tell me something," Dan paused. "Jack, is he just a pawn to deliver vengeance on your father, or do you have some liking for him?"

Richard smiled. "You know the answer to that." Dan didn't, but the grey gaze, which did not quite see him, stopped him from asking further.

Chapter Eight

Hazeldene – June 1553

Jack was called to go to Richard's room in the late evening when they all had retired from the hall. There had been some scant entertainment provided by Judith, accompanied by one of her ladies on her lute. The lady clearly thought she could sing, and, clearly, she could not. Thankfully, for the audience's sake, after only three tales of courtly love, Edward bid his wife rest her voice. Had Jack been present, he would have been blowing bubbles in his beer as Judith warbled through her tales of chivalry and romantic love.

Jack found Richard with a cloak draped over his arm.

"Going somewhere?"

"We are going somewhere. Do you fancy a walk before bed? It's a new moon and a pleasant evening," Richard said.

Jack smiled; Richard sounded in good humour. "It's a fine night for a stroll," he agreed. He lifted the latch, pulling the door open a fraction, but Richard was shaking his head and pointing behind him. Closing the door again, Jack followed Richard to the opened window.

"And what great offence has the door committed that you no longer wish for its services?" Jack enquired quietly as he leant from the window to observe, respectfully, the long drop to the ground.

"The door, none, but the passage has eyes," Richard replied lightly. "Go on then, drop to the sill and go round the corner to the right; it's like walking down stairs after that."

Both men stopped at the sound of the knock on the door.

"Who the hell is that?" Jack whispered, concern in his voice.

"God in heaven, why now?" Richard glowered at the door, and then at Jack. Taking a tight hold on Jack's doublet, he pushed him back behind the door, saying under his breath, "If you laugh, I will put a knife through your ribs."

Jack, confused, stood quietly as the knock was repeated for a second time.

Richard opened the door, but didn't step back, and remained blocking the entrance.

"Judith, my love, have a care. Edward has summoned me to talk to him," Richard said in a hushed voice.

Jack crammed a fist into his mouth.

"Surely not? He's gone to bed. I was so careful," Judith said, trying to take a step forward into the room.

"Please my love, let him not catch us together. Another night will be ours."

Jack bit down hard onto the back of his hand as he heard the unmistakable sound of his brother kissing his employer's wife. A moment later Richard had released her. The door was closed, and Jack could hear the soft sound of her feet on the wood boards outside the room.

"Not a word," Richard warned.

There were tears of mirth running down Jack's face, wiping them away as he made his way from the door towards the window, still having difficulty containing his laughter. He held it in for as long as he could and then collapsed against the desk, shaking with laughter.

Richard stood, arms folded, observing him coldly.

"Another night will be ours..." Jack mimicked, dissolving into yet another fit of uncontrolled hysterics.

"I am so pleased I have amused you." Richard's voice was heavy with sarcasm.

"Oh, you have. How long has that being going on?" Jack wiped the back of his hand across his eyes again.

"It's not going on," Richard replied evenly.

"Well, it certainly looks like it is," Jack said, still laughing.

"It's not, she's barely old enough to be his wife, she's a child married to an old man, and I have not taken her to my bed," Richard stated, and then added, "why am I even telling you this?"

"I don't know, I really don't. This is so funny?" Jack sniffed loudly and grinned at his brother.

"And why would it be so amusing?" Richard said, but he could not help smiling at the absurdity of the situation.

"That there's something happened that you didn't plan for. I bet that really annoys you," Jack said.

"Oh, you've no idea. That was something that even I did not see coming," Richard replied, laughing as well now. "Get out of that window before I push you."

Richard's room occupied the corner of the house. Directly to the right of the window lay the sharp turn in the stone, signalling the end of the wall. Looking thanklessly at his brother, Jack lowered himself out, his arms bearing the weight of his body until his feet found security on the upper frame of the window below. Keeping his body hard against the contoured stone, breathing shallow and even, Jack slid his feet carefully along the ledge until his fingers finally found the corner. The roughened masonry felt cool and coarse against his cheek. Moving by touch, he edged closer to the worn corner, extending his arm to the invisible. The northern facing wall was subject to the full punishment meted out by the weather and his fingers felt the scooped-out sandstone blocks, eroded away under pressure from the wind, and the slits between the blocks where the mortar had crumbled. A good hold secured with his left hand, his fingers locked into the stone, he moved to step around the corner. It was the trickiest part of the journey; his right foot was unable to find secure purchase on the smooth west-facing wall.

The north wall provided no window embrasure to apply his weight to but offered cracks, dusty with crumbling masonry. He rubbed his foot in the unseen joint, seeking a more secure hold, and heard pebbles skittering from their lofty perch. He moved to the left, allowing room for Richard to join him on the makeshift stairs, smiling a silent greeting as his brother rounded the corner, and together they began a careful descent.

Richard's progress was quicker, his moves made with a confidence born of familiarity, giving his brother the notion that he had travelled this route before. Jack was slower, more cautious, testing the firmness of cracks and fissures offered by the wall before trusting his full weight to their temporary keeping. He dropped finally into the long grass where his brother waited. The vertical descent had brought them to the foot of the mighty Norman defences outside the security of the curtain wall, and no longer within the stone embrace of Hazeldene.

It was a mile and a half directly across the fields, and Richard led them quickly to their destination. Dressed in folded grey, the incandescent disc of the moon showed little light to reveal their passing.

Finally, Richard signed Jack to stop, pulling him down low. Before them, Assingham was picked out in relief, depthless black against the dulled pearl night. The only detail not lost to the dark was due to a defective shutter from where leaked the pale yellow light from a taper.

Richard, dropping to sit in comfort, turned to Jack. "Well, this is Byrne's chosen spot. What do you think?"

A rustle of stems as Jack settled beside him. "I am, in more than one sense, in the dark."

"Byrne has been instructed to relay the messages, messages which will support Northumberland's cause. To throw the hounds a foreign scent, we are using

Assingham to relay messages. With such as Byrne at the helm, if this venture succeeds, it will be a bloody miracle that the Pope should be interested in. He fears to forge the links too firmly in case the day goes Mary's way and has shirked his task to me. Any questions?"

Jack merely shook his head in response.

"Well, dear brother, what you don't know is that Assingham's Lord is a staunch supporter of Mary and, I believe, currently at that lady's side."

"This is not sounding so good," Jack commented. "In fact, I think it sounds like more trouble than it's worth. Why not have your meetings in the forest over there?" Jack asked, pointing in the direction of the trees he knew were there, but he could not see.

"Because he pays, so, unfortunately, he calls the tune, and the tune–as unpleasant as those created by his wife–is here," Richard said dryly. "It does, however, have one or two curious advantages, doesn't it?"

Jack couldn't see what advantages there might be, but didn't voice the thought.

"So, who do you suppose will take the day, Mary or the Duke?" Richard changed the subject.

Jack shook his head in the dark. "I know not and care not as long as we get paid."

"Point well noted, although your desire may be thwarted if the Duke loses." He paused long enough to give Jack time to absorb that. "If you were to lay a bet, where would you place your coin?"

Richard's enquiry was a little too lightly put. Jack's guard was raised; the question was not as idle as it seemed. "Can't say. I know something of the Duke, but what strengths Mary has, I don't know."

"I agree," Richard said, shocking Jack and pleasing him with his concurrence.

"Who would you choose?" Jack asked, interested in his brother's thoughts, and wondering if for once he would share them. There was no reply, only Richard's laughter, and Jack turned from interested to irritated.

"Both," Richard said after his laughter had subsided. "Come on, let us deliver a message."

Deft fingers produced a small square of neatly folded parchment, dazzling brightly against the grey of the night. Richard did not share the cause of his amusement. Pushing himself up and beckoning Jack to join him, they set out to Assingham.

Later that night, after Richard and Jack returned to Hazeldene, there was a fire in the empty stalls in the stables. The alarm was quickly raised and all the animals were safely removed, but before the fire was put out, it took with it a good section of the roof and the end wall collapsed.

Anne De Bernay had been working on the household accounts since early morning. Tired, and with a back stiffened by immobility, she laid the pen to rest and straightened from the desk, groaning. A satisfied smile beheld the ink drying on the last entry in the accounts as glossed wet faded to matt black. The book closed. She laid it on one side of her desk. It was at that point that Gavin came to announce Judith Byrne's unexpected arrival.

The mean hall provided for its owners and guests with six high-backed chairs pulled in a semi-circle around the fire. The wall they made providing the only seclusion from the rest of the hall, which, by necessity, was where all ate and slept, save its lady and absent lord. Judith was there now, her embroidered skirts arranged to spill in neat and even folds over her knees, silver threaded flowers finding themselves picked out in the firelight. Judith did not stand to greet Anne; it had taken too long to arrange her dress in such a fashion as to avoid most of the filth on the floor.

"I am here to ask a favour, Anne. You can say no. I don't mean to impose on our friendship, but part of our stables burnt down last night," Judith said, carefully pulling her riding gloves from her fingers.

"I am sorry to hear that. How can I help? If it's labour you need, or materials–we have plentiful supplies of timber, now that Peter has added Markham Woods to the Assingham estate, certainly..."

Judith interrupted. "Nothing so costly to you, my dear. We need some space." Judith saw the puzzled look on Anne's face and continued.

"Edward is having the stables rebuilt, but on a different plan. They were too small for our needs and much in need of renovation, as it was, so Edward wants to pull the remains down and start again. Well, it was my idea really, and Edward liked it. We would much appreciate it if you could spare some space in your paddocks. I noticed they were half empty, and if you could, it would save us much trouble. Don't worry about feed. Edward said he'd send up one of his men to look after them, plus a cart of food so it wouldn't cost you anything." Judith stopped suddenly, convinced of a positive result.

"We have plenty of space, and I do not suppose a few more horses around would make any difference. Of course I don't mind, Judith." Anne smiled.

Richard left Hazeldene shortly after Judith had departed for Assingham and headed into the forest. He approached a clearing where a stone circle from another age still showed through the briar of the forest floor. In the centre, another horse was tethered loosely. Its rider sat on top of one of the druids' stones, impatiently tapping a whip against a riding boot and occasionally cast his eyes around, expectant of a visitor.

"Well, you're Derby's man, I believe. What a pleasant morning it is, do you not agree?" said Richard conversationally.

"Do you have it?" the man snapped. "The time is late. I had thought you were not going to arrive. I have a hard ride ahead of me, so if you will hand it over, I would be on my way."

"Oh yes, I have it." Richard handed over a sealed square of white parchment. The other took it without paying any attention to its contents.

"Next time, see if you can arrive a little earlier, man. Otherwise, I shall have words with your master." Mounting his horse, he swiftly disappeared from view.

Richard watched him leave, gazing thoughtfully after him, and made no effort to depart for some minutes. "I own no master save my poor self," he said, his only audience the trees. The network, albeit small, was established.

Messages were received from Whickham and left in simple code for collection by the other conspirators' lackeys. On arrival from Whickham, the man was directed to deposit them in the stables, as directed by Richard who intercepted all communications, as he must, to keep Edward informed.

Richard was also in communication with Derby, who was both a sworn supporter of Mary and a man very interested in receiving letters from an informant in the Duke's camp. Eager to cover all possible angles, Derby had agreed to send regular messengers to meet with Fitzwarren's man and collect what information he had. Richard took what pieces of information he gleaned from Whickham and his own network, elaborated on them, and penned letters to Derby. That was how Mary, soon to be Queen of England, first heard the name Richard Fitzwarren, offering what small service he could, along with his ever-lasting loyalty.

The first news that Northumberland's supporters were preparing to back his cause with physical force was no news at all to Derby and Mary. They had their own sources and more than a few of the powerful were less than confident of the Duke's success. Viewing him as a less than desirable leader, which was what he aimed to be: a king without a crown.

Catherine, returning from the kitchens, saw a man she did not recognise unloading a cart drawn by a tired, dusty-looking horse.

"M'lady." The fair-haired man said respectfully as he saw her approach.

"Has Lord Byrne sent you over from Hazeldene?" Catherine asked; her mother had told her of the fire.

"Yes, M'lady," the man replied.

"When are the horses coming?" Catherine asked. She was harbouring a secret hope that there might be a suitable replacement for Clover that she could lay claim to while they were housed at Assingham.

"The horses are already here. We brought them over early this morning."

"Oh, I see." Catherine walked round the cart and entered the stable, eager to see the horses. Where only three pairs of nostrils would normally have appeared from the stalls, there were now eight. A pair of enquiring eyes looked down at her as, open-handed, she offered some food from the hay box. A gentle, velvet mouth rubbed across her palm to take the offering. The whiskered skin brushing her hand made her giggle.

"You want some more?" Catherine put her head on one side to match the horse's own attitude. "Here then, but don't think I've a mind to stand here and feed you all day." The horse returned for a third helping, the large nose snorting as its mouth found nothing in the open hand. "One last one, then no more. Your friend here will get jealous, and I can't show any favouritism. That would not be fair, would it? I must treat all my guests alike," Catherine said, giving the horse an extra large handful.

"Assingham must be a tiresome place, lady, if you find you have to resort to conversations with horses, and my horse at that."

Catherine spun around to face the speaker. The voice, lazy and arrogant, was unmistakably that of Edward's cousin, Richard. Catherine hurriedly brushed the stray strands of grass from her skirts, trying to regain her composure.

Please let him not have heard all of that. The man must think me such easy prey.

"Why, Richard, good morning. I had not expected to see you at Assingham." Catherine fought to keep her voice level.

"My horse is being stabled here for the time being, so I wanted to reassure myself he was suitably housed." To her horror, Richard walked towards her down the narrow passage in front of the horses, blocking her exit.

Recognising his master, Corracha moved back to where he had stood earlier, his head now between Richard and Catherine, nuzzling affectionately at Richard's hand.

"Well, as you can see, perhaps this is not what he is used to, but I am sure he will be comfortable. If you would excuse me, I have other things to attend to," Catherine replied briskly.

"Of course," Richard said absently. Rather than retreating down the passage to allow her out, he merely stepped to one side, leaving her no choice but to squeeze past. Skirts in hand, Catherine hurriedly closed the gap between them, turning slightly sideways to move away and make good her escape.

Richard caught her arm by the elbow, trapping her between him and the stable wall behind her.

"Please, Sir..." Her voice was high, holding the shake of nerves, but still, he held her elbow fast against her tugs. She felt his breath on her face. He was so close. Suddenly, smiling broadly, he released her arm and turned away, leaving Catherine staring at his back. Red-faced, composure shattered, Catherine fled the stables in a flurry of skirts.

Catherine avoided the courtyard, having no wish for another encounter with Edward's cousin. The mere thought of him still made her anger rise, and the ever-present possibility of an unexpected meeting anywhere around Assingham made her nervous. Twice, whilst embroidering that evening, she had looked up, sure someone was watching her. The meeting that afternoon had more of an effect on her than she was prepared to admit.

It had been a difficult decision. Harry had wanted the snivelling piece of filth under his foot, a bleeding pile at his feet, but luck, it seemed, had saved him. Byrne was a name Harry had heard but, until now, he had never noted it. He knew that Byrne, like himself, was among the Northumberland's supporters. And it seemed that Richard Fitzwarren and his men were the support Byrne hoped to offer. Harry, similarly placed by his own ambition, could not act. He needed his men near. Edward was ill. The country held its breath, knowing the king's death could be upon them very soon.

The alternative was to wait, but Harry feared that Richard would disappear from Byrne's side, or worse, he could perish in the fighting before Harry's knife could be applied to him. Thus torn, he had decided to reap what immediate benefit he could from the information he had, and this decision brought him to the current conversation.

Invited by an urgent message, Robert Fitzwarren sat perched on a table edge while Harry poured him wine. Retrieving his own glass, Harry seated himself, though not too closely, to the other man.

"Well, Harry," Robert raised the crusted cup and drained half its contents. "What's so secret a tale as makes you dismiss your servants?"

"I have news," Harry said slowly, "much to your liking, I would think."

"Don't tell me that doxy Annie, has a sister?" Robert was bored, and it showed in both his manner and his voice.

Harry was annoyed. He had wanted to show Robert how clever he had been in tracking down Richard, but instead he blurted, "Your brother is back."

"That had better not be spoken lightly," Robert said menacingly.

Harry sensibly heeded the warning edge and avoided prevarication. "He is employed by Lord Byrne and resides at Hazeldene." Harry gave Robert all the scant facts he had and then waited. Robert, hands clasped white-knuckled behind him, gazed from the open window at the pin-pricked night of London.

His words Harry did not hear.

"This time, Richard. This time..."

A nail-bitten hand turned the letter over again. Within the elaborate sentences was Northumberland's decision to keep Edward's imminent death a secret, and details of his supporters who were gathering forces to help the Northumberland hold the city. These she knew to be true. Edward still lived, teetering on the brink, but as yet he had not breathed his last. Mary lifted the page and, before she sent the sheet spiralling to the eager lick of the flames, observed the penned name once more: Richard Fitzwarren.

Chapter Nine

Hazeldene – Late June 1553

Jack took the offered card, storing it tightly behind the other three he held; a thumb and forefinger slid the edge to peek at him from the back of the hand. With great effort, he prevented himself from scowling at the three of clubs. His other cards were two lousy fives and an errant knave. Was he prepared to lay more on a pair of fives? Looking up, Jack hoped to read his opponent's face, but instead he found a pair of grey eyes already watching him intently.

"Well?" Richard enquired.

Jack sighed. Releasing his grip on the cards, he let them tumble from his fingers. "It's yours."

Richard collected the discarded suits, placing them with the rest of the deck, and added to the pack the few cards he had held.

"Hey now, no!" Jack exclaimed. "It's only sporting to let me see what I lost against."

Richard smiled. "I think not."

"The game is up. There is nothing left to win," Jack protested.

"There is always something to win; there are always stakes left to play for." Richard expertly split the deck in two and reunited the parts.

Richard moved to re-deal, but Jack motioned to stop him. "Would you have me in penury?"

Richard stopped and shuffled the deck instead.

"What's our move? Do you know yet?" Jack enquired, wondering if Richard would share his knowledge.

"We wait." Richard idly started to sort the cards back into their houses.

"I begin to wonder if this is folly," Jack muttered as he reached for the jug.

"I don't see why that should bother you, as we shall be paid either way, folly or not." Richard was placing aces on top of the kings. "Another game?"

The game ended when Jack laughed bitterly at his misfortunes, casting the cards towards the victor in defeat. "I should have known better than to be further tempted. You are begotten of the devil..."

"We are our father's sons," was all Richard said flatly.

"Well, that's true enough," Jack accepted. And then, "What's he like... Our father?"

"Arrogant, selfish, cruel, miserly are only a few of the words that come to mind... There is much of him in Robert," Richard supplied.

"I often wondered what would happen if I turned up at his door. There's always a possibility he might not turn me out on my ear. After all, he placed me in his brother's household; a lot do worse than that, you know," Jack sounded thoughtful.

"If I was in your place, I could see how tempting it would be," Richard observed. But William Fitzwarren is not a kind man and blood ties, as I know to my cost, don't mean a lot to him."

It was not the reply Jack had wanted. "It might not be like that."

"Jack! Once, I turned back up at his door, cap in hand, and the man left me for dead! My own father! He had not an ounce of pity in his soul as he laid the lash on me." Richard replied, his voice level, his tone patient.

"Jesus! It was your own father who put those marks on your back!" Jack blurted, letting Richard know his secret was no more.

Richard's eyes narrowed. "Dan told me I had had a midnight visitor. Nothing is bloody sacred. Anyway, that is my... our father's handiwork."

"Surely there must have been some reason for him to do that! You don't set at someone like that without good cause," Jack protested.

"There was, and brother, you are not going to find out tonight what it was, so don't bother asking. But the crux of the matter is that you can expect nothing less if you cross his path. Please believe me on that," Richard spoke earnestly. "Being tied to the Fitzwarren clan is no way forward for us; the way forward for us is money."

"And, as you can see, a surplus of gold coming out of my arse is one of my constant worries," Jack replied sarcastically.

The reply, when it came, was five neatly dealt cards landing atop of each other. Reluctantly, Jack took them into his keeping, meeting Richard's mild enquiring eyes over the top of three knaves and two smiling queens.

"Have my name, and all the curses it so rightly deserves, if you can win it." In Richard's hand was not a coin, but a ring. Gold and black-crested, it was stamped with seeded rubies and emeralds. In the centre of the shield was a sun, represented by a cold diamond.

Jack smiled, his eyes sparkling with more warmth than the crushed coal. "I have, by your own hand, three knaves." With precision, he laid them face up. "And two pretty queens." He set them separate from the laughing trio. "I think the test for us both would be to see what you hold."

"Nothing," Richard laughed, loosing his hands he let tumble a poor array of unmatched low-numbered cards, not a painted face among them. "You look disappointed?" Jack indeed did. "You expected aces? I have none. This time, you hold all the cards. It's a game of chance, Jack."

Richard had the final word. He rose from the table, leaving Jack alone with the disarray of cards and the sparkling monogram of power.

Catherine sat staring from the open shutters in her room as the day outside drew to an end. The trees in the foreground found themselves still painted by a dipping sun, while those more distant had cloaked their branches already with evening shades.

A rider emerged, breaking the neat undisturbed edge where trees met the meadow, and urged his horse on to a gallop, heading towards Assingham. He was too distant for her to make out the rider's features. A messenger from her father, she thought, but then, no, it was only recently that they had received a letter from that quarter. Perhaps it was something from Judith, her neighbour at Hazeldene, but Judith's home lay not in the direction he came from.

Puzzled, Catherine watched as the rider disappeared from the view afforded by her window. By now, he should be in the courtyard. No one came. Leaning out of the window, she saw no movement below, heard no exchange of voices; even the snorting horse and jangle of bit and bridle were absent. Puzzled, she made her way downstairs. Emerging from the hall, Catherine found no sweating horse and dusty rider; only John, a bucket of water in either hand, making his way to the kitchens.

"John, there was a rider approaching. I saw him from the window," Catherine asked.

"I'm sorry, M'lady, there's been no rider stop here, not that I knows about anyways, and I've been working out here all the while." John, stopping to speak to her, slopped water over the rims of the filled buckets.

"I must have been mistaken. It did look like he was coming here, but I suppose he must have ridden past."

John didn't reply and Catherine watched his retreating back for a moment. Then an unmistakable snort and stamp met her ears: the disobedient but highly forgivable Clover. A soft-shoed foot moved automatically before she winced at the memory of her last visit; indecision delayed her advance.

Silently, she spoke to her flagging courage. It's my home and I shall go where I wish.

Martha, the kitchen maid, watched the girl make her way towards the stables until John blocked her view. "And where's lady long legs off to now then, eh?" Martha received one of the pails from John's hand.

"Ah, now, leave the lass alone, Martha. You've never got a good word to say for her." John tipped the remaining bucket, allowing its contents to join Martha's in the tub in the kitchen corner.

"Well, she's hardly a fit daughter for his lordship now, is she? Of marrying age and she slides around the place and hardly ever has a word to say for herself. The master will be hard pushed to find any to take her off his hands."

"God love us, woman. With a tongue like yours wagging, there's no room for anyone else, is there?" John ducked and avoided the fist aimed at his ear.

"Get away with you."

John grinned as he reached the door.

Some four miles distant, Alan was employed, but on his own business, not his master's. He smiled as he watched the rumps of the two retreating horses move away down the dusty road. Cold silver near his skin warmed his heart, and his blood surged with the force of his victory. His only regret was that when Harry's men fell on Jack, he would be ignorant of Alan's part in his downfall. However, the purse he held more than made up for that loss of satisfaction.

"Alan, are you coming or stopping?" Froggy Tate called. Alan glowered at the short-barrelled man. The horses he led behind him were already saddled and loaded with their possessions. "Who was that then?" Froggy continued, and spat in the direction of the retreating horseman.

"Nothing. Give me that horse." Alan pulled the reins roughly from Froggy's hand and led the horse away before mounting.

Froggy spat again. Thoughtful eyes flicked between his companion and the distant movement along the road which marked the departing riders.

Courage renewed, Catherine made her way to the stables. Looking down the passageway in front of the stalls, she saw a figure emerge from halfway down the paddock's length. It appeared as only a darkened shape in the dim light and Catherine assumed it was one of the stable lads, but what light there was caught on polished metal, revealing a sword at his side. As she watched, he dropped to his knees and pulled the planking from the front of a stable door. Moments later, he seemed to finish his unknown task and moved away quickly, disappearing inside a vacant stall.

Five long minutes passed, and still he did not show himself. Catherine took a step into the gloom but hurriedly changed her mind. He must still be in there somewhere and she had no wish to meet an armed man in the dark. The only sounds that met her ears came from the horses at the far end. The first two stalls in front of her were empty, and the remaining ones housed the horses from Hazeldene. Behind her, she heard John making another trip with pails of water, and this gave her a measure of reassurance. Summoning her courage, she made up her mind to walk forward and identify the person who was trespassing within the stables. If she screamed, John would hear.

It was likely only a man sent over by Lord Byrne. Her feet, in soft leather shoes, made no noise on the clean straw, and the rustle of her skirts on the wood wall was camouflaged by the noises from the beasts within. From several paces away, she could see into the stall her visitor had moved into; it was empty. What had he been so interested in? It was a simple door of heavy construction made to withstand more than the occasional insult from a hoof. Vertical planks, a hand's span wide, were fixed with nails to a wooden frame. Her fingers felt up the door. She had seen him remove a plank and lay it momentarily on the floor before replacing it, but nothing gave-way to her touch.

Some minutes later, a smoking candle from her desk on the uneven floor, she was searching in earnest, determined to find its secret. The wood that had been removed was clearly visible now. The doors were half height, allowing the horses to peer over them, secured by a slide bolt at the top and an iron kick latch at the bottom. Most of the planks ran from the top to bottom of the short door, but one in the corner was cut a foot or so from the sill and the timber was bruised where it had been levered out, and on more than one occasion judging by the damaged grain.

Pushing a knife between the planks, she found that little pressure was needed to force it out of place, and from behind it fell a parchment that settled quietly on the floor in front of her knees. She pushed the paper quickly into her pocket and, wood back in place, made a hasty retreat to her room.

The candle re-lit on the desk, her door locked. Catherine stared at the paper lying in front of her. In the centre was a wax seal, the blurred impression a testament to a hasty application. Sliding a flat knife gently between wax and paper, she encouraged the seal to pop away intact from the lower sheet. Her hands hovered over the parchment.

Well, you have stolen it and opened it; you might as well read it.

The few lines it contained were hurriedly written, the haste proven by the splutters the protesting pen had left on the page, but the script was still legible and neat.

The single sheet contained a few lines in all. It was neither addressed nor signed.

We would be pleased to accept your gift and look forward to your visit soon. The weather has been unpleasant here, but we hope it will improve when you join us. Hopefully, there will be some good hunting to be done, which will entertain you during your stay.

Catherine read it twice. Had it been addressed and signed, she would have believed she was reading some private correspondence between friends or maybe businessmen meeting to discuss trade and pass away some of the summer months in each other's company. But these vital marks were omitted, and the method of its delivery placed further suspicion on the meaning of the words. Reaching for more wax, she refolded the sheet, adding a few drops under the seal before pressing it closed again.

One more person was thus admitted to that small ring privy to the information sent north from London.

"I'll not ask how you got that." Dan took the offered ring from Jack's outstretched hands.

"Would you believe me if I told you I won it at cards?" Jack offered, smiling.

"Somehow, no, but I'll give it back to him." There was an odd expression on Dan's face.

Jack continued. "All right, would you believe me if I told you I was forced to win it at cards, and that is the truth of it."

"I would believe that." Dan grinned.

"It was Richard's poor idea of a joke." Jack made to leave.

Dan caught him by the arm, stopping him. "Are you sure...?"

"Yes Dan, I'm sure. Richard likes to remind his half-brother of his bastardy; it keeps me in my place. He spun me a yarn about how bad our father is. I think he only said it to stop me turning up at the family manor and finding out about his shameful past." Dan could tell from Jack's tone he wasn't being serious.

"Ah, you're wrong there," Dan warned.

"What? Wrong about our father or Richard's shameful past?" Jack laughed.

"Stop being bloody clever," Dan said hotly.

"He told me that it was his father who had tried to whip him to death. I don't suppose you'd know anything about that, would you?" Jack said, folding his arms.

"No," Dan spoke too quickly. "I know nothing about that."

"I'm sure you don't," Jack said sarcastically. "I'll find out one way or the other, mark my words. So why don't you just sit yourself down and tell me now?"

Dan sighed. "There is something, what I cannot tell you, but it colours the way your brother treats you."

Jack was a little shaken. Here was something indeed. "Tell me."

"That family of his, and yours for that matter, have a lot to answer for. I've known your brother for a lot of years, and he's not as cruel or as arrogant as you sometimes think."

"Tell that to Robby," Jack said quickly.

"Well, he should have kept his thieving fingers to himself–better some quick justice than having the bloody assize involved."

"True. Don't think I haven't noticed you're trying to change the subject. Now just what is it you won't tell me?"

Dan had already begun to retreat, and despite the pleas, he would supply Jack with nothing else. Jack had no intention of giving up, though. If Dan wouldn't tell him, then perhaps Richard might.

The note she had replaced had vanished, she was sure, at night, and if there was to be another, Catherine wanted to see its delivery. John had assured her that tonight would be clear, but cold. As it turned out, it was more than that; it was windy, and the gusts of air carried a mist that drenched fields, trees, and animals.

A blanket wrapped tightly around her, Catherine sat and watched. The only activity was that of the rabbits emerging from burrows to graze nervously. She was about to abandon her perch on the window ledge, becoming uncomfortably aware of the damp working its way through her wrap, when her eyes were arrested by a movement in the tree line.

Water darkened the leather glove that held the pine branch aside as the heavy cob stepped lightly from the fold of the trees. Assured that all was quiet, he pressed his heels lightly into the horse and it trotted out. The branch, when released, sent a shower of heavy rain to soak the carpet of sponged needles. The mare was fresh, and she covered the distance to Assingham quickly, the sound of her passage dulled by the soft earth beneath her hooves. Cautiously though, the rider dropped from the saddle and led her the final distance, bringing her on foot to the back of the stables.

Even at that pace, he covered the ground almost as quickly as Catherine could pass through the house. She left her room and quickly descended the wooden stairs. The hall was quiet; the fire burnt down, the dim light picking out the sleepers who were all laid near it to gather the last of its warmth. Lifting her skirts, she silently trod across the hall and then dashed quickly to the pitch-dark entrance to the stables.

He waited, listening, silencing his mare with a calming hand. Tying her reins to the soaked wood, he dropped to his knees and disappeared inside Assingham. Still low, he waited, his eyes adjusting to the blackness. Knowing then where to go, he moved swiftly and with a purpose to deliver the message to the keeping of the woodwork.

Catherine felt sure the man had left. His mission complete, she told herself; he was unlikely to wait around. Quietly she moved into the space running in front of the stalls and looked down nervously at the planking forming the door to the empty stall.

Was there another message? Yes! Even in the dark, the whiteness of the paper when it fell to her feet was unmistakable. Snatching it from the floor, it disappeared inside of the folds of her dress. Hastily replacing the panel, Catherine headed directly for her room. Neither the sleepers in the hall nor the dogs arrayed with them heeded her as she alighted the stairs.

The small square of parchment looked much like the previous one. It bore something akin to a seal, but the impression was again blurred and gave no hint as to the crest or letters. The short, flat blade hovered over the parchment. She had lifted the seal on the previous one without breaking it.

Could she manage it again? The edge of the knife went under the soft wax. The last had sprung apart from the paper, whole and intact, with little persuasion, but this one was firmly attached. A different angle with the knife failed also to persuade it to free itself. Her attempts had damaged the seal and little curls of red showed where the knife had scored the moulded wax. It was obvious to anyone now that it had been tampered with.

The sealing wax on her desk was a markedly different colour from that attached to the letter, but... Catherine smiled. Taking the candle from the pewter holder and cleaning the debris of wax from its circular dish, she scraped the seal from the parchment into it.

The square of parchment, when unfolded, revealed an even briefer message than the last one. It stated simply:

Three nights hence.

Carefully, she held the pewter dish near the fire's dying flames; the wax returned to a liquid that could be poured back onto the parchment where the original seal had been.

Catherine watched the blob of red begin to solidify before taking her ring and pressing it lightly into the wax, turning it so as to remove any impression of the crest. The seal, she had to admit, was not as substantial as its predecessor. Much of the wax had remained in the bottom of the candleholder, coating it in a dull red veneer, but the impression was like the previous one, indistinct and unclear.

The courtyard was lit by a dim and uncertain light heralding the coming of the dawn when Catherine returned the parchment to its hiding place. Small fingers pushed a stem of straw into the wood of the door; she would know now if the planking had been removed. Catherine slept well into the morning until she was woken by Martha enquiring after her health. Further investigation revealed the note gone.

A day later, upon employing the same tactics, Catherine found another short note, which read:

Our hearts are heavy.

Catherine was mystified.

Jack threw a saddle up onto the back of the horse, leaning under it he retrieved the girth strap. He recognised the polished boots that he could see approaching across the courtyard. "I told you Assingham was too much of a risk." He said when his brother had come to stand close to the horse.

Richard, one hand idly smoothing the Arab's mane, fixed a hard stare on his brother. Jack noted that amongst the rings he wore was the one he had given to Dan. "Why do I get the feeling I am not going to like this? Go on, tell me what happened."

"What happened, my oh-so-well-planned brother, is that a lady who, I will remind you, had been dissuaded from visiting her stables, is not only still frequenting them but was, in fact, occupying one of the stalls when I paid a visit last night."

"Ah!"

"What do you mean? 'Ah!'?" Jack stood and faced Richard.

"Well, I think we can fairly assume Lady Cate was not on a midnight stroll, but by all accounts, we should make our move soon. She may know something is going on, but not what. I doubt the pretty lady can read, let alone make any headway with the code. Her father's away. I can see no real problems. Next time you go, find a diversion," Richard finished pleasantly.

"A diversion? Like what exactly?" Jack enquired.

"I leave it to your imagination," Richard smiled. "I slipped with a lit torch in the stables. Now it's your turn."

"Thanks, thank you very much," Jack's words were laden with sarcasm. Richard turned to leave, but Jack stopped him. "Richard?"

"Yes," Richard was mildly curious at the other's tone. They were in the middle of the yard, and somehow this didn't seem the right place.

"Nothing, nothing that can't wait until you get back." Jack watched as Richard threw himself into the saddle and set the horse towards the gate.

Jack could feel eyes upon him. Turning, it was with relief that he found the inquisitive gaze came from the yellow eyes of the cat, watching him on the edge of a saddle rack.

Chapter Ten

Assingham – Early July 1553

Catherine was sitting in the hall after darkness fell, promising herself one last look in the stables before retiring. She had to admit that if her visits became any more frequent, it would begin to look extremely odd indeed. John had already given her a queer sideways look when he caught her crossing the courtyard for the third time that evening.

She had just got to her feet when she heard shouting and screeching coming from outside. Running from the hall, she found the kitchen boy standing in front of the open hen house door, surrounded by feathers, which were escaping from within. As she watched, a cat, fat tabby and with its tail in the air, left the henhouse, running straight between the boy's legs and then past Catherine, so close she felt it brush against her skirts.

"How the devil did that beggar get in there?" John yelled as the lively animal made a neat escape round the back of the kitchens.

John followed, pitchfork in hand. "It's fenced off–he'll not get out now."

His confidence was misplaced. The newly constructed fence, which had been built to protect the chickens from predators, showed a wide breach. Some hundred yards on the other side, the cat could be seen in the moonlight, making for the safety of the woods.

"How on earth did that happen?" John stabbed the fork into the ground and advanced towards the fence. "That post has been pulled out. A bloody cat didn't do that!"

On the other side of the broken fence they could see the cat making its final bound for the safety of the woods, a large prize in its mouth.

"Someone has broken the fence down. That's the only way that crafty bugger could have got in here." John had retrieved the post that had been pulled free, his eyes scanning the mud for further traces of the culprit, muttering under his breath, "Who'd want to do such a thing?"

The kitchen boy retrieved three dead hens. Carrying them by the feet, a twitching wing protruding from the mass of untidy feathers, he took them to the kitchen.

"We've lost some good layers there. That fence was fine this morning when I brought the feed round. I've no idea how that happened. I need to tell Gavin, someone is to blame for it and I'll have to get it fixed, or we'll end up with foxes in here and we'll have no hens left at all." John came up beside Catherine, as if to reassure her, but she was not listening.

Walking back across the courtyard, she turned towards the stables, leaving a bemused John behind the kitchens to effect hasty repairs. Inside the stable block, it was too dark to see if the straw was still in place, and she reprimanded herself for not having the foresight to collect a light from the hall first. In the dark, she had the eerie feeling of being watched, but she barely hesitated before dropping to her knees and pulling her knife from her waistband. Inserting it into the crack between the planking by feel, the wood slipped through her fingers, dropping to the hardened earth with a clatter, but it was followed by no paper, no telltale white square. Catherine felt on the floor in front of her skirts for the parchment, but found nothing. The message was gone.

Replacing the board, she realised exactly when it had been taken. It had been quickly removed, unnoticed by anyone, whilst a cat was wreaking havoc in the hen house. "Our hearts are heavy" had to mean something to someone–but what? Rubbing her hands down the front of her skirts to remove the dirt from them, she returned to her room with an angry look on her face.

The invite to attend Hazeldene for a meal with Edward and Judith in a few days time arrived at midday for Catherine and her mother, delivered by the blond stable hand Catherine had seen at Hazeldene before. Anne bid him go to the kitchens whilst she penned a reply.

"I don't want to go, mama." Catherine bleated.

"Why not?" Her mother asked, exasperated. "I thought you were becoming friends with Judith."

"She doesn't like me; she was horrible last time I went. Please don't make me go." Catherine pleaded. She had no intention of being absent from Assingham any evening in the near future.

"Alright, we won't go if you are so set against it. I myself would rather not either. Edward is rather tiresome, and Judith never stops talking about herself–I can think of better ways to spend an evening," Anne conceded. She penned a reply and gave it to the callused hand of Hazeldene's man.

Jack was taking his time on the return journey from Assingham, Anne de Bernay's note tucked inside his doublet. The reins were slack in his hands, and the mare stepped on quietly, following the track. Jack stared ahead, unseeing.

That Robby had suggested he should take his brother's place did not surprise him. After he had been caught stealing, he had plenty of reasons to want rid of the Master, and Jack was fairly sure that after this current venture was completed Robby would find himself needing a new employer. That Richard hadn't rid himself of the man was only because it was expedient not to.

Jack tapped his fingers idly against the pommel.

Could he take his brother's place?

He had executed his brother's orders well after he had taken the men to Carney Bridge. Even Richard had been unable to find fault with him on that score.

Did he want to take his brother's place?

A smile twitched at the corner of Jack's mouth. He'd certainly enjoy seeing the look on Richard's face if he lost his role of command. To see uncertainty in his brother's eyes would be satisfying indeed. Although it was a look Jack knew he was unlikely to witness, there was little chance he could take his brother's place, not for any significant time, anyway. People like Lord Byrne would not deal with the likes of Jack. Richard had the connections, the manner, the skill to lead, and Jack recognised that once this current endeavour was over, he would have little idea where to take the men next or how to obtain more paid work for the group.

Judith received Anne's note where she sat sewing in the garden. Edward, seeing the messenger's return, had hurried to enquire if their guests were coming.

"Anne says she cannot come." Judith was trying to pull the needle through several layers of unyielding material, and gestured with her head to where the letter lay discarded on the table beside her. "See for yourself."

Edward scanned the brief words. "I was looking forward to a bit of good company and a reason to break out some decent wine," he spoke absently, before turning and walking back to the house.

He found Richard in the stables, talking to one of his men.

"I know," was all Richard said as Edward approached.

"I cannot see them harmed, Richard," Edward said, a sorrowful expression on his face.

"There are a dozen people at Assingham. Old men, women and boys. I feel they will not closet themselves in the main house and make us lay siege on the place." Richard turned now to give Edward his full attention. "They will fall to their knees and beg for mercy, the lady and her daughter included."

"Using Assingham to exchange messages was one thing, but now that Whickham wants to use it as a centre for us to gather, well, that's quite another." Edward's anguish had increased. "Why choose it?"

"As yet, no-one knows what strength Mary has. It makes sense to amass your support behind defensible walls. Once your forces are all together and the location of Mary's troops are known, then a decision can be safely made as to where to move," Richard explained patiently.

"Assingham is hardly defensible, you've seen it," Edward countered.

"Use Hazeldene then," Richard shot back.

Edward conceded defeat. Assingham had, through no fault of its own, been committed.

"I know all the glory and none of the guilt; that's why you pay me." Richard's tone was harsh, but then he added the words Edward wanted to hear: "I will see to them."

Edward's mind was eased. "Everything is as we arranged. I have heard from my son Geoffrey; he is moving as planned. He has thirty of his own men, added to what I have here we will be able to provide Northumberland with some credible support. All will go well, I am sure." Still muttering to himself, he rose and left.

Jack watched Byrne retreat, a look of open loathing on his face. Crossing the yard back to his brother, he said, "If weak-willed men like that aim to take the reins of England, then I'm worried."

"He is a small man with a loud mouth and big ambitions," Richard explained. "But you'll not have to put up with him for much longer; it's a soldier's life for you again, Jack. That, at least, should mean I have one happy person around me."

"Would you lay a wager on us getting out of this in one piece?" Jack asked mischievously. And then, after a thoughtful pause, "And paid?"

"The outcome of a race to claim a throne is never a safe wager. And whether you like it or not, we are part of it. Poor fools that must act within the rules laid by others," Richard lamented. "So we shall have to wait and see. We meet as arranged tomorrow," Richard said, eyes bright, "from there it's in the lap of the Gods."

Jack stood. "You want me to go and pass the word?" he asked.

"Indeed, let us relieve your companions from their daily toil, and make sure we play our part well. I don't want them running into Edward's son, Geoffrey. You know where I want them and you to be?"

"I do," Jack replied quickly.

"Make sure you are where you are supposed to be, collect the men and secure Assingham before everyone else arrives," Richard instructed.

"That won't be hard," Jack said.

"Well, let us just hope that Byrne's companions are as well organised as we intend to be." Richard replied.

"Richard?" Jack hesitated. "I've spoken to Dan. There's much both he and you won't tell me. Would now not be a good time to tell me?"

"What, before we die in the foray? That would be incredibly noble of me, would it not?" Richard scoffed, and then added, "But today I don't feel particularly noble."

Jack tried another track. "Dan has told me much already."

Richard's eyes narrowed, but he said nothing.

"Tell me. I think I have a right to know." Jack was closer to the truth than he knew.

Richard was no longer smiling. "It sounds as if you know everything already."

Jack avoided the trap. "I just want to know why."

"Why?" The word came out in an angry gasp. "What exactly did Dan tell you?"

"He told me why you couldn't accept me." Jack hoped he hadn't betrayed his ignorance.

"For God's sake, Jack, there is much at stake. Can you not leave this? We have been paid to perform a service for Byrne. I do not have time to argue with you," Richard snapped at his brother before turning to leave.

Jack stood, scowling at Richard's retreating back.

"He's an argumentative bastard," mused Robby, moving from the back of the stables. Jack spun around at the sound of his voice. "What did he catch you at, then?"

Jack was relieved that Robby had not heard the exchange. "Questioning his actions, as usual."

"Aye, well, he's a bad-tempered cur, that one. If you ask me, he's waiting for a knife in the back, and it'll happen, mark me." Robby moved to lean against the cart where the master had so recently stood.

"Do you think so?" Jack's thoughts were elsewhere.

"I do. Alan says he'll not last. What do we need him for, anyway? He does nothing, he's just an idle bastard. If we were on our own, we could make twice as much and not have him on our bleeding backs." Robby spat in Fitzwarren's direction.

Jack's attention was now most fully Robby's. "You might be right there, but I can't see what we can do about it."

"Aye, well, maybe there is something. Alan has a plan. We'll just have to wait and see, but I can tell you I'm with him," Robby confided.

"What exactly is Alan doing?" Jack moved closer to Robby.

Jack recognised the uncertainty in Robby's eyes and his voice was hesitant when he replied. "I can't say, but my money is on Alan. What about you?"

Jack was shocked. He was being asked if he would stand as a challenger against Richard. He was careful. "I hear what you say, but I can tell you I don't think Alan has a chance of getting rid of Fitzwarren. Do you?"

"He doesn't need to. There's someone else that will do that for him." Robby replied, though his voice had become uncertain, and Jack read the apprehension on Robby's face.

Jack moved to allay it. "Well, that would change things, wouldn't it? But who?"

Reassured, Robby continued, "Well, that I don't rightly know, but Alan said it had something to do with what happened before he left London. What I can't say. But does it matter? If someone is happy enough to get rid of him for us, all the better. You couldn't do a much worse job than he does? Alan would back you and quite a few of the other lads as well."

Jack wondered if Robby knew he had recently levelled Alan to the ground. He doubted it. Otherwise, the man would not be so eager to share Alan's plan. Alan would not be planning to replace Richard with Jack, Alan would have designs on the role of leader for himself. "Well, there is much in what you say, Robby. Who else is with you? Dan? Mat?"

"Nah, not them. Mat's a right shifty bastard, and Dan—nah—he's Fitzwarren's man all right. But Gavin's with us and so is Froggy Tate, and Alan thinks the rest'll follow when he's gone."

Jack grinned. "I think Alan might be right."

It was enough for Robby, who clapped him on the arm, being careful to use his good hand.

The following day, while Jack was busy organising the men, Catherine was less well occupied. The needlework had lain in front of her, untouched, for hours, and she had retired to her room early, for she could not stand to sit in the hall and watch the slow evening routine of the household. She knew she had another hour to wait before the house was fully asleep, and even so, she had prepared already. Wearing an old dark-grey dress, she had folded two cloaks, both dark in colour; one to warm her and one to spread over the gaps in the planking to ensure she would not be seen, and both lay ready on her desk. She was confident that in the gloom of the stable, even if someone did look up, they would be unable to see her up in the stable roof.

Finally, she dared to venture down the stairs and move quietly through the sleeping hall and into the stable. During the afternoon, Catherine had looked carefully at the route she would take to climb to the roof. But, in the dark, the foot and handholds could not be seen at all clearly. Hoisting the cloak above her head, she threw it upwards to her hiding place. She misjudged it and it came straight back down, providing an unwelcome slap in the face. The second attempt was successful, leaving her hands free to make her ascent.

Jack was supposed to be on his way to deliver final directions, but it had taken longer than he had thought to find Dan who, at the Master's direction, had been to the village.

"Thank you for your words of wisdom." Jack sat down heavily next to Dan. Leaning across, he helped himself to a greasy slice of mutton.

"Aye, I heard. Did I say to you to go and share it? No, I bloody didn't. If it helps you any, what you got is nothing compared to the roasting he gave me. I regret it as much as you do," Dan muttered through a mouthful of chewed meat.

"I'll not be putting up with it any longer anyway," Jack declared.

Dan's eyebrows raised. "How's that then?"

"I'll leave. It's as simple as that. He doesn't want me here and I bloody well don't want to be here having my arse kicked every time there's something to answer for. No, my mind's made up." Jack had no intention of leaving, but he hoped the threat might prompt Dan to say more.

"Aye, well, it's your choice," was all Dan offered.

It was not the response Jack had wanted. "I thought you might have something to say."

"Like what? You want me to persuade you to stay? To run and tell the Master? The world has more in it than the likes of you." The big man left the table.

That went bloody badly.

Jack realised he was going to have to try a different tack. He didn't much fancy asking Richard again. He had much more chance with Dan; he just needed to find the right approach. Jack's thoughts were interrupted as Robby moved into Dan's seat.

"I heard you're leaving. Is that right?" Robby questioned quietly.

"Maybe." Jack was in no mood for Robby's company.

"Well don't. Anyhow, not just yet, eh?" Robby's words reminded Jack of his earlier conversation with the would-be plotter.

"Oh, aye, and Alan's going to lead us," Jack shot back.

Robby missed Jack's sarcasm. "Aye, and soon. Alan says it'll not be long now."

Jack's attention was riveted on Robby. "You've seen Alan then? I thought he was waiting in the village?"

"He came over last night to have a word with a couple of us," Robby confided.

"You and Pierre, am I right?" Jack probed.

"Pierre, he's with us, I reckon." Robby's head bobbed enthusiastically.

"So what's Alan's plan, then?"

"Oh now, he said I couldn't tell anyone. He only told me. All you need to know is that we'll be rid of him bloody soon." Robby sounded triumphant.

"I thought you were gone," Mat called from the doorway.

Jack turned as Mat moved in and sat down. Robby had already slid down the bench, away from Jack. "I was just going." Jack stood moodily.

"What was up with him, eh?" Mat asked Robby when Jack had gone.

"Nothing that I know about." Robby returned his attention to the platter in front of him.

Jack knew that the "something to do with London," of Robby's previous conversation was probably Harry, but how Alan had made the connection he didn't know. He knew he should tell Richard.

But that would require talking to him.

It was not as easy as she had thought it would be. Standing on top of the stable partition, Catherine had thought she would be able to pull herself over the edge of the protruding platform. The distance was much greater than she had judged, and she could just get her hands firmly around the edge of the wooden structure. She tried to pull herself up, getting half an elbow over the edge, but her feet swinging in mid-air above the stable partition could find nothing to push against. The dry wood forced splinters into her hands as she tried to pull her weight over the edge, but fear of falling into the dark stable below overcame the increasing discomfort in her hands as she heaved herself up, pausing for breath when she felt secure with one knee firmly on the planking.

The structure groaned under the new weight, but it did not give way. Spreading her cloak out over the wood and arranging the straw around her, Catherine settled down to wait, laying flat on her stomach so she could peer easily down the length of the stables.

Richard's mind was preoccupied with the puzzle of what fresh information he should send South to Derby as he walked slowly up the stone spiral steps from the hall to the corridor leading to his room. Had he walked faster, had he not paused before he pressed the door open, he would not have heard footsteps in the corridor on the other side of the door. Light footsteps that he at once recognized.

Judith.

His fingers had already pressured the door open an inch. Gently, he pulled them away, and the door moved back silently and closed against the stone frame. With more speed that he had used during his ascent, he dropped back down the steps. Edward had still been in the Hall when he had left. He hoped to find him still there when he returned. However, the high-backed chair that he had occupied was now empty.

He set foot across the hall in the direction of the stable block and the bunk house on the end that Jack shared with the rest of the men. Light and noise seeped around the edges of the badly fitting door, and from inside, he could hear the sound of singing. Jack's voice was carrying the solo part, and the rest of the men were joining in the chorus. Richard leant against the wooden wall and listened.

It was an old song, *Good King Hal*, older though than the last King, even though he had adopted it. The King went hunting and, separated from his men, he finds himself in a haunted hall and sets his wits against the witch he finds there. She sets him challenges, but each time the King outwits the crone. Jack certainly had the voice for the part, strong and melodious, and the listeners leant him silence, joining in only for the chorus.

Jack finished and received shouts of approval from the audience. Richard smiled slightly, he knew Jack well enough to know he would be declining their request to take up another song until they begged him sufficiently. Jack had never been one to disappoint an audience. The noise from the men subsided and Richard correctly guessed Jack had accepted, however, his choice of song did surprise him. "All and Forever" was a song he had not heard for a long time. Indeed, he'd never even heard Jack sing it before.

Staring into the darkness, he listened.

"If today was your last ever day
Would you turn and walk away..."

The tale told of a father dying and calling his sons to him one by one. For each, he had a different message and a final farewell. The song went on, the lyrics melancholy, the voice clear and precise. Richard realised his shoulders had sagged when Jack reached the final verse when the old man passed away, grieving as his son's set to fight each other even as he drew his last breath.

Groaning inwardly, Richard pushed himself away from the wooden wall, about to walk back to the hall, when the door opened. Light spilled into the courtyard and Jack stepped through the doorway. Seeing Richard, he frowned, then pushed the door closed behind him, leaving them both in darkness once again.

"An interesting choice of song," Richard said.

"I hardly thought you would be listening, did I?" Jack replied defensively.

"No, I suppose not." Then he added thoughtfully, "It could be a truth though. All of us fighting after he dies."

Jack watched his brother carefully. "Haven't you told me repeatedly that if it is worth having, it is worth fighting for?"

Richard laughed, "I'm not so sure that it would be worth fighting for, and Jack, I'm not in the mood for fighting with you tonight."

Jack, cautious, changed the subject. "What are you doing out here, anyway? Did you want me?"

"I'm hiding."

"Hiding?" Jack repeated, sounding confused, then seeing the grin on Richard's face, he began to laugh. "You are hiding from a Byrne's wife? Do you really fear women that much?"

"I fear that one! Christ, she's spent the whole evening staring at me. It would somewhat spoil our endeavour if it came to nothing because we were kicked from the door by a jealous husband."

"You have a point," Jack conceded. "Can't you think of something to deter her?"

"How do you deter a love-sick girl?" Richard asked, exasperated. "If I upset her, then the consequences could be just as unpleasant. We've not long left. For just a few days, it is safer for me to just avoid her."

"Aye, perhaps."

"And your tasks?" Richard asked. Jack had spent the day making sure the men were ready.

"I've spoken to them all. They will be where you want them, God willing, in a day," Jack replied, taking a step closer towards his brother.

"Well, hopefully not God willing. I would hate to trust this venture to a fatalistic hand or to God's fickle will." Richard paused, then added, "Do you want to join me at Assingham tonight?"

"The meeting tonight? You want me to go?" Jack was a little surprised but pleased none the less.

Richard nodded confirmation. "And I apologise for my earlier behaviour."

"Accepted," Jack was relieved. "And as for tonight, you leave me little choice. To stay is to frustrate myself by asking you questions which you will, for the sake of it, never answer."

"That is exactly why I wish you to go, to save myself from being hounded for morsels of information half the night. Anyway, you do me wrong." Richard grinned at Jack. "I am most forthcoming, helpful, and amiable."

Jack recognised the apology and, although surprised by it, grinned back. "And a bloody liar." Then he added, his voice sounding serious, "Richard, I think Alan is about to cause trouble amongst the men."

"Alan is always causing trouble," Richard replied, leading the way back across the yard to the main house.

"I think this time is different," Jack said, stepping quickly to catch his brother by the arm.

"What has he done?" Richard asked, not sounding particularly interested.

"He's planning on getting rid of you," Jack said bluntly.

That did stop Richard, and he turned to face his brother. "It's idle drunken talk. He's full of it. Thank you for telling me Jack, but Alan just likes to hear the sound of his own voice."

"I'm not so sure. I was talking to Robby, he's siding with him," Jack replied.

Richard laughed quietly, then said with sarcasm, "That is a coup to be worried about! Alan and Robby couldn't get the upper hand in a card game. Thank you for telling me, but really, can you see them doing anything but talk?"

When Richard put it like that, Jack had to agree it sounded unlikely. "You are probably right."

"Good, let's see if we can get back to my room before Lady love spies us." Richard said, setting his feet back onto the stone steps in the spiral stairwell he had descended earlier that evening.

Jack followed, and a few moments later, they were in Richard's room. "It looks like you've missed your visitor," Jack said, chuckling, as he remembered Richard ejecting Judith from his room some weeks ago while he had been stifling laughter and hiding behind the door.

"At least I'm not forced to part with coin," Richard replied, grinning maliciously.

"Go on, get your arse out of that window before I help you with a push." Jack found himself berating an empty room, for his brother had already vanished from sight. Tucking his gloves into his jacket front, Jack prepared to join him on the dark traverse.

Edward had been dead for a little less than a day. The young King's body lay still in the royal bed, one hand flung behind the pillowed head and the other resting palm up on the coverlet, looking only a little less alive than the Edward of a week ago.

Northumberland had known he needed to suppress the news of the King's death for as long as could. The plan, now in place, had been one devised between himself and Suffolk months ago and two of Northumberland's most loyal servants were set to carry it out. One of his captains and a trusted steward took complete control of his royal apartments while Northumberland slipped away to make the first moves in his bid for the throne.

The physicians who had attended Edward were secured in locked rooms in the palace, guarded by men handpicked from Northumberland's household. They had no need to fear for their lives, they would be released when news of Edward's death finally broke. A heavy guard remained in the royal chambers and Edward's personal servants were secured inside his private rooms, also unable to leave.

The success of the plan revolved around ensuring the routine of the past weeks continued. Food was sent for and empty dishes were returned under the watchful gaze of Northumberland's most loyal officers. Laundry went out in woven baskets and fresh snow-white linen returned. His physicians, sworn to silence, were escorted from the rooms they occupied to Edward's suite where they sat on hard chairs in an ante room until such time as they were escorted back again. They were instructed to keep up the ruse until they received a message from Northumberland.

The news, however, did leak. One of Northumberland's men had been heavily bribed. He had little opportunity to get a message out from the palace, instead, he devised a way to send a signal. In Edward's bedchamber, the hangings had been drawn around the sides of the bed so the corpse could not be seen. The man gave the servants blunt orders to extinguish the fires and open the windows to make the room as cold as possible to preserve the King's flesh and stop it from putrefying.

The three full length glass paned windows were pushed open to admit the cold winter air, the agreed upon sign to those watching that the King had breathed his last. The young king had been dead less than an hour before the news of it began its rapid journey across England.

Mary was asleep, but soon the house was alive with tapers and fires. The courtyard was lit by torches in brackets as men led sleepy horses from the stables to dispatch vital messages to inform Mary's loyal followers that the time was now.

In the dark, time is difficult to calculate, especially if the moon cannot be seen to provide guidance as to the passing of the hours. Catherine had no idea how long she had lain in the loft. The stable roof, she was surprised to find, was warmer than she had thought, and several times she had to stop herself from getting just too comfortable and falling asleep.

When a man came crawling through the hole made by the removed planking at the back of the empty stall, followed quickly by a second man, Catherine was instantly alert. She had a perfect view of the vacant stall and watched as they moved swiftly to the security of darkness in an unoccupied box. They had disappeared so far into the shadows that, after a time, Catherine was unsure if they were still there; there seemed to be no movement, and the horses were surprisingly still. It was some time before three more arrived, less carefully than the first two, and with no fear of being observed. The three stood in the stall propped against the partition wall, but their low mutterings were not decipherable from the distance of her lofty perch.

Then one of the first to arrive spoke from the darkness. "Well, gentlemen, good evening."

The effect was physical. Catherine's eyes widened, and the breath caught painfully in her throat; immobile, she watched, transfixed. The three men turned instantly, seeking the speaker.

"Fitzwarren," one of the later arrivals said, "I hear our plans have changed. So when do we move?"

"Tomorrow," Richard replied. "Assingham is an easy target with women and old men. If the work is done right, there will be no escapees to run and tell of the happenings here. I will lead the advance as planned; everything is as we agreed. Geoffrey, you will follow us as arranged?"

Geoffrey Byrne, Edward's son, inclined his head in confirmation.

"So, it's come; the King is dead," one of the other three, darkly dressed, voiced what everyone was thinking.

There was a quick guarded conversation amongst the three. "We meet tomorrow, then."

The business of the night concluded, the three left through the back of the stall and Catherine heard the noise of horses moving away into the distance. Richard also appeared to be standing quietly, listening for the retreat of the visitors before moving to leave himself. His companion moved from the shadows to join him.

Catherine lay unmoving in the dark, listening to the last retreating horse.

Assingham to be taken by force! The King dead! Tired though she was, sleep was beyond her as she tried to think what to do, for even now that she was aware of their intent, she could find no plan of action that would frustrate it.

His brother's apology and, for once, openness, had fired Jack's determination, and he had made up his mind about something that had plagued him all afternoon: Robby. He was going to find out what was being planned and stop it.

Jack found him easily, woke him and pulled him, half asleep, outside and into the shadows near the kitchens. Robby rubbed the sleep from his eyes and swayed a little, the evening's ale having not fully left him.

"Robby! Robby!" Jack gave him a good shake.

"God, Jack, what do you want? What's happened?" Robby groaned.

"Nothing as yet. I want to know what Alan's up to?" Jack demanded.

"I told you earlier that Alan said just to wait. I can't tell you anything more than that. Is that what you got me up for?" Robby was getting angry.

Jack ignored Robby's irritation. "Come on, there's no harm in telling me, is there? It'll be done in a day. I want to know what's happening. We all need to know when to act." But Jack was not fooling Robby, who took a step back.

"I dunno. I dunno. I'm not too sure I can trust you. So leave it, Jack, I'm not going to say," Robby hissed.

Jack smiled. "Robby, ah... no, Robby." Jack quickly caught hold of the man's arm as he made to duck past him. "Tell me and I'll let you go. I'll say nothing to Alan or Pierre, but if you don't..."

Robby understood the threat, but the terror of what might happen to him at Alan's hands was worse than his fear of Jack, and he writhed against the grip. He was no match for Jack and in a few moments, he found himself face down in the yard with the weight of the other man on top of him.

"Now," Jack spoke through clenched teeth, "tell me."

A break in the arm just below the elbow encouraged Robby to tell Jack everything he wanted to know, the pain of shattered bone too much.

Jack set off to put an end to Alan's insurrection, reasoning that it was the route he would have used later in the day anyway, so if Robby had not spoken the truth, he could continue and carry out Richard's bidding.

Hal and Spratty knew the road he would take. They knew him as one of Harry's household, tied now to a worthless master, Richard Fitzwarren, and not as the bastard brother of the same. He was not their goal, but a goodly prize, and one which, with sufficient persuasion, would lead them to Robert's own brother.

Alan had set the trap for Jack, not for the Master. He reasoned that this way he would get rid of both of them. He'd told Robby to let Jack in on his plans and had guessed rightly that Jack would beat the rest from Robby to protect his worthless brother. From Jack, Hal and Spratty would find the Master, and once he was gone, no one would stand in Alan's way. He didn't tell the others that Jack was to be the first target. He knew many of the men liked the Master's bastard brother.

Chapter Eleven

Assingham – July 1553

Jack saw them before they had recognised him as their target. They were Harry's men, mounted and waiting, near enough where Robby had said they would be. Jack knew he was right when both of them pulled their horses together and blocked the road, steel drawn, watching him intently.

Bringing his mare to a stop and holding her on a short rein, he cast his eyes around for more, but it seemed there were just the two in front. The man on the right began to advance. Jack pressed his heels into the soft flanks and she obligingly stepped backwards down the track. Only a dozen paces, but it had lengthened the distance between the two men. If the one before Jack realised that he now faced him on his own, it did not show in his visage, which was creased with eager delight.

Jack's gaze switched between the short blade he held and the man's face. He could only pitch a swing if he brought his horse to the right of Jack's. It was a matter of position, and only one of them had ridden in a melee.

Jack tightened his hold on the mare, shortened reins, pulled her head down and around, a simple ploy designed to convince his opponent that he was in retreat. His attacker took the opportunity and kicked his horse hard. She lunged forwards, his blade raised he bore down on the fleeing man.

Only Jack was not in retreat. Wheeling the mare round, her flanks crashed into the other horse. Too close now, his attacker could not swing the blade, and Jack got in a painful jab to his ribs with the hilt of his own sword before the two horses separated.

Jack had his horse turned back to face his aggressor before the man had even begun to bring his own horse back to the fight.

With the drawn blade in his right hand, reins tightly held in his left, Jack guided his mare sideways slowly. Keeping his opponent in front of him, preventing him from moving to his right, and at the same time quickly gauging the skill of his attacker. Jack knew now that the mounted man before him was both incautious and badly skilled. He should be no match for himself as long as he didn't make a mistake. Knowing he needed to finish this before the second man joined the fray, Jack spurred his mare forward, hind quarters kicking out as she agilely passed the other horse. The speed took his opponent by surprise, as did the back swing that Jack delivered in the moment before he turned the mare back to face his attacker.

The blade had run the full length of the back of the man's arm and the tooled edge had sliced through leather and linen to deliver a neat bleeding cut. The injury was to his right side, and as Jack readied himself for a second attack the man, shrieking in pain, dropped the blade from his hand. His horse, lacking commands, bolted across the road, threatening to unseat her rider.

Jack turned his attention back to the second mounted man, who had hurriedly stowed his blade and was preparing to abandon his companion. Jack prepared to follow, but sense stopped him. He might end up with neither of them if he gave chase, and the easy quarry was the man on the spooked horse in front of him.

Catherine knew she couldn't go to the Byrnes for help. If Edward's cousin Richard was involved, then so might Edward. Instead, she turned to John, hoping he would know what to do, hoping he would believe her.

"What do you mean you've locked her in her room!" Martha exclaimed.

"Just that. I've locked her in. It's for her own good. Such things as she's raving about would have her tied to a stake and her heels warmed. She's lost her wits, shouting and ranting she didn't make much sense. What can bring such things on, Martha?"

"Well it could be the black arts, you never know." The possibility of gossip was too much for her. "Tell me what she said."

"Well, I did get from her that the King's dead," John sat down heavily on the only chair in the kitchen.

"No..." Martha rounded the table, all eyes and ears. "She said that?"

John ran his hand through his hair, nodding,

"Lord have mercy, no..." Martha interrupted. "What else?"

"She has been meeting with men in the stable at night!"

"Men! What's his lordship going to say about that?" Martha gasped.

"Aye. I went straight to Lady Anne, she was terribly upset and told me to lock the girl in her room." John threw his arms wide, "What else could I do?"

"You did the right thing, John, telling Lady Anne. It's probably no madness that's beset her; she's probably breeding!" Martha folded her arms.

"She said she'd been there many nights. I pray you're not right, Martha. What should we do?" John was appalled.

"Send one of the lads to get Mistress Stump from the village, she'll know what to do with her," Martha suggested. "I'll tell Lady Anne that it might be an idea for the best."

"Mistress Stump, yes–yes, I'll do that."

Mistress Stump was duly called on and agreed to see the lady first thing the following day.

Anne, with a wide-eyed Martha in tow, had unlocked the door, and listened with growing horror to her daughter.

"But mama..." Catherine pleaded, "It's the truth."

"Your imagination runs away with you, child. Martha has been telling me you have been playing childish games in the stables. It's time, Catherine, that you started to act like a lady. You'll have your own house and children soon."

Catherine continued to try to protest, but her mother had pressed the door closed and, taking the key from her belt, slid it quickly into the lock. She could hear their muffled voices in the corridor outside, shortly after she heard the footsteps of the pair walking away from her room.

She knew there was little she could do. Experience had taught her that when she had been locked in her room for previous transgressions she would be in there overnight. There would be no food until the door was opened early the next day and she would be admitted back to the company of her mother, penitent and hungry.

Catherine ran her hands through her hair. What was she going to do? She wanted to believe she had imagined it, she just wanted everything to go back to the way it had been. This time it was going to be different; Martha would not come with the key and her mother was not going to be waiting for her in the morning in the hall.

The man's horse had stepped from the road and into the tangle of briar, ears flat she tossed her head and spun, her rider's curses making her jittery and nervous. Secure in the knowledge that the second rider had left, Jack dropped from his own saddle, looped the reins of his own horse over a branch, and set out to catch those of the one carrying the bleeding man.

A moment later he had the mare's bridle in his hand and a second after that, arms flailing, the man fell howling from the saddle to land with a crunch on the forest floor. Pulling the horse clear Jack's boot made contact with his stomach, achieving the momentary paralysis he required. Two more kicks ensured he stayed down and another to the head delivered the man's mind to blackness.

Jack secured the man's horse, and then dragged him towards a tree, dumping him against the supporting trunk. Quickly he relieved him of a blade he found at his belt and a worn leather purse that contained very little.

Jack stared at the man's face.

Did he recognise him?

He wasn't sure. Lank greasy hair spilled from underneath a tight leather cap, he had a nose that had been broken more than once, and through his parted lips Jack could see a row of chipped front teeth. Consciousness returning, the man groaned.

Jack rocked back on his heels and waited patiently.

When the man's eyes did flicker open and focus on his face they were filled with terror, and despite the pain from the lacerated arm he dug his hands in and tried to push himself away from Jack.

Jack shook his head, his eyes never leaving the man's face. Reaching down, he wrapped his hand around his ankle and tugged the leg hard, unbalancing the man and pitching him on his back.

"Who do you work for?" Jack growled the question.

He received in reply only a shriek of terror as his erstwhile attacker still sought to scramble away from him.

"I'll only ask one more time," Jack said, his voice low and threatening.

Locked in her room with no one answering her desperate pleas, Catherine finally climbed from the window and hid in the only place she could think of: the hayloft. She did not hear the arrival of the riders. The effect of the last two sleepless nights had overtaken her, and she was blissfully unaware that the advance party, which should have been led by Richard, had been overtaken by an impatient and overzealous young man. Geoffrey Byrne, Edward's son, was eager to show his mettle to his men, and he led them down on Assingham before Richard had made his move.

Richard leapt down from his horse and flung the reins in the face of someone standing in the gloom. He quickly crossed to where a man sat arrogantly on top of a barrel of beer, most of its contents spilt across the ground.

"Ah, Fitzwarren, it seems I have saved you a job!" The man on the barrel grinned triumphantly. "Join us, there is plenty for all." He indicated the barrel with his full flagon.

The upraised vessel was violently ripped from his hands, its contents spilt over jacket and hose before landing with a metallic clank against the kitchen door.

"Geoffrey, I would be appreciative if, in the future, you did as you were told, rather than doing as you wish to satisfy your childish temperament." Fitzwarren's voice was hard.

Byrne's son resorted to bravado. "You should thank me. I have saved you a task. The men were restless. To have delayed further would have been to ask for trouble," he blustered.

"Geoffrey, I shall certainly not thank you. This is a matter I have not finished with, as there is much to do, so I shall postpone the moment which, when it arrives, is one you will most sincerely regret," Fitzwarren's said coldly. Then he added mockingly, "So, prepare to provide me with a full account, if you will, of how you heroically and with much danger to yourself took and subdued this well-manned and armed manor."

Geoffrey looked relieved. The confrontation was to be postponed and Richard's attention was turned back to the night's work. Richard had already set off towards the hall and Geoffrey was left with no option but to step quickly after him, following like a puppy, his arrogance left behind on the beer barrel.

The fire still burned in the grate in the hall and several tapers were still lit, the wan light enough to clearly pick out the bodies, laying in the sticky mass of their own blood. The half-naked form of Martha, her milky eyes open and gazing sideways blindly, lay spread like a starfish on the floor, her face partially obscured by the quantity of blood that covered it from the gaping wound at her neck. The Lady Anne lay on her front, bereft of her dress with only a shift pulled up under her arms. Hands outstretched in front of her as if she'd been trying to crawl away before the blade in her side had ended her escape. Richard's face hardened as he saw the scrapes her nails had made on the wooden floor as they had raped her.

John was a small distance away, dead at the foot of the table where he had been playing cards, an ugly incision at the nape of his neck visible as his body lay over the scattered sticky deck.

Geoffrey was silent as he stood behind the unmoving Richard, waiting for his next instructions. When Richard did move, he was so fast that Geoffrey never saw the blow coming, felt only its force as it knocked him backwards.

"You knew my orders," Fitzwarren blazed above him. "Don't tell me this farmhouse provided such resistance that it required the murder of all those who were in it!" Richard's boot connected accurately with Geoffrey's body causing him to gasp in pain.

"It seems I no longer feel like postponing the moment." He gave him another kick and the prone man gasped. Richard leant over Geoffrey, his face betraying nothing, contrasting sharply with the contortions that were exhibited on the boy's pain-stricken face. "A simple question, Geoffrey, and I would like a simple answer, and the one you give I hope, for your sake, is the one I would like to hear. Tell me, are there any survivors after your little show of force to impress your men, or did these poor folk put up such resistance that it necessitated the death of all of them?"

Geoffrey refrained from answering, his body rigid, braced for the next impact.

"You are not talking to me, Geoffrey. Am I to take from that, that you saw fit to slay the entire inhabitants?" The look on Geoffrey's face told the world clearly that no one had been spared when they burst into the Manor.

Richard hauled the protesting man to his feet, pushing him hard against the wall. A moment of wavering uncertainty robbed Geoffrey of his freedom. Too late he attempted to pull from the hold, but all he could do was struggle against the fierce restraining grip. The forearm rammed hard across his throat held the useless breath in his lungs; eyes widening in panic, he could neither expel it nor take another.

Geoffrey stopped trying to pull the arm from his throat. A trembling hand found the dagger in his belt, and desperation aimed it at his attacker. Richard intercepted the blow, vice-like, his fingers dug into the younger man's wrist, slamming it against the wall. The pommel grazed the masonry. Geoffrey's fingers, opening, lost their hold on the hilt, and the knife slipped from his grasp to rattle on the stone floor.

Richard's own dagger was in his hand, the point of it pressing up under Geoffrey's chin.

Geoffrey stood immobile. The fight was lost.

"You killed all of them?" Richard growled, his dark eyes, lit with menace, glared into Geoffrey's.

Geoffrey swallowed hard, his head tipped back, avoiding the steel point.

His silence was his answer.

"All of them?" Richard repeated, his tone hostile

"They were Mary's supporters," Geoffrey spoke quietly, fearfully aware of the blade pressuring his throat.

"For God's sake! They were women, children, and old men," Richard's words were taut with temper, fury burnt brightly in the stone grey eyes.

The knife's point had pierced the skin, blood ran down the blade in a thin red line.

"Stop!" It was Edward Byrne's voice.

Richard's hand tightened on the hilt. The pressure on the tip increased. Geoffrey yelped, pressing himself back harder against the wall.

"Stop! Damn you. Do you hear me?" Byrne yelled as he ran across the hall.

Breathing hard Richard released Geoffrey, who dropped heavily back against the wall, hands to his throat. Not finished with him, Richard delivered a punch to the stomach that had Geoffrey on his knees retching, and a kick to the head sent him rolling across the floor to fetch up against Martha's body.

Richard turned from the son to the father. "None here deserved this." The blooded dagger still in his hand he pointed it towards the bodies.

Edward paled, a nervous stare casting around the wreckage of the hall. "What's happened?"

"Your son is what happened." Richard still fuelled with rage strode past Byrne and, as he drew level, he swung the blade down, impaling it in the wooden top of the table.

Edward flinched, backing away a step. "Anne, Catherine? Surely not!"

"I cannot save them for you now. Thanks to your son, there is a certain irreversible finality about the situation." Richard wrenched the knife from the split wood and turned his back on Edward.

When the man had finally spoken Jack recognised him. His smashed front teeth leant a whistling lilt to his words that he remembered as belonging to one of the men he'd seen occasionally in Harry's London household. Spratty was his name.

That Harry had tracked them down, and that somehow Alan was involved in this, felt like a physical blow. Jack knew he needed to get back to Richard as quickly as possible.

Jack was about to ask the man another question when the unmistakable sound of approaching riders met his ears. Swearing, Jack got to his feet. It wasn't, thankfully, more of Harry's men, but Richard's, lead by Dan and Mat.

The rider's brought their horses to an abrupt stop.

"Bloody hell Jack, are you alright?" Dan, concerned, dropped from the horse and stared down at the man at Jack's feet. "What did he want? Jesus, he's in a right state. Did he try to rob you?"

Jack shook his head.

"What then?"

"He's Harry's man. There were two of them and they wanted Richard," Jack said, his voice still angry.

"We need to warn Richard, he's taken the rest of the men and ridden to Assingham already," Dan asserted, and then looking down at the man at Jack's feet, added slowly, "and you can't leave him there either."

There was a terrified howl, followed by a plea from the man as he realised his fate had just been sealed. The noise was cut off abruptly a moment later.

Chapter Twelve

Assingham – July 10th 1553

Soon the Manor was the scene of organised activity. The looting, drinking, and raping, which had been the tone whilst Geoffrey had briefly been in control of Assingham, were replaced by order and military efficiency. Riders left with messages; horses were stabled in the stalls below Catherine; tables in the hall were righted and the floor cleared. Geoffrey, enlisting the help of those who had arrived with him, moved the bodies and piled them in the courtyard, away from the food and drinking water. Byrne's co-conspirators who were to join those already at Assingham had not yet arrived.

Edward, his expression stony, had been unable to watch as the dead were removed from the hall.

"This is not Geoffrey's fault. This was my doing," Edward said bleakly. "I committed Assingham and these are the results.

Richard regarded him with a cold stare. "If you cannot control him, then yes, the blame is yours," he replied harshly.

Byrne did not answer. If Richard could feel the older man's discomfort rising, he did nothing to allay it. Edward was, however, swiftly forgotten as Richard's eyes had alighted on the figure of Jack dropping from his saddle. It was obvious from the expression on his brother's face there was something he wished to urgently impart.

Jack had been challenged before he reached Assingham, and it was Marc's shout that was his pass through the gates and into the courtyard. The plan had not been flawed and appeared to have been executed well.

Sliding from his saddle, his eyes settled on the piled bodies.

Dear God! How could this have happened?

Marc moved in and took the reins of Jack's horse.

"What happened?" Jack asked with urgency, nodding towards the bodies.

"Byrne's son got here before you and slaughtered the lot of them," Marc supplied, grubby fingers tugging at his beard.

Jack rubbed calloused hands over his face, swearing, as he suddenly realised the cost of his delay. The cost of sending Dan and Mat to collect the men.

"Master was madder than Hell. I thought he was going to kill Byrne's son, and so did Byrne," Marc continued.

Jack's heart beat loudly in his chest.

This is all I need.

"Master nearly cut his throat, so I heard." Jack did not appear to be listening, and Marc added, "Do you hear me?"

"He hears." Both men turned to see the Master, his face dark, eyes without humour, approaching across the yard. "Jack. A word inside, if I may."

The words might have sounded formally polite, but there was an all too clear edge of anger behind them. Jack stepping quickly after him, followed Richard into the empty hall.

Richard rounded on him as soon as they were alone. "I don't know whether it is the eight dead bodies outside that angers me so much, or the fact that you didn't do as you were instructed. Again!"

"I was trying to keep you from Harry's men. I told you Alan was up to something, didn't I? But you wouldn't listen," Jack shot back, his own anger rising

"Harry's men?" Richard repeated, his manner instantly changing, the anger gone from his voice.

"There were two of them. One got away," Jack replied.

"And the other?"

Jack shrugged and said, "He didn't."

"Are you sure there were just two of them?" Richard asked.

"Fairly sure," Jack replied. "Robby told me of Alan's plan to get rid of you."

"Dan told me what was going on, I knew what Alan was up to," Richard said, then pressing a hand to his temple and meeting his brother's eyes he added, "what I didn't know was when he was planning to execute them."

"You knew...!" Jack blurted.

"Froggy Tate told me days ago that not only had Alan met with someone, he didn't know who, but that he was spreading the word that they would be rid of me. Surprisingly enough, not everyone wants to see me cold in the ground. Alan told Froggy that I had committed murder when I was in London and that it had finally caught up with me. Froggy wasn't convinced that the pair Alan had been talking to were the King's men and came to tell me so."

"I don't believe you knew and did nothing! Why didn't you tell me?" There was utter disbelief in Jack's voice.

"What exactly would you have me do? Froggy was to tell me if he heard anything else, and in the meantime, I decided to avoid riding out alone." Richard replied. "Dealing with Harry's men was a secondary issue. I needed the men here to support Byrne."

"Christ! I told Mat and Dan to bring the men here. If I'd got here sooner this wouldn't have happened." Jack's voice was filled with regret.

"Perhaps." Richard studied his brother's exhausted face. "Though Geoffrey set out much sooner than he was meant to, even if you had arrived when you were supposed to, it would still have been too late."

Both men heard the commotion in the yard. Richard, striding past Jack, headed for the door. Two of Richard's lookouts had intercepted a rider who wouldn't answer their questions. When they found a heavily sealed letter on his person, they had dragged him back to Assingham.

"Take him inside and lock him up," Richard ordered, taking the papers into his keeping. Pierre and Robby, the messenger pinioned between them, headed towards the main house.

Richard, the letter in his hand, ignored Byrne's inquisitive glances and walked towards the fireplace, breaking the seal as he went. Jack, crossing his arms across his chest, blocked Byrne's passage across the Hall, and the older man, grumbling, left the room. Dan appeared at the open door and crossed to where Jack stood.

"What a bloody mess this is. No wonder the Master was madder than Hell," Dan said under his breath.

"I know, I've seen it," Jack replied more roughly than he intended. "But it was Harry's men. They'd tracked him here. What else was I supposed to do? I couldn't have stopped this."

"I know," Dan said in reply. "Where is the Master now?"

"Over there," Jack gestured behind him to where Richard stood near the fireplace, the remains of a smouldering fire still smoking in the hearth.

"Well, it appears, brother, that we are on the wrong side." Richard spoke from where he stood near the fire. He'd thrown on one folded sheet and was watching as embers flared and the flames turned it to ash.

"Now that's nothing new, is it?" Jack's tone was resigned. "So what's changed?"

"London has declared for Mary. We have been lucky enough to intercept a messenger carrying this news to her at Framlingham. The ships have mutinied and turned on Northumberland, stopping his advance. He's at Cambridge now. His mistake was leaving the city," Richard mused. "He should have held London."

"Who knows?" Jack asked, coming to stand close to his brother.

"At the moment? Northumberland and a few others. We must change sides, and quickly; we are only hours ahead of the news." Richard pulled two more letters from his doublet and added them to the fire, the paper curling in the heat before the flames blackened the sheets.

"It does not surprise me at all that our plans have been ruined again," Jack stated bluntly. "So how do you plan to get us out of this, then? Exactly what do you intend to do?"

"Ride for Mary. Take this," Richard held up the recently won letter, "kneel and place myself and my men at her disposal. She knows not as yet that her position is so strong."

"And do you think that Lord Byrne is about to let you ride out of here once he realises you have turned against him?" Jack pointed out.

"He will have no choice. Half the men here are mine. He is unlikely to be able to prevent us from leaving if we wish to, is he now? Who is going to stop me? Geoffrey? I doubt it."

"True," Jack observed.

Richard turned his attention to Dan. "Did you find her?"

"Like you said, she's in the stable. She was bloody lucky," Dan replied.

"Did she see you?" Richard asked, his attention straying back to the course-altering letter he still held.

"No. She's up in the roof, right back in the corner like a scared mouse. What are you going to do with her?

It's only a matter of time before she either comes down herself or someone finds her up there, and tomorrow the place will be swarming with men. Someone will see her," Dan replied.

"You have met her before at Hazeldene – haven't you?" Richard was forced to turn more of his concentration to the issue.

"Well, I suppose she would recognise me. I've been around when she has been visiting and once I escorted her back here." He grimaced. "I know where you're heading, and I'm not sure that she'll trust me. I can get her out of here, but only if she agrees to come with me, and I'm guessing she'll be kicking and screaming."

"Well, out she must go and stay, at least until the country declares for Mary. My charity knows no ends, does it? I entrust you to save the lady and take her somewhere safer. Take Jack with you. She knows him as well," Richard instructed bluntly.

Dan faced Richard squarely. "And where are you going to dispose of her now that you have arranged her untimely death? Edward thinks his son killed her, right?"

"I hadn't given it much thought. It wasn't at the top of my list of current priorities. Any suggestions?" Richard asked wearily.

"I'll think of something, I suppose," Dan replied.

"Meet us at Framlingham, if we are still there," Richard told him.

"And if you've still got your head," Jack mused darkly.

"Have some faith. I believe the lady will give me a hearing," Richard said, then added, "go with Dan, Jack. Get out of here before the place starts falling over itself, trying to stop us leaving. I'll see you again at Framlingham," Richard said dismissively.

"Wouldn't I be better with you? I am sure Dan can manage a girl on his own?" Jack protested, not liking the idea of the task at all.

"She's the daughter of Peter de Bernay, and he's one of Mary's supporters. His gratitude might be quite valuable to us shortly," Richard responded levelling his gaze on his brother. "Her safety could be key to ensuring ours."

Fixing what he hoped was a reassuring smile on his face, Jack popped his head over the edge of the hayloft. Thankfully, she didn't scream as he had feared she would. The girl looked at him; her face drawn, resignation painted on its features. Fear appeared not to be there as she matched his stare, but not his friendly smile as she listened.

"We need to get out of here as soon as the horses are ready. I'll come back for you," Jack assured her.

It took some time, even under the cover of the mass of men and activity, to manoeuvre three horses from the courtyard and tether them at the back of the stables. Catherine wordlessly allowed him to lift her from the perch and lead her out through the stable to where Dan held the reins of the horses. The three mounted and made their way in no great hurry across the fields and towards the sanctuary of the woods.

Richard, as he said he would, pulled his men out of Assingham. By the time Geoffrey and his father realised they had been duped and that the hired troop were abandoning their cause, it was too late. They could only shout at the backs of the disappearing men.

Assingham was placed in Bedfordshire. On a map, to the South of Cambridge was to risk running into the Northumberland's troops and those riding North from London to support him. To ride to the North of Cambridge was to take a longer route, and Richard knew that the letter he held was one he needed to deliver as soon as possible.

They took the southern route.

The company rode close to the City where the land was flat, though the riders were exposed as they crossed the Cam near Grantchester. Richard, in the lead of the troop, saw the flash of sun on steel to the south first. Riders. He pulled hard on Corracha's reins and a raised hand brought the men behind him to a jolting halt.

"There's hundreds of them!" Mat supplied, pulling his horse closer to the Master's.

"At least." Richard was looking closely at the group moving towards the City. Were they supporters of Northumberland? There were no banners that he could see. "Come on."

Richard dug his heels in and forced his horse back to a steady canter, back on the course they had been set upon. They were going to cross the path of the riders from the south, of that there was no doubt. After an order from Richard, the men spread out and rode abreast. There was now no doubt that they would be seen.

The banner, when Richard saw it, was green, tipped with crimson, and flying at the front of the advancing column. It was the Earl of Oxford's pennant flapping in the sun. Richard turned his horse towards the standard and drove him on. The column had split. The rear riders had stopped, but the front had continued forward, separating the front fifty riders from their vanguard. The lead group concertinaed around the banner. Richard had already set his sights on the men he was riding towards. Liveried, wearing the colours of Oxford, and with the Earl in attendance.

A shout from Richard slowed his men. Richard continued to ride forward, straight towards the banner. Eighteen pairs of eyes watched as their Master pulled his horse to a stamping halt, and even at this distance, they could see the quick and urgent exchange.

A moment later, Richard pulled his horse away from the column, and as he did, the riders turned and set their horses back in the direction they had come. By the time Richard returned to his men, the head of the column had reunited with the straggling second half and a crush of confusion arose as the mounted men strove to obey orders to turn their horses back south, away from Cambridge.

Richard summoned his men to ride towards him, and in a moment he had turned his horse back on the path they had been originally set upon, towards Framlingham. They rode hard across the flat fen landscape, putting distance between themselves and the retreating column before Richard slowed his horse and brought Corracha back to a trot.

"Christ! I thought we were about to run into the Earl's army then? Where have they gone?" Mat asked, pulling his horse next to Richards.

"Like Pelops," Richard said, smiling. "They have failed to appear where they should."

Mat gazed at him in confusion.

"They've returned to London," Richard said. He allowed his horse to carry him at a slow canter until he was recovered, before setting a hard pace as they continued on their journey to Framlingham.

Richard was the first to abandon Northumberland, the early warning of disaster being provided by Mary's messenger. Others too would leave, some too late to save themselves. He was confident of acceptance when he arrived in Framlingham, sure that the dispatch he held would smooth his path. At this point, the Queen's party, although resolute and confident, did not know the full extent of their strength. Had they known, they would have moved to the capital immediately. As it was, they waited in Suffolk.

The date was the 16th of July, two days since Northumberland had reached Cambridge. Richard knew time was not on his side. He had to change allegiances before Mary became aware of the full breadth of her victory. This would occur whenever the news broke that the crews on the ships that Northumberland had sent to Yarmouth to cut off her escape had mutinied, and London had declared for Mary; likely within a few days. Richard finally arrived at Framlingham and bid his men camp outside with the other forces billeted there. With a hasty tidying of cloak and hair, he went to deliver the dispatch and declare his allegiance to Mary Tudor, Queen of England.

The Earl of Derby was a shrewd man who had not waited to see the tide turn and had placed himself with Mary from the outset. She had declared herself Queen on July 9th, and Derby had the comfort of knowing he was one of the first to refer to her by that title. He had received communications from Fitzwarren before, so the name was a familiar one.

Now he considered the latest communication. The man, whoever he was, was now at Framlingham and craved a personal audience to "Bring her Majesty most welcome news." Derby couldn't dismiss him, as Fitzwarren had proved most helpful before. If there was a report, he needed to know about it sooner rather than later. He sent for Richard.

The lady had not slept for two days, and neither had Derby. The legs that transported him up the stairs to the rooms she was occupying were weary ones. One of the guards posted at the door bid him enter. He knelt.

"Do not stand on ceremony at a time like this. What news have you?" Mary snapped.

"Nothing but good news, Your Majesty." He smiled.

"Tell us, what developments?" she asked eagerly.

"Word has finally come that London has declared for Your Majesty," Derby spoke quietly as he brought her the first firm knowledge of her accession to the throne.

"Praise Mary," she spoke on a hushed breath, her right hand steadying her on the desk. "Can it be?" Then, "How has this news come?"

"From a source that we know to be reliable," said Derby, then he added, "although the delivery was not via our normal courier."

"What do you mean? Could this be false news, a ruse to make us leave this stronghold?" Mary asked sharply.

"I don't think so. The document appears genuine, and the code used proves this. However, if you remember, we received a communication two days since from Richard Fitzwarren detailing Northumberland's movements from London," he began, before pausing.

"Yes, I remember," Mary said slowly. "There was little in his report that we didn't already know, but it confirmed our other sources. Anyway, what's he got to do with this?"

"Well, Fitzwarren delivered the dispatch. I haven't, as yet, had a chance to question him properly. I wanted to bring you the news as soon as I could."

"Who is he?" Mary enquired.

"Little known by all accounts. Richard Fitzwarren is his name. I believe he has a mercenary band with him, camped now with your other followers. I suspect he is probably a soldier of fortune who craves advancement, but to be fair, he's not alone there."

"It is not always easy to separate the wheat from the chaff," Mary agreed. "He has performed us a service." She hesitated. "Bring him to me..." She turned back to the papers before her and the Earl, cursing his tired limbs under his breath, prepared himself, once again, for the stairs.

The Earl did not descend fully into the hall but remained a dozen steps up the stairwell, inviting Richard to join him, saving his legs the extra work. Richard handed his sword over to the guard in response to the outstretched arm and lightly bounded up to join him, receiving a twisted smile for his youth.

"Your Majesty." Richard knelt in the firelight; he spoke no more, waiting for her words.

"Rise, please. You have, it appears, tried to do us a service with your reports, and the news you have brought to us is most welcome," Mary said, standing now behind the desk. "How did you come by it?

"Your messenger was set upon by some of Northumberland's men. Myself and my men were on our way to Framlingham and were able to offer assistance," Richard lied smoothly.

"Hmmm..." Mary was unconvinced. "And the messenger?"

"Injured, Your Majesty, but he bid me at any cost to bring this letter to you at Framlingham."

"A convenient story. I wonder if the messenger was lucky, or unlucky, to come across you on the road?" Mary gestured for him to stand.

"These are hard times, Your Majesty. It is difficult to determine friend from foe," Richard said evenly, rising in one smooth movement.

"An extremely shrewd observation, especially from one who comes to join us so late in the day, and who has been able to pass us information that can only have come from the heart of Northumberland's camp. The Earl tells me you have further news," Mary probed.

"Your Majesty, Northumberland had marched to Bury St Edmunds. However, scouting parties have shown him the strength of Your Majesty's support and he has been forced to drop back with his main force to Cambridge, where he resides now. He awaits reinforcements, which will not come. His initial intentions were to attack and capture Your Majesty, but the Earl of Oxford has withdrawn his support and marches, as we speak, back to London, a blow that will make Northumberland surely falter."

"How do you know this?" the Earl demanded, rounding on Richard.

"I have my own lines of communication, and I am most willing to place them at the disposal of Your Majesty."

"Are you certain about Oxford?" Derby continued, his brow furrowed.

"Yes I am," Richard replied.

"How can you possibly know this?" Derby demanded immediately.

"I know this because we saw his men returning to London," Richard explained, then added, "riding south, away from Cambridge."

Derby turned to Mary. "If Oxford has abandoned the Duke and leant his support to your cause, that is indeed a blow to the usurper." He turned back to Richard. "We believed he was bringing a significant force himself to strengthen Northumberland's position at Cambridge before they pressed on to try and capture Her Majesty here at Framlingham. Oxford's remaining larger force is in London, securing the city."

"Send a messenger to Oxford. It will confirm my words," Richard urged.

Derby nodded. His reply though was for Mary, not Richard. "Oxford is holding London for Northumberland, if it is true that he has changed his allegiance, then the city will be ours."

The Earl moved close to Mary. "Your Majesty, there is much to do. We need to quickly find the truth of these claims and consolidate our position..."

"Yes, yes, we must take counsel." Mary said, "Derby, go and confirm this report and take...?"

"Richard Fitzwarren, Your Majesty."

"Yes, Fitzwarren... with you," Mary added absently.

Richard returned to the camp his men had set up on the grounds of Framlingham and waited to see if the news he had brought would secure his position. Lying on the dried summer grass, his saddle for a pillow, he closed exhausted eyes and slept. He awoke when Mat gently shook his shoulder. "You're wanted, Master," the accented voice told him.

The Master sighed and turned to look up at Mat, whose form made a good shield from the midday sun. "If I had wanted to sleep all day, I would have told you, idiot," but there was no malice in his voice.

"We took a vote," Mat grinned, then added, "and none were brave enough to wake you. It's your own fault."

Richard gave him a withering look and forced himself to his feet. Looking down at his clothes, he sighed. They looked ridden in, fought in, slept in, and worse: not a happy state in which to meet your new employer. He strode off to requisition a tent, which was where the Earl's messenger found him, stripped to the waist over a pail of water. Mat told him to enter at his own peril; the messenger chose to ignore the dishevelled soldier, and throwing back the tent flap, stepped inside.

"I'll have your ears, Mat," growled the man inside, water running down his body. A pewter ewer, trailing a spray of water, hurtled towards the man's head. A quick hand deflected its flight, the edge of the rim bouncing off the wooden tent pole and bruising the wood.

Richard, turning to face the newcomer, looked even more unimpressed when he realised it wasn't Mat who had stepped inside the canvas.

"Sir, my name is Robert Ashley and I have a message from the Earl of Derby," the man announced, taking a precautionary step backward.

Richard took notice of the averted eyes and knew Ashley had seen the lash marks on his back. Casting a dark look at the man, he pulled a shirt over his head, making no hurry to cover the telling scars.

"The Earl bids you attend him at once." Ashley dropped his eyes from Richard's cold stare before adding, "I will await you outside."

Ashley, emerging from the tent, found one of Fitzwarren's men grinning at him.

"You've still got your ears then," Mat observed as Ashley emerged.

"How did he get those scars? It's a wonder he lived," Ashley asked, moving far enough away from the tent so that his words would not be overheard.

"Dunno," Mat replied, folding his arms. "But you can bet that the man who gave them to him isn't breathing."

Ashley chose to stand some distance away and wait for Fitzwarren, and wait for some time he did.

"I've met you before, near Hazeldene," Ashley blurted, sounding surprised.

Richard met his gaze and inclined his head in acceptance of the words. "A pleasant surprise. Let's not keep the Earl waiting."

Richard summoned Mat to him and said something quietly in his ear before joining Ashley to obey Derby's summons.

"You proved accurate in the finest detail." The Earl motioned for Richard to be seated. "How did you have such information in advance of us, man?"

"That is my trade, my Lord. You would not steal it from me, would you?" Richard replied casually.

The Earl guessed correctly that Richard would probably say no more. "Her Majesty is preparing to move to London, and her followers will bring her to the city. Do I take from your words yesterday that you still intend to lend your support to our queen?"

"Those were my intentions," Richard confirmed.

"Your men? They are retainers, tenants on your farm?" he ventured.

"No, they are my men: soldiers in my pay." Richard knew the Earl had by now ascertained that he belonged to no household within the area and would have already tagged him with the all-encompassing name of mercenary.

"Mmmm," was all the Earl offered.

Richard waited.

"Would this be a correct assessment?" The Earl leant back in his chair. "Stop me if I am wrong. I know not where you come from; however, I venture that you arrived in the area at Northumberland's bidding, hired to rise against Her Majesty and support the Greys." The Earl stopped Richard from speaking with a raised hand. "But, for whatever reason, you changed sides, left Northumberland and paved the way for your acceptance here with what I grant was useful information. Ensuring that dispatch reached us from London was vital, as was the timely news that Oxford had withdrawn his support for Northumberland. Have I accurately assessed the situation?"

Richard smiled, palms open. "You have me, my lord."

"And Oxford? How did you know he had changed sides? Were you perhaps in his pay before arriving here?" The Earl queried.

"I wasn't in Oxford's pay, however, I have been in communication with him over the last few months," Richard replied truthfully.

"I thought as much." The Earl was smiling openly, pleased at his accurate assessment.

"Well, despite that, sir, your presence here has been noted by Her Majesty and she would receive you before she leaves for London. Loyalty is a changing commodity at the moment. Can you give me assurances that yours is not of a fleeting nature?" the Earl enquired.

"I can give you lengthy assurances as to my good character and my loyalty, expound upon my virtues until you fall asleep. However, they would remain unproved, would they not?" Richard said. "An empty truth is but a lie, my Lord, and I am sure you do not want to listen to them."

"Well said. I have listened to far too much fawning recently. Be off. I will send for you again." The Earl spoke good-humouredly. "Before you go, I would like to know a little more about you. From where do you hail?"

Richard, in a corner for once, was forced to recount his personal history, with enough hard facts for the Earl to later substantiate. At the end of the interview, the Earl was convinced Fitzwarren would be a valuable asset, and he was determined to have him working for him.

It was just over a week later when Jack started picking his way through the tents and bedrolls of Mary's variously sleeping and celebrating supporters.

They stretched out in every direction and he had not seen the like of it since the battlefields of Europe. It was well we changed sides; he thought to himself. He would not have liked to fight this mass, even though the majority were badly armed tenants. The sheer weight of them would have forced the Duke into quick submission, and Jack never liked being outnumbered. It was some time before he spied a face he recognised among the many. Froggy Tate was crouching down at a fire, poking at the dying embers.

"Where is he?" Jack led his horse up to Froggy.

"You're back then." Froggy pointed at a tent behind him. "I tell you," Froggy continued, "this is not a bad change of scenery." He waved around him; the air of celebration led each night to drunken revelry, which was to most men's tastes.

Jack smiled. "I'll not be long and I'll join you." He ducked inside the tent to find Richard on the bed, propped up on his elbows, writing. It was still pleasantly warm inside. The night air and the slight chill of the July evening had not yet snuck beneath the canvas folds. Jack dropped to sit cross-legged on the tent floor. He had decided not to tell his brother where they had left Catherine. Dan had persuaded Jack to keep the information he gave to his brother as minimal as possible. "The less to pick fault with," he had reasoned, to which he had agreed wholeheartedly.

Richard looked up at length. "Well?"

"Done. She's safe. And us? Have we changed our colours?"

"It does appear so, for tomorrow I have a private meeting with the Queen," Richard said, smiling.

Jack was impressed. "Better wear your best boots then." Then Jack put forward the question, the answer to which he dearly wanted to know. "Well, may I ask where Alan is?" He had not seen him and was sure he would not have survived the discovery of the scheme.

"Ah, don't be too disappointed, Jack, but he's here and still believes his intentions remain undiscovered. If he still has contact with cousin Harry, I would like to be the first to know about it. He still believes Tate is one of his devotees," Richard replied carefully.

"That's if Froggy doesn't change sides on you," Jack pointed out, "there seems to be a lot of that happening right now." Richard ignored his gibe. "That cur Alan should be cold by now."

"I've told you why he isn't, and I've told you my reasons why I want him to stay hearty, hale, and after my blood. Do you not understand?" Jack did not reply. "As for Froggy, I have not relied entirely on my natural charm. Silver is the coin to Froggy's heart, and I do not believe that Alan could outdo me." Richard laid a hard gaze on his brother.

"Well, whenever you have what you want, promise me the opportunity of a personal score I wish to settle." Jack's eyes flashed blue and his voice was angry. "I am lucky to be here. If that shit had his way, I would be cold in the ground by now. I did try to warn you, remember?"

"You will, I trust, be able to wait peaceably for your vengeance?" Richard asked, his voice deliberately calm.

"We will have to see, won't we?" Jack stood, stretching. "If you don't need me, I am off to find some ale with Froggy." The implication of his words was clear; Froggy was Alan's shadow. Richard sighed.

The camp mood was one of battle victory, which Jack found odd because there had been no battle. This had its pleasant side, for the dead and dying which normally accompanied soldiers' camps were absent. Froggy had spotted Alan and beckoned him over. Jack's face hardened at the sight of him, his temper began to rise and the hold on the ale cup tightened.

Froggy, sensing a change in his companion, asked, "What's up with you?"

"Nothing," Jack said quickly, his eyes on Alan's approaching form.

Froggy's eyes narrowed, and he looked between Alan and Jack before he whispered, "What's happened?"

"Just leave it," Jack said, a warning tone in his voice.

Froggy shrugged, and the pair joined Alan as they wandered, ale in hand, through the myriad tents and camps that composed this forest of Mary's loyal supporters.

"There's Mat!" Alan pointed to the man they knew, standing at the front of a ring of cheering spectators.

"Aye, what's this then?" Froggy enquired as they pushed companionably to the fore to find the reason for the noise.

Mat moved back a pace to stand near them. "Good to have you back, Jack. That one there's been in for four turns now. Go on, my money's on you."

The game they'd come upon involved fighting with staffs and the current victor stood in the middle of the ring, waving the purse he had just taken over his head, grinning broadly. Jack appraised him; a broad man, he wore only hose and shirt, which clung to him with sweat. Thick veined forearms showed beneath sleeves that were pushed back. He fought on strength, Jack guessed.

"Come on, who'll come and give Dale here a bashing?" challenged a man entering the ring.

Jack waited.

A man was pushed into the ring by his friends. Obviously drunk, he tripped over a divot, much to the mirth of all watching, before staggering to face Dale.

"I'll not fight you," Dale laughed, and dodged a drunken swing that threatened to pitch his assailant face down in the mud. "Get him out of here." He pushed the man backwards, gently sending him into the arms of the laughing crowd. "Come on," he held the purse above his head, "I'll bet the lot against the next man to enter the ring."

"Go on!" Mat jabbed Jack in the ribs, receiving a hard look, but Jack remained unmoved. Mat, full of ale, yelled, "Here, he'll fight you," and pushed Jack. The attention of the crowd was drawn, and they fell back respectfully around Jack.

"I will have your balls for this, Mat," Jack growled angrily, his arms still folded, unmoving.

"Ah, a challenger!" yelled Dale, moving across the ring. "And you are, sir?" he asked with mock formality.

Jack didn't move.

"Having second thoughts? A little shy, eh? Well, that's to be expected," he laughed. "Come on, anyone else? This pansy won't do."

Jack, resigned, stepped forward.

"Ah, you've changed your mind." Dale was delighted. "And you are?"

"Why do you want to know?" Jack asked pleasantly.

"Oh, I like to know the names of the men I've beaten," Dale said with good humour. "There's been Davey Norton who gave me a fair fight. Cob Hobson, who has got a few less teeth today, which'll serve him right for trying to take me down when I had my back to him." There was an appreciative laugh from the crowd. "Then we had Berin Haylan, who should've known better than to try and fight me with a skin full of ale,"

Dale ticked off another of his opponents on his fingers, "and the last lad who fancied his chances was Crispin Cartwright, and he'll be feeling those two cracked ribs I gave him come the morning."

"More like three!" called back one of spectators, grinning. A hand protectively across his bruised torso, and a grazed cheek marked him as the aforementioned Crispin. Dale returned the grin before looking back at Jack. "So what's your name, then? Why don't you tell me now while you've still got a mouthful of teeth?"

"I'm the man who'll take your money," Jack replied.

There was an "ooh" from the crowd. It was spoiling for another good fight.

"You're a sure one," Dale lifted his staff from where it was impaled in the mud and moved in on Jack.

Jack unbuckled his sword belt and laid it on the ground. Dale's eyes narrowed as he viewed its fine finish and the jewels adorning it. "Who'd you steal that from then?" he asked, circling Jack.

Jack ignored the comment.

"Let's see if you're as pretty a player as your sword suggests." There was a brief pause, and then they began. Dale launched into an attack, which Jack parried with ease, taking his time to judge his opponent's strength.

Mat leant with a drunken sway towards Alan. "Easy money! I got ten on him to win."

"If he knew that, he'd lose to spite you." Alan's eyes had not moved from the contestants. His money was on Dale, who he hoped would give the bastard more than a good beating.

The game was over quickly. Dale waded in with heavy strokes meant to drive his opponent backwards until he could take no more of the hammering. But he only made two attacks. Jack smoothly forced the first away and stepped under the second, swinging his staff neatly into the back of Dale's knees to deftly take the big man down.

Jack stepped back; the crowd cheered. Dale went to toss the purse to Jack, but Jack stopped him, yelling, "Hold! Best of three."

Dale's grin broadened. "A gentleman as well! You'll not catch me out again."

And he was right. Jack took the fall in the second bout and lay prone on the grass with Dale's staff pointed at his throat. The crowd roared their appreciation at the champion's resurrection.

"He did that on purpose," Mat complained loudly.

"Two silver pieces. I take the winner," Richard yelled as Dale raised Jack to his feet. This drew a murmur from the crowd; this was half a year's wages, bet by a man too well dressed to be of their kind.

Mat visibly cringed as he heard the silken voice of his employer behind him, and he stepped aside to let him into the ring.

"No," Jack snarled, walking towards Richard.

"Hey, if he wants to lose his money to us, let's not stop him," Dale called.

"I can't change my mind; they'll skin me," Richard told Jack affably. Mat was already scraping in his jacket for fresh coins for his next bet. He'd put all in. He paused in thought. Master or Jack? He had no doubts Jack would overcome Dale. Master was a right cunning, dirty bastard when he wanted to be. The Master, he concluded.

Jack, sighing, turned back to the ring and grinned at Dale. "Ready?" he called, Dale smiled back.

Dale lost, as Mat had predicted, but he kept his self-respect, for Jack prolonged the game. This time, he offered his arm to Dale to raise him from the grass. "Well won..." Dale paused; he still did not know the champion's name.

"Jack," the winner provided.

"Good luck to you!" Dale slapped Jack on the back as he departed the ring. "My money is on you."

Richard handed his doublet to Mat and, leaning over his ear, said too loudly, "If you bet with this, I'll not pay you for a year."

Jack and Richard moved close. "Shall we give them a good show?" Jack enquired quietly.

Richard smiled, "Most certainly, my sweet polynices." Word had spread and more of his men had joined the spectators. The pair turned their backs on each other and took up stances a few paces apart.

"To the death," yelled Richard.

"To your money," yelled Jack, and the fighting began in earnest, with a speed the spectators had not witnessed that night. Dale, standing on the sidelines, realised quickly that he had only won his second bout and remained in the ring so long during the third due to Jack's grace, and not his own skill.

Richard continued to force the point.

Jack's blue eyes narrowed. *All right, so that's how you want to play, is it?*

Jack hardened, forced to place the full weight of his body behind the swings, as Richard was doing.

They fought for five minutes, sweat pouring down both men, the crowd variously silent and cheering. Jack almost managed at one point to disarm Richard but was forced away before he could complete the move by a hard kick in the stomach, which sent him staggering backwards. It was becoming painfully clear to Jack that the game his brother was playing was a deadly serious one.

Their staffs locked and Jack used all his strength to pull his brother close. "What the hell are you doing?"

The reply was a flashed smile, and for his moment's inattention, he received an elbow jammed painfully hard in his ribs. Gasping, Jack backed away. He bloody means it, thought Jack. Despite the effort, Richard was still breathing evenly, waiting for Jack's move.

The brief interval gave Jack time to look around. He recognised many of the faces in the circle that had grown about them. He didn't want to lose in front of them all. But winning would not be easy. If he dropped his guard, a lethal blow would get through. Richard would expect him to stop it; he had made that clear. Jack finally bowed out by wrong footing himself and falling backwards to land on his back inches beneath an aimed swing. He stayed down, a hand on his ribs, feigning a minor injury from the fall. The crowd cheered. Mat smiled and staggered off to collect his money. Alan scowled, and Dan, in the ring of spectators, shook his head.

Richard, staff still in hand and breathing hard now, stood over his brother. "You didn't have to do that."

"I know. It has not made me a rich man, has it?" Jack scowled up at his brother. "What the hell were you doing?"

"I was curious." Richard extended his arm, and Jack took it, pulling himself from the earth. The crowd cheered at the generosity of the victor.

"What do you wish me to prove to you, exactly?" Jack demanded, anger in his voice as the pair stood close. Richard did not reply, but released his grip on Jack. "Another test of my loyalty?" Jack left the ring, retrieving his sword as he went, and received another cheer from the crowd for his entertainment.

Dan saw the master approach. He was not an easy figure to miss in this crowd. Taller than most men, his lithe, darkly dressed form stood out amongst the thick, farm-bred peasants and the liveried colours of household servants. He had been searching for Richard for almost an hour, and now that he had found him, he wondered what to say. Dan had been Richard's sworn servant since he had been so appointed by Richard's father. In the man now approaching him, Dan saw nothing of the boy he had cared for save for the confidence of manner, which had always been there.

Dan squared his shoulders and made to stop Richard's advance. "I have looked..."

Richard cut in, "Seek, and ye shall find; knock, and it shall be opened unto you," he quoted.

"Richard, we must talk." Dan caught Richard's arm.

Richard turned to look at him, his face dark. "Ask," he said sardonically, "and it shall be given to you."

"Be serious," Dan growled, in no mood for the others feigned frivolity.

"Only the insane take themselves seriously." Richard did not pull from Dan's grasp.

"Aye, well I wonder sometimes if you're not..." Dan released Richard. "Tell me why you did it."

"Did what? I was unaware that I had done anything on this fine day," Richard replied amiably.

"You know what you did." Dan glowered at him from under thick, dark brows.

"I am afraid you will have to enlighten me," Richard's voice was still light.

"I saw the fight you had with Jack. What exactly are you trying to do? Drive him from you?" Dan was angry now.

"Nothing passes you by, does it? He bloody well deserved that after what happened at Assingham," Richard replied wearily.

Dan ignored him. "And another thing... weren't you going to tell Jack once this was over?"

"Was I?" Richard asked.

"You bloody well know you were!"

"So you keep telling me. Look, soon enough Robert will find out from someone that my bastard sibling is with me. He will know straight away who he is. If I tell Jack, don't you think that would force the hot-headed fool to confront him sooner rather than later?"

"Jack's not the prize idiot you keep making out, you know." Dan was angry now. "You're not the only one who can play games. Catherine, the girl from Assingham, you want to know where we took her?"

"Where?" Richard asked warily.

"She's at the Abbey," Dan growled. "So, are you going to do anything?" he pressed the point again.

"What would you have me do?" Richard questioned. "No, no, don't tell me; I can guess. However, I am not my brother's keeper."

"You're right there for once–but he's sure as hell yours. He nearly got himself killed trying to save your neck! For Christ's sake, don't make an enemy out of him as well," Dan exploded. "I know your reasons, but you're wrong, very wrong."

"Alright, I'll talk to him," Richard conceded.

"You'd bloody better." Pushing his hands into his jacket, Dan turned his back on Richard and headed for the camp. Richard watched him go, a slight smile at one corner of his mouth. It was Dan's unerring mission in life to prevent him from stepping from the path. The problem was that it was the right path, as Dan perceived it, and not as Richard saw it. The man would now expect nothing less from him than to put right the wrong he reasoned Richard had committed. And, as he believed that Dan would carry out his threat, Richard had no choice.

The Abbey! He should have seen that coming. Jack believed his mother to have entered the Abbey after giving birth to him. A few questions or a simple enquiry would start Jack down a new path. Richard assumed correctly that this hadn't happened... yet.

Chapter Thirteen

Framlingham – Suffolk – July 19th 1553

"We will leave in two days, when the appropriate arrangements have been made, and move to London." Mary observed the man kneeling before her. "It is our wish that you join us on our procession south."

"As Your Majesty wishes," Richard said, still kneeling at her skirt hem.

Mary held out her hand absently to Derby. He knew what she wanted and retrieved the roll of parchment from the table, placing it in her small hand. "As a sign of our appreciation, and your continued good service and loyalty to our cause, it is our wish that you have this," Mary proclaimed royally, and handed the Latin script to Richard.

"Your Majesty is too kind," Richard replied humbly.

Mary looked down at him, but she offered no reply. Few could blame Mary for trusting little. Her whole life she had been subjected to her father's whims and desires and she had borne witness to his harsh and cruel treatment of her mother. Constantly unsure of her position, her status never secure, she had been left tight-lipped and with a hard face.

"Your Majesty," ventured the Earl of Derby quietly, "there is much to attend to if I could..." He let his words trail off, his hand indicating the pile of waiting papers.

"Yes, yes, of course. Richard Fitzwarren, we shall look to see you on our journey to London."

Richard heeded the dismissal and bowed his way from the chamber. Walking down the stairs to retrieve his sword from the guard below, he absently tapped the scroll against the palm of his hand, the vaguest trace of a smile at the corner of his mouth.

Jack, waiting for Richard, leant idly against a wall amongst the throng of Mary's supporters gathered around the main gates. Finally, he saw his brother's unmistakable form emerging from between the door in the gate, flanked by two guards, and moved quickly through the crowd to intercept him.

"Well?" Jack was impatient.

"Here." Richard handed the papers to Jack, who unfurled the heavy vellum pages.

"It's in Latin." Jack's pace slowed as he tried to read. "Here," he handed the papers back. "It's legal Latin. I cannot fathom it."

"You should have paid more attention to your tutor, Jack," Richard said absently.

Jack scowled. "All right, suppose you tell me what is says."

"I can't," Richard replied. "I haven't read it myself."

"You must have some inkling," Jack protested. Getting no reply, he continued sarcastically. "So, you just strolled in there, no one said a word, they merely handed you that and, not remotely inquisitive, you asked no questions and left?"

He received only a withering look and was forced to wait until they returned to Richard's tent before his brother decided to finally study the documents. After a lengthy read, which tried Jack's patience immensely, Richard looked up, smiling.

"Come on then, tell me," Jack growled.

"It appears I have a manor and land at Burton near Lincoln, with a forest, a mill, and all rents from the village and farm land thereabouts," Richard finally volunteered.

Jack was amazed. "How you managed that I don't..."

"I thought you wanted to know." Richard looked up from the papers darkly.

"Sorry, continue," Jack muttered through tight lips.

"And a house on Chapel Street in London," Richard concluded.

"Well, that's an improvement on our present situation. What will you do next?" Jack asked eagerly.

"I have little choice in that. I have to accompany Mary to London as she makes her triumphal entry into the city. However, in view of this," Richard indicated the papers, "I think I shall send half of the men to Burton, to find out what I have and what it's worth."

The bestowal had piqued Jack's curiosity, and if asked, he would have left straight away. Burton was not more than a day's ride from Framlingham. They could be there tonight, appraise the place, and be back here before the procession to London. "So when do I leave?"

"Did I say you should go?" Richard responded shortly.

"No. I just thought that as you were going to London, I would..." Jack's words trailed off.

Richard relented. "Alright, I would like you to go to Burton, find out what we have and what it's worth and send a report down to me in London. I'm following Mary as she enters the city and it could be a long journey, so send one of the men with the report to Chapel Street and I'll pick it up when I get there."

"You'll need to give me a letter of representation. Otherwise, no one will take me seriously when I get there." Jack sounded as if he liked the plan.

"Not a problem. Find out what kind of annual income we can expect from this manor, if any. I suspect it's a fairly small place and not up to supporting much more than its own upkeep, but it's a start."

"It's a bloody good start, I'd say. You have certainly moved yourself up in the world. This time let us try to hang on to it, though," Jack said warningly.

"If I was ever cautious, Jack, we would not have ended up with Burton in the first place. It's a game of chance we are playing, and as the rewards are high, the stakes must be as well," Richard replied.

"Well, let's hope your luck holds out, eh?" Jack said, then asked, "Mat told me you almost rode straight through the middle of the Earl of Oxford's men on the way here. What happened?"

Richard regarded him with serious grey eyes. "I told the Earl that Mary had already turned her sights on London and had taken her supporters and left Framlingham."

Jack's brows furrowed. "And he believed you?"

Richard nodded slowly. "He did. The Earl has been receiving and sending messages through Whickham to Byrne and the rest of the supporters. I'd added my own messages, so he had no reason to disbelieve me."

Jack still remained confused. "But how? What did you tell him that made him believe you?"

"Just enough, Jack. He had been sure Northumberland had been a fool to leave London, and as soon as he heard Mary was marching there, then it was the excuse he needed to return himself. His was a half-hearted rebellion, at best."

"I never know which side we are supposed to be on!" Jack sounded exasperated.

"I would have thought the answer to that was fairly obvious," Richard said, rubbing a hand over his face.

"No, it's not obvious. One moment we are working for Byrne supporting Northumberland, then we've swapped to Mary, and then when you rode here, you swapped back to supporting him again when it suited you," Jack sounded utterly confused.

"You are getting too caught up in the details. We, Jack, are on our side."

The pair returned to the camp raucously drunk. Dan received the body of Jack as it slid from the horse's saddle, and Richard hauled him to the tent, his own feet a little unsure. He dumped Jack on the bed none too carefully and slept soon after on the rug-spread floor.

Hal clearly saw that Richard Fitzwarren was surrounded by his own men and heading to Framlingham. So he cut his losses and returned to his master with what news he had.

London had declared for Mary, with Cecil himself making the declaration. Harry knew his father had pledged himself to the Queen, so he had no worries about the change of policy. That had little effect on Harry. What really did annoy him, though, was that Richard had allied himself to Mary long before the tide had changed. Richard had been playing both sides for as much as he could get, and that he had ended up the better for it, Harry did not doubt.

Chapter Fourteen

Framlingham – 22nd July 1553

On the 22nd of July 1553, Mary, Queen of England by the Grace of God, left Framlingham, her household and supporters, moving with no great haste toward London. Many of those who had gathered followed her; others returned after the revelry to their farms and villages. Harvest time was upon them, and that would wait for no man and certainly no queen.

Richard was bound for London and left with the gaggle of supporters that followed the triumphant Mary, whilst Jack made for Burton. It was Jack who arrived at his destination first and Jack, desperate to find out what the place was like and to prove his own worth, had left quickly.

Burton was a small fortified Manor house, nestling in a lap of green land surrounded on three sides by forest and on the fourth by a stream. A mile, maybe two, from the Manor was the village of Burton. It was small, centred around the church and an open space that served as both an area for communal grazing and as the marketplace.

It had been with a cold humour that Richard had found out that Robert Hastley, the previous owner of Burton, and apparently loyal to Mary, had been feeding information to Northumberland's supporters. When he had realised the folly of his actions, Hastley had fled to Scotland, leaving Mary free to give one traitor's property to another of the same kind. Richard had not shared this information with Jack.

There remained a small staff at the Manor house. When Jack dismounted in the courtyard he was met by a fat man and a priest. Jack had bid Mat ride ahead by a day and inform the inhabitants of his pending arrival, and he saw him too, accompanying the overweight retainer. Jack looked around the confines of the walled courtyard, his eyes taking in the defences, maintenance, and structure of the heavy curtain wall.

"I am Guy Thomas. I used to be Robert Hastley's cofferer. I am now..." The man paused, unsure now he faced Jack, who he erroneously assumed to be the new master of Burton. "...At your service," he completed, bowing stiffly, the top half of his body pivoting with difficulty around the unyielding bulk of his ample girth.

Guy saw that Jack was fairly well dressed, a soldier by the looks of him, tall with sun-bleached blond hair, his manner hinting at the power that beat beneath the surface. Guy's throat and mouth were dry, his eyes flicking uneasily over the group of armed men at Jack's back.

"You have books of account?" Jack enquired.

"Of course," stammered Guy.

"Good man, show me the property and then we can have a look at them over a beer?" Jack said, smiling and clapping Guy on the arm. "Have someone stable these horses will you and show my men around?"

Guy motioned for the two men cowering in the doorway to comply.

Jack made to follow him, but the priest stepped in. "A word if I may," he ventured. Jack cast his eyes over the man of God who stood in his way. Although ageing, he had an active air about him. Jack had little time for the clergy. It was, after all, they who had cursed him, but this man looked like he might have had to work for his living, unlike the fat religious upholders he despised. There was also something strangely familiar about him.

"Of course," Jack said amiably, regarding the priest with a slightly puzzled expression. "But perhaps after I have looked around."

The priest seemed to be in no hurry. "I will wait if that is acceptable."

Jack raised his hand in assent and followed Guy in. The courtyard contained only two exits, one through the main gate by which they had just entered, and another up wide steps that led into the main body of the Manor. Jack followed Guy up these and through wooden doors, directly into the main hall. It was not large; the main features were a fireplace along one wall and a dais at the far end. Jack looking up at the eastern wall and found the remains of a decrepit minstrel's gallery. The remaining exit from the hall led into a corridor which, Guy informed him, went to the kitchens. He followed Guy up narrow spiral stairs to the next level.

The first room was clearly awaiting the return of its master. Books lay on the table, clothes still hung over a chair, and the remains of the last fire still lay black in the grate. It was obviously the room occupied by Robert Hastley and his wife. The next was a similar layout, the furnishing simpler, and the bedchamber contained three beds. Again the room seemed to be sadly awaiting the return of the children who would never come back. The third room was where Guy kept his books and Robert had obviously used it for conducting his business. The final chamber on this floor had been converted into a family chapel, the ornaments of prayer still stood on the altar.

Jack spent most of the day poring over the books, asking questions and receiving answers from Guy. When he looked up to stretch his aching back he saw from the window that the light of the day was disappearing fast, but he felt at last in a position to inform Richard of what he had at Burton. He rubbed his tired eyes.

"Can I assume that my services will still be required?" Guy ventured nervously.

"Ah, Guy, there is a question," said Jack fishing inside his jacket for a document. "Here, this is from your new master."

Guy took the document and read the short words from Richard Fitzwarren, authorising Jack to act on his behalf.

"It does say that in his absence that you are to act for him," Guy said, laying down the page.

"Does it indeed?" Jack was tired; he knew exactly what it said, having stood over Richard as he penned it, pleased with the trust placed in him.

"Am I to assume he will often be absent? I know little of this man. Perhaps he has lands elsewhere?" Guy ventured. His confidence growing, he tried to find out a little about Robert Hastley's replacement.

"What he does, Guy, is his own business. However, since I appear to be in charge at the moment, consider yourself hired. How much did Hastley pay you again?" Jack had seen the amount penned in the books and recalled it instantly.

"Ten a year," Guy answered.

Right answer, thought Jack. It had been a minor test of the man's honesty.

"Can I assume that ten would still be acceptable?" Jack enquired, his tone making it plain that there would be no bartering.

"Yes, sir." Guy had a genuine smile on his face.

"Oh, damn!" Jack exclaimed. "I forgot. I need an inventory of all the stores. Can you do that for me by the morning? I've ten men down there; they'll riot if the beer runs out. I take it there is enough for a day or so?"

"I believe so," Guy replied.

"Good, otherwise you'll find me lynched in the yard," Jack said good-humouredly. "Shall we continue in the morning?"

Guy's head bobbed in agreement and the pair made their way downstairs to the hall where he found his men had been amply supplied with beer already, and then he spied the priest, still waiting.

Jack had forgotten him. "Forgive me. You wanted to talk. Please sit. I'll stand if you don't mind; I've been stooped over a desk too long."

The priest sat; glad at last to take the weight off his feet. "You don't remember me, do you?"

Those words gained him Jack's full attention and his clear blue eyes roamed over the seated man. "I can't quite place you." Jack said slowly.

"Oderint dum metuant," the priest said, his face splitting into a grin.

"You!" Jack exclaimed shaking his head. "That was a night I do remember. You put my brother in a foul mood."

"I don't think it was me who did that. How is he anyway?" Jamie enquired, his manner friendly.

"Not here, I'm sure you'll be saddened to hear. So what are you doing in Burton?" Jack asked, dropping into a seat opposite Jamie. Elbows planted on the table, he regarded the priest with a steady blue gaze.

"Burton? This is my parish," Jamie supplied.

"We met in Dieppe?" Jack responded, "That is a long way from here."

"We are both a long way from there, aren't we?" Jamie said, leaning forward. "I was on a pilgrimage to St Trophimus' Church in Eschau, St Sophia is interred there." Jamie crossed himself as he spoke the saint's name.

"I'd not thought we would ever meet again," Jack said, and then smiling added, "If I remember correctly, I owe you for a jug of ale."

"You do remember correctly, and I'll gladly accept your hospitality," Jamie said quickly.

Jack, shaking his head and smiling at the priest's presumptuousness, obtained from one of the servants a full brown earthenware jug. It was set upon the table between them and cups followed a few moments later.

"What did you want to talk to me about?" Jack asked. His throat dry, the first cupful of ale disappeared in two quick swallows and he was already reaching for the jug to refill the cup.

"I know nothing of Fitzwarren," said the priest, "and I would like to know your intentions so I can convey them to the village. They are worried by such change, and know not how you lean."

"Lean?" echoed Jack, confused.

"Yes, Robert Hastley was a Catholic and most of the village hereabouts is too," the priest said, as if that supplied sufficient explanation.

Jack took another drink. "Ah, religion," he said.

"Well?" the priest asked.

"Sorry, I am a little tired. I care not and I think I can say with some certainty that my brother will care little either. As long as the rents get paid, do as you please," Jack said.

The priest looked relieved.

Jack continued, "I am sorry you had to wait so long to know that."

Jamie nodded. "It looks like you are faring much better than when we last met," he said, raising his cup and gestured around the hall.

"It's my brother's, not mine," Jack supplied. "He's not here yet, and I am in charge."

"Seems he is doing well for himself." Jamie sipped from the cup, and then added, "You, on the other hand, don't look much altered from the last time we met."

"What's that supposed to mean?" Jack said, his voice a little too loud.

"Exactly that, you don't look like you own Burton," Jamie said bluntly.

"Well, I don't, this is my brother's, as I told you," Jack said defensively.

Jamie sighed, "Well you don't even much look like his steward either. Martin, the blacksmith's simple son, looks better dressed than you do."

Jack slammed his cup down into onto the table, bruising the wood. Before he could pull his hand away Jamie had fastened a bony hand around his wrist.

Shaking his head and smiling he said, "I see you've also still not managed to tame your temper."

"My temper was fine, until I met you again," Jack replied through gritted teeth. He managed to resist ripping his hand from Jamie's grasp.

Jamie released his grip and smiled. "The Lord will have a reason for our paths to have crossed again. I think we should both wait and find out what that reason is." Then conspiratorially he added, "I can tell you lots about Burton that you'll not get from Guy."

"Like what?" Jack said, still sounding annoyed.

"Oh. like how Guy's cousins have had preferential rental rates for years," Jamie said, "and how the beer supplied by Smythe, Guy's wife's brother, is watered down so he can charge more per keg."

Jack's eyebrows raised, and he was silent for a moment. Then reaching for the jug he refilled Jamie's cup. "So tell me, then, everything you know about Burton. Maybe the Lord did indeed make our paths cross for a reason."

The jug was emptied and refilled four more times before Jamie left and Jack returned to the company of his own men.

Elizabeth was still resident at her London house, Durham Place, having been in the city to take part in Mary's coronation procession. Her position had in recent times been elevated from one of minor royalty to the heir to the throne.

But Elizabeth recognised it for the hollow sham it was. Mary would marry as soon as she could, of that Elizabeth had no doubt, and then she would then be returned to her former status. The Princess also recognised the danger of her position. Mary had no liking for her half sister and saw her as an imminent threat, something that secretly pleased Elizabeth.

Furthermore, there was the religious clash. Mary, devoutly Catholic, could not abide Elizabeth's Protestantism. Elizabeth understood the strength of her position, and gaining the crown was, to her, a real possibility. To achieve it she had only to keep her head. However, that might prove a none-too-easy task.

Kate Ashley, Elizabeth's confidant and governess, had advised they move to the Buckinghamshire house at Ashridge, and Elizabeth agreed that it would be safer to retreat there and remove herself from court life. This was exactly what Elizabeth intended to do after a decent interval had elapsed. She did not want her departure to be seen as overly hasty and borne from a desire to be at a safe distance from Mary.

"Not that one, Kate, it makes me look fat," Elizabeth said, pointing to one of the dresses laid out on the bed.

"It does not," objected Kate.

"Well, it doesn't matter. I shall wear the green one anyway," Elizabeth said. "I will better blend into the scenery."

Elizabeth was preparing to attend Mary at a masque in the palace gardens that evening. Kate left the room, taking the dress to have a hem repaired.

Elizabeth, idle for once, wandered from the bedchamber into her drawing room. The windows were flung wide open, and the sun played on the pond in the garden below. Elizabeth stood looking down for a long time, unaware of grey eyes watching her intently from the corner of the room. The room was silent. Suddenly Elizabeth's back straightened. She'd sensed she was not alone, and a moment later she turned to face the intruder. Elizabeth's hand went to her chest, and she inhaled sharply, but the call she could have made caught in her throat.

Richard, leaning against the panelling, smiled at her.

"So I was wrong." Elizabeth met his grey eyes and returned his smile, the shock of a moment ago now gone from her face.

"Wrong?" he echoed.

"I had thought you were long dead by now. So you are either a ghostly apparition, a product of my imagination, or," she paused, "I was wrong." Elizabeth stared at him for a long moment, then added, "How did you get in here?"

"The same way I intend to leave," Richard said, pushing himself away from the wall and removing a chestnut leaf that was lodged in his sleeve.

Elizabeth turned to look at the opened door leading to the balcony. "You didn't?" She laughed. "You haven't changed. You will break your neck. If you ask, I shall allow you to use the door." Elizabeth moved two more steps forwards.

Between them was a small round table, three books sat on it, one of them bookmarked with an embroidered linen ribbon. Richard picked it up and flipped it open to read to the title page. "Erasmus, you do surprise me."

"Why?" Elizabeth asked.

"Your preference and obsession was always Greek philosophy," Richard said, replacing the book on the table.

"They have a broad audience, however Erasmus had a particular insight into a future we are now occupying. It is always wise to look before you step forward, don't you think?" Elizabeth replied, her eyes never leaving his face.

"True, I would have thought Erasmus a little heretical at the moment. His observations were not always ones your sister would wholeheartedly agree upon," Richard said evenly, rounding the table to move closer to her.

Elizabeth let out a loud breath. "Her faith is blind, and that is not necessarily a good thing." Then, changing the subject, she said, "I have not heard your name mentioned for so long. The last I did hear was that you were in France."

"That was true until recently," Richard replied.

Elizabeth stepped back and sat down in one of the high-backed chairs, her hand patting the cushion of the vacant one next to hers. "Richard, don't stand there. I pine for good company. Sit down. You look like you'll leave me at any moment."

Richard, sighing, complied. "The lady still likes her own way, I see."

Elizabeth ignored his comment. "So what brought you back to England's shores?"

"Northumberland's money in the main," Richard said. He could still see the girl's face in the woman's features.

"No! You opposed Mary? Ah, now, that's funny," she said, laughing.

"I don't think Northumberland would share your amusement," Richard said.

"It was a fool's plan based on greed. He deserved the result," Elizabeth observed caustically.

"Avarice has never provided a good foundation for stability."

"Ambition is often avarice when you turn a blind eye to the facts," Elizabeth pointed out. "So what was your ambition when you were working for Northumberland, or did you honestly believe he could succeed?"

"The lady gets straight to the point still," Richard responded, shaking his head slightly.

"Don't prevaricate, answer me," Elizabeth pressed.

"I did not turn my back on the facts, however I needed an employer, and the simple truth of the matter was that the Earl's supporters were hiring and Mary's were not. However, when it became apparent that there was about to be a rapid and crushing defeat, like Achilles, I withdrew my services.

"Ah, but Achilles did not change sides, did he? Did you? Or do you still support his faction against Mary?" Elizabeth's assessing eyes never left his face.

"In truth, I don't think there is much of a faction left," Richard said.

"So, where are you placed now?" Elizabeth questioned, her brow slightly creased as she waited for his answer.

"I offered Mary some service, nothing of any real significance, and ostensibly I am working for Derby at the moment."

Elizabeth's face hardened as she repeated the name slowly. "Derby."

Richard, reading her thoughts, added. "I said working for, I did not say loyal to, did I?"

Elizabeth, seeing the mischievous glint in his eyes, reflected his smile with her own. "And where does your loyalty lie?"

"You need to ask?" Richard's voice bore a serious edge, and for a moment there was cold silence between them.

"Yes, I do need to ask," Elizabeth said, her words clipped and her eyes holding his.

"As always, my loyalty remains yours," Richard said solemnly.

"Good. Let's talk about other things. We are still friends, I think?" Elizabeth entreated, the furrow between her brows lessening.

"I would always hope so." Richard returned her smile and watched a moment of relief flit across her face.

She continued, reassured. "Tell me then how you deserted the Earl and how you lent some insignificant assistance to my sister."

"I am, like you, adept at self-preservation. I changed sides in the final hour, rendered the lady some service, pledged my loyalty, and here I am," Richard said. The summary was far too brief, too evasive, and the look on Elizabeth's face told him as much.

"Why do I have the feeling there is slightly more to this than you are saying?" Elizabeth enquired.

It took an hour, in the end, to answer all her questions. Elizabeth was a political animal with a voracious hunger for news from Mary's court, and Richard took the time to provide her with as much detail as he could. They ended by discussing the Spanish match. Both of them were in agreement that it could be political suicide for Mary, and that she would have a hard time convincing Parliament that the alliance was a good one for England.

Sometime later, after Elizabeth had watched his departure through the garden, she was still musing over her visitor when Kate returned with the dress, its hem repaired.

"Elizabeth, come on, you shall be late," Kate said, laying the dress on the bed and smoothing out the creases. "Elizabeth?"

Elizabeth turned. "Kate, sorry, I was elsewhere,"

"I can see that," her governess said carefully. "What's happened?"

Elizabeth smiled mischievously and swept across the floor, her skirts swirling around her. Kate, surprised, followed her. "I've had a visitor," Elizabeth announced suddenly.

"A visitor! Who? I saw no one admitted!" Kate sounded puzzled.

"A most handsome gentleman, Kate. Ah, if only you had been here," Elizabeth said as she skipped away from Kate's advance.

"Tell me. Do not play games," Kate added, more authority to her voice.

Elizabeth contemplated her reply for some moments. "Lord of the forest, by all accounts; an elfin form he was, and one I thought long lost to me," she said, still twirling round, skirts spinning.

Kate stood, hands on hips, and observed the other woman with a worried look on her face.

Elizabeth, seeing that Kate was beyond comprehension, said, "Richard! You remember."

Kate still looked at her, nonplussed. "Elizabeth, you are confusing me. No one called this afternoon. Who are you talking about?"

"You are slow, Kate. Richard Fitzwarren."

Kate looked aghast for a second. "Fitzwarren! Here in this room? No."

"Yes, indeed," laughed Elizabeth, continuing to dance around the room.

"How did he? He didn't..." Kate, lost for words, advanced on Elizabeth.

Elizabeth turned on her governess, a hard light in her eyes. "He was most charming, as he always was. He was nothing less than a gentleman, and do not accuse him of being anything else."

Kate heeded the warning. "How did he get in?"

Elizabeth didn't reply, but merely pointed to the open window. Kate walked to look out into the garden. They were two floors above the ground; it would have been a perilous climb. Her eyes were caught by a green leaf on the balcony and a snapped twig from the towering chestnut that dominated the back of the house.

"That would be some feat to make it the distance from the tree to the safety of the balcony." Kate turned back to Elizabeth. "That boy always did like the dramatic."

"Oh, I think you'll find he's no boy, Kate." Elizabeth grinned.

"Now you be careful. He was not sent from you before without good reason. We all saw what he was like. Mark my words, lady," Kate chided.

Elizabeth's face darkened as she descended on her governess from across the room. "Who am I, Kate?"

Kate didn't answer, but bit her lip.

"Exactly. And I shall, for a change, do as I please. Anyway, it is too late, he serves me now. I have little enough at my disposal, Kate, and what poor stuff I do have I must make use of as best I can," Elizabeth finished.

"What have you done?" Kate said.

"I have done nothing. It is Mary who has raised him up. If only the cow knew what she'd done." Elizabeth, her eyes bright, stared into Kate's, forcing the older woman to look away.

Later, when Elizabeth picked up the book from the table, she smiled when she saw that her bookmark had been replaced with a leaf from the chestnut tree.

Elizabeth had consigned his memory to the deepest recesses of her mind, sure he was by now dead. There had been no mention of his name, and she had not seen him for five years when they had both been part of Sir Thomas Seymour's household in Chelsea.

William Fitzwarren was, at that time, close friends with Thomas Seymour, and his son, Richard, was attached to his household. Seymour married King Henry's widow, Catherine Parr, and Elizabeth was then taken into his care. Richard and Elizabeth had become close companions; Elizabeth had little opportunity to make many true friends, and Richard had been among the few.

Then, what had started out as a game with Seymour asking for Elizabeth to kiss him, as a daughter should her stepfather, ended with him tearing her dress from her shoulders. Richard had intervened and the blame for her dishevelled state Seymour had quickly and efficiently laid upon him. The truth didn't come from Elizabeth, who was too afraid of Seymour, but oddly enough, from Seymour's own wife, Catherine. By then, it was too late. Richard had been banished from the house and had returned to his father's estate, his reputation permanently tarnished.

Hal was still on his master's business, and in London now, trying to track down Richard Fitzwarren. So far he had not had much success.

Hal's feet were hurting him. When he wriggled his toes, he found that only two on the left foot could move, his foot was so jammed into the leather boot. Hal cursed himself for throwing away his old boots, the conviction that these would slacken with wear had been wrong. Hal hopped from foot to foot as he waited for his new companion, David, to join him. Robert Fitzwarren had sent one of his own men to help to track down his brother. Hal didn't particularly like David, but if he had been asked, he would have admitted that at least he wasn't as witless as Spratty, whose company Hal did not miss in the least.

Robert had suspected Richard would go to London, and in this he had been right. He set his men to find him by enquiry, and they were also to ask for Anne and Catherine de Bernay, who might be with him.

David arrived back. "Nah, nothing. This'll take forever," he snarled. He had no love for the task and was sick of asking questions of people, sure that if the man they sought did not wish to be found, he would not be using his own name.

"Where next?" Hal asked as the pair walked through the filth of London rotting in the July heat.

"How should I know?" David said hotly, spitting into the gutter.

"Master said he was with Mary." Hal was talking to himself; thought was not one of David's strong points. "Well, my brother's wife, Nancy, is a cook in Derby's house here in London. Maybe she could find out," Hal concluded.

"How's that going to help? She's not likely to know him, is she? And Derby's not in the bloody city, is he?"

"No, damn you, but she might know someone who might be able to ask someone, who might be able to get someone to find out," Hal growled though clenched teeth.

"That's a lot of mights," David pointed out, spitting again.

"Got any better notions?" David shook his head. "Come on, then." Hal wanted to get his weight back on his arse in the saddle and off his sore feet.

John Somer, Minister for State in fact, but not in name, backed through the door to his private office. One hand clutched two parchment rolls to his chest, the other held a lit lamp emitting a steady yellow glow. Using his elbow he pressed the door closed, let the parchments roll onto his desk, and set to lighting the other two lamps in the room. Placing all three on his desk, Somer seemed satisfied with the level of light and set about organising his papers.

"You would have told me that I'd be paying with my eyesight if I tried to work in such a dark room," the voice came from the shadows, the tone quite light and carrying with it a sense of amusement.

Somer exclaimed, made to stand quickly, and in the act knocked one of the clay lamps from the corner of his desk. Quicker than Somer, Richard stepped forwards saving the lamp from its descent into the floor rushes. Somer, lunging for it at the same moment, found his hand closing over the wrist of the other man. Face to face, their hands together on the lamp, their eyes locked.

"It's hot, can I let go?" Richard Fitzwarren said.

Confusion flittered across Somer's face for a moment before he realised Richard was referring to the lamp and he lifted his hand away. "Are you burnt? You gave me a shock."

"Like Althaea, I have, it seems, put the fire out." Richard fitted both halves of the extinguished lamp back together, the pungent animal fat coating his hands. Pulling a square of linen from his doublet, he carefully cleaned them while regarding Somer. "I have saved us both from a burning."

Somer, recovering from his initial shock, dropped back into a chair behind his desk, waving at another for Richard to take. "I dare not ask how you got in here. I should have my steward's hide for his carelessness."

Richard inclined his head, but didn't answer the question.

"Back in England then? I'd heard you'd gone to France after the Seymour affair."

"I wasn't left a lot of choice," Richard replied matter-of-factly.

"I know," Somer agreed, "he was a man who deserved to fall. He set his sights too high, refused to take any counsel, and put his trust in a child." Thomas Seymour's attempt to kidnap the King, even though he maintained he had acted with the boy's consent, had led him to tread the cold boards towards the block.

"I'd left his service by then, as you know." Richard replied.

Somer held up his hand, and smiling, said, "You can pull me into an evening of Court gossip, but first let me call for food and wine. Richard, it is good to see you. I want to know everything you have been doing since you left England."

"Everything?" Richard echoed.

Somer pressed his palms to the table and stood. "Everything."

An hour later there were empty plates on the desk, their wine cups full, and Somer, enjoying the companionship, finally turned the conversation in the direction he knew was of interest to the other man. "If you've come to see me then, at a guess, you are on the trail of some of Seymour's old associates?"

Richard raised his eyebrows. "It would be a fair assumption."

Somer's tone became practical and businesslike. "Times have changed. Who, who have you been in touch with so far?"

"There was only Cardon I knew I could trust. That was why I came to you next," Richard replied honestly.

Somer nodded. "Cardon will serve you well. There's also Finbrook and Cleater. Both men are still well placed and I use them on occasion, although Cleater is not at Court as much as he used to be, so what he can provide can be a little thin, but he is still..."

"What about Clandyke?" Richard interjected.

"Have you not heard?" Somer looked at his old friend, surprised, then seeing the look on Richard's face, he continued. "He was executed two months ago on Tower Green for treason."

Richard's eyebrows raised, but he said nothing, sipping at his wine and waving for Somer to continue.

"He was found with papers implicating Northumberland in a plot to take the regency. There was no way that was going to be allowed to stand." Somer concluded. "He was, of course, working for Northumberland but also for Derby, his silence was a matter of urgency, and now it is assured."

"Nobody ever said it was a safe game to play," Richard replied, placing the wine glass carefully back on Somer's desk.

"Who do you work for now?" Somer asked directly.

Richard met Somer's enquiring look and smiled. "I work for myself."

"That's an honest reply at least," Somer said as he tapped his fingers against the rim of his cup, his face thoughtful. At length he said, "You can add me to your list of clients."

"I was hoping you would say that."

"My loyalties are fixed. Just remember that," Somer warned, "I'm saddled with a role I didn't ask for, and pleading old age, it seems, will not release me."

Richard knew why they would not release him. Somer was fiercely loyal, dedicated, and trustworthy, a fact known by the current elite. To have a man like that in place as the de facto minister of state provided a block against many of the self-seeking members of the Privy Council. He was dedicated to the Crown, no matter who was wearing it. Trusted by Henry, he had been an automatic choice to continue to guide the administration of the Kingdom under his son. Now Mary was availing herself of his steadfast services.

Their meeting concluded two hours later. Richard leaving by the same route he had used to enter, unseen through the orchard at the rear of Somer's house.

A short while later, he was back in his house in Chapel Street. Two candles burned on his desk, both of them thick with triple wicks, and the light from them cast a steady glow over the papers before him. Richard looked at the folded letter carefully before he broke the seal, a seal that was both nondescript and small.

The unfolded parchment revealed a sheet with a detailed order upon it for cloth. The top section described the quality, quantities available, expected arrival dates, and below it was a list with a proposed order. At first glance, it appeared a merchant's missive, a tally of stock and orders. Richard pulled from his doublet a second sheet; opening it, he placed it over the first. Holes in the top sheet showed him certain sections of the document below. In a neat hand, he copied out the revealed text.

There was a code in place, but if you did not know which sections of text it applied to, then it was impossible to break. The cipher applied to less than half of the text on the page. It was a process he himself had provided for Seymour, it was both simple and effective. Even if the cipher was cracked, without this sheet, without knowing which parts of the document to decode, it could not be cracked. These sheets could be changed, and so an old code could be used over and over.

The velum also bore a series of numbers next to the cutouts. These determined the order in which the exposed text was to be decoded. So even if the whole document was decoded, little sense could ever be made of it as the relevant sections would be out of order.

The sections copied out Richard, folded away the top sheet and began the process of decoding. It was a cipher he had committed to memory, not a difficult task, as the cipher was one he had designed.

Richard read the message on the sheet before him for a second time. Then he pushed himself from the chair and, crossing the room, delivered both the original message and his own decoded sheet to the fire. He watched the sheets quickly curl, blacken and turn to ash.

Chapter Fifteen

Lincolnshire – 30th July 1553

Jack set to work again to try and absorb all there was to know about Burton. He had viewed the books of account kept by Guy and satisfied himself with the basic fabric and security of the place; now by degrees he needed to acquire a more detailed knowledge.

His evening with Jamie had ended up as a drunken one, but along the way, he had picked up quite a lot of knowledge. The priest inferred that Guy was running Burton to his family's advantage, and that was generating a lot of bad feeling amongst the tenants and villagers. Supplies came from Guy's preferred sources, usually in Lincoln, and the village was suffering financially now that it had lost the opportunity to supply Burton with their own local produce.

Jack was once again in the company of the fat retainer.

"So let's look at the land. How is it apportioned?" Jack asked, his hands holding open on the desk a map of the manor and the surrounding area.

Guy went to retrieve a small ledger from the shelf. "It's all in here." He opened the book part way through. "The rents are here." Guy tapped a column with a round fleshy finger. "This is those who've paid." He moved his hand to another neat row of figures. "And this is those who are still owing."

Jack could see that the paid column was nearly completed. That was a shame, he thought. Hastley had already had the income for this year. Gathering a candlestick and an ink pot, he dropped them on the edges of the map to keep it open and took the ledger from Guy.

"Mmm..." Jack turned the page back over. "When's the next rent due?"

"January each year, but it's a poor time, and we don't often see much coming in 'til later in the year." Guy reached over and turned the book back to the current year.

Jack turned the pages back again and looked at the rents. "There's been a bit of a rise, wouldn't you say? What's the tenure?"

"The demesne lands, all at will, with the exception of here," Guy pointed to two entries at the bottom of the page. "These are leasehold: one to the blacksmith and one to Geoffrey Hugh."

Jack didn't reply, but he peered closely at the list of names, then raising his eyes and meeting Guy's, he said quietly. "Isn't Hugh your wife's brother?"

Guy stammered. "Yes, but look, he's a good payer, always first," Guy sounded defensive. "He always pays up promptly. Previous master, begging your pardon, thought it a profitable arrangement."

"Do you think rents need to rise?" Jack flipped the pages backwards in the book and then forwards again. "these two leaseholds have not had a rent rise for three years, yet the other tenants have all suffered one. Any reason for that?" Jack asked, looking up, closely studying Guy's face.

"I'm sure they have risen," Guy mumbled, and reached for the book.

Jack closed the book with a firm hand and pulled it towards him. "No, Guy, they haven't."

"Well, the land on the leasehold portions is poor. That's probably why Master Hastley didn't put the rent up," Guy spluttered nervously.

"Make you mind up Guy. Either they've had a rent rise, or they haven't." Jack glared at him and Guy dropped his eyes to his feet.

Jack opened the book again and ran his finger down the list of tenants and the rents paid. The two large leasehold tracts were worth nearly as much in rent as all the rest of the tenants put together. Jack was about to say as much and managed to stop himself. He would do this properly and not jump to conclusions. So instead he said, "Do you think we should put the rent up again next year?" Jack's finger tapped the list of tenant's names.

"I am sure you know prices are on the up, but if you want to do it, well, that's not for me to decide," Guy supplied carefully.

"You don't think it is a good idea?" Jack enquired.

"It's been a poor harvest for the last two years, another and I don't know if you'll get the money in," Guy answered.

Jack wondered whose side he favoured. Had Guy been Hastley's man, or did he side with the tenants? Or was he on his own side, as Jamie had insinuated? He would have to wait and see.

"I will think about it," Jack said, and then asked, "The markets, when are they held?"

"Last Saturday in the month," Guy supplied, sounding relieved at the sudden change of subject.

"What sort of trade is there?" Jack's eyes were still roaming over the pages.

"It's very small. Most of the tenants take their produce to Lincoln; the market sells the usual wheat, corn, beets, sometimes animals if they've some to sell."

Jack placed a level stare on Guy's face. "Does the market supply Burton? Do you buy in from there?"

"The quality is poor. The master preferred for me to bring in produce from the Lincoln markets," Guy answered, licking his lips, one hand fidgeting with the material on a frayed sleeve.

"You will ride out with me. I would like to see for myself the extent of the land, see exactly what there is,"

Jack said, snapping the book closed. He wondered idly how many men it would take to get Guy in a saddle. Two probably, he concluded. Jack was sure he would find out soon enough if what Jamie had said was true.

They had been out most of the afternoon. Jack was mildly amused by Guy's growing discomfort on the horse he was riding, and he had been unable to resist coaxing his own eager mount into a quick trot. Mat's horse, on loan to the large man, had moved quickly of its own volition to keep pace, and Jack had to turn his face away to hide his mirth as the man slid from side to side in increasing danger of meeting the grass.

Guy had introduced Jack to the tenants he called over from the fields. Some stood nervously without looking up from the soil, some eyed him suspiciously, and a few, he noticed, had even hidden. He was not enjoying being on display and tired quickly of his new role. They passed the church on the return journey. Jack turned to Guy. "Didn't you say Jamie had land hereabouts?"

"Yes, up there. Can you see?" Guy said, pointing.

"Wait here, Guy, I won't be long."

There were three men working in the field, and initially Jack did not recognise one of the stooped men as Jamie. He was filling a bucket with rocks from the turned mud.

"Hello, lad, and how's your head?" Jamie grinned as he straightened up.

Jack returned the man's grin and slid easily from the saddle. "Not as bad, I bet, as yours," he replied, tying his horse to the remains of a gatepost.

"Out seeing what's yours and what isn't, eh?" Jamie was rubbing his filthy hands down his stiff back.

"So, is this mine, then?" Jack kicked at a stone at his feet.

"Aye, that's yours. And this one," Jamie tapped another with his boot, "and all these rocks over there." Jamie waved his arm towards a pile at the end of the field. "If you want them, I'll not stop you coming and taking them."

"What are you doing working in here?" Jack asked, noting the other men in the field had all backed away towards the far fence. He added, "friendly lot aren't they?"

"You're making them nervous," Jamie replied.

"Me!" Jack sounded taken aback.

"More Guy than you, to be honest," Jamie said, sounding exasperated, "They're just waiting for another one of his rent rises, or to have another tariff slapped on them on market day."

"Now hold on," Jack said defensively. "I've done nothing yet."

Jamie cast a dark look in Guy's direction. "Not yet, you haven't. That's true enough."

"Do you rent this land?" Jack asked, changing the subject. "I didn't see your name in Hastley's ledgers.

"This section here is rented by the Church and some of those who can't afford to rent on their own work it, and I help them," Jamie supplied. "It'll be in your ledger under the name of St Marie's and it's the worst piece of land Hastley had."

Jack, casting his eyes over it, had to agree. He was no farmer, but it was fairly obvious that the uneven ground, thick with rocks, was poor farm land.

Jamie saw him looking over the tract and said, "It's not so bad over there." He pointed to where the field banked down towards the stream. "But up here it's always been poor. The rain washes the soil off," he continued, shaking his head. "I had a thought to plant hawthorn or the like over there, give it a bit of shelter from wind, but I don't know. It'll bring in birds."

"I'm no farmer. Don't ask me for advice," Jack said.

"I can tell you're no farmer; this does give that away, you know," Jamie lifted his stick from the mud and tapped the sword at Jack's side with it. "What are your plans, then?"

"Plans?" Jack echoed. "I've made none yet."

"Ah, you'll be waiting for your brother to arrive and make the decisions, will you?" Jamie queried.

Jack turned a hard gaze on the priest. "Don't press me. I know what you aim to do. I am no fool."

Jamie's face split into a wide grin. "Good, I am glad we are in accord." After delivering his words, he stooped to pick up his bucket and, turning his back on Jack, stomped off across the rock-strewn field.

Jack wanted to shout after him, but managed to contain his words, and instead retraced his steps to where Guy was nervously waiting for him.

The next stop on Guy's tour was Burton's mill.

"Master Hastley had this built last year," Guy said proudly. "We used to have to take all the grain from the local area to Lincoln, but now its ground here. The Master had a group of masons come from London, it took a year to build."

Jack gave the structure a sour look.

Guy looked confused. "It's good for the Manor, sir. We charge farmers to use it and even take in grain from as far afield as Ashford, which is nearly eight miles away."

Jack tipped his head back to look at the top of the water wheel, that was in perpetual motion, driven by a stream that had been cut away from the side of the main river. "I don't doubt you, Guy. It's just that I've had a bad experience with mills before."

"Let me show you, this one is very ingenious. Hastley designed it himself." Guy ducked inside the open door and Jack followed him. On the inside, he could feel the noise of the mill coming up through the soles of his boots. Disappearing through the roof, the central shaft secured to the millstones was turning slowly.

"The miller can vary the speed, and also disengage the mechanism when it's not in use," Guy had to shout to be heard over the noise of the turning stones and creaking of the wood structures that held them. "If you go up those stairs, you can see where it is connected to the water wheel."

In the corner, a set of steps disappeared through a hole in the ceiling leading to the mill's upper floor. Jack made his way up them and tried not to laugh as he heard Guy heaving his bulk up the steep stairs behind him. As he emerged through the opening, he could see the wooden shafts attached to the water wheel turning above his head. His brother would be truly fascinated by this. It made Jack feel less than worthy that the mechanics didn't stir his interest at all.

Guy had made it up the final few steps and huffed over to stand next to him. "That door over there leads to some steps down to the millpond, and this opening here means you can get to any part of the main wheel easily if it needs repairing." Guy had to shout to be heard over the noise coming from the huge wheel, turning ponderously on the side of the mill. The opening was enormous and the full width of the wheel could easily be reached from it. With a cautious hand on the sill, Jack leant out and looked down at the enormous paddle wheel being turned by the constant flow of water from the stream.

"There are sluice gates, and they can be dropped in place to stop the water flow," Guy pointed to them upstream from the mill.

"Why would you want to do that?" Jack shouted.

"If the wheel becomes damaged, it won't run smoothly and then the whole mechanism can be affected, that door in the corner gives you rapid access to them. Sometimes, especially during the winter, large rocks can come down with the water and they can break the paddles off," Guy said loudly in his ear.

Jack, intent on making a rapid exit, headed for the door in the corner and the steps leading to the sluice gates. They were steep wooden ones, leading down to a narrow door at the bottom. Guy didn't follow him, Jack noted with a wry smile. Opening the door, he could see beyond it the wooden gates that were held out of the water by a pulley mechanism. They could be dropped quickly to stop the flow of the river and the wheel. Water on the other side would back up until it was forced into a currently dry channel and diverted back to the main river.

It wasn't a decision he had reached lightly, and he hoped it was not one he was going to regret. Jamie's assessment of Guy was proving to be a little too accurate. The rent books confirmed favouritism towards his family members, merchants in Lincoln were all connected to him, and Jack was in no doubt that he would be getting well paid to ensure they remained the chief suppliers to Burton for everything needed to run a small manor.

A week ago Jack had instructed Froggy Tate, who he believed to be one of the less intimidating men in their group, to become Guy's shadow. He didn't want to turn the man off and then find out he couldn't access his own cellars, with no idea which keys fitted, which locks. To Guy he had told a different story, Froggy Tate was to ensure his safety, the implication being that the sometimes raucous troop of men under his command could not always be trusted.

Froggy had taken his work seriously. Before long he knew the name of everyone of the servants who worked at Burton and what their roles were. He had poked his nose into every nook and cranny of the damp stone manor and was sure that it held no secrets he needed to know about.

Jack had summoned Guy to him, still uncertain about what he was about to do. If he did turn him off, then the sole responsibility for Burton and its day-to-day management was about to fall squarely upon his shoulders. Jack groaned. He knew he had little choice.

Five minutes later Guy was walking through the hall, a look of shock on his face.

Jack's report, when Richard received it, was extremely detailed. He has been busy, mused Richard, who for once found himself impressed with the results of Jack's endeavours.

The spade sunk into the top crumbly layer of soil easily but stopped abruptly as the iron edge on the wooden blade struck solid, unyielding stone below. For the umpteenth time that day, Catherine used a word she would have been hauled before the 'Abbess for using. Removing the spade, she tried again, and again hit something solid, jarring her shoulders painfully in their sockets. Kneeling down, she cleared the top surface to expose the rock. This one was too big to lift out. Wedging the spade under an exposed edge, she tried to prize it from its spot. It didn't move at all. Too much of it was still held secure by the damp brown earth around it.

Catherine stabbed the spade down into the soil in a frustrated circle. The metallic clang that answered her told her how far the slab's bulk extended. Scraping with the spade, Catherine cleared most of the surface soil away, allowing her to lever the rock from its earthy grip. The stone removed, she picked it up and hefted it to a pile of rubble at the end of the vegetable garden to be. Her fingers were sore. Splinters from the spade handle had penetrated into her palms and blisters stood out from the skin on the pads of her hands. The sun had begun to dip in the sky. Please, she prayed silently, let it be time to leave the fields for Vespers and, more importantly, after the church service, a meal.

"Laborare est orare," the Abbess had said. "To work is to pray," and had ordered Catherine to work in the fields. It was not her normal daily pastime, but she supposed she had brought it on herself. A sour attitude and her thanklessness for the temporary home provided to her had led her to incur the displeasure of the Abbess. She could not remember the whole of the lengthy lecture delivered by the austere woman, who forced her to kneel on the stone flagging throughout, but "Laborare est orare," she had been told would remind her of the need for purity in thought, word and deed, which, she decided, was wrong. All day she had stood outside and, on reflection, concluded she had very few pure thoughts at all. In fact, most of them were most definitely blasphemous. It was as well the Abbess was not able to read minds as well as the novice's scrawled Latin.

The spade went in again. And again it struck a rock, her hand sliding down the rough-hewn handle gathered more splinters as trophies of "Laborare est orare." Catherine threw the spade across the part-dug patch and sat down on the earth, her back against the pile of stones she had excavated. Closing her eyes, she allowed her muscles to finally relax. Stopping work was sure to bring her before the Abbess; some nearby tattletale would be quick to note her inactivity and report Catherine's shortcomings. After her failure at labour, they would lock her in a cell, and in this weather, the protection of stone walls from the wind seemed most attractive.

"You have been with us...?" the Abbess paused, expecting the kneeling girl before her to provide her with the answer.

"Three months," Catherine sullenly replied.

"Yes. And you repay our kindness and care of you like this? By contriving to be disruptive? Why, Catherine, why?" the Abbess enquired.

"I have told you, I am not..."

The Abbess cut her off. "Yes, not part of this order, I know. Not that line again, please, Catherine. It is becoming a little tedious, and you cannot deny the fact that this order has held out the hand of friendship to you, given you a home and, if you would allow it, a purpose in life. My dear girl, what do you want?" The Abbess waited but no reply came. "Should I turn you out of the abbey, free you as you perceive it? Where would you go? You are penniless, you would starve soon enough. You have to accept that the only home for you is here, with us. Accept that and accept your life."

Catherine continued to stare sulkily in front of her. "How do I know I have nowhere to go?"

"Well, it sounds as if the world of men may have destroyed your life. I have sent letters at your request, and we must await the replies. For the moment, Catherine, accept what the Lord has given to you: a good and productive life. Now, I am sure you have lots to think about and I propose you do so over the next few days. Go to your cell and remain there, then come back and see me on the morrow. I am anxious to hear your thoughts." The Abbess dismissed her and Catherine hid a smile: no more digging.

Catherine lay on the hard bed and stared up at the whitewashed ceiling above her. It felt good to lie still. Outside she could still hear the noise of work around the abbey: the creak of the cart carrying firewood to the warming room, drawn, she knew, by the stooped form of Sister Agatha. It reminded her of the hard work required of the nuns. Distant kitchen noises met her ears, as did the pungent aroma of cooking as it began an assault on her, reminding her of an urgent need to feed her rebelling stomach.

Catherine turned on her side, away from the window, away from the abbey, away from the inhabitants, and stared fixedly at the wall. Should she give in? Should she make this her home? No, it was not her home, but then her home, Assingham, had been destroyed and everyone she knew slain. Probably her father was dead too, for she had heard no word from him yet, but there was still time; she just had to wait.

"I just want to go home, please God, please let me go home," Catherine spoke aloud to the empty room, salty tears sliding down her cheeks, vocalising the silent prayer she had made every night since she had arrived.

Jack turned the letter over in his hand and then tossed it back on the table, where it had already lain for eight weeks. It was from Richard to Peter de Bernay. The contents he could only guess at, and he had been instructed to deliver it when he returned Peter's daughter to Assingham. What Richard was unaware of was that Catherine's father had been involved in one of the few skirmishes with Northumberland's men and was numbered amongst the few who had lost their lives.

Jack had found plenty to occupy himself to avoid taking Catherine back to Assingham; it was a task that didn't appeal at all. He knew he would eventually have to go, but not today. Jack delayed the journey until the letter was twelve weeks old, and only then did he find himself at the gates of St Agnes's.

He was aware of the cold morning air, heavily laden with damp, which had already soaked into his riding cloak, causing it to hang even heavier on his shoulders. Jack was still pondering Dan's enigmatic words, hinting that there was some mystery here surrounding Richard. What it was he couldn't guess at. His mother, he knew, had gone to the Abbey, but he had never known the woman and had never cared to find out anything about her. He would enquire after her this time. She had been a part of his father's household and perhaps she could tell him something about his family that he didn't know.

The abbey was in a quiet valley recess outside the village of Marsden, and Jack saw its towering church spire for a long distance before he reached the main door.

"Well here goes, Jack," he said to himself, and dismounted at the gate.

His presence was announced to the Abbess, and he didn't have to wait long until he was admitted to her private quarters. Bowing after he entered, he kissed her ring and then rising, said, "It is good to see you again."

She grinned a little toothlessly. Leading him to a chair beside the fire, she bade him sit while she busied herself pouring wine.

The lady saw no need to run through time-honoured pleasantries. "I can find little reason for you to come calling other than the lady you so kindly, if a little hurriedly," her tone was acid, "left with us."

Jack, who had been settling down for some general conversation, which he could use to steer round to the subject he was interested in, was a little taken aback by her bluntness.

"You'd be right," he replied, unable to think of anything else to say at the moment. "Richard wishes me to take her back to Assingham."

The Abbess paused while he took a drink and pretended not to notice the grimace on his face produced by the crude beverage. "Ah yes, your brother. We had no chance to talk when you were here last. Tell me about him. Believe me, goings on here are mundane, to say the least. You left in such a hurry last time that I was left only with questions." Wriggling her shoulders, she settled back into the chair.

"You were left with only with questions! I think it's me who has the questions," Jack said. "My mother came here in..."

The Abbess interrupted. "I knew Marie extremely well. We were friends, she and I, close friends. I was saddened when she died last year."

"Last year!" was all Jack said.

"Yes. Why? Did you want to see her? Left it a bit late, didn't you?" the Abbess said with deliberate cruelty.

"It looks like I did," Jack sighed.

"Why? What did you want to know? Perhaps I can help," the woman prompted, almost eagerly. "Don't be so worried. What have you to fear from me? Nothing you say can be heard outside these walls. Satisfy my curiosity." Jack still did not look like he wanted to share his thoughts. Sighing, she continued, "She remembered your brother, Richard. Of course, he was a babe then."

"That was when Marie was Eleanor's waiting lady before I was born." He was a little curious, but his voice still bore an edge of resentment.

The Abbess ignored it. "No, no, it was after you were born. She kept Marie with her until she was brought to bed of Richard."

Jack sat forward.

"I thought he was older than me?" Jack said, a bit shocked by this revelation.

"Where did you get that from? You're the elder by a year and a half."

Jack sat back in the chair; it was of no matter really; he supposed.

"So, how do you find Richard, then?"

Jack's eyes narrowed at her direct question. "Why do you want to know?" he snapped back.

"Idle curiosity, I told you. I suppose there could be nothing but discord between you. Richard has reasons to resent you, and you have plenty yourself against that family," she sighed, shaking her head. "He told me that you were not easy company, and I can see why."

Jack's confusion stopped him from speaking. The Abbess took it as an acceptance of her words and continued, "What will you do now?"

"What do you mean? You've seen Richard? When? Where?" Jack was now bolt upright in the chair.

"He came to see Marie a month or so ago, I suppose. I find it hard to keep track of time," she replied, smiling a little toothlessly at her guest.

"Why did he want to see you?" Jack asked quickly.

"Family secrets," she said, and then added, "he knew you'd be back here again, and he'd asked me to keep the past to myself."

"Tell me? What is it I don't know?" Jack leant forward.

"Just one simple fact, that's all," the Abbess replied.

"Why will no-one tell me?" His words were edged with pain and resignation.

"Your brother told me that he'd tell you in his own time, but it seems he's yet to do that," she said, her voice calm and patient.

"I've asked him time and again. He won't tell me. It is a secret he jealously guards." Jack dropped back in the chair, his eyes fixed on the floor.

"Does he now? I can see why that might be the case," the abbess said.

Jack looked up from the floor, his shoulders slumped, his voice heavy with regret. "I believe he does not trust me enough to share it with me."

"I don't think that's the reason. If anyone should be questioning trust, then it should be you. Do you trust your brother?" she asked, her brow furrowed, watching him carefully.

Jack opened his mouth to speak, but her raised hand stilled his words. "Search your soul. Don't offer me hasty words."

Jack's eyes wandered to the fire, the dancing orange flames the only movement in the room. Unseeing, he stared at the burning logs.

Did he trust his brother?

The fire's white hot centre lit his eyes with an incandescent glow.

Could he trust his brother?

One of the logs shifted in the hearth, sending a shower of orange sparks to dance and die on the stone flags.

Looking up he met her steady gaze still observing him closely, the heat from the fire still set in the depths of his eyes. "Yes, yes, I do."

A thoughtful expression settled on her face, and the ringed fingers on her right hand drummed on the arm of the chair. "I believe you do."

A smile twitched at the corner of Jack's mouth. "I'll just have to persuade him that he can trust me."

"That might be difficult," she observed.

"I have little choice, do I? How else am I going to find out?" Jack said wearily.

"Did I say I'd not tell you?" The Abbess replied quickly.

"You said Richard asked you not to," Jack replied.

"He did, and as I recall, I don't actually remember agreeing. I'm bound by higher orders than those your brother can command." The Abbess's voice was edged with the authority of her office.

Jack looked at her, apprehension plain on his face.

Did he really want to know?

"I'll tell you. And for no other reason than someone else won't. Just still yourself, Jack, and shush, it's not a time for you to talk." She stopped, considering carefully how to continue. "A painful truth is often better than a hidden lie."

"Please, tell me," Jack's voice was hoarse.

"You are not only Richard's older brother, you are William's son, and the child of his wife." The Abbess delivered the truth swiftly.

"What!" Jack exclaimed. "I can't be."

"Your mother was pregnant with you. William took one of her serving women to his bed, and she gave birth to his bastard a month after you were born," she continued.

"I don't understand. Why would I end up in his brother's household?" Jack's face was clouded with confusion.

"Eleanor didn't want his bastard in her house. So to teach his scolding wife a lesson, William switched the babes. There was little difference. You were a month older, but Eleanor had left you with a wet nurse, so she was easily deceived. You, my dear, are Eleanor's son," The Abbess explained.

"Who knows?" Jack managed to ask, his eyes wide with shock.

"Very few. I thought only Marie and William knew of it. How your brother found out he didn't tell me," she answered.

If he was Eleanor's son, then this meant...

Jack stood so suddenly that the chair behind him tipped and banged back loudly against the wooden floor.

"If I'm older than Richard, then..." Jack paced across the room.

"You are William's heir," she finished for him, pity on her face. "Marie's bastard son who, by all accounts I have heard, is marred by Marie's sin, is accepted as William's heir. And you, Eleanor's lost child, are equally coloured by William's sin."

"And Richard knows this?" Jack managed at last.

"Of course." Her words were a little sharp. "Why else would he come to see me? He wanted the same as you will want now. Proof. And I have none. There is only my own word, which is worth little, and as I told him, I will not speak outside these walls. So, knowing the truth is of little help."

"How did he find out?" Jack's face was ashen. He returned to the chair and dropped heavily into it.

"I don't know, but such family deeds as William committed have a habit of returning to haunt the living." She looked closely at him, but his eyes were unfocused and he did not see her.

"I don't know whether to believe you," he said at last, his face still pale.

"Why not? Why should I lie? If I were you, I should be asking myself what your brother is likely to do," she said quietly.

"Hah," Jack choked. "Which one would that be? I seem to have a few to choose from."

"One that is heir, one that would be, and one that can never be," she said quietly.

Jack turned his eyes sharply on her. "Are you saying that is why Richard was here? Does he intend to make himself heir over Robert?"

"That is not what I said." She was smiling again.

Jack stood, his temper risen too far for him to sit still. "Tell me, is that why my brother keeps me at his side—so he can remove Robert and make himself Fitzwarren's heir?"

She did not recoil from the outburst, but her face hardened. "Don't walk back into the world with that conviction. I don't know what is in your brother's mind any more than you do, so don't judge him on your own presumptions."

Jack dropped back into his chair, head in his hands. "How can all this be?"

"Quite simply, she said. "Unfortunately." The sight of him saddened her; all this trouble wrought on him by deeds long since past. "I knew your mother and I can tell you something which may cheer you. For a start, she didn't name you Robert—no, that was William who insisted on naming the child after his father. No, she named you John for her brother. Smile John Fitzwarren, for that is your name. And if any of that family ever saw you who remembered Eleanor, they would know you for a son of hers. All the others were coloured for William, but not you," she said, her eyes on the bowed blond head.

Jack was the only man to have got thoroughly drunk at St Agnes's since the masons had finished laying the stones. She supplied him with the means and left him to take what solace he could in it.

Catherine was forgotten. Told swiftly by the Abbess that she was to be escorted back to Assingham, she was left all night unable to sleep, in her room, denied the chance to ask questions.

The ride to Assingham was one that Jack could never remember. There was too much going on in his head, he had so many questions and his thoughts were utterly confused. He paid little attention to the route they travelled and even less to the girl who rode next to him. He was eager only for one thing: to deposit his charge at Assingham and return to find his brother. Jack needed, more than anything else, to confront Richard.

Why had he not told him?

Why had he kept this to himself?

And where was the proof of the deed that had denied Jack his rightful place in the world?

He made the pace cruel. Arrival at Assingham, though, was not the end of his problems. There they found four men who were guarding the manor, awaiting the arrival of Peter de Bernay's brother's steward.

They had little time for Jack and the girl he was travelling with and barred them both from access to the manor. Informing Jack curtly that the manor was empty, it had been overrun during the recent troubles and everyone had been slain, even the lady and her daughter. The master, Peter de Bernay, had died in a run-in with Northumberland's troops as he fought to put Mary on the throne. They told Jack that if he wanted to wait until the steward came, he could, but he wasn't expected for another few weeks, and Jack would need to find lodgings in the village.

Jack knew he couldn't leave her there. He was going to London: he was going to talk to Richard and the unwanted burden joggling beside him was his brother's problem as well. He would just have to take her with him.

It was two hours later when Jack was dragged back from his brooding thoughts by the sound of the girl's voice.

"Stop. Stop please..." Catherine wailed.

Jack looked over at her. She looked cold, wet, uncomfortable and her eyes were red and swollen with crying. Jack felt an immediate attack of guilt. He wasn't being fair to the poor girl. She'd not long since found out that her father had died and he'd spared her little thought. Jack knew he was better than that.

Dropping the reins into his right hand, he pressed his horse closer to hers. "Here, give me your reins." Both horses had slowed and Jack took the leather and tied a knot in the straps, keeping them short around the horse's neck. Then he produced a lead line and clipped it to the bridle of her horse. "I'll lead her now. You tuck your hands inside your cloak. They look blue with cold."

Catherine wiped the back of her hand across her wet nose before pulling the thick cloak tightly around herself and tucking her frozen hands under her arms.

"We'll stop when we find somewhere. It won't be long. There's smoke rising above the trees over there. If we are lucky, the village won't be far ahead of us." Jack smiled, and the horses set off again at a steadier pace.

Catherine slammed the door of the room they had rented for the night and turned on her companion. "What are you doing? You have no idea where you are going to take me—have you—no idea at all? We should have stopped at Assingham; it would have only taken a small while to sort things out."

Jack looked at her sadly. "Please, Catherine, I couldn't leave you at Assingham. They believe that you are dead. Nothing I said was going to persuade them that this was not the case. Come and sit down over here." He patted the seat in the snug near the fireplace. "I'll light a fire, we'll have something to eat, and I will try to put your mind at rest." Jack busied himself building a fire while Catherine stalked moodily around the room.

It was typical of most inn accommodations. It had a low ceiling and a floor that meandered from the horizontal with a mind of its own, a bed and no other furniture, but it did have the luxury of a fire in one corner.

Catherine sat on the edge of the bed in the rapidly chilling room and watched Jack as he laboured with flint and steel.

"Who are you? I saw you when you were at Hazeldene, and then when Edward's horses were brought over, do you work for Edward Byrne?"

Jack didn't immediately reply. He wasn't entirely sure what he should say to her.

"I know you helped me from the stables that night, but I can remember so little, it's only after I got to the Abbey that my memory seems to return," Catherine said, her voice shaking.

"I'm not surprised. Sometimes it's better to not remember." Jack spoke with his back to her as he fed the dried kindling to the eager flames.

"Will you tell me please, sir? Who are you, and where are you taking me?"

Jack was saved from having to answer when there was a knock at the door. He looked sternly across the room at Catherine and gestured for her to remain seated while he collected the tray of food that had been delivered.

Kicking the door shut with the heel of his boot, he turned back with the tray. "Come and join me by the fire and have some wine and food." He knew Catherine must be hungry; neither of them had eaten all day.

Stepping over to Catherine, he lowered the tray so she could see the steaming bowls of food, hoping to tempt her. "Please come and have something to eat with me. Let's call a truce." He smiled, and Catherine involuntarily found herself smiling back.

They ate in silence, both of them hungry, and the bowls that had held a simple pottage were soon emptied, only crumbs where the warm coarse bread had been.

Jack pushed the tray away and poured two good measures of wine from the jug, holding one of the brown earthenware cups out to Catherine. "Feel better?" he enquired, settling down on the floor in front of the fire, using his cloak as a pillow. It was a planned move. Catherine had the seat and sat over him; the reverse seating arrangements might have intimidated the girl further.

"Yes, thank you," Catherine said. "I didn't realise I was so hungry."

"I always know when I'm hungry. It's a curse." Jack raised his head and emptied half the cup of wine before looking Catherine in the eyes. "Please trust me. While you are with me, no harm will come to you. I will look after you," he assured her. "I will take you to London and Richard will help you, I promise."

Catherine jerked her hand back as if she'd been burnt.

"Richard? Not Edward's cousin?" There was terror in her eyes. After that, the conversation was loud and short. It ended when Jack left the room, slamming the door behind him.

It's not my bloody fault, is it? No. If anyone was to blame for the lady's current situation, it was probably his brother.

Hands on the balustrade, Jack's eyes roamed the common room of the inn below; it was several minutes before he realised where his eyes had come to rest. His mouth twitched into a smile. The girl, sensing the gaze from above, smiled invitingly up at him. Pulling her shoulders back, her breasts, only partly cupped within her bodice, added to the invitation which played across her face.

Jack was busy when Catherine, her temper cooled, went in search of her escort. She found him in the inglenook, buried beneath a woman who was sitting astride him, skirts round her waist and bodice unlaced and falling on its way to meet them. Catherine watched, her mouth hard. If Jack saw her, he gave no sign. Turning, she stomped heavily on the boards and returned to the room.

Jack did not knock when he returned. He threw his doublet onto the bed. His shirt was untied, the neck wide and hanging lopsided, exposing a shoulder. "You wanted me, my lady?" Jack's words bore an edge of inebriation.

"You're drunk! Get out! Get out!" Catherine yelled, but Jack did not obey. He was tired, and this room was warm with a fire still lit in the hearth.

Catherine slept, fully dressed, on the bed, while Jack sprawled out on the floor in front of the fire.

Jack, his head pillowed on his arm, woke as soon as he heard the creak from the bed. The dying fire cast a poor light across the room, but it was enough for him to see the girl. As he watched, she swung her feet to the floor and began to move quietly to the end of the bed. There was a small bag of her possessions on the floor and she leant over to silently pick it up. Jack groaned inwardly. He was going to have to get up and stop her from leaving. His palms flat on the floor, he pushed himself up and moved to block her exit.

Catherine had her back to him, collecting her cloak from where it lay over a chair back. A moment later, her eyes in the direction of where she thought the sleeping man lay, she advanced towards the door and walked straight into him.

"Where are you going?" Jack said.

Catherine, shocked, dropped her bag.

"You've nowhere to go, Catherine, please," Jack reasoned.

"Let me go! Get out of my way. I don't want to stop with you."

She tried to push past him, but a firm hold prevented her, not finished, she kicked out wildly in the dark. The first one missed his body, and she nearly fell, but the second one connected, drawing an exclamation. Spurred on by this success, she persisted. Jack received three good kicks before he decided that enough was enough.

"Stop it or you will force me to... Ah!" Kick number four was enough. If she made any more bloody noise, the whole inn would be awake. Releasing one wrist, he hit her on the side of the temple—not hard—but enough, he judged, to stop her. The blow connected, and Catherine reeled from the impact. Jack still held one wrist and caught her before she hit the floor. Stunned by the blow, her body sagged against him. Picking her up, Jack dropped her none too gently on the bed. It creaked ominously at the impact. Seating himself on the edge, he examined one shin, which still stung with the force of her kicks. Jack's eyebrows raised; the bitch had drawn blood. He had tried to help, and if this was the thanks he got, well damn her to hell. The girl on the bed groaned. Jack smiled evilly.

I hope your head hurts in the morning, lass.

A partial truce was called the following morning. Jack was too good-humoured for her to continue to be angry with him.

"Look." Jack showed her the cut on his leg. "You're a bloody vixen, woman." At that, she had grinned, and the remainder of the journey was easier.

Chapter Sixteen

London – August 1553

Alice knocked gently on the door and then admitted herself to Kate's presence after an appropriate interval. "Yes, what is it, Alice?" Kate said, without looking up from the needlework on her knee.

"There is a man in the kitchen, madam. He says it's about the bill for the cloth you ordered last week, says it wasn't settled, madam. He's causing a right fuss and Frederick thought it best to send for you, madam," Alice said, sounding agitated.

Kate pushed the needlework roughly aside and pulled her sleeves down, sighing.

"I'll be down directly, Alice," Kate said, rising. "I am sure I have the account here," she murmured to herself, pushing papers aside on the table, which doubled as her desk when they were at Durham Place. "Ah," she exclaimed, the account coming to hand instantly.

Kate descended the steps to the kitchen. "I do not know on what authority you come, but this was most surely paid, and I have the account here," she said briskly.

"Ah, well, me master says as how it's still unpaid m'lady and I have this here, but seeing as I can't read…" The man held out a paper in his hand and Kate moved to study the document. She looked at the words, confused for an instant. It told of a sale of five horses, two pigs, and of fodder for the feeding of stock.

"But this is..." her voice trailed off as she looked up and stared with instant recognition into the slate grey eyes under the hood. Fitzwarren! There was a moment's silence before she continued, stepping back from him. "Yes, you are right. There has been an error. It will take me but a moment to calculate this right, and I will send you back with a note for your master. Come, follow me and bring that bill with you," Kate said, and led him from the kitchen, and the watchful eyes of Frederick and Alice, into her temporary office. Once behind the closed door, Richard pushed the hood back from his head and bowed, smiling at Kate.

"Elizabeth told me you'd visited her," Kate said roughly.

"Only with the best intentions," Richard said. "You still cannot trust me—can you, Kate? Do you still blame me?"

"No, it was not your blame to take, Richard. I knew the truth of it as soon as you were gone," Kate said, appraising the figure before her. "Well, Elizabeth was wrong," she said, stepping back from him.

"Yes, she did say that she thought I breathed no more," Richard said.

"No, not that; she said you'd not changed. Well, I don't know whose eyes she looked through, but you're not the young rogue I remember," Kate said.

"I can assure you, Kate, I am more of a rogue than ever." Richard reached forward to catch her hand, and smiling, lifted it to his lips. Kate blushed.

She turned quickly from him and made a pretence of putting the unneeded account back amongst her papers. Her composure recovered, she faced him again. "So what brings you here this time?" she enquired, moving to settle herself back in the chair she had occupied before Alice disturbed her needlework.

"News for your mistress, and..." Richard paused. "... I wanted to see if you still held me in such low regard."

"News first, then we'll discuss my feelings toward you," Kate said quickly.

Richard settled himself easily on the edge of Kate's desk. "Mary rejects Courtenay and instead turns to Spain and Philip. It is expected that a proposal will be received from that quarter soon. The marriage will need to be approved by Parliament, and there are many who think that they will not allow it. The Council, anxious to secure an heir, however, has not rejected Courtenay and are considering him as a suitable match for Elizabeth. He remains Gardiner's favourite, which stands him in good stead. There is movement afoot to unearth again the evidence collected against Anne Boleyn, and use it now to question Elizabeth's legitimacy. It is the same as before; there is nothing new. Renard, the Spanish ambassador, is hoping to possess the evidence to force Mary's hand, but it seems he has an interesting adversary in Gardiner, who wishes to use the papers to persuade Elizabeth into the match with Courtenay. Also, Elizabeth is attracting Mary's disfavour. It appears she failed to attend Mass again and the Queen questions her belief in the faith." Richard delivered his news efficiently and watched with some satisfaction as Kate regarded him with a new expression on her face.

"I told her to be careful. She only needs to make a show to keep Mary happy. I did not know she'd done it again. Her actions are so foolish; sometimes I wonder at the girl's sense," Kate said angrily.

"It's probably a small matter, but one close to Mary's heart," Richard agreed.

"I will talk to her. Is that all?" Kate enquired.

"I have no other news, but when I do, I will most assuredly bring it to you," Richard said, and paused before continuing. "So Kate, do you still dislike me so?"

"Ah, Richard, no—I suppose not. When they told me it was you who attacked Elizabeth in the garden that day and tore her dress, I was a willing victim of their words, too ready to believe. I didn't know it was Seymour." Kate regarded him in silence, an apology in her eyes if not on her lips. "Elizabeth didn't confide in me for months and then, of course, it was too late, and the poor girl had to face the knowledge that everyone knew."

"That was not your fault, Kate." Richard took her hand gently and held it between his own.

"Elizabeth has placed her trust in you, so I shall do the same," Kate said seriously.

Richard returned her smile and, lowering himself from the desk, took her hands and raised her from her seat. "Now," he said, pulling her close, "about that note you were going to write for my master."

Kate pulled away, blushing again. Taking up a pen, she wrote a few words on a scrap of paper and handed it to him. "Now get you from my rooms and stop being such a rascal."

Richard pulled his hood up again and bowed before Kate led him back to the kitchen and saw him from the house.

She returned to her room, passing Elizabeth's door. On a whim, Kate turned back and opened it. Her mistress was reading by the fire and looked up.

"What is it, Kate?" she enquired.

"I just thought you'd like to know that I've had a visitor," Kate crowed, laughing. She made a rapid exit, closing the door with a slam as Elizabeth rose to pursue her.

Nancy was Hal's sister-in-law, and she worked in Derby's household. Hal was hoping that there might be a chance that she could set them back on the trail of Richard Fitzwarren.

"And what would you be doing here, you no good bleeding thief? I told you last time I saw you that if we met again, it would be too soon." Nancy scowled at him. "It was a bad thing you did, Hal Mercer, when you stole your poor mother's belongings that should have gone to my David, her eldest son."

"Oh come on Nance, that was years ago." What she said though was true, Hal had spirited away most of his mother's meagre possessions when she died before his brother's wife could lay claim to them.

"Time doesn't make it right!" Nancy replied angrily.

"Ah now, Nance woman, don't be so..." Hal tried.

"I'll be what I bloody like! You're not coming through my door. Anyway, he's out." Nancy referred to his brother, Will.

"I don't want Will. I've come to see you," Hal said, leaning against the doorway, which was blocked by the wide woman his brother had wed.

"Now why would that be, eh? If it's money, you can take your tail and be off." Nancy's white fists were balled on her wide hips.

"It's money, Nancy, aye," Hal grinned, and held out his hand with four coins in it. Nancy looked from him to the money suspiciously.

"These are yours; I won't tell Will either. I want to know where a friend of mine is, that's all." Hal told her who he was looking for, his name, and what he looked like. He mentioned the de Bernays as well. Nancy, much to Hal's annoyance, told him to come back in a week.

When he returned, he was disappointed. Nancy stowed the coins under her apron, but all she told him was that Fitzwarren had been at Framlingham. From there he had come to London, but where she did not know. One of Derby's grooms had remembered a fight at Framlingham or some such incident.

Finally, though, a week later, Hal did have a stroke of luck. One man, now a resident at his master's new house at Chapel Street, had wasted no time in finding Hal and informing him where he could find the man he sought.

Chapter Seventeen
London – October 1553

The Thomas Wyatt, who came to Richard's house in London, was a very different man from the one he had spoken to earlier in the year. When they had discussed Northumberland's plan to secure the throne, Wyatt had been Mary's man, more from a dislike of Northumberland than from loyalty to Henry's daughter. Now this had changed.

Wyatt was a man who had fought for England in the Italian wars and later played a prominent role in the siege of Boulogne; he had little intention of standing by and watching Mary hand his country to Spain. His view of the situation was very simple: if Mary married Philip, then all control would pass to him and his Spanish courtiers. It would be a surrender by marriage. Parliament would have no power, all the decisions made would be Spanish ones, and the ruling elite would be switched to favour the new King.

If Richard was surprised by the visit, he did not show it, instead he led the way towards the room he had adopted as his own towards the back of the house.

Wyatt peeled the leather gloves from his hands and slapped them down noisily on the desk in front of him, ignoring the seat Richard had gestured towards. "You know why I'm here?"

Richard shook his head slowly.

"Damn it, man! This Spanish match. It's been confirmed today that the wedding will go ahead. I don't think any of us thought it would actually ever happen." Wyatt paced across the room, clearly agitated.

Richard paused for a moment before seating himself on the opposite side of the desk, watching as Wyatt stalked back across the room towards him.

"Do you realise what will happen? Do you?" Wyatt questioned, coming to stand before Richard.

"There are a few possibilities. However, it is often hard to know the future, especially without the services of a good oracle," Richard replied dryly.

"This is serious," Wyatt reprimanded. "Parliament is up in arms. I've just come from Somer's house where we've been holding a meeting. There seems little we can do to stop it."

"So why are you here?" Richard asked patiently.

Wyatt fastened a hard stare upon the other man. "Information can flow both ways. You've ears and eyes at Mary's court. We need to know how this marriage will play out politically–we want to know if she intends to make this Spanish husband a King. It's an abomination. Trust a woman to put herself before her subjects and her country."

"Maybe you should have backed Northumberland?" Richard pointed out unhelpfully.

Wyatt rounded on him. "That, sir, is not amusing."

"It wasn't meant to be," Richard replied, rising, his hands on the edge of the desk.

"I need to know where your loyalty lies?" Wyatt had come to stand facing Richard. He was watching him closely.

"My loyalty?" Richard repeated slowly.

"There is a division, and I'd like to know on which side you stand. If any," Wyatt said. Richard recognised his words were carefully chosen ones, the conversation was moving towards treason and Wyatt would rather not have his words quickly reported back to Richard's employer, Derby. Opposition to the Spanish match was one thing, but opposition to the current monarch was quite another.

"Are you questioning my integrity as well?" Richard replied.

"You backed Northumberland, and when the tide turned, so did you," Wyatt pointed out.

"Shall we agree, then, that a degree of expediency guides my loyalty?" Richard said.

"Just expediency?" Wyatt questioned.

"Alright, expedience and profit," Richard provided, letting Wyatt clearly know that his loyalty had a merchantable quality.

Wyatt nodded. It seemed to satisfy him sufficiently to place the next question. "Once you stood for Elizabeth. Do you still?"

Richard's eyes narrowed, his face expressionless. "Why do you ask?"

Wyatt looked exasperated. "For God's sake, man! I know why you were expelled from Seymour's house. Somer told me how you ended up as his scapegoat. I want to know if you are still in communication with her?"

Richard's eyes never left his face. "Tell me why you want to know?"

Wyatt spoke through gritted teeth. It was obvious he was not enjoying being interrogated by the younger man, and he wished to provide as little information as possible. "There are many who would oppose this Spanish match, and a Queen who allies herself so closely with a foreign power."

"And... these people... think that Elizabeth could take her place?" Richard stated the words Wyatt had avoided.

Wyatt nodded slowly, a slight smile on his face. It had been what he had wanted to hear. "She would have many supporters."

"That would be treason," Richard said.

"Aye, it would."

Richard's grey eyes met with Wyatt's. "I would like to meet them."

"Would you, now?" Wyatt said, the smile that lit his face a sure sign he was pleased in finally having raised Richard's interest. "Well, there'll be a meeting at my sister's house in two days. Come then, and bring me any information you have on how this Spanish match is to be imposed on the rule of England."

Richard was left alone shortly, wondering how it was that words, and sometimes so very few, could change the whole fabric of the future. If Wyatt was right, then perhaps Mary had fatally underestimated the unpopularity of her marriage to Phillip. If Parliament was willing to back Elizabeth, then there might be a power shift from one sister to the other.

Richard arrived promptly and found himself shown into a backroom where three other men waited. They eyed him suspiciously and a conversation that had been in full flow ended abruptly. Wyatt was absent, and Richard took up a station near the window to await their host's arrival.

Wyatt had evidently been out collecting more men, and they arrived together, their loud laughter in the corridor outside of the room heralding their entry. The heavy oak door opened, admitting three men along with Wyatt. Richard knew one of them, the Duke of Suffolk. He had been occasionally at Seymour's London house and the eyes that Suffolk lay on Richard told him of recognition, although they were devoid of a welcome.

Richard remained at the back of the room and listened. Wyatt was firmly against Mary's wedding. He and several of the other men were in passionate agreement that it would mean Parliament and the Privy Council would be eradicated in favour of institutions wholly controlled by Philip and Charles V.

A man seated at the table, the oldest of the assembled, trod a less passionate route, urging caution. There was no firm reason as yet, he argued, to assume Mary would dispense with the services of her English nobles once married. Wyatt, however, refused to accept this, and as the evening continued and a quantity of wine was consumed, the doom that was upon England raced home as if it were a grim reality upon those assembled. Even the elderly gent seated at the table abandoned his cautionary tone and declared that it was now his God-given task to save England from the yoke of Spain.

Richard, remaining sober and silent, watched and listened with clinical detachment.

At the end of the evening, when he was filing towards the door with the others, Wyatt put his hand out to stop him. There were now just three of them left in the room.

"This is Sir Peter Carew," Wyatt supplied, nodding towards the other man who had remained. "He is the member of Parliament for Devon, and he is a staunch supporter of our cause. You once gave me this," Wyatt went to a writing desk in the corner of the room, and pulling out a draw, produced the red leather purse Richard had given to Wyatt months before. "It is now my turn to use it. I would have you keep Elizabeth informed of our cause. She will have her own supporters, and should the time come, all will need to be ready. And we will need as much information as you can get on how this new political alliance with Spain is going to be executed." Wyatt released his hold on the coins, and the purse dropped into Richard's hand.

"I will inform the lady," Richard replied, stowing the money away inside his doublet.

Wyatt nodded. "There will not be another meeting after tonight. If so many of us gather again, we will attract attention. Derby and Mary have eyes everywhere. Carew here," he nodded to the other man who had remained, "meets with me regularly, and we will use him as the route for information. Send your missives through him and I will relay information back to you in the same way."

Richard turned to look at Carew. He had a good ten years on Wyatt, his doublet stretched with the evidence of good living, and reddened cheeks told that he had indulged in a quantity of Wyatt's wine that evening. Richard was about to speak, but Carew spoke first, dismissively. "Call on me tomorrow and we will establish how we shall do this. I'd like a private word with Thomas."

A moment later Richard found himself outside in the corridor, the panelled door closing behind him on the two not so loyal members of Her Majesty's Parliament, Thomas Wyatt and Sir Peter Carew. Richard was led back to the yard at the back of the house where his horse had been stabled. One of Wyatt's grooms had saddled Corracha and stood holding him by the reins. The Arab's ears laid back flat against his head, nostrils wide and an iron clad hoof clattered loudly against the rounded cobbles in the yard.

The groom, seeing Richard approach, tightened his grip on the animal's reins and pulled the horse's nose down a fraction. "He's nothing but a bag of temper mounted on four hooves, this one."

Richard reached out patted the horse's tightly arched neck. "I'd have him no other way."

The horse communicated its dislike of being kept standing in the yard by pulling even harder on the reins and snorting loudly.

"Are you so sure about that?" The groom said, pleased to be able to loosen his hold on the animal as Richard swung into the saddle and drew the reins tight.

With a rider on his back, and one he knew, Corracha stood still, the breath still snorting noisily from his velvet nose. His eyes fastened on the groom standing before him. Ears now pricked up straight and alert.

"I'm very sure," Richard replied, leaning down to pat the horse's neck. "He's a loyal beast."

The groom neatly stepped sideways, not totally convinced that he wasn't about to be either bitten or kicked. "He's a sight. I'll give him that. But you know what they say about beauty, don't you?"

"No, what do they say?" Richard said as he prepared to leave.

"You can't trust it," the groom replied.

"Appearances can deceive," Richard cast the remark back towards the man as he applied his heels to the horse and they rapidly departed Wyatt's house.

Catherine had never been to London and was shocked by the city.

"It's just street after street and still we have not reached the middle," Catherine exclaimed as she rode next to Jack,

"What did you think it would be like?" Jack turned towards her, his voice amused.

"I expected the centre to be open land in the middle, like most towns and villages, where the markets would be. Londoners seem to sell their wares just anywhere they want," Catherine gestured to the side of the street they were travelling down.

Dotted along the edge were stalls poking out from the fronts of houses and crammed into alleyways. Business was conducted all over London, and loudly, judging by some of the arguing merchants they had passed. Jack, seeing that Catherine was paying little attention to where her mare was going, took hold of the reins of her horse. After obtaining the directions he needed, he led her skilfully through the mire that was London, leaving her free to gaze around.

Jack grinned as he continued to answer the barrage of questions she threw his way. He was grudgingly coming to admit a liking for the little brown mouse he had brought from St Agnes's. She had a shrewd mind and a ready wit, which went some way to compensating her for a plain appearance. When she confessed how she had intercepted his brother's messages, it had told him that within that flat chest must be a fair degree of courage. By the time they had reached London, he felt thoroughly sorry for any part he had played in the destruction of her life. Catherine de Bernay, now believed dead, could be in a far worse position than she believed. Jack had persuaded Catherine that, whether she liked it or not, the only person he could think of who could help her was Richard.

Jack had not seen his brother for three months. He had parted from him at Framlingham in July and it was now October. The Chapel Street house was a good one, at the back there was a sizeable courtyard with stabling for a dozen horses, and beyond that a large kitchen garden. The house itself, timber-framed and rising to three stories, was both imposing and large. Jack shook his head in wonder, his brother always seemed to land on his feet.

Quick enquiry of the men in the yard told him that Richard was in the house, and a few more pointed questions directed him to the room he needed.

Jack's hand instinctively reached out to knock on the panelled door, then a memory of the Abbey and what he had learnt changed his mind. Instead, he reached for the round iron ring on the door and opened it.

"Jack!"

It was immediately plain from the expression on Richard's face that Jack was an unexpected visitor.

Jack stalked into the room like a hungry dog.

"Well, I see you're alright then?" Jack said, pushing the door closed behind him.

Richard's brow was furrowed for a moment only. "So, Jack, and how fares Lincolnshire then? Harvest in, stored and safe, your toil at an end, the folk poor but happy?"

"Why would you care? You've never been there." Jack's voice was hard.

"And have little intention of ever being there often, but I see it suits you well. Perhaps you have farming stock in you?" Richard continued in the same light, negligent tone.

"Stop! Not this time. You'll not raise my temper again." Jack buried his anger. Fastening a hand around a chair back, he pulled it from under the table. The growling of wood on stone scored the air between them. Dropping into it, he leant back, feet crossed, arms folded, and observed his brother with an unyielding scrutiny. When he spoke, his words were reasoned, even calm. "Sit down and tell your *elder brother* why you kept me ignorant of the truth?"

Richard, the false smile abandoned, stared at his brother. It took a moment to regain an outward appearance of self-assurance. When he spoke, his voice was taut. "So you've been to the Abbey."

"I have," Jack admitted. For a brief moment, he recognised indecision in Richard's expression, betraying the fact that he was having difficulty deciding how to deal with the situation. Jack felt a satisfaction that, for once, he managed to keep from his face. "Why didn't you tell me?" Jack asked when Richard remained silent.

"A few reasons," Richard replied at last, grey eyes alight with a degree of uncertainty.

"I think it's time you shared those. Don't you?" There was a wine flagon on the table along with a set of fine glass goblets. Jack selected two, filled them in silence, and slid one across the table. "Sit down."

For the first time, Richard obeyed a direct order from his brother and lowered himself into the chair opposite Jack, his eyes never leaving the blue ones that were watching him intently from across the table.

Jack lifted his glass and drained half of it before setting it back quietly on the table. "It steadies the nerves, or so they say."

Jack watched with satisfaction as Richard collected the glass from the table and drank. If Jack had entertained any misgivings about this meeting, they were suddenly gone.

"There is nothing left to hide, Richard. *I know the truth.* I know who I am. And *you* should have told me," Jack stated with an iron directness.

"I know," came the quiet reply, the words heavy with regret.

"Why didn't you? I thought at the start it was because you planned to expose Robert for what he is and take his place. But now I'm not so sure," Jack continued, his temper fully defused by his brother's remorse.

Richard's eyes dropped to the glass in his hands, staring into the depths of the wine. "In the beginning, perhaps I did. I wanted what he had, knew that if I had the proof of it that I could oust him and force William to recognise me as heir."

"But you didn't," Jack pointed out.

Richard shook his head. "I realised after a very short time that it was greed that was driving me. If I took Robert's place, then there was a risk I would become him. He wastes away his life waiting for an old man's death with no idea what he is going to do with his inheritance when he receives it."

"But you're not like that." That Richard compared himself to Robert at all was wholly objectionable to Jack.

"No, and I didn't want to be. And I don't want you to be either." Richard rubbed his fingers across his forehead, his eyes closed for a moment.

"Do you have any idea how much I want to shake you until you break? I set out from the Abbey with a desire to do nothing more than shatter your bones. We are equals and you've never accepted that," Jack said roughly. It was an honest admission, the edge of anger that would have tinged those words until so recently though was absent.

"What stopped you?" Richard asked.

"The lass, Catherine. It's hard to remain in a bad mood in her company, and if my situation is unfortunate, hers is a sight worse," Jack conceded, then added truthfully, "and you are, for once, treating me with a degree of honesty I rarely receive."

"Honesty is a trait I find hard to adhere to, it seems," Richard's voice was filled with a weary resignation.

"Well, honesty is, for the most part, less profitable than dishonesty," Jack cast back the quick reply.

Richard looked up, delighted surprise on his face. "When I hear you quote Plato to me, I know I have lost."

"You've lost nothing," Jack replied. "You have the opportunity to gain a brother, one you don't need to keep at arm's length. Should you want one?"

Richard's eyes flicked to the fireplace, as if considering the offer.

Jack felt his stomach twist - *had he gone too far?*

"Trust must be earned, honesty proved, and loyalty reciprocated." Richard's voice was serious.

An uneasy silence settled between them. Jack broke it. "Was that Plato as well?"

Richard smiled. "No, my own poor words. I should earn your trust, prove my honesty and loyalty."

Jack reached for the wine flagon and blindly filled both glasses, a quantity spilling onto the wood. Raising his glass, he said, "You have already. If you were Robert, I would not be here now."

"There's a truth in that," Richard accepted, taking his own glass into his keeping. After a thoughtful pause, he asked, "So, what are you planning to do now?"

"I was going to ask you that question. You will, I've no doubt, have given this a lot of thought," Jack accepted the change of subject.

"The situation is not an easy one," Richard sat back in his own chair, firelight playing on the glass in his hand. "William is not likely to admit to what he has done, and if Robert finds out who you are, he'll have no choice but to have you killed," Richard stated bluntly. "You might think we are doing well. Burton and Chapel Street are a huge improvement on where we were six months ago, but we are not in a position to pit ourselves against William and Robert. Perhaps in time, but not now. Do not dwell too much on what could have been, Jack."

Jack emptied his glass, studied it for a moment before setting it back on the table and folding his arms. "You have no idea how hard that is."

"I've had a hundredfold opportunities to place myself in your position. Don't you think I've not thought about it as much as well? I couldn't tell you. I didn't want to drive you to William's door. That would have been unfair."

"I can't just ignore this," Jack leaned forward, his hands on the edge of the table, "and you cannot expect me to either."

"I know," a slight smile played on Richard's face. "Trust me, in time, together we will confront them."

Jack nodded, "Alright, in time. I trust you."

Richard looked at the girl Jack had left him with. She had her back against the door and her eyes were filled with a volatile mixture of hatred and fear. Letting out a long breath, he pulled a chair from under the table.

"Come and sit down. There is no need to stand over there. I'll not hurt you." Richard was preparing himself for what was to come: how to answer the expected volley of questions and accusations and the inadequate and unwanted answers he would give.

Catherine dropped, rather heavily, into the offered chair. Richard could see her hands were shaking so fiercely that she dared not take the glass he placed in front of her.

"I am most sorry about the circumstances of your recent life. It was not by my design that you should be here now," Richard said, simply and evenly.

Catherine turned to look at him. Richard saw in the depths of her brown eyes that anger was very soon going to be the triumphant emotion.

"Could you tell me, sir, what happened to my father?" Catherine asked, her voice unsteady.

Richard answered her with a simple statement of fact. "Your father, my lady, appears to be dead and has been since you were placed in the Abbey. His lands and Manor at Assingham have passed to a kinsman, I don't know who. I know only what Jack has just told me. More I will endeavour to find out. You are, in simple terms, believed dead. It was assumed you had perished when the Manor was taken by Northumberland's supporters. Do not doubt me, my dear, for it was I who identified your body as one of those in the courtyard. It seemed a good idea at the time because it meant that no one would set themselves to look for you. The hope was to return you to your father unharmed. However, circumstances are such that this cannot be."

Richard was sorry for his choice of tableware. He neatly side-stepped the expensive Italian glass as it was hurled at him, smashing against the stone wall behind him, a stain spreading down the stone from its ruby contents.

"You, your family... Judith and Edward... they were our friends. We trusted you."

"Did we not do as friends would have done? We took you to a place of safety away from Assingham." Richard's voice held the edge of a patience tried. For a moment, he considered telling her that he had not had anything to do with her father's death, but the expression on her face told him he would never be believed.

"I do not, nor ever have trusted you," Catherine yelled at him. "I don't want to stay here with you."

"Where exactly will you go? This is London. Do you have friends or family here?"

Catherine answered by avoiding his eyes and mutely shaking her head.

"As I thought. So, I will do what I can. Meanwhile, consider yourself my guest, and do your best not to try my patience any further or you will find yourself on the street." Richard walked past and left her. From the courtyard, he looked back through the window to the room. Catherine was still clearly visible where he had left her, leaning over the table, one hand to her eyes. Sighing deeply, he turned to leave. He would find somewhere for her to lodge and try to contact her family, as he had promised he would.

Then his thoughts turned to Jack. Jack! Damn him. His brother's timing could not have been any worse. He would have to get Dan to make sure the fool did not get himself killed. Jack's words might have sounded reasoned and considered, but Richard was not sure how much he could rely on Jack's newfound restraint, especially if it were introduced to alcohol or argument.

Richard already had an appointment with Sir Peter Carew that evening, and he had no intention of missing it. Jack was going to have to wait.

The meeting had gone on long enough for Richard after only a few minutes had elapsed. It was clear that Sir Peter Carew was a man who thought a lot of himself and he liked the world to know it. Richard felt like he had just been through the longest sermon of his life, the whole time on his knees, and they had yet to talk about God.

By the end of it he knew of Carew's status at court, of his links to Henry VIII's sister, Margaret, through his marriage to his wife, of his estates in Surrey and Devon and of his two houses in London, of the military success of his eldest son and of the cleverness of his other son who ran his own legal firm in the capital. Richard was also sure by the end of the summary that Wyatt had made a bad choice. Anyone who liked to talk as much as Carew was not a man to trust with secrets.

When Carew had finally finished, Richard attempted to instruct him on the methods that ensured the safe transportation of news, of the codes, and how these would, if applied correctly, keep both Carew and the rest of Wyatt's group safe. It was not an easy task, Carew clearly felt that any form of administration was beneath him, and it was only when Richard reminded him of his obligation to Wyatt and the higher cause that they were aspiring to that he finally got Carew to cooperate long enough for him to explain the process of the cipher.

When Richard left an hour later, he was relieved the meeting was over.

In terms of a plan, Wyatt's could only be described as basic at best. That Mary was to have ruined England with her poor choice of husband was not going to be allowed to happen. A suitable candidate for marriage to Elizabeth had been found in Edward Courtenay. With his own royal blood linking him to the throne, it was felt that this reinforced both his and Elizabeth's claim.

Courtenay was part of the English nobility, however, he was also a man of little wit and easily led. Should he marry Elizabeth, he would be a man Parliament and the leading elite could easily bend to their will. He would be a lot more pliable than Philip would ever be, for the son of Charles V, The Holy Roman Emperor, was a man who had been destined to rule and prepared for such a role.

None of Wyatt's supporters were under any allusion as to how the process would play out should Mary have her way. England was wealthy in wood and textiles, its ports and shipyards produced both formidable warships and merchantmen and the temperate climate and fertile fields husbanded high yields of wheat and barley. England was a storehouse to be robbed to supplement The Emperor's European cities, it would be stripped of both produce and gold in the form of taxes to increase the wealth of Spain.

Wyatt's plan pulled together both Catholic and Protestant reformers, all of them united against the threat to England's sovereignty. With the help of Richard's network, there were to be three planned uprisings. Wyatt was to lead the one in the city, but it would be backed by two others, one in the Midlands, and one in the West Country. It was assumed that once it was known that the rebels held the cities in these key areas, then Wyatt's success in the capital would be assured. Wyatt was confident of the support he would draw to their cause from the Londoners, who did not favour the Spanish match.

Richard had put his network at Wyatt's disposal. Carew in the city was to relay the messages by riders when the time came to the outlying cities.

Richard's next destination was Ashridge in Buckinghamshire. It wasn't a quick journey, walking for most of the time next to a horse that the vendor had assured him would butcher well. Over the animal's hollowed back were loosely tied two bundles of possessions and his wares: ribbons, buttons and trinkets.

Elizabeth resided at Ashridge in a state of constant agitation, always on the edge of conspiracy, with Renard trying to find concrete evidence against her. More by luck than by design, she managed to distance herself far enough to evade implication. Although she was currently allowed her freedom, she knew her mail was intercepted, and that spies had infiltrated the ranks of her household. Richard's visits, if discovered, could be enough to orchestrate her downfall.

"My lady," Kate said, "there is a peddler downstairs; cook has made him a meal in the kitchens. Why do you not come and see what he sells? you may enjoy the distraction."

Elizabeth's eyes narrowed. "A peddler you say, Kate?"

"Indeed, my lady," Kate replied. "Today I believe he only has wares for yourself."

"Has he?" Elizabeth's heart raced. "Perhaps you are right, Kate."

Elizabeth went to the coffer at the end of her bed and lifted the lid, retrieving a dozen coins from her dwindling supply. Then she thought better of her rash action and replaced all but one.

The pair made their way to the kitchen where, as Kate had rightly said, there was a peddler seated at the servants' table. Stepping inside, Kate soundlessly closed the door behind them.

"We have but a few moments. I am constantly watched, and they have changed my household so often I know no longer who is spying on me," Elizabeth said hurriedly.

"Well, it appears your sister will wed. The date they imply is next July; Renard, the Spanish Ambassador, will feel a little safer when the Queen is married," Richard supplied.

"Not much. He will feel safe only when my head rolls from the block," Elizabeth said bluntly.

Richard quickly imparted Wyatt's plan for rebellion, eager to get to his more personal news.

"Do you think he may succeed?" Elizabeth enquired quickly, brow furrowed.

"He might. He can raise a fair force to fight with him. He has support of Carew and the Duke of Suffolk, who between them can provide a good number of men to champion your cause. They are planning three simultaneous uprisings against Mary, in the west country, the midlands, and Wyatt himself will lead his men into London. To succeed Wyatt needs to take and hold the City, and that is no mean feat," Richard replied, his voice thoughtful.

"I will make a note then not to be in London at the time," Elizabeth said, smiling.

"Renard, I believe, is changing tack. He cannot seem to persuade the Queen to dispense with you, and so he is now trying to persuade the Church to intervene on his behalf." Richard paused for a mouthful of food. "He has papers, false or true, I do not know, relating to the circumstances of your birth. He hopes to use them to have you removed by Parliament as the rightful heir."

"There is nothing new in those rumours," Elizabeth responded.

"Ah, but what is new is that someone is going to try and use them to press home their cause. This approach may gain sympathy from the Queen. Her hatred of your mother is well known. If Renard is careful, he may be able to make a sufficiently damning case to make Parliament move against you. This will not happen straight away, and times do change. If by then Mary is married to Philip and conceives, Parliament may be persuaded, it has little use for you," Richard said.

"Harsh words," Elizabeth replied. "Is there anything else you can tell me? News is not a commodity to which I have access anymore."

"There is still a move to marry you to Courtenay. It is seen that this would provide England with an English heir if Mary leaves no issue," Richard told her.

"Yes, I know this. And Courtenay? Has he been involved yet in making advances for my hand?" Elizabeth asked.

"No, in fact, he has been especially quiet on the matter. I believe he fears the wind may change and you are too dangerous a lady to be linked with, despite his personal ambition, although I think you will receive a visit to discuss the matter in the near future," Richard advised.

"Courtenay is no man at all. Have you met him?" Elizabeth asked.

Richard smiled. "Confinement in the Tower for most of his life has left him..."

"A complete fool!" Elizabeth finished for him. "The man has no wit and even less intelligence."

"Despite that, they believe you will agree, as it will secure your position. However, should you produce an heir, the crown would miss you out and go to your issue with the Earl as protector," Richard said.

There was a light tap on the kitchen door, Kate's signal that they would not be alone for much longer. Richard produced some coloured ribbons and passed them to Elizabeth.

"He what?" Robert's eyes were wide, and David winced, involuntarily backing a step away from his master.

"Like I said, Sir..." David tried feebly.

"Shut up, man, I heard you. Get out. I want to know where he goes and what he does." David obeyed, eager to no longer be in Robert Fitzwarren's presence.

"What will you do now?" Harry asked stupidly. He was seated by the fire, doublet unbuttoned, streaks of grease gracing his shirt front.

"What can I do? He's bloody ingratiated himself with Mary, a loyal and obedient servant. Not exactly easy to have him killed, is it? No one would have noticed or cared before if one more piece of snivelling filth bled to death. But now my clever brother has Mary's favour and is at court. Would you believe it? She does not know what a viper she has near her!"

"Well maybe a word here or there would help; your father knows Cecil, doesn't he?"

"Don't be bloody stupid. Richard would see that coming." Robert was livid, sure now that his brother was just waiting for the right moment to trade the information he held over him. Damn the man! At court? He could hardly believe it; the shit should be dead by now.

"Apparently, he's there with that bastard he calls his brother. I tell you, Robert, that is one man I wish to see at my feet," Harry prattled.

"Who's with him?" Robert snapped.

"Jack. You remember, he turned on me on Harlsey Moor, stole my bloody horse and felled me from behind just as I was about to..."

"Jack! Harry, stop. Who the hell is Jack?" Robert demanded.

"I told you before." Harry was more than a little put out. "Jack was reared in my father's house, some bastard of your father's. Didn't you know?" Robert shook his head and Harry continued, "Well, as I said, he's with Richard now, and the man has the audacity to call that low-life his brother." Harry's voice droned on, but Robert was no longer listening. The circle had been completed, and it had been completed first by Richard, it seemed. The man, Jack, that Harry spoke of, if he was with Richard, calling him his brother, had to be the one! God damn his father. The child should not have lived. He should have thrown the wretch in the moat.

Chapter Eighteen

Lincolnshire – January 1554

Christmas came and went and was little marked at the Manor in Lincolnshire. A quantity more ale than usual was consumed and Jack lost more than his weekly quota of money at cards, but there was little else to mark the season. Richard had neither been seen nor heard from. Jack had waited at Chapel Street after his brother's disappearance and then had moodily taken himself back to Lincolnshire. There he waited until he could stand it no longer. When the first snows of December finally melted, he made a cold and unpleasant journey back to London, and that was where he had hoped to find Richard. His brother, it seemed, was in London, but no-one appeared to know exactly where.

Elizabeth, as she had told Richard she would, remained at Ashridge in Buckinghamshire, and as predicted, trouble broke soon after Christmas. So soon was it after the festive season that Sir Thomas Wyatt had an unforeseen advantage in his hands. His substantial band marched quickly, its ranks ever increasing, on London. As Richard had foreseen, he had no mean feat ahead of him. To succeed, Wyatt would have to take and hold the city, forcing Mary into submission. Elizabeth was safer than Richard had hoped, for although any rising against Mary would implicate Elizabeth, Wyatt's main cry was "No to the Spanish wedding." It would have been far more dangerous had the cry been "Elizabeth for Queen," a sentiment that luckily remained largely unvoiced behind the more immediate goal of preventing an alliance with Spain.

Richard had received the message in the form of one of Carew's servants who delivered the summons verbally. It breached every rule of Richard's, but he was left with little choice but to obey.

Arriving at Carew's London house on Appleby Street, he was shown into the main house and a servant led him through the dark panelled corridors to the yard at the back. They passed a wooden building Richard supposed must house pigs given the squeals and snuffles that escaped from the slatted walls, then across the cobbled yard to the stable block attached to the house. Carew, it appeared, was in there. The door was opened a moment after the servant's knock. Richard entered, quickly closing the door behind him and taking in the scene.

Carew had risen abruptly from his seat. Another man sat on top of a barrel, his hands lashed behind him with leather straps, his mouth gagged, and a more than capable man sat next to him levelling a knife at his chest.

"Fitzwarren! Thank God you've come." Carew threw his hands to his head and ran them through his untidy hair.

Richard turned, making sure the latch was in place.

"It's all gone wrong. I knew I should never have got involved..." Carew wailed,

Richard cut his words off, his own slicing through the air like steel. "Still your words. Who are these men?"

Richard looked at the pair, jailed and jailor, and it was the man holding the knife who spoke and not his master, Carew.

"I'm Hanwyn, Master Carew's Steward, I caught this man," he stabbed the air with the knife, making the bound man flinch and his eye's bulge. Hanwyn continued with his story. "I found him in the Master's study. He was no match for me sir, and I got him down here and sent for the Master."

Richard looked at the man. He was certainly no match for Hanwyn. A cut above his left eye was leaking blood and his right cheek was swollen and grazed. Thinning sandy hair, in his middle years, and slightly built, he had not stood much chance against Carew's steward.

"Carew, I think we perhaps should continue this discussion between ourselves." There was a warning note in Richard's voice, one Carew chose to ignore.

"Hanwyn is my most trusted man. We can speak before him," Carew said, and then before Richard could stop him he produced from his doublet several folded sheets and threw them on the table. "He's Carter's man. He normally delivers his messages, and we found these on him."

"Christ!" Richard exclaimed, his eyes widening. "You left these where they could be found?"

"I hardly expected a thief in my study, did I?" Carew said defensively. "Remember you yourself said that we'd be safe if we kept to the process, and I did!"

Richard, shaking his head, examined the bound man. "You knew where to find those, didn't you?" Even though he was firmly gagged, his eyes widened and his head shook in denial.

"He knew where they were, and worse, he knew what he was looking for," Richard stated, pausing while his eyes bored into Carew's. "How did he know this?"

Carew paled. "He's Carter's messenger. He'd wait while I penned the replies."

"He waited while you penned the replies," Richard repeated slowly, an unmistakable edge of anger in his voice, "and he'd watch how you did this, and where you kept these?" Richard roughly flipped over the code sheets that lay on the rough wooden table.

The look on Carew's face was answer enough.

"But he's Carter's man, isn't he? Carter already knows what's in them, so why would he get this man to break into my study?" Carew said, confusion clouding his features.

Richard had difficulty containing his temper. "I think that is fairly obvious. He doesn't just work for Carter, this man has another master." Turning to Hanwyn he said, "Un-gag him. We need to find out who he's working for and for how long he's been helping himself to your master's secrets."

It took only a short while, the force used was brutal, and the small man's refusal to speak did not last long. Hanwyn, releasing him from a tight hold, let him drop back onto the top of the barrel, where he sobbed out his confession. He told them he'd been forced to work for another master, forced to break into Carew's house. He begged for clemency, asserted that his very life had been in danger and he'd been given no choice. Eventually, he told them who it was that had coerced him. "Master Prentice, I meet him in the Swan's Neck Tavern off Meek Street."

"And did Master Prentice pay you well for your duplicity?" Richard asked, folding his arms and observing the man coldly.

He shook his head, and Richard's glance towards Hanwyn had the big man's arm back around the captive's neck in a hold that blocked the air from his lungs.

"Please, please..." the man gasped, struggling against the hold, his body writhing from side to side, his hands helplessly still tied behind him.

Hanwyn slackened his grip but did not let go.

"He did pay me. But I still had no choice," the messenger pleaded.

"We are all faced with choices. It seems coin paved the way to disloyal ones in your case," Richard observed, then asked, "how much and how often?"

He spoke freely from then on, telling them of the brief meetings he had with Prentice, of the amounts he had been paid. Any messages he was to deliver first went via Prentice, and any replies were delivered after he had visited the Swan's Neck Tavern. He had a meeting that evening planned at the Tavern when he was supposed to be handing over the papers he had taken from Carew's study.

Richard pressed the heels of his palms into his eyes, then looked at the man seated on the barrel. His words, however, were for Carew. "Well, we are going to need to let him reach his meeting with Prentice."

"What!" Carew blurted, "but you just said..." Richard's raised hand stilled Carew's words.

"He has a meeting planned at the Swan's Neck, if he doesn't keep this meeting then whoever he has been giving this to will know they have been discovered and we will stand no chance of finding out who it is that has been intercepting them. Isn't it obvious?" Richard stated again, his voice sounding weary. "I will take him to the Tavern and find out who Prentice is."

It was Hanwyn who spoke then, "Sir, the Swan's Neck isn't a gentleman's tavern. You'll look out of place. I'm known there. If I go with you, no-one will give you a second look as long as..." Hanwyn let his words trail off.

"I don't look like this?" Richard finished for him.

Half an hour later, Richard, dressed in borrowed clothes, set off with Hanywn and the messenger to The Swan's Neck. The man, when he was released from his leather bindings, was in no doubt as to what they would do to him and agreed readily enough to the plan. They had returned to his keeping some of the stolen papers after Richard had made some neat incisions in the parchment so the overlay could no longer be used as the cipher key.

Richard and Hanwyn took a table together, and the messenger sat a little distance away, nursing a cup of ale. Cold water applied to his face had removed the trails of dried blood and in the gloom of the inn interior, the purple stain on his cheek bone from the beating Hanwyn had given him was hardly noticeable.

While they waited, Richard mused on what he had found out. The amounts of money the messenger had been paid were not insubstantial, and he had been relaying information back to Prentice for two months. Two months. Richard's head spun. That was about the whole time that the planning for Wyatt's rising had been in place. Whoever Prentice was supplying the information to was potentially primed to know exactly what was planned. Despite the precautions with the code, Richard could not discount the fact that it might have been cracked. All the planning, the coordination, the work to rise against Mary had been wrecked by the work of one stupid man, and one greedy one.

Hanwyn's elbow nudged Richard to revive his attention. The man that the messenger was to meet, Prentice, had, it seemed, arrived.

Richard looked at Hanwyn. "When the meeting is over, can I rely on you to follow the messenger and take him back to Carew's again?"

Hanwyn nodded. "Yes sir."

Richard clapped him on the arm. "Good man, let him leave alone, but follow him."

"You can rely on me," Hanwyn said. It was obvious from his tone that he was enjoying this immensely.

Richard observed Prentice without looking at him. He was surprised by the man who met the messenger. He strode in with a proprietary air and sauntered across the room, calling for ale as he went. A large man, too well dressed to be a servant or a labourer, he wore a tight leather jacket that strained over a well fed paunch, knee high leather riding boots, and a dark brown cloak of close spun wool held in place by a large, round silver clasp with a twisted leaf design pinned on his shoulder. Whoever Prentice was, he wasn't afraid of being seen, and he was not a man to hide in the shadows.

When the meeting was over, Prentice remained behind, joined immediately by several others, and it was another two hours before Richard could absent himself from the Swan's Neck and follow Prentice to his destination. He did not have far to go, and the big man was an easy target to follow through streets. They arrived at the informer's eventual destination and Richard found himself reaching out for a wall to steady himself as he watched Prentice admitted through a postern gate and into the confines of Derby's London residence.

Richard felt sick. The wave of nausea flooded through him and threatened to overwhelm him.

Derby! Christ, why did it have to be him?

Derby knew of Wyatt's plan, at least Richard had to suppose he did.

Richard did not have much time to waste. Hanwyn would, he hoped, be back at Carew's now with the messenger, and that was a more immediate problem he needed to deal with.

What to do with the man?

Quickly he made his way back towards Carew's, little of his mind on the journey, most of it on this new and unwanted problem. He had to assume the code had been cracked, or at least part of it. Derby had experts at his disposal, and despite Richard's precautions, he was sure that if they had put enough hours into decoding it then there was very real danger that Derby was fully informed of Wyatt's planned uprising. If he was, then that put Elizabeth in a very real danger. She needed to disassociate herself from Wyatt and from Courtenay.

The more immediate issue, though, was what to do with the messenger. Very little physical pressure had been needed to get him to talk. It had to be assumed that he would buckle equally as easily if asked any searching questions by his master or Prentice.

Returning to Carew's, he was admitted again to the tack room where Hanwyn waited with the messenger. He was sitting back on top of the barrel, though this time his hands were not bound.

That he had been in conversation with Hanwyn and Carew was obvious when Richard opened the door and the pair looked towards him. The messenger had completed his part of the plan, since his confession and subsequent cooperation, they had treated him well. He was obviously hopeful that he was going to walk free from Carew's tack room, maybe even a little optimistic that he could continue to profit from the venture.

"Well done," Richard said, closing the door at his back and sliding the wooden latch into place. "I was able to follow Prentice, not an easy man to miss in a crowd."

He'd walked behind the messenger and lay a hand on his shoulder, squeezing it slightly. If Hanwyn's face had not creased in horror, the man would have had no warning. The knife in Richard's hand would have sliced his throat before he had been aware of the assault. As it was, he twisted violently under the increasing pressure on his shoulder, his eyes seeing the blade coming towards him.

It was neither clean nor quick.

The knife missed its mark and stabbed into the side of his neck. Not a killing blow, missing the arteries and sliding into the corded muscle and tendon encasing his spine. Hanwyn was immobile for a moment only, the man's scream brought him to his senses. Throwing himself on the messenger, he brought the man to his knees and held him fast, pushing a handful of sack cloth into his mouth to stifle his guttural animal shrieks.

Richard, a hand in the man's hair, held his head as still as he could and reapplied the knife, the blade this time stabbing through his throat, the point impaling itself with a thunk in the wood of the barrel beneath him.

It took time. Two of them held him down as his violent struggles lessened.

Hanwyn, his arms wrapped around the dying man, met Richard's eyes. "How long is he going to..."

Richard wrenched the knife hilt sideways, opening a menacing gash in the side of the man's neck and splattering them both. The struggles lessened immediately as soon as the knife had cut through the heart's supply of blood to the brain.

Despite being covered in blood, Hanwyn's expression was one of relief as he felt the body grow limp in his grasp.

"You can let go," Richard said. "He's dead."

Hanwyn did let go then. Removing his arms carefully and slowly from around the leaking body. Looking very much as if he expected the lifeless corpse to turn upon him.

"Why did you kill him?" Carew asked in a hoarse gasp.

Richard regarded him coldly. "I didn't. You did."

"What?" Carew regarded him in confusion.

"Did you want me to release him? At some point or another, he is going to lead someone else back to your door. You let him know too much," Richard replied matter-of-factly.

"What shall we do with him?" wailed Carew. Throughout the man's murder he'd stood in the corner, his back pressed to the wood, and when Richard had pulled the blade through his flesh, he'd vomited and globules of it ran still from his mouth and down the front of his doublet.

"You've got pigs, haven't you?" said Richard, rising from his knees and rubbing his hands down his hose.

"Pigs!" Carew looked at him incredulously.

Richard wiped his blade clean. "Well, you can either try to dispose of his body under cover of darkness when the watch are abroad and after the curfew bell has rung. Or you can feed him to your pigs. Your choice."

Back at the house in Chapel Street, Richard sat with his head in his hands. In front of him, the cipher keys lay on the desk.

What the hell am I going to do?

It had always looked like it was going to be difficult. Thomas Wyatt had, for a moment, held in his hands the promise of change. He'd had the chance to propel Elizabeth onto the political stage, to take her from pawn to Queen. While that was a possibility, Richard knew he'd had no choice but to back him.

The board had, however, changed.

Richard had known from the outset that Wyatt's plan was weakened simply by the complexity of it. The three rebellions were to occur at the same time. In theory, if there were risings in Kent, the Midlands and Suffolk, Parliament would not be able to stop them all and popular support would flood towards the ones not being suppressed and the movement would grow organically.

Wyatt's efforts were going to fail, though if the rebellions outside of London failed to gain the support they needed, if they posed no risk to the status quo, then Parliament would not be moved to divide its forces to suppress them. Parliament, he feared, would now be warned of Wyatt's plans, they might not have the dates but he had to suppose that Derby was aware of the plan, and he was sure that the conspirators were being closely watched.

With a quick movement, Richard pulled all the cipher pages into his hands and balled them, then standing he moved quickly to the fire and fed them to the flames. Watching the paper curl and blacken.

It was now more than likely that the riders dispatched to send the messages to spark off the risings in the Midlands and Suffolk would be intercepted. Richard pulled from his doublet another letter, one he had not consigned to the flames, one detailing Wyatt's plan and the names of some of those complicit in it. Whether he liked the task or not, now he needed to ensure Wyatt's plan failed quickly, for he needed to prevent Elizabeth's name from being linked to the plot.

Shortly after, Richard had called for his horse and was setting it in the direction of Derby's house. When he arrived, he was not kept waiting long. The urgency in his voice had persuaded Derby's staff that they should convey their master's visitor as quickly as possible to the man he wished to see. It was a household where unannounced guests who arrived and left after dark was the norm.

Richard strode confidently into Derby's room, his hand already inside his doublet, he pulled free the letter and held it out for Derby.

Derby's eyes flickered between the folded sheet and Richard's face. "Tell me quickly."

Richard did, and Derby, his mouth pressed into a cold hard line, had nodded solemnly. "We have intercepted riders leaving the city. We have their messages, but the code we could not break. The Duke of Norfolk is to take a government force and ride south to stop his advance, but we don't know if the troops he has will be enough to halt Wyatt."

Richard knew then that Wyatt's plan was doomed. The messages had not made it out of London. There would be no support outside of the city, the risings in the Midlands and Suffolk were going to fail.

Wyatt was on his own.

"He plans to bring his men straight across the Thames near the Tower," Richard supplied at the end of his summary.

"Does he now? We can be prepared. We have men across the City, we can pull them back to the Tower and mass our forces there," Derby said, his hand tugging at his chin, his brow furrowed.

"A map. Do you have a map of the City?" Richard cast his eyes around the littered surfaces in Derby's study.

"A map? Yes, here." A moment later, Derby had shuffled through a pile of papers and produced a wide vellum sheet with the city penned out on either side of the snake that was the Thames. "I had it drawn up outlining the new borough boundaries. Why do you want it?"

Richard traced his finger along the river until he found the point he was looking for. "Here is the bridge near the Tower."

Derby peered closer. "Yes, and the land on our side banks down to them. We can easily defend that side by placing a force here," his finger stabbed the map on the river's south bank, "we can even stop them from crossing the bridge in the first place. If we take a force across, we can block them at Southwark, that way we keep the bridge safe and Her Majesty."

Richard looked up from the map, and his eyes met Derby's. "I agree. What if I told you there was a way to stop them from getting to the north of the river without shedding blood and crossing swords? What if I could free all the men from guarding the bridge and prevent Wyatt from crossing?"

Derby's eyes widened. "I would like to hear it."

The Duke of Norfolk had headed south with a band of soldiers over eight hundred strong to stop Wyatt from bringing his force anywhere near the city. Several of the officers had served under Wyatt in Italy, and that, combined with the sight of four thousand advancing rebels, caused five hundred of Norfolk's government troops to defect.

Wyatt, confident of success, and unaware that the risings in the Midlands and Suffolk had failed, was convinced that there would be two more forces, equal to the one he lead, advancing towards the Capital. He was sure the country would be in chaos with Parliament unable to decide how to react - should they hold the capital? Should they send out troops to quell unrest? Should they divide their forces?

Wyatt's encounter with the government troops furthered his rising confidence that his cause would be successful. Those that had not defected they chased back North towards London. Wyatt was convinced the city would lend its support to him when he arrived.

Wyatt couldn't use outriders when he approached the capital. The troops instead rode unopposed all the way up the Southwark Road towards the bridge that led to the Tower.

"Sir, there are no troops on the bridges." It was one of Wyatt's captains who spoke, having just ridden back from the front of the leading troop.

As he approached the bridge, Wyatt soon saw the truth of the captain's words himself. The City had a sixth sense for unrest, and London had not been taken unawares. The population who lived in the streets leading to the crossings were gone, the streets were empty, and there were no government troops lined up to prevent them from crossing.

"Maybe London is siding with us," the captain sounded excited.

Wyatt, more cautious, motioned for his men to advance, and slowly they made their way towards London Bridge. It was an impressive structure, rising sixty feet above the water line. The bridge was erected on top of a set of piers, and both sides of the crossing were crammed with wooden buildings. Only the central route was cleared for the traffic to make its way from the south to the north of the river.

"The tower is open, look!" Wyatt heard another of his men shout as he pointed towards the bridge.

At the Southwark end of the bridge, a large defensive tower rose, and below it were the double gates that could be sealed shut as part of the city defenses.

Wyatt's eyes narrowed. "Would a fleeing force not have closed the gates against us?"

"London is for us. I think they are open in welcome," his captain stated with confidence.

They rode closer to the derelict bridge, and on through the open gates of the tower. When their horses passed under the tower, it became painfully clear, why there had been no need to close the gates against them.

The central section of the wooden bridge between the two central piers had been ripped up. The defenders had used oxen and chains and rived a twenty-foot hole in the middle of the road. The remaining spurs of wood that jutted from the sides were too narrow to use to get an army across, there was no way to safely to take horses over and the gap was too long to shore up with available materials.

London Bridge, and the crossing, had been defended by fifteen men and two teams of oxen that had been hurriedly herded onto the wooden structure.

From the vantage point on the North side, Derby watched as the whole of Thomas Wyatt's force was brought to a crashing standstill.

Shaking his head in disbelief, he looked at Richard. "You were right. He is turning to take his rabble across Lambeth Moor and cross at the bridge there."

"He has little choice. That's the only way he can get into the city now. His troops will need to come up The Strand, let them. The land there is open and wide, then they will pass down The Fleet and into the city near Blackfriars. Set your men up to block every exit once they are in the streets and beyond St Paul's," Richard supplied.

"We would be better meeting them head on in the open fields near St Clement's Well, after they cross the bridge." Derby objected.

"No, let them enter the city. Let their force press forwards and sense victory, then block the streets. The rear will press the front against your defenders and the streets are so narrow there that there'll be no communication between front and rear. Keep a force of men out of sight near Aldergate and then use them to push Wyatt further into the trap," Richard explained. "They will have nowhere to go. The front and the rear flank will be under attack and if you press the troops forward from Blackfriars, you will crush them, literally."

"Christ man, it's a filthy way to win a campaign," Derby said, although it was clear from the look on his face that it was a plan that offered a degree of certainty that he liked.

"It's not a campaign, is it? It is not even insurrection, it is nothing but a criminal act of treason if it lacks popular support, and Wyatt lacks support. Set your blocks up after St Paul's. That way they will be unaware until they are upon them." There was a bitter edge in his voice.

Wyatt's popular support had been lost when Derby's men had intercepted his messengers. Carew's carelessness had thrown Wyatt to the wolves, and Richard had no doubt that he would soon be torn apart.

Dan heard the noise and moved to the courtyard gate. The streets of London were empty, doors were closed, shutters pulled tight and valuables stashed beneath floors and stairs. The screaming and pounding on the gate continued. Dan slid the small shutter in the gate open and peered out, looking straight into Catherine's wide eyes.

"Let me in!" Catherine shrieked.

Looking past her, he saw the first of the mob rounding the corner at the end of the street. Dan slid the bolts back and opened the postern gate. Catherine tripped on the step, but Dan, eager to close the breach, hauled her through the narrow gap and slammed it shut as Catherine fell on her knees in the courtyard.

"Arms!" Dan raised the alarm. Grabbing the girl's arm, he pulled her to her feet, propelling her towards the house.

"I didn't know they were so close." Catherine wailed, and ran up the steps straight into Jack who, running to obey Dan's orders, was still buckling on his sword belt and not looking where he was going.

"Jack, take her in and look after her; they are upon us," Dan yelled. The noise was increasing behind him.

"Come on." Jack took her arm, pulling her into the house and heeling the door closed behind him. They ran down the hall and then through a low-arched stone doorway, twisting down a set of narrow steps to emerge in the cellar. A door in the corner took them back to the same level as the house and they emerged in the stables.

"We can take horses from here and get out of London if we need to." Jack peered through the slatted stable wall to see what was happening outside. All seemed quiet. "I thought I'd seen the last of you," he said, moving quickly to the other side of the stable to peer again through the slits.

Dan burst through the door. "Get her out, Jack. They are through the gate and I'm not losing good men to that rabble; we're going to pull back. Go," he ordered, disappearing.

"Bloody hell!" Jack saddled two horses in record time. "Here, take the reins. When I open the gate ride..."

Catherine struggled to clamber into the saddle.

"Christ! Are you sent to kill us both? Come on, get up." Jack threw her up into the saddle and they sped from the stable and into the still empty streets behind the house.

Jack pulled the horses up when they were outside the city. Catherine sat shivering on top of the lathered horse.

"I didn't know what to do. It all happened so quickly. I didn't know... and then I saw them coming 'round the corner..." Catherine wailed.

"Slow down, lass. We will worry about the circumstances of our meeting later. Right now, we are going to concentrate on getting somewhere a little safer and a lot warmer." Jack's mind raced as he tried to think of where to move from here. They were on the north road and there would be a good chance of running into more of the rabble making their way to London if they stayed on this route. Allowing the horses a few minutes to recover, they continued their journey cross-country.

The Queen continued to receive information as soon as it became available and spent the rest of the time in her private chapel, variously pacing, wringing her hands, and praying to the Lady.

"What news?"

Three armed men followed Thomas Howard, Duke of Norfolk, into the hall. He knelt before the Queen.

"They have moved to cross the river at Richmond, Your Majesty. We have troops deployed across the city to stop his advance."

"Praise Mary," the Queen said, kissing her rosary cross.

"The day will be ours, your Majesty. They are poorly equipped and badly organised. Wyatt's band is chiefly composed of beggars, thieves and vagabonds. They will be more concerned with looting than championing his cause. When they sense the full danger they are in, or have filled their packs, they'll leave and we shall chase them down," Norfolk stated flatly, any shame he felt about leading a troop of men that had defected to the rebels was one he had hastily buried.

"You think they will advance any further?" Mary enquired.

"No. We have made a stand and hold all the central roads; they'll not manage to pass us. The aim," he gestured with his arm, "is to block the main roads, allow them into the edge of the city, and create around them a trap from which they cannot escape."

"And Derby?" Mary pressed.

"He's taken men already and positioned them near Aldergate to close the trap behind them. Within a few hours, your Majesty, we will have Wyatt's men contained."

Seventy miles away from London, the half-sister of Her Most Gracious Majesty was playing cards with Kate at Ashridge.

"I don't know what has happened but sure as the Devil, something's afoot," Kate said, turning over a three of clubs. "Mary's guard was strengthened this morning when another troop of men arrived," she added sotto voce.

"I know. I have seen them myself, and I believe you have already told me five times at least. I should be flattered that they take such pains to secure my whereabouts," Elizabeth said cynically.

"It must be that Wyatt has ridden against the Queen," Kate said. The debate, consisting in the main of wild conjecture as they had no hard facts to go on, was into its third hour. "Think, my lady, he may triumph. Remember, the people oppose Mary, particularly now she plans to marry Philip."

"Richard said he thought Wyatt would fail, and until I hear otherwise, I will trust his judgement. To do anything else will give Renard the final excuse to persuade Mary to have my head," Elizabeth said.

"I would like to be a fly on the wall now in the palace," said Kate maliciously. "I would bet my best dress the old cow is scared to the bone."

Wearing a cuirass and with a red sash tied to his shoulder identifying him as part of the government forces, Richard took control of erecting the block across Cheapside. There was a slight bend in the road, and it was after this that they erected their defenses. It would work better if the advancing men were not forewarned until they were too far down the narrow street to retreat. Any reverse at that point would be impossible, prevented by the press of men behind them.

They'd used a cart, turned onto its side and a line of empty firkins to block the advance. Their makeshift barrier stopped Wyatt's men and the front row, pressed from behind, were forced onto the blades of the defending troops. Within minutes the dead themselves were the blockade, and the men forced forward were crushed into the narrow street, unable to defend themselves, and with no space to draw a sword they were trampled, or if they made it to the front they were hacked down by the men manning the barricades.

The street ran with blood, it poured through the mass of trapped, writhing bodies, and still the men at the rear forced them forwards unaware of what was happening at the front.

Richard wheeled his blade round again in front of him; it was an execution, not a fight. The blade he held ran with blood, it had made it beyond the hilt and his gloved hand was soaked with it.

The fight was over in less than an hour. The dead remained where they had fallen. The rest of Wyatt's supporters, surrounded by Derby's troops, were being herded back from the city where they were going to be secured outside of the city gates. If Wyatt himself was dead, Richard did not know. He had not been among the men who had advanced towards the Tower down Cheapside.

The grass around St Paul's was littered with the immediate aftermath of the fight. The dead and dying laid out next to bodies of horses and abandoned weapons. Walking through them, Richard's eyes fastened on the heavy riveted doors of the church and he made his way into the dark, cold interior.

He made ten steps inside the Cathedral before he groped blindly for the support of the wall and a shaking hand found it. It wasn't enough. He felt the whole force of what he had done course through him like fire, burning his nerves, making his chest tighten and his heart beat painfully.

There was noise inside St Paul's. Feet were running on the ochre floor tiles, men were trying to find sanctuary inside its solid stone walls. He supposed he, too, was trying to find sanctuary as well from the carnage in the streets. A hand leaning heavily on the back of a wood pew, he walked unsteadily from the main aisle towards one of the small chapels on the western side of the church. A gated one offered him the peace he needed, pressing the ironwork open he entered and sank to his knees, his head on the stone bench set in the alcove, his cheek against the cold grey granite, he tried to face what he had done.

Wyatt was either dead or he had been captured, of that there was little doubt. Richard had blocked his entrance to the city, forced him to Blackfriars, and then ensured he was boxed inside an effective trap.

He had stopped him. Did he have the right to stop him?

Wyatt's men were being hunted and butchered like rats in a barn. He'd done that. It had been of his making.

Derby and Norfolk would have held the bridge, taken the fight to Southwark and to Wyatt, of that Richard was sure. What would the outcome have been then? Wyatt had over four thousand supporters, Derby and Norfolk had half that number. Derby had wanted to take the fight to Wyatt. He would have crossed London Bridge, the bridge's narrow roadway would have denied him any kind of quick retreat and then Wyatt would have had him in the trap. If he had pressed his advantage, and Wyatt was an able commander, there was no reason to suppose he would not, then Derby would have found himself cut off from the capital. It would be highly likely his force would have been divided.

Oh God! All in the cause of damned efficiency.

Richard rolled his head sideways and was sick on the tiled floor.

✝

"Hold." Jack slung the reins into Catherine's hands. "Right, we'll stop here tonight. Get yourself down."

Catherine, getting no help to dismount, slithered inelegantly from the saddle and followed Jack to the door. It was dark now, the yard of the inn lit only slightly by the moon.

"Come on, let's get you dry," Jack said as they crossed the inn and ascended the low stairs to a room appointed to them above. Jack sat on the bed and looked closely at her for the first time that day.

"Now, pray sit and tell me what I have done to deserve this. Spare no detail: I am an eager listener," he said, dropping his wet boots on the floor before kneeling to light the fire.

"I was lodging with Christopher Haden and his wife, two streets away from Richard's house on Chapel Street," Catherine supplied.

"Pass me the tinder box. It's in my pack," Jack interrupted, then asked, "Who's Christopher Haden?"

"He used to be a tutor in the Fitzwarren household when Richard was younger and they had kept in touch. I was stopping with him while Richard contacted my family." Catherine flipped open the top of the pack. A quick rummage brought the wooden tinder box to the top, she placed it in his open hand before she continued. "Richard had written to my family, and he was waiting for a reply, but so far I have heard nothing."

"So what brought you to the gates of Richard's house?" Jack asked as the first sparks from the tinder box began to turn to small, bright flames in the hearth.

"There was fighting in the streets. Master Haden had barred all the doors to the house, but then he feared for our safety, and we left the house in the back of a cart driven by two of his servants. We rounded a corner, and the servants saw the armed men running towards them and abandoned us. Master Haden shouted for us to run for our lives, and I found my way to the house in Chapel Street," Catherine explained, wiping the back of her hand across her dripping nose.

"You were lucky Dan let you in," Jack observed as he added several more pieces of wood to the growing fire before rocking back on his heels.

"My thanks are his," Catherine said sincerely.

"Come and sit over here near the fire, lass. You're shivering with cold," Jack said, turning to look at her.

Catherine joined him and sat on the floor next to him.

"So, what are we to do now?" Jack dropped to sit cross legged next to her, his blue eyes meeting her brown ones.

"I don't want to go back to London," Catherine said quickly.

"A return at the moment is not an option. The City is not safe, and it is Richard who has the contacts, not me," Jack said, holding his hands out to let the orange flames warm them. He could take her back to the abbey if she would go, or he could take her to the Lincolnshire Manor. Although he did not really want the responsibility for her, and he couldn't see Richard being pleased that he had taken her there, either. It was not a place for a woman. Since he had turned Guy off the place was little more than a soldier's barracks. Jack could well imagine the ribald comments and attention that she would attract. "Where would you wish to go, Catherine?" Jack asked, hopeful that she would have a destination in mind, and that his responsibility for her would be a short one.

"I don't know," she simply replied as she took one of the logs from the stack near the fire and added it to the pyre. "My family still believes me dead. And who wants me resurrecting from the grave to get in the way of a nice inheritance?"

Her tone told him that Catherine was aware now of the seriousness of her situation, and he grimly accepted her words. "Wait here, let me see if I can find some food," Jack pushed himself up from the floor and left her alone.

She was still seated where he had left her when he returned carrying a tray laden with beer, bread, cut meat, cheese, hot pottage – Jack was hungry, he never liked to deal with a problem on an empty stomach.

Catherine helped herself to food from the tray, and they sat in silence while Jack ate enough to stop his stomach from complaining.

"You are not much help. Here..." Jack leant across and refilled her cup with beer.

Catherine set the full cup down on the floor next to her. "Richard told me you were a knight. Surely you must know somewhere I could lodge as a guest..." Catherine waved a hand in the air and did not continue.

Jack choked on his beer.

"What?" Catherine blurted, annoyed.

Jack was still laughing loudly.

"Tell me!" Catherine demanded.

Jack's body was still shaking with mirth, tears in his eyes. He couldn't answer her.

"Tell me what I said that is so funny?" Catherine wasn't amused.

"Do I look like a knight?" Jack finally managed, wiping tears of laughter from his eyes.

Catherine did not reply.

More seriously, he said, "Tell me what you see, lady?"

"I see..." she paused. "This is stupid. What are you trying to say? Just tell me, what was it I said that you found so funny?"

Jack, still smiling, refilled his empty cup. "I'm no knight. I am landless, penniless and nobody's heir. I am quite simply no one."

"That sounds like someone feeling pity for themselves. I am well acquainted with that feeling," Catherine replied, bitingly.

Jack looked up sharply, about to tell her that she had no idea how it felt, then realised before he spoke that she probably did. "I am Richard's brother," he said simply. It seemed like confession enough.

"Well, I can be forgiven if I had not noted the family resemblance." Catherine was still annoyed. "Go on, I guess there is more to it than that."

"We are a pair, you and I," Jack dropped back on the floor, propped up on one elbow, and observed her levelly. "We have, and yet we have not."

"And what's that supposed to mean? Don't talk in riddles. If you have something to say, speak it. Do not make me guess at the edges of it. I am in no mood for word games," Catherine snapped at him.

Her directness shocked him. "All right, lady, I shall tell you, and perhaps you can tell me what to do."

Catherine listened in silence as Jack told the story he last revealed to Jamie with the addition of the information he had recently received from the Abbess.

"Well, I think that we are, as you say, a pair, and both of us need recompense from one man. I will place myself where you best think I can meet him," Catherine said quietly. "Where will you go?"

Jack didn't answer.

"Where would you go if I were not with you?" Catherine persisted.

"To Richard's manor at Burton," he replied at last, rolling to his back. Jack stared at the ceiling, his eyes unfocused.

"Well, I should wait there for him as well. Send word to Richard that I am safe outside London and request that he continue to try to contact my family," Catherine said simply.

"I cannot take you there," Jack protested, sitting back up quickly.

"Why not?" Catherine said.

"Burton is not a place with pretty rooms and waiting ladies. It's where Richard trains and keeps his men, it's little more than a soldiers' barracks. I could not close my eyes there and guarantee your safety," Jack said, sounding exasperated. Catherine was simply a problem he didn't want.

"Well, it seems to me it doesn't matter where I am. At the moment, no one can guarantee my safety, and I have been coping without the assistance of a waiting lady for quite some time." When he didn't reply, she added, tears springing to her eyes, "Please, I've no-one else to turn to. You are the only person I can trust."

It was a plea Jack knew he could not ignore. "My lady," he said ceremoniously from where he still lay on the floor, his arms spread wide, "I am at your service. Which still, I would like to point out, does not solve our present problem."

"Take me to Burton. You know the way and you are known there. Surely if you are with me, I can come to no harm," Catherine continued persuasively.

Jack grunted. "It's only a day's ride, I suppose."

Catherine smiled at him, relief plain on her face. "Thank you, thank you."

"You might not be thanking me after you have been there for a few days," Jack said, returning to gaze at the dark-beamed ceiling in the room. The beginnings of an idea were starting to form of how he could take her to Burton and keep the men's hands and cruel words from her, he certainly couldn't watch over her all day. He did feel sorry for her, the girl had not had a good time recently, and in a way he felt partly to blame for her circumstances.

Turning his head sideways he caught her looking at the sword that he had unbuckled and now lay on the floor near the fire. Catherine smiled at him. "That could be a knight's sword. My father has one he let me hold sometimes, but this part here," Catherine reached over and placed a finger on the cold steel, "was different."

"The pommel," supplied Jack, rolling onto one side to better observe her, "how was it different?"

"It was just round, and plain, this is beautifully engraved." Catherine peered closer, "There is a dragon carved into the metal, look, here's its head and its body twists round this side and the tail winds right the way down to the hilt."

The sword was Jack's most prized possession, and he was pleased. "Turn it over, and on the reverse you can see the wings and the dragon's eyes are rubies. It was, by all accounts, my father's." He paused, staring at it. "Richard gave it to me."

Catherine met his eyes, her smiled genuine, "What does the Latin say? It's too dark for me to read it properly."

"Let them hate so long as they fear," Jack stated, then added, "it is the family motto."

Catherine laughed then, "Well that's very fitting for your brother, I can imagine there are plenty that hate him."

Jack grinned back. "You've no idea, and he doesn't give a damn.

When they arrived at Burton, the gates were closed, but the two men on guard duty hurriedly moved to open them to admit Jack and Catherine. The hour was late, and apart from those on watch they saw no-one else in the enclosed yard. Jack unbuckled his pack from his horse and handed both the horses to one of the men who had opened the gate.

A guiding hand on Catherine's elbow he led her to the main door of the tower. There was a route to the third floor that avoided the hall, opening the heavy wooden main door he hurried her up the wide spiral stairs. As they passed the door that opened onto the hall the sound of the company's voices met their ears. They passed another door leading to the rooms and when they reached the next one Jack pressed it open, relieved that they had made it without encountering any of the men.

Behind the door was a wide corridor with two doors off it on the left-hand side and ahead of him another door that led to his room. Letting go of Catherine's arm

Jack produced the key he needed and applied it to the lock, a moment later they were both in the dark room that Jack had taken as his own at Burton.

The wooden shutters were open, but the moonlight provided little light. Catherine stood alone in the middle of the room while Jack busied himself lighting an oil lamp that sat near the fireplace.

"Right lass, there's a tinderbox on there, get the fire lit. I need to go and see the men, let them know I'm back." Crossing the room he used the key again to lock the door they had entered by, though in the opposite corner was another, smaller door. "Drop the latch on this one after I've gone, I'll not be long."

Before Catherine could complain, he'd gone. The smaller door lead to a tight spiral staircase set into Burton's thick walls, and it led all the way down to the main hall.

Jack listened for a moment before he pressed open the door and stepped into the hall. Rush lights lit the interior, and the fire, well fuelled, adding its own light. Cold air spilled into the room from the stairwell and Mat, seated with several of the other men near the fire, sensing the draught, turned.

"Jack! When did you get back?" Mat said loudly seeing him in the doorway.

"Just now," Jack replied, pushing the door closed behind him. He crossed the room to where a barrel sat on a trestle table, selected one of the pewter cups sitting next to it and slopped the contents from the cup onto the rushes. He filled the cup from the barrel, pulling the bung away and tipping the wooden cask forwards. "I hope there is more than just this left."

"There's more, down in the cellar," Mat said, then asked, "how was London? We've heard about Wyatt, news came in earlier today from Lincoln."

"Come and join me Mat," Jack had dropped into a chair on the dais, away from the main group of men.

Mat reluctantly cast in his hand of cards and, collecting his ale cup, moved to join Jack.

Mat was one of the few other men, apart from Dan, who had seen Catherine at Hazeldene, and Jack needed to talk to him before he became aware that the girl was here.

"I've something I need to talk to you about," Jack said, his voice serious.

Mat's brow furrowed, leaning closer he said, "Go on."

"You know the girl I helped get away from Assingham?" Jack asked, his voice quiet.

"Yes, the de Bernay lass," Mat said, sounding puzzled.

"Don't ask why, the story is too long to tell, but she's here," Jack said quickly.

"What for?" Mat asked. "Did the Master send her here?"

"There was fighting in the streets in London, it wasn't safe to leave her," Jack answered.

"The fighting was bad then?" Mat took a large swig of ale. "There were riders came into Lincoln today, so we heard about the rising."

"I had no choice but to bring her with me," Jack said, his voice resigned.

"What's she like?" asked Mat, a lascivious grin on his face.

"You can take that look off your face for a start," Jack's voice was low and serious.

"Oh, come on, a woman here? The lads aren't likely to leave her be are they?"

"She's little more than a child, Mat, but yes, she's going to be trouble," Jack replied morosely.

Mat grinned. "You should get on well together, having something in common."

Jack ignored Mat's comment. "So guess who's got the bloody job of making sure she stays in one piece?"

"Good luck to you," Mat laughed, "the only women round here are Tilly McDrew in the kitchen and she must be ninety and her niece Ada whose soft in the head and has a face that looks like a goat's arse."

Jack leant across the table. "No, it will be a joint effort, Mat. Pass the word that she's too precious for horseplay. Richard will start lopping limbs off if it's otherwise."

"And how do you propose I do that?" Mat enquired, his eyes opened wide.

"Tell them she's Richard's niece..." A smile suddenly crossed Jack's face, "No... tell them she's his sister; that'll stop anyone going near her." It was partly Richard's fault that her life was in ruins, so she might as well join the family properly.

"His sister!" Mat laughed, snorting beer back into his cup. "I'd like to see Master's face when he finds out about this. But I agree; it'll stop the lads going within spitting distance of her. His sister..." Mat continued to chuckle.

Jack changed the subject. "Anything happened while I've been away that I need to know about?"

Mat shook his head. "Nothing. Marc was in Lincoln yesterday so we heard about the rising against Mary. What's happened in London? Is it true that the rebellion has been put down?"

"You probably know more than me, there was fighting in the streets, and I left and brought the girl north."

"And the Master, where's he?"

"In the thick of it, would that be a fair bet?" Jack growled.

Elizabeth's household was preparing to move again. It was a regular occurrence and the packing arrangements were well practised, the disruption just part of everyday life.

She had received a correspondence, delayed somewhat, from Wyatt who had urged her to move to the more fortifiable residence at Donnington. His messenger, the Earl of Bedford's son, had arrived with a flourish born of his unwavering belief that Wyatt would triumph over Mary, believing he was bringing Elizabeth the first news of her succession.

Elizabeth had greeted him less than enthusiastically, dismayed by this direct contact, damning Wyatt for his carelessness. Her sense of foreboding had been proved right when a letter arrived, summoning her to Mary's court. It seemed that, as Elizabeth had feared, Mary was well aware of the communication Bedford's son had delivered.

Elizabeth had taken to her bed, convinced at last that she was undone. Wyatt had unwittingly linked her solidly to the uprising. She was convinced Mary would condemn her to the Tower and shortly after take her head. Kate could not shake Elizabeth's melancholy and urged her to go to London and state her innocence before Mary. To do otherwise was to confirm her guilt; it was her only chance. Elizabeth refused and lay in bed succumbing to a severe depression. She remained in bed and pleaded illness as her reason for ignoring the summons, which had arrived from the Privy Council on 29th January.

"Please, Elizabeth, you have ignored them for long enough. They will not tolerate it much longer. Ride to London and plead your case with Mary," Kate begged; she was beside herself now.

"I daren't," Elizabeth wailed from beneath the bed sheets. "I wish I had advisors to tell me how to act."

"We have waited long enough; we must make our own moves. By staying here you are just playing into the Council's hand and confirming your guilt." Kate was close to tears brought on by days of fruitless reasoning, cajoling, threatening and arguing. She had slept little since the summons to court. Leaving the princess, she made her way to the kitchen and found Alice running to meet her, skirts held high and a look of terror on her face.

"Alice! Slow down. What news?" Kate said taking the girl's shoulders.

"A delegation from the Queen, my lady, to see Mistress Elizabeth. They have just ridden in. Lord Effingham is with them and they demand an audience."

Kate, too weary for hysterics herself, squared her shoulders and sighed. "I will see them, Alice. Go to the kitchen and make sure Cook is aware of our new guests." Alice turned to obey. "And, Alice, find out how much wine we have left. I intend to serve a quantity to our guests tonight."

Kate rose from her curtsey. Lord Effingham came forward from the delegation, all still standing in their travelling clothes in the hall. "I insist on seeing my niece," he said without pleasantries.

"She is greatly unwell, my lord, and has been in bed for two weeks," Kate said, eyes downcast: the picture of obedience.

"Go and see your lady and tell her that the time for excuses is long past. I demand an audience. Tell her if she will not see me I will personally have the door to her bedchamber broken down," Lord Effingham said.

Kate bobbed a departing curtsey. "I will go and see how she fares, my lord."

"My God, they've come to convey me to the Tower." Elizabeth's face was stricken.

Kate was taking no more of Elizabeth's excuses and bullied Elizabeth to dress. "I have ordered wine for your guests, told them you have just woken and will see them presently. You will apologise for your delay and insist they stay at Ashridge as your honoured guests. Have strength, Elizabeth. Take courage; all will be well. Your illness was a little convenient following on so soon after Wyatt's failure and suspicions have been roused. You must play your part well, lady," Kate said. "You can do it."

Elizabeth, finally forced into a corner, came out fighting. She did indeed play her part with brilliance. Lord Effingham, on leaving his audience with her, announced to his son that he believed Elizabeth would remain a thorn in Mary's side for not much longer at all. A messenger was dispatched to London and Mary, stating that the princess was indeed in ill health, and perhaps even mortally so.

Elizabeth had turned the tables brilliantly on Effingham. After their second meeting, he conceded that she was too ill to travel and said she should remain at Ashridge until more fully recovered. Elizabeth insisted that she must go to London and see Mary. She told him it was her dearest wish, punctuated with so much coughing that Lord Effingham had backed away from the bed. He was convinced she wished to make her peace with Mary and that this could be her dying wish.

Elizabeth smiled widely when he was gone, feeling she had managed to reassert a small degree of control over the situation. While she remained at death's door, preparations for her departure took three days to complete and the journey to London, a scant thirty miles, took a further eleven, so slowly did they have to travel. Of her illness, there was no doubt. Following two more reports from Effingham, there was a feeling that Elizabeth was not long for this mortal world. Mary, devout and pious, convinced herself that Elizabeth must be afforded a final opportunity to save her soul and sent a priest to accompany her on her journey. Elizabeth believed her ploy would save her, but a twisted fate would soon force to her to tread the same cold stone steps of The Tower that her mother had walked upon.

Chapter Nineteen

Lincolnshire – January 1554

A letter had been dispatched by a rider to Catherine's lodgings in London, bearing the lady's word that she was safe outside the city. A second brief note was sent to Richard, at Jack's insistence, telling him that she awaited news from him at Burton. Meanwhile, Catherine remained within Jack's rooms, reading what books there were, occasionally playing chess and arguing.

Convinced that Richard would send for her as soon as the city was safe, Jack forbade her to leave the rooms, having reservations about Catherine's continued security. There was, in fact, little else to do; the weather was foul. Gales hugged the manor for a week and rain tried to penetrate every room, and in some places it had a good degree of success.

Jack found Catherine seated on the floor by the fire in his room, legs drawn up and chin on her knees.

"I hope this is good news," he announced, holding out the parchment that had just arrived from London, the handwriting on the outside unmistakably Richard's.

"So do I. Another week in here and I shall go mad. My chess has improved though." Catherine tore the seal open without looking up.

"That wouldn't have taken much, you've gone from terrible to just bad," Jack hovered expectantly, trying to read the words over Catherine's shoulder, hoping that very soon he would be rid of his responsibility.

The note was a brief one from Richard, he bid her to remain where she was until he sent for her. There was a PostScript for Jack, telling him in no uncertain terms what he thought of his actions in taking Catherine to Burton.

"Come on, what does it say?" Jack said impatiently.

Catherine looked sheepishly up at him, holding out the letter for him to take, "It appears your brother likes us not at all on our own and combined, well..."

Jack took the letter and read for himself. "What!" he exclaimed, looking down at her accusingly. "You said he would send for you! Sweet Mary, I knew coming here was a fool's idea." Angry he cast the letter towards her and ran his hands through his untidy hair.

"I thought he would. You know him better than I do. Don't lay the blame on me," Catherine replied angrily, standing to face him, her hands on her hips. "Do you think I want to spend any longer locked in here?"

"What the hell am I going to do now? Richard in a bad mood is not good. I told you he would object to you coming here," Jack complained, more to himself than to the girl in the room.

Robert tapped his fingers thoughtfully on the edge of the desk. This was news indeed, but how to use it? He could not confront Richard; if he did that he risked being undone. No, it had to be someone else. But how? Richard, he now knew, had been seen visiting Elizabeth's house twice. He knew about the time Richard had spent at Thomas Seymour's house, and how he had taken the blame for that man's assault on the young princess. That Richard had kept in touch with Elizabeth surprised him a little, but the reasons for his actions could be none other than his brother's own treasonous intentions. All he had to do was prove it, and prove it to the right man. Harry had been right, his father did know Cecil, but that was of little help, his father was becoming useless as his invalidity increased. He also had a secret worry that his father, if he saw his younger son's success, may revel in it to Robert's detriment.

That left Renard, the Spanish Ambassador. Robert did not know the man, but it was clear from what he had heard that he was pushing hard for Mary to consign her sister to the block. Others, like Gardiner, were still erring on the side of caution, arguing for the marriage of Elizabeth to Courtenay. Robert cared little, but wondered if Renard would be interested in a man, professed as loyal to the crown and to Mary, who sought out Elizabeth's company.

Jack's bad temper continued, during which time he avoided Catherine's company. This wasn't difficult as Catherine remained confined in the room he had appointed to her. If she thought his moodiness was solely directed at her, she was wrong: Jack's thoughts were on his family. While he accepted the truth of Richard's arguments that his father would want little do with him, and that there was a real danger from Robert, he could not help but dwell upon what could have been. It would have been such a simple thing for his father to correct. Why hadn't he? Why had he left Jack to struggle through life? Was there a chance that he would recognise him as his son now? Or was it, as Richard maintained, too late?

Since Framlingham, some seven months ago, they had met only once. Thereafter, Jack was sure Richard had made efforts to avoid another meeting.

Jack stood now in the open doorway of the room Catherine occupied.

"So, have you recovered your humour then?" She spoke from where she sat on the floor, idly turning a bishop in her hands from the chess set.

Jack moved in and closed the door. "My present problem is you, sweet lady." Jack eyed her critically. He was sure no one would believe there was a woman's body beneath the clothes she wore; in fact he was not entirely sure there was. The appearance was a gangly youth whose limbs had not yet filled out, and a good covering of grime had removed any polish there might have been.

"It appears we are most wholly stuck with each other until I hear otherwise. However, you cannot stay up here any longer."

"I tried to tell you that before," Catherine replied a little petulantly.

"I know. The persuasion, however, for my change of mind has come from elsewhere." Jack smiled. "You are ruining my reputation as a rogue and a womaniser."

"How?" Catherine was not following his reasoning.

"It's thought I am keeping you up here for my own lewd pleasure." Jack grinned as he saw revulsion on her face.

Catherine said nothing.

"Oh don't look so struck." Jack moved to sit opposite her. "I am, as it happens, teasing you, which is nothing compared to what those beggars down there will do to you. However, they believe that you are Richard's sister, and you can be fairly sure fear of him will keep their hands off you."

"Sister! Is that the best you could come up with?" Catherine looked horrified.

"Welcome to the family," Jack said, smiling evilly.

"And you are only fairly sure that will keep me safe?" Catherine asked, real concern in her voice.

Jack laughed. "How fast can you run?"

Elizabeth's fears were finally quietened when she was installed with her household at Whitehall. However, she resided there under heavy guard. "A precaution for her safety," Lord Effingham had said lightly. Mary's plans to wed were now taking shape; Philip had arrived in England and the wedding was scheduled for July. The Queen was, on the advice of her council, taking great pains in the time available to finally quash all traces of the rebellion. Wyatt was in the Tower and as yet had not implicated Elizabeth in his plotting. Courtenay, as Richard had predicted, was also residing there; Wyatt had obviously felt he should not share his final months alone. His implication of Courtenay frightened her yet further. She knew well that the means existed within the confines of the Tower to extract any convenient confession. Elizabeth waited for the moment when he would break and sign the document that would include her as a co-conspirator in the plot to overthrow Mary. The Council, not finished with Wyatt, had yet to examine Elizabeth for her version of events. She knew their summons would indicate that Wyatt had finally been forced to make a confession. There was nothing to do but wait.

"She can't play!" Mat announced loudly as Jack and Catherine joined him at the table in the hall where a card game was about to start.

Catherine took an automatic step backwards, but her retreat was halted by Jack's firm hand on her arm.

"Sit down next to Martin," Jack instructed. Martin obligingly made space and Catherine slid into the space next to him, her eyes nervously flicking between Jack and Mat.

"She can't play!" Mat said again, his voice louder this time. "It's against the law."

Jack glowered at Mat. There was a brown ale jug in the middle of the table, Jack picked it up and put it down in front of Catherine, his eyes holding hers. "There's a barrel in the corner over there, fill that and then make sure Mat's cup, and everyone else's is kept topped up all night." Then returning his attention to Mat, he asked brusquely, "Happy now?"

"It's still bad luck," grumbled Mat.

Jack produced a handful of coins and put them down with a loud chink on the table, Mat's face split into a wide grin at the sight of them. "Now I'm happy," he announced. A few minutes later the cards were spinning across the table and in the dim light from the fire and the rush lights the card game ran on for hours. Catherine didn't see the end of it, her head pillowed on her arms she fell asleep on the table, one hand still linked through the handle of the jug.

Martin, fearing the jug would be tipped over by the sleeping girl, pulled it from her grasp, and Catherine woke with a start.

"Go to bed, lass," Jack said as she raised her head, his eyes on his latest hand. He didn't pay her much attention as she rose and headed for the small door in the corner of the hall leading to the two floors above them.

Jack lost again. Casting his cards on the table, he pressed his palms to the wood and rose. "I'm not playing another hand in the dark, the fire's burnt down and I can hardly see what cards I hold."

Mat was grinning as he raked his winnings towards himself. "Ah well, you can try to win these back from me tomorrow night if you like."

"More like tonight," Jack said quietly as he made his way towards the door Catherine had used.

The stairwell was nearly black, the small windows let in a little moonlight but, not enough to see the steps clearly. They were even, and Jack, one hand on the stone newel post in the centre made his way up them steadily.

The first floor up had the room where the books of account were kept, where a small chapel still existed and there were two rooms that had been adopted by Dan and Mat as the more senior men with the troop. About to pass the doorway he paused, beyond it he could clearly hear the sound of feet scuffling on the wooden floor. Jack was about to take one more step upwards when the unmistakable sound of a woman's cry came through the door.

Jack didn't even feel for the latch on the door in the dark, a shoulder against it and he was through in a moment, the wood swinging back and slamming noisily into the wall on the other side. The room he was in was Dan's, moonlight spilled in from the two open shuttered windows, and in the opposite corner of the room was another door. Crossing the room in three quick steps he yanked it open, beyond in the corridor he found Catherine, on her knees, and behind her, one hand wound in her hair and another about to land a blow, was Alan.

"Let her go," Jack growled.

Alan straightened immediately at the sound of Jack's voice. Catherine, his hands still caught in her hair, screamed as she was pulled backward. Alan untangled his hand and levelled a boot towards the girls back, kicking her forwards. She fell sprawled on the floor screaming between them. Alan headed along the short corridor and towards the wide stone steps that led back down to the hall and then to the yard. Jack jumped over the girl and was about to take the first step down in pursuit of Alan when the noise of Catherine's sobbing stopped him.

Cursing under his breath he let Alan go, and turned back to the girl who was still laid on the floor. "Are you hurt? What did he do?" Jack was on his knees on the floor next to her in a moment.

"I'm alright," Catherine sobbed.

"Come on, up you get." Jack had a hand under her arm and pulled her quickly to her feet. He couldn't leave her in Dan's room, it didn't lock. The room with the books of account did, but he didn't have the key. Jack realised he'd no choice but to lose valuable time and take her up another flight of stairs to the room she used there and lock her in.

"I'll be back soon, give me the key." Jack said quickly as he opened the door to Catherine's room and deposited her inside. Quickly she passed him the key, Jack pushed the door closed and locked it before running down the corridor taking the stone spiral steps two at a time. As he passed the hall, his shouts brought the card players tumbling out after him and in a moment they were all in the yard. The gate stood open, and the confused form of Froggy Tate was standing in the middle staring at them all.

"Where's Alan?" Jack demanded.

"He said he'd an urgent message to take to the Master, I helped him saddle a horse, and he's just left," Froggy provided.

"Which route did he take?" Jack shouted, heading towards the stables.

"I didn't look," Froggy replied, "the Lincoln road I expect."

"Martin, Marc, you are with me," Jack ordered.

The men exchanged uncomprehending glances but moved to obey and soon three more horses thundered through the open gateway.

They returned when the first light of dawn was breaking over the low fields. Whatever direction Alan had taken had not been the one they had chosen, and after two hours of pointless pursuit it became obvious that they had lost their quarry.

Jack, exhausted, unlocked the door to Catherine's room. She was asleep on the bed, dressed, her face red and it was obvious what she had spent the night crying. Her eyes opened when she heard Jack opening the door.

Jack leaning against the door frame smiled and shook his head. "At least one of us got some sleep!"

"Did you find him?" Catherine asked, her voice quiet.

"No," Jack shook his head. "Come on, I'm going to the kitchen, and you can tell me what happened while I have something to eat. Tilly is about to take some bread out of the ovens, chasing Alan half way to London has made me hungry." Jack extended his hand towards her and Catherine, sniffing loudly, took it and he led her down to the lowest floor where the kitchen was located.

Catherine sat opposite Jack in silence while he gave his undivided attention to the food placed before him. Half a loaf of warm bread, cheese and ham slices disappeared before he raised his eyes to look at her.

"Tell me then, what happened?" Jack asked before he folded another slice of pink meat into his mouth.

Catherine sniffed. "I was going up the stairs when Alan opened the door to Dan's room and pulled me in, I think he wanted to..."

"Did he say anything?" Jack pressed, watching her closely.

"No, he threw me on to the bed, I crawled off the other side and got through the door into the corridor near the chapel and that's where you found me," Catherine swallowed hard, her red-rimmed eyes meeting his.

"Alan's a cur. I told Richard to get rid of him." Jack had returned his attention to the platter in front of him.

"Is he gone?" Catherine asked.

"Oh he's gone alright, there's no chance he'll come back here again, not now he knows I'm after his hide," Jack replied, then looking up from his food he added, "I'll have a word with Froggy, he's nice enough, got a daughter of his own somewhere or so he keeps telling me, so if you are not in your room you can keep Froggy or me company."

Catherine nodded. "Thank you."

"Hungry?" Jack asked. Catherine nodded, and he slid his empty platter towards her, grinning. "Me too. Fill that for me while you get yourself something."

At the end of March Dan rode into the manor courtyard, his horse mud-spattered, where he encountered Mat.

"Where's the master then?" Mat asked, taking the reins as Dan dropped from the saddle.

"At court, if you please," Dan replied.

"Too much of the bloody good life! He'll come back fat and with manners," Mat quipped.

"Well manners wouldn't be such a bad thing, would they?" Dan replied absently as he looked around the yard. "Where's Jack? I have a message for him."

"In the yard round back with Catherine," Mat replied as he began to lead Dan's horse towards the stables.

"Catherine! Jesus! Is she still here?" Dan exclaimed.

"She is, and she's a tongue on her like a viper's, wonder where she gets that from?" Mat called back over his shoulder.

Jack was leaning over the fence, a foot on the lower rail, watching as Martin and Marc swung wasters at each other, iron reinforced wooden training blades.

"For the Lord's sake, Martin, I've seen women in the bedroom fight better than you," Jack jibed.

The men round the ring laughed: Martin's face flushed. He was a man whose swordplay was basic and his wit equally so. If there was heavy work to do, it would fall to Martin, his skill at arms was certainly of secondary importance. His eyes narrowed, goaded by the insult he turned on Jack, exposing his back to his opponent. Before he could make a retort Marc had neatly kicked him in the back of the knee, and Martin collapsed into the mud. A moment later Marc, laughing himself, had the wooden point of the blade prodding none too gently into the fallen man's back.

"You bastard!" Martin cursed, twisting his head to observe Jack from where he lay. "That was your fault!"

"The lesson is, do not get distracted, and do not lose your temper." Jack grinned as Marc pulled Martin from the mud. "Richard has yelled far worse than that at me over the years," he said to himself.

"Mat said I'd find you here," Dan said, coming to stand next to Jack.

"Dan! It's good to see you. Any news from London?" Jack smiled broadly at the big man coming towards him.

"Master's still there. I don't know what he is up to and I don't want to know. Wyatt's in the Tower and not long for this world. Mary's got Elizabeth under armed guard at Whitehall and my money says she'll not be long behind Wyatt." Dan pushed himself away from the fence to look past Jack at the girl that stood to his left. His head close to Jack's he said quietly, and with some passion, "Have you lost your bloody mind? What's she doing here? You must be mad bringing a woman here."

"Not mad, Dan. Believe me, I had no choice." Jack looked around him; there were too many about now. "I will tell you later, now hush."

"You still look a mite too clean over there, Jack. Get in here." It was Martin, still mad at Jack, and covered in mud.

"You've had one good lesson for today; are you sure you want a second?" Jack said lightly, his blue eyes bright with amusement.

"You'll not be giving me any lessons! Get in here. I'll show the lassie there what you are really like," Martin gestured at Catherine. "With your fancy clothes and your fine manners, you're no man, that's for sure."

"It does look like you've annoyed Martin," Dan said, then added, "Mind you, he has a point. You are starting to look a little too well fed and too well dressed to be standing around tilt yards."

"Angering Martin is hardly difficult," Jack scoffed loudly enough for Martin to hear, "teaching him some skills in the tilt yard, on the other hand, is a task I am not equal to."

"I heard that," Martin growled from the other side of the fence.

"You were meant to, you dolt," Jack shot back.

Martin's face, red already with anger, deepened in hue as his brain acknowledged the insult.

"Go on, teach him a lesson. I could do with a laugh," Dan said quietly and grinned.

With a flourish, Jack unwound his cloak from his shoulders and dumped it in Catherine's arms. "Hold that, and stay with Dan." Agilely vaulting the fence, he turned his attention to the muddy Martin.

Martin grinned back at him. "You're not going to forget this, Jack." He had in his hand one of the wooden wasters, with their iron cores they carried the same weight as a real blade and were capable of breaking bones if not cutting flesh.

Jack had in his hand another of the training blades that had been propped against the fence post. Hefting it in his hand he gauged the weight.

"Come on, man," Martin said, annoyance and impatience in his voice.

Jack had not made any move. He stood, weight on one foot, sword pointed down, watching Martin and smiling.

"I'm ready whenever you want to start," Jack said idly.

"Go on, Martin, flatten him," Marc urged from the sidelines.

Catherine had moved up to stand next to Dan, Jack's cloak still bundled in her arms.

"So how are you, Catherine?" Dan asked, his eyes still on the players in the ring.

"Very well thank you," Catherine replied quietly, her eyes also on Jack and Martin.

"It's getting dark. Get on with it or we'll be here all night," Dan called over loudly to Martin.

Martin finally made his move. Stepping forward he swung the wooden edge towards Jack, who adeptly shifted his weight to his other foot, side-stepping the swing. The wood whistled menacingly but harmlessly through the air inches from his ear.

Martin swore. "Fancy footwork will not help you." He swung again and this time Jack's blade engaged. Catherine watched, hardly breathing. The venom in Martin's strokes looked too real for her liking. Jack continued to deftly parry Martin's advances but made no attack of his own.

"You bloody milksop, have you no balls?" Martin jibed as his attack continued.

"I think," said Jack lightly, "I have had enough of your insults."

The speed of Jack's next moves was not one Martin was prepared for. In two steps and four lightning-fast blows that were heard but not seen, Jack's erstwhile assailant stood disarmed, with a sword-point at his throat. He moved backward as Jack continued to walk towards him. Jack grinned and lowered his weapon, turning back to Dan and Catherine.

Martin, obviously not finished, decided on wrestling as his next tack, so determined was he to get Jack on the ground. He lunged. Jack caught his arm around his neck and deposited him with a rib-jarring impact in the mud in front of him. "Lesson two: don't be so bloody predictable," Jack said from where he stood over Martin.

"One of these days they'll have you, by foul means or fair," Dan said, laughing from the side-lines.

"You wanted to see me?" Jack looked around the church interior, it was the first time he had visited Jamie's stone church in the village, and the priest, now in his vestments, looked wholly different to the one he had spoken to in the fields.

"I did, come with me lad," Jamie who had been stood near the font, headed towards a door in the wall behind the altar.

Jack, given no choice, followed him, walking up the aisle of the Norman church towards the altar and then setting his steps towards the door Jamie had disappeared through. It was low, and he ducked through it, finding Jamie on the other side already setting two wooden cups on a table next to an earthenware jar with a leather stopper.

"I'm assuming you'll not object," Jamie said, pouring out two measures from the bottle.

Jack took his and sniffed it before he put the cup to his lips, a moment later he gasped as the liquor hit his throat. "God's bones, what's it made from."

Jamie grinned. "I knew you'd like it. It's made locally in the village."

Jack took another tentative mouthful and held his cup out for a refill. "I am assuming you didn't ask for me to come here to sample your village aqua vitae?"

Jamie poured another good measure into the cup Jack held out. "No, you are right. It's Guy."

"Guy?" Jack exclaimed. "I turned him off, on your advice, if you remember."

"I know," Jamie's tone was conciliatory. "It seems there was more to it than I first thought."

Jack groaned and pulled out a chair from under the table, the legs scraping loudly on the stone flagged floor. Dropping into it he turned his sapphire blue eyes on the priest. "Go on then, tell me what's happened."

Jamie placed his hands palms down on the table and regarded Jack with serious eyes. "Guy had been charging the villagers a fee to use the mill, and that was on top of what Hastley had charged. When you turned Guy off Knoll, the miller, started charging it instead. So there was no benefit to the village in turning Guy off, it just swapped one thief for another."

"What's this got to do with me?" Jack said coldly.

"It's your mill, you need to stop Knoll of course," Jamie explained patiently.

"It's not my mill, it's my brother's," Jack pointed out accurately, "I don't want to get involved in your local disputes, take this to the assize."

"You are right, it's not your mill, but you are acting as Fitzwarren's steward, and if Knoll is taking money then it's money you are not getting. I know several of your tenants are in arrears," Jamie stated bluntly.

Jack drained the cup and held it out in front of Jamie, who obligingly filled it, his eyes never leaving Jack's. "I hate mills," was all Jack said.

Jamie smiled. "So you'll do something about it then?"

Jack emptied the cup and placed it on the table. "Yes, old man, I will."

Jamie beamed and filled Jack's cup for a fourth time.

Jack stood on the bank to the mill pond and let his eyes run over the structure before him. The mill was made of whitewashed stone, contrasting sharply with the dark wheel that turned, dipping its paddles into the pond. Hastley must have had some money, Jack mused, to have had this built, it was a shame he'd taken his wealth with him when he had abandoned Burton.

John Knoll was the master miller, and he worked with the help of two assistants, when Guy had given him a tour of the manor and the surrounding lands he had been introduced briefly to him. Stepping through the open door into the dusty, dim interior, he found the man he was looking for shouting at his assistant who was hastily threading cord through a flour bag to fasten it shut.

Knoll looked up at the intruder and scowled until he recognised Jack standing in the doorway. "Master Fitzwarren," Knoll greeted Jack.

Jack nodded in acceptance of the greeting, and said simply, "A word if I may." Jack promptly stepped back through the door and waited outside for the miller to join him.

"How can I help, Sir?" Knoll said, emerging and dusting the white flour from his hands.

Jack laid a cold blue stare on the miller. "I've been advised that charges are being levied on my tenants for using the mill."

Knoll regarded him with an equally cool look. "That might have been the case, Sir, when Guy was the steward, but it's not something I know anything about."

"So if I question some of my tenants they'll deny paying you for use of the mill?" Jack asked slowly, watching Knoll carefully.

"That's right, Sir, they don't pay me for use of the mill," Knoll stated bluntly.

"That's good then," Jack replied, casting another hard look over the miller before he left. Now he had to talk to the tenants. He'd ask Jamie which ones to approach, he had, after all, set him up for this task. It would remain to be seen who got to speak to them first— Jack or Knoll. Jack's hope was that the practice would cease and that he would not have to go the trouble of finding a replacement miller.

Chapter Twenty

London – February 1553

Richard found himself quickly admitted to Derby's presence, he was however surprised when he found the Earl wasn't alone but was involved in a heated conversation with a man he recognised. The man was John Somer, plainly dressed, as was his habit, in dark clothes that did not mark him out as a man of note. Richard had taken a few steps back respectfully and waited for the Earl to conclude his business.

The conversation closed soon after with Somer collecting papers from the Earl's desk. "I will see what I can do, if you wish to get this past Parliament they will scrutinise every word, every turn of phrase, I am warning you." Somer concluded.

"I agree, and that's why I wish you to take it to them all beforehand so when it is formally presented there won't be any trouble. Mary wishes for her nobles to be united," Derby concluded, already looking in Richard's direction. His business with Somer, as far as he was concerned, was concluded.

Somer turned, his eyes caught Richard's for a moment, but there was no spark of recognition and he merely inclined his head in greeting as he moved past him towards the door.

The Earl waited for the door to close in the frame before he turned his attention to Richard. "Busy times I am afraid, and I am getting too old for court life." He heaved a sigh and ran a hand through his thinning hair. "Mary is pressing for her marriage to Philip and it seems the job of placating Parliament has fallen on my shoulders."

"I am sure you are equal to the task," Richard replied carefully.

"Let us speak candidly. There are many nobles who support Mary, but the marriage and alliance with Spain is one they fear. They fear what they do not understand, they are like children in the dark," the Earl said.

If Richard thought the Earl's assessment of the situation was slightly too simplistic he did not say so, he just nodded in agreement.

"The terms of the deal are to be drafted by Somer, and he will, I hope, provide the Queen with a settlement that all parties will be happy with. Renard, the Spanish Ambassador, as part of the marriage negotiations is seeking a permanent solution to the issue of the lady Elizabeth," Derby concluded.

"A permanent solution?" Richard echoed the Earl's words.

"There are two. The woman is married off and removed from the political scene that way, any claim to the throne then would be vested in her offspring, or she is tied to Wyatt and follows him up the steps to the scaffold," Derby stated bluntly.

Richard nodded, his face thoughtful. "The latter course does prevent a political volte-face should the need arise."

"You are right, and that is exactly what I want. You have a shrewd mind. So tell me, if Elizabeth is removed, where will the doubters turn then?"

Richard paced across the room to the window and stared through the small leaded panes, what lay beyond was obscured by the raindrops that blurred the view.

"Courtenay would be the logical answer," Richard replied slowly, "although his claim would only really be viable if he was tethered to Elizabeth, without that his lineage is a little tenuous being only Edwards VI's second cousin, and..." Richard paused.

"And the man is a fool," the Earl interjected.

Richard, ignoring him, continued. "Any claim the Gray name had was obliterated by Northumberland's botched plot. Ideally you should remove Courtenay and Elizabeth." Richard stroked his chin, then added, "But after you get Parliament's approval for the match."

"Why after?" Derby demanded.

"If Mary dies in childbirth, you will have handed England to Spain, if Elizabeth is named as heir then you will get your deal. Then remove her from the succession after Mary is married." Richard supplied.

"It's a different matter marching the heir apparent up to the scaffold," Derby replied.

"Not really, she is already closely linked to Wyatt, if he confesses now then it will be a little inconvenient, however if evidence is unearthed after the union with Philip then the case could be brought against her," Richard said, turning back from the window to face Derby. "Courtenay has been linked with the conspirators already, so ideally a single trial and the removal of them both together would be an ideal solution. If that was known by those who disfavour Elizabeth as heir it will ensure their support. It will also make those Parliamentarians who fear to support Mary's marriage because they dread a loss of sovereignty sign as well, they will see Elizabeth as the bulwark against a Spanish invasion."

Derby looked at Richard in dismay. "You cannot broker a deal to two factions who are so closely linked. These men do talk to each other, you know. We'll be made to look like fools."

"Men will believe what they wish to believe, and additionally they will believe in something that they can influence. Those who believe you will send Elizabeth to the scaffold a suitable time after Mary's marriage will choose to believe that because it will be Parliament who will finally approve the executions, especially if there is a rumour that Wyatt has made her complicit in his plans. Why then would they not believe it?" Richard supplied, his voice reasonable.

"And those who wish to keep Elizabeth as heir?"

"Will be relieved that Wyatt's confession has not been revealed, and the very fact that it has not also reinforces the fact of Elizabeth's survival as heir."

Derby's brow furrowed.

"As long as there remains conjecture both sides can draw from it the conclusion that best suits them, and Mary will get the support she needs from Parliament to sanction Spain's marriage deal. What happens afterwards is very much a different issue as Mary will then be wedded to Phillip and the process will have served the cause," Richard concluded, his eyes meeting the Earl's.

"I can see how this could work," Derby pulled thoughtfully at his beard, "it would need to be carefully managed." The Earl walked to the front of his desk and faced Richard, "And where does your loyalty lie I wonder."

Richard frowned, "Have I not proven myself to be a loyal servant?"

"You have, however I am well aware that you were part of Thomas Seymour's household and of the incident that occurred there." The Earl said.

"And why would that effect my loyalty? If anything, I would have thought it would have ensured it," Richard said, an edge in his voice.

"How so? You supported the lady Elizabeth, how do I know that you no longer do?" The Earl asked pointedly.

It was now Richard's turn to adopt a look of utter dismay. There was an undercurrent of bitterness in his words when he spoke. "Sir, I tried to save a woman's honour, and I admit I would act again the same way if those circumstances presented themselves. However, after that event I was banished by Seymour, disinherited by my father and left with nothing as a result. I do not owe that lady any loyalty."

"Lady Elizabeth, does she know you bear her such ill will? You were, by all accounts, close friends." Derby said.

"She would have no reason to know, I have not spoken to the lady since, it was many years ago. We were childhood friends, that was true, but time has severed that bond," Richard replied.

"Perhaps you are someone she might believe she can trust," Derby continued.

"She might," Richard said slowly.

"I believe that our problem with Wyatt wasn't a singular event, there are rumours that Elizabeth is involved in another plan to take the capital. Your idea that we can use her to secure Parliament's approval I can agree with, however it would all amount to very little if the lady did indeed involve herself with yet more insurrection."

"There is a truth in that," Richard agreed. "I am assuming you would like me to see if I can find anything out?"

"Elizabeth is resident at Whitehall, under guard. Her visitors are recorded and closely guarded, so how you get to speak to her I shall leave with you," Derby said.

"I shall find out what I can," Richard replied seriously.

Derby regarded Richard in silence for a few moments before he spoke again. "Good, join me tomorrow and let me see if we can together convince Somer. The man has no liking for his task, and he may see some worth in what you propose."

Richard finally went to see Elizabeth at Whitehall, it had taken longer than he had wished. The relief on Kate's face when she had seen him had been painful to see, and he was sorry he had so little comfort to bring.

The meeting with Elizabeth had been a brief one, there was little news to pass on, he had only wanted to reassure her of his loyalty, no matter what she heard.

When he emerged from Elizabeth's room he found Kate was outside, pacing nervously in the corridor, her hands knitted together, waiting for him to emerge.

"Kate," Richard said, taking her hand in his, "Elizabeth is lucky to have you with her."

"You brought good news, I hope," Kate said earnestly.

"No doubt she will tell you soon, but I have a favour to ask now," Richard told her, as he led her down the corridor.

"If there is anything…"

He lifted his fingers to her lips to still her words. "I know you would do anything, there is no need to say it. There are a limited number of people *you* can trust, and I know even fewer." He led her to a window and pointed to a house in the distance. "You see that attic room with the light in it?"

"Yes, I can clearly see it," Kate said as she looked at the distant window lit with a pale yellow light.

"When it is lit as it is tonight I will meet you in the garden near the briar gate at ten o'clock. You can get there?" Richard asked.

"Yes, I am allowed into the small garden, but it is heavily guarded. How do you propose to get in and out?" Kate replied, a worried expression on her face.

"Don't worry about that." Richard smiled and turned to leave, crossing the dark garden and disappearing noiselessly into the foliage.

Kate, watching his retreat, could not see where he had disappeared to, and after a few moments switched her eyes instead to the lit window in the room Richard had pointed out, its dim light clearly visible across the housetops.

After a moment Kate lifted her skirts and returned to her mistress, keen to learn of any news Richard had brought. When Kate found her Elizabeth was standing, arms folded and a look of consternation on her face, staring at the lit fire in the hearth.

"Well?" was all Kate said as she closed the door behind her.

"Not much, Kate. It appears Wyatt has not confessed just yet, but that is probably a matter of time only. Renard is still pressing Mary to condemn me to the Tower, but the Council feels there is not sufficient evidence. I am safe here for the time being. I will be requested to stand before the Queen's Council as I expected, probably after Wyatt has been executed and there is no danger of his final words being changed," Elizabeth said matter-of-factly.

"Should you petition Mary again for a hearing?" Kate asked, her hand on Elizabeth's arm.

"She didn't reply to my last letter. However, I can but try. It might be that I can get my case heard, before Mary's Council is set upon me," Elizabeth replied.

"I had hoped there might be more," Kate said, sounding disappointed. "I had hoped to hear that Mary might have finally granted you a private audience so you could personally put your case before your sister."

"Unfortunately not," Elizabeth replied, staring again into the flames.

Richard left the way he had entered, climbing easily over the ivy-clad wall. The sandstone beneath the vegetation had powdered and crumbled providing easy hand and footholds. After peering into the quiet street below for some moments, he dropped noiselessly to the ground. If he knew he was watched as he made his way from Elizabeth's house, he gave no sign.

"Feet!" yelled Jack, exasperated. Marc altered his stance obligingly, moving his boots back two paces to where they were supposed to be.

"Oh no, I think I shall die. Please save me, Jack," Dan said, backing off from Marc's erratic blows.

"Dan, this is not supposed to be amusing," Jack said, annoyed, and then to Marc, "feet, for the love of God, do you take no notice of me?"

Catherine was leaning on the fence, her arms spread on the top bar and her head resting upon them. Jack moved to stand near her, picking up his own sword from where it was propped against the fence.

"You make it look so light," Catherine said, her eyes looking at the blade.

"What, this?" Jack asked, turning the sword over expertly in his hand. "It is. Here," Jack offered the hilt to Catherine.

Catherine wound her hand around the grip, and Jack let go. The sword plunged to the ground, so unready was she for the weight of it. Jack grinned.

"Damn!" Catherine swore, Jack laughed, and she immediately flushed, trying to ignore the chorus of laughter from the men on the other side of the ring. "That wasn't funny either," she complained.

"Sorry," Jack returned half-heartedly.

"Is this a private game or can anyone join in?" There was no mistaking Richard's silken voice. "Dan, if you please." Richard threw his riding cloak at Dan who obeyed the unspoken order and left the yard.

"The rest of you can get out of here as well." Richard commanded.

"Richard! So you've finally decided to join us." Jack's attention was riveted on his brother and his eyes were wide with expectation.

Richard, ignoring Jack, carefully removed his gloves, laying them on the fence post. "I am pleased to find the lady suitably entertained."

Catherine stood still, eyes wildly staring at Richard, the sword dropped at her feet.

"Pick it up," Richard said conversationally. He stood in front of her, arms crossed. Catherine did not move. "The first lesson you will learn today is that you do as I say." Richard drew his own sword. "The second is that contrary to popular belief, I do have some family loyalties. Now," the point hovered in front of her face, "pick it up."

Catherine stooped to obey.

"Richard, no!" Jack protested, "What are you doing?"

"Stay out of this, Jack. Patience, I know, is not one of your virtues, however the lady is not all that she seems," Richard said. Then, addressing Catherine, "Are you?"

There was a long silence during which Jack forgot to breathe.

"Now, let us see what Master Jack has been teaching you, shall we?" Richard smiled maliciously at her. "You do not move? Perhaps you feel I have some advantage over you?" Richard placed his sword in the mud, point down and stepped back. "Now, does that even things up a little? I am unarmed. You have the advantage."

"Richard, no!" Jack knew where this was leading but Richard ignored him.

"Come on, Catherine, you have no liking for me and I give you the opportunity to strike at me. Why do you not take it? This is what you've waited for, isn't it?" Richard continued. "Perhaps you think Jack will come to your rescue, do your work for you? Well, I hate to disappoint you there, but he won't."

Catherine shook with rage. "You are a bastard," she hissed.

"No. I think you'll find that is what they call Jack, not me," Richard said in the same light tone.

"Ignore him," Jack shouted the warning.

Tightening the grip on the hilt, rage swelling within her, knowing she would lose, she still swung the blade true at his head. Her expression changed to one of surprise. She heard Jack yelling; felt the impact of steel on steel jarring her right shoulder and the sword flew from her grip.

"Oh dear," Richard said. "You missed."

"What do you want?" Catherine yelled back.

"A bloody explanation, lady, and make it a good one." Richard's sword point was pressed against her shoulder.

"Richard, it's my fault she's here. You have no argument with her," Jack tried.

"Leave it, Jack. She knows what I am talking about, don't you?" Richard pressed the point a little harder into her shoulder but she kept her ground. "Well?"

"I don't have to answer to you," Catherine yelled. The steel point was getting close to her skin.

"Perhaps, but under the circumstances, I think I have the upper hand, don't you agree? Now tell me what you've done or believe me..."

"Back off Richard. Now!" Jack leapt over the fence.

"Very well." Richard did step back from Catherine, but not before he'd forced the sword's point though the final layers of fabric and deep into her shoulder. Catherine screamed and dropped to her knees.

"You bastard!" Jack stepped towards his brother, his intention clear.

"Do you think so? I have had enough of swordplay for one day. I believe that the lady is in need of some assistance," Richard said and cast the sword he held into the mud at Jack's feet.

Jack hesitated, then dropped to his knees in front of Catherine and pulled her unwilling hand from the blooded shoulder.

"Let me see, please?" Jack asked, his voice quiet and level.

Dan watched Jack, with Catherine in his arms, return to the house then went to find Richard. "What the hell did you do?" Dan grabbed Richard's arm.

"I don't know," Richard pulled from Dan's grasp.

"Shall I tell you now, or shall I let you work it out for yourself when your clouded brain clears?" Dan growled. "That was a hard lesson, a graver one than many of the men here have suffered at your hands."

"I have good reason."

"Maybe, and if so, share it with Jack before he puts a well-deserved knife in your ribs," Dan growled. "I might even hold you while he does it."

"All right, go and fetch him then," Richard snapped.

Dan had duly brought a reluctant and still angry Jack to where Richard waited in the empty hall. Richard's calm reasoning had begun to dampen Jack's murderous rage.

"Ask her? Ask her who pursued her down the streets of London. It wasn't Wyatt's rebels, no; it was Robert's men. Alan set her to plead at the gates and have them opened, and they were. Fortunately, Dan didn't throw them as wide as Alan had planned, so they had to mount an attack on the walls. And you, dear brother, helped the angel who nearly killed you escape neatly from the back of the house."

Jack shook his head, but his brother continued. "Ask her, or ask yourself; it's all there. She doesn't like me, and with reason. She thinks I put her household to the sword. Alan knew, and she made a willing participant in his scheme. I am not sure yet how Robert found out where she was; that's the only piece of the puzzle I have yet to fit into place. Most inventive of my brother to use Wyatt as a cover for his own plans though, don't you think?"

Jack's face was pale. "Alan!"

"Yes Alan. That you were in there then didn't matter to her at all," Richard cruelly pointed out. "And now you know why the lady wished so much to be at Burton. She hoped to find me, and as you know I have been elsewhere, neither in London nor at Burton. She was waiting for me to come here."

Jack rubbed calloused palms across his face and paced across the hall. This was all fitting too well together. *Alan!*

A dark looked crossed Richard's face. "What's happened that I don't know about?"

Jack didn't answer.

Richard's voice adopted a sterner edge. "Jack, what's happened?"

Jack turned back to face his brother. "If you didn't keep everything to yourself all the time, then none of this would have happened. Alan's gone, I caught him trying to beat the daylights out of Catherine, he escaped. I tried to track him down, but he got away from me."

"Well, that fits. He wouldn't want her telling you about what had actually happened in London. If he saw that she had a liking for you, then it was a risk he couldn't take," Richard mused. "He would need to get rid of her."

"I don't believe you," Jack said, his words lacking conviction.

"Yes, you do, or you wouldn't still be here, would you?" Richard said, the harsh edge gone from his voice.

"But... you think she still means it?" Jack stammered.

"I'm sorry Jack. Judging by the fact that she lost her temper when I threatened you, I don't think she wants you dead, if that helps," Richard replied.

"She believes she has every reason to want you dead, and Richard, you have never done anything to change her mind. Today will not have helped any. How can I persuade her now that she was wrong?" Jack sounded tired, his voice strained.

"Jack," Richard, moving forwards, caught his brother's arm. "Won't you even allow me, for once, my temper? It is something you revel in yourself often enough."

"What family loyalties did you refer to by the way?" Jack sounded confused as he pulled roughly away from Richard's hold.

"The lady almost succeeded in killing you, it is not a state of affairs I found myself happy about," Richard spoke through clenched teeth; his temper had not left him.

There was a silence between them for a moment, then Richard murmured, "Such facts as the ones you had learnt need time. Have I given you enough?"

"I don't know. Richard..." Jack buried his head back in his hands. "What you did today..."

Richard sighed painfully. "For you, for what might not be, for what I have not done, I will try, heaven knows why."

Richard moved towards the dais and dropped heavily into one of the chairs.

"I will go and see how the lass is, and I'll soon know the truth of your words," Jack said and left his brother alone. After only a few minutes with the tearful girl he knew the truth of Richard's words.

It was an hour before Jack returned. Richard was still seated alone at the dais when Jack stepped up and lowered himself into a chair next to him, pulling from his pocket a deck of cards.

"Why do you try me so?" Jack asked quietly, his hands riffling the cards.

"Do I?" Richard raising his head looked at Jack, his hand held a half-empty cup, and the gaze that held Jack's was less than perfectly focussed.

He's drunk, thought Jack, an unusual state for Richard. *Perhaps the tables may turn tonight.*

"Yes, you bloody do!" Jack placed the deck of cards face down. "Cut."

"What are the stakes?" Richard's words bore an edge of inebriation as he lowered his eyes to the deck.

"If you get the highest card, you can beat the living daylights out of me for this; however, if I draw the highest card, then I get to take my retribution. You should have told me," Jack's voice was weary now rather than angry.

"If I had, you would have denied her the opportunity to change her mind, and I think she may have." Richard's hand hovered over the deck. "Is she alright?"

"What do you think? No, I think we can say she has not taken it too well," Jack said, watching his brother's hand about to cut the worn deck.

"A little dramatic, I agree. Sorry, I was drunk," Richard ventured, then laughing. "Come on, she wasn't exactly bleeding to death. It was only a scratch."

"Were you?" Jack hadn't realised.

"Very. Allow me some weakness. I fancied meeting neither you nor the lady sober," Richard smiled, but with little humour. "So, to the cards, if I get the highest card..." Richard cut and held up an eight of clubs.

"A fair hand brother," Jack cut the remaining deck and held up a queen of diamonds.

"I am undone. Would you like to extract your penance now? I am deep in my cups so it probably won't hurt so much, or shall we wait?" Richard slurred resignedly.

"I probably should, but not tonight. Richard, promise me instead that you will tell me in the future. I cannot make the right decisions if I don't know all the facts," the anger had gone from Jack's voice.

"A fair comment, alright." Richard conceded. "Anything else?"

"No more tricks with Catherine," Jack said, "that was fairly cruel."

"Ah, the Chevalier protects the lady to the last," Richard said, his grin a little lopsided.

"Careful," Jack warned.

"Sorry, yes, I will improve my behaviour," Richard replied quickly, his hands raised in a gesture of conciliation.

"What would that be then?" said Jack asked darkly. "From the wholly unacceptable to merely slightly unacceptable?"

"Something like that," Richard grinned.

Jack could, for some reason, not stop himself and smiled back. "You really don't care what anyone thinks of you?"

"Not really," Richard accepted, then his brow furrowed, and he asked, "Why, by the way, did you make the unhappy lady's state worse by saddling her with the brand of being my sister? Was that to teach me another lesson as well by any chance?"

"Ah no. I just thought that it would keep straying hands off her. Both from fear of yourself and a worry that she might share some of your more unwelcome characteristics," Jack said, unable to resist a malicious smile.

"I'll not ask what those are," Richard said, raising a hand to still Jack's words.

"Probably best not to," agreed Jack.

"You want to know about Robert as well, am I right?" Richard reached for the pitcher and refilled his cup.

This was unexpected, and Jack's eyes narrowed.

"It's a most unhappy state; you find yourself between nothing," Richard slurred opening one empty hand, "and nothing." The other joined it. "It's no different for me. The Lady Elizabeth has moved from legitimate to illegitimate at the stroke of a pen; the same is true of you, and there is little that can be done. Have you thought about what you would do?"

Jack shook his head.

"There is only one way you can go. Legally establish yourself as heir, sue through the courts of chancery." Richard dropped back in the chair and regarded his brother with an unsteady gaze. "You could not win. Your family is backed by too much wealth. Such a claim would fail and fail maybe after many years. Do you wish to wait your life out on such meagre hopes?"

"There must be something. Surely you can't expect me to..."

Richard cut him off. "No, I cannot expect you to let it fall from your mind. Robert will track me, of that I am sure and," a delighted smile wandered onto his face, "it is an encounter I most surely will enjoy. There can be only two outcomes."

Jack looked up at that. "Go on."

"Either I shall be overcome, in which case these problems will be your own, or... or my father's favourite bastard will die at my feet," Richard said evenly. "So, as you can see, Jack, the chances of me becoming heir slightly outweigh your slender hopes, and on that, and on me, you will have to trust."

"What are you saying?" Jack delivered each word carefully.

"I am saying, if I succeed, for a reckoning will come, that I can defer to you," Richard spoke quietly, his eyes never leaving his brother's.

"You mean if Robert dies you would give me all that you inherit!" Jack's voice was incredulous and loud.

"Shhhh! Do not share my intended generosity with the rest of the hall, or else I shall have them all placing suits at my door and I have only a limited stock of potential inheritance," Richard said quickly. "As I said, on that you will have to trust me." Then, after a lengthy pause, "Will you?"

"You give me little choice," was the unsatisfactory reply.

Richard dropped his head into his hands, his hair fell to obscure his eyes and his voice held an edge of anguish. "Is it so hard? Trust is not based on choice or lack of it. It is belief, pure, simple belief, and something that neither you nor I can inspire."

"I will..."

Richard stopped him. "Do not sully such with mere words; they assure me not at all. Actions are what you shall be judged by. Can we not, for once, stand united?"

Jack tipped the ale jug towards him. "How many of these have you had?"

"So is your answer no?" Richard replied, the smile falling from his face.

"Yes, the answer is yes. But..."

"Here comes the caveat! Go on," Richard groaned.

"Tell me next time. Alan would not have escaped, if you had told me," Jack said.

"It's a shame he did. That was a score I was looking forward to settling," Richard murmured.

Richard reached across suddenly, clapping Jack on the shoulder and jolting the cup in his hand, sending beer to soak the wood.

"Careful!"

Richard ignored him. "Here, drink, and I will tell you a tale that will cheer you." Richard filled both their cups, none too steadily, from the pitcher, ale sluicing over the side of Jack's pooling on the table.

"And what would that be, then?" Jack said, moving his arms to avoid the spreading pond.

"One of loyalty," Richard announced grandly. "Marriage is the tale, who and what and where and why. Surely you did not think I had come to Burton because I craved the country air?"

"I can fairly assume that as it would be impossible to find a creature willing to tie themselves to you, this must not be your own state of wedlock you are referring to," Jack replied dryly, but his eyes were alight with eager curiosity. His brother rarely shared anything, however, when he did, it was often news worth listening to.

"Most wholly unfair," Richard rebuked good humouredly. Then, his tongue loosened by the ale, he told Jack much that he already knew of the planned Spanish match. Jack listened without commenting, giving Richard his full attention. "So, Renard, the Spanish Ambassador, perceives that the Protestant threat is too great," Richard concluded.

"By that I am assuming you mean Elizabeth?" Jack questioned.

"Something like that. The current grand scheme runs thus: when Northumberland set Lady Jane on the throne he did it via 'The Devise for the Succession.' How he got Edward to sign this is still a mystery. However, this purports to make Jane and her heirs the successors to the throne," Richard mused, tapping his fingers on the table.

"Which would have secured Northumberland's place. Yes, I know, but it didn't work, and I still haven't quite forgiven the shit for nearly taking us with him." Jack's tone was acid. "Can you get back to what you were going to tell me about?"

"Yes, yes," Richard said, then a confused look on his face, he asked. "What was I going to tell you about?"

"Christ! A marriage, remember?"

"Ah yes. So, the facts are well known. Northumberland fell and Mary is Queen and so on. However, when Northumberland wished to secure Edward's signature, he went to a lot of trouble and produced a lot more evidence, I suppose, with the intent of using it to persuade Edward to sign. The Archbishop of York secured these documents, and I know of only part of their contents. They contain, amongst other items, documents relating to the circumstances of Elizabeth's birth, and Renard has a desire to use them to have her removed from the royal scene, playing at great lengths on Mary's hatred of her mother's successor," Richard explained as he twisted the cup in his hand.

"Anne Boleyn's indiscretions are legendary, Henry made sure of that. There is nothing new there," Jack observed.

"The new thing is that someone has dug out some documentary evidence. False or true, it doesn't matter. Her parentage has been called into question and someone is prepared to use it. They are being brought south to London for that very purpose. It plays on Mary's fears and her hatred of Elizabeth; it might be all she needs to finally make a decision. Renard hopes so." Richard drained his cup, inspected the empty interior, and refilled it.

"So, for whatever reason, and I am sure you have a good one, we are to either help or hinder with the delivery of these documents," Jack observed, his words carefully placed.

"Correct, almost," Richard answered, smiling.

"Go on." Jack groaned. "I knew I'd get it wrong."

"Renard has requested they be brought to him in London. The Archbishop of York, as you know, fell at Mary's hand. Whether from a desire to save his own neck, I don't know, but he divulged the existence and whereabouts of these papers. Renard, being everywhere and anywhere, became aware of them, and they are to be transported from York to London by some of his men."

"So you want to intercept them?" Jack wished his brother could be straightforward, just for once.

"Ah, there is a final complication," Richard countered, the words blending together, an apologetic expression on his face.

"God! Go on," Jack exclaimed.

"Bishop Gardiner does not want Elizabeth to fall. He would much rather see her wed to his favourite, Courtenay, and for their heirs to secure an English succession should Mary fail to produce a child of her own. It would be more than a little inconvenient if Courtenay's intended either lost her head or was finally barred from the throne by the curse of bastardy, wouldn't it? Furthermore, he believes possession of these papers may persuade Elizabeth to wed," Richard explained, tracing a circle on the table using spilled ale.

"So you are here to stop the papers reaching Renard, and you are working for Gardiner?" Jack had a feeling he was wrong before he had finished.

"Not quite, but almost. Some of Gardiner's men will join me here soon, and with my help, they are to stop them being delivered to Renard and at the same time take them to Gardiner. Who knows when they could be useful in the future? Plus, I feel that Gardiner does not entirely trust me with the task," Richard said, sounding more than a little hurt.

Jack smiled. He thought he had finally fathomed it. "Ah, so we are to help ensure that they fall into the correct hands, then?"

"An excellent observation," Richard declared drunkenly, then leaning towards his brother added confidentially, "however, there is one final player in this little scene who also wishes to obtain the papers, and prevent them from reaching either Gardiner or Renard."

"He's right not to trust you. I bloody well wouldn't. So why do you want them?" Jack said; now he had the truth of it.

"Well, despite your accusations, I do have some loyalties. Pass the jug," Richard said.

"Ah yes, Lady Elizabeth," Jack said, shoving the jug back across the table towards his brother. Richard had suffered at her hands, and why he still stood by her, Jack was unsure. "So you're playing Queen against..." Jack paused, "... Queen?"

"Maybe. They are, after all, most deadly pieces," Richard answered.

"You will not survive this game for long," Jack said wearily.

"If Mary knew..." Richard left the sentence unfinished.

"Can I ask one question?" Jack ventured, wondering if his brother, as drunk as he was, might answer.

"Go on, why not?" Richard looked up and met his brother's gaze.

"Does Elizabeth know what you do?"

There was a lengthy silence before Jack received an answer. "No," Richard finally said.

"I thought not," Jack said. "I am assuming you have a plan to palm them away from under Gardiner's men's noses without them noticing."

"I am working on it. The cargo will pass this way, which is useful. I have already told Renard that there is a scheme to waylay them and his own spies have confirmed the truth of what I have said, and I have a letter from him to the courier, Henry Walgrave." Richard explained slowly.

"So, both Renard and Gardiner think you are working for them?" Jack said wearily.

Richard grinned.

"Tell me something: how is it that you know so much? I've always wondered and never asked," Jack said carefully.

"It's a trade I learnt when I worked for Seymour; it seems like it was a lifetime ago." Richard paused.

"Well?" Jack pressed.

Richard remained stubbornly silent, his hand bringing his cup back up to his mouth, a quantity dribbling down his chin and onto his open doublet.

"Patience is not one of my virtues, as you keep on reminding me. Get on with it," Jack prompted.

"When I was in Seymour's household, I was involved in his ring of spies and confidants. I took some pains to endear myself to them, and we continue to correspond, shall we say?" Richard supplied.

"It's a dangerous game, but you know that, don't you?"

"I have little else to use to make our way. It's served us quite well so far. But yes, the path is becoming a little treacherous," Richard admitted.

"Don't you mean a little treasonous?" Jack interrupted.

"Well, yes, that too, although I suppose it depends from which side you look at it. It's a matter of seman ...semanti..." Richard hiccupped loudly, "semantics."

The next day, the brothers rode towards the Lincoln road, on a route chosen by Richard. There, high in a tree, was a lookout post. From a rocky outcrop to the trunk of an oak tree were tied two ropes, a top one to hold on to and a bottom rope for feet to slide along. Both were pulled taught, but Jack knew that as soon as any great weight was applied to them, they would stretch and sag.

"I had Froggy and Marc set this up. We have the first watch," Richard said to his brother, "So go on, you go first," Richard said, gesturing towards the rope strung between two trees.

"Why do I have to go first?" Jack asked as he peered over the edge. He didn't have a fear of heights, however he had a healthy respect for them, and the drop from the rope between the tree and the cliff was not one he was likely to survive if he fell.

"Well if it will take your weight, then at least I know I will be safe," Richard replied in a matter-of-fact voice, leaning forward himself to observe the drop.

"I cannot fault your reasoning. However, I can't say I am overly happy about it." Jack wrapped his hands around the top rope and gave it a hard tug. It *felt* firm. "Do we really need to go over there?" Jack asked, not being able to quite see the need for this unnecessary risk.

"From here we can see as far as that line of trees there," Richard pointed towards them, "but from over there we have a vantage point all the way down the Lincoln road."

"Do both of us really need to go?" Jack was still not convinced.

"For God's sake Jack, move." Richard was already putting his feet on to the bottom rope and twisting the top one around his wrists to steady himself.

As Jack watched Richard placed all his weight on the bottom rope, as Jack had suspected it stretched far more than the first lengthening the distance between them, the top rope went from waist height to head height, and it was now no longer as easy for Richard to use to keep his balance. Jack stepped back from the crumbling rocky edge and, folding his arms, rested his back against the rock the rope was lashed around and watched Richard's passage critically.

"You'll need to go up the rope now you've reached the middle. It'll not be as easy now," Jack observed.

Richard stopped midway over the rope and cast his cool grey eyes back to his brother. "Thank you for your words of wisdom. I think, however, that I can grasp the rudimentary principles of a rope bridge without your help."

Jack shrugged. "I was just trying to be helpful."

Richard didn't say another word, the second part of the traverse was the hardest, his boots slid on the rope and it was his arms that needed to take his weight and pull him up the last of the rope so he could reach the massive, out-flung branches of the tree. A moment later, the ropes bounced loose as his weight left them. Richard was sitting on one of the branches, his feet swinging in the air, regarding Jack across the short distance.

"Come on, then."

Jack pushed himself away from the rock and wrapped his arms around the top rope before he placed his feet on the bottom one. A handful of pebbles skittered from the rocky edge and Jack's eyes couldn't help but follow their descent to the rock-strewn ground at the bottom of the stony outcrop.

"It's best not to look down, or so I've been told," a cheery voice called helpfully from the leafy confines of the tree.

"Bugger off."

"I was just trying to be helpful," Richard mocked.

Jack ignored his brother and put one foot on the rope, testing the effect his weight was going to have. He was heavier than Richard, and the rope was going to stretch away more beneath him. After taking four sideways steps along the bottom rope, he realised just how much more it had stretched. One more step and the top rope was going to be above his head and of very little use to him in keeping his balance.

"That does look like it's going to be awkward for you," mused Richard from where he sat on the tree branch.

One more step and Jack knew he would be at the bottom of the ropes stretch as he arrived at the middle, and he also realised the top rope would be at the full extent of his outstretched arms above his head. He had two choices–go back, or transfer all his weight to the top or bottom rope.

"Jack, take the top rope, it'll not have suffered as much strain as the bottom one," Richard's voice had lost its mocking tone, and the words were seriously spoken.

With the agility of a horseman, Jack took his feet from the bottom rope and hooked them around the top one. From there, he began the short hand over hand climb up the angled rope to the perch Richard was sitting on.

Neither Richard, with his eyes on Jack, nor Jack with his eyes on the rope he was climbing up, saw it unwinding from the oak branch where it had been secured. Jack's extra weight on it had broken a securing peg holding the rope in place. Jack was the first, however, to be aware of it.

The rope dropped a foot, the unwound end snagging for a moment on a notch on the tree trunk. Jack grabbed for the branch Richard was perched on as the rope freed itself and dropped away beneath him to the forest floor.

The branch was too wide to wrap his arms around. Jack felt his grip on the rough bark slip.

Richard's hands grasped around his left wrist, the hold like iron. "Reach up with your right hand. There's a hold just above it."

Could he hold on with one hand? He had no real hold on the bark, all that was holding him up was his brother's grip.

"Come on, Jack, I can't hold you!" Richard's voice was strained with the effort of supporting his brother's weight.

Jack took a breath and let go with his right hand. Richard grunted against the pain of the extra weight and, for a moment, Jack felt his wrist slipping through his brother's grasp. An instant later, his right hand had located the hold and his tortured muscles dragged him towards the safety of the branch top.

His chest heaving, he curled on top of the branch, his brother still with his hands tight on him. Suddenly, Jack realised how his brother had saved him. Richard had used his own weight and was hanging from the tree. His only hold was the one he still had on Jack. If Jack had fallen, then they both would have. Jack leant down and fastened a hold into Richard's doublet and hauled his brother back to the top of the tree branch next to him.

A moment later, Richard knelt next to Jack, his body shaking from the exertion. A cut on his right cheek from a knot in the wood was dripping blood in a steady stream.

"You could have let me fall," Jack managed.

"I nearly did," Richard replied, his breathing still coming in ragged gasps.

Jack's fist was still tightly balled in his brother's clothing, and he dragged him close, wrapping his arms around him.

"You didn't. You could have, but you didn't." Letting go of him, Jack sat back on the branch and said in a serious voice, "I am sure you weighed up all the outcomes very carefully. It would be so much easier without me. You remove Robert and that just clears a path for you. You were raised for it, you could be the heir so easily, and if you had let me fall, you could have taken it. No one would blame you. But you didn't, and I am grateful you made that choice."

"Jack. I just meant I wasn't strong enough to hold you," Richard stated bluntly.

"Oh." was all Jack could manage.

An hour later, they had safely climbed down from the tree, slowly traversing the branches rather than trusting to the remaining rope. Mounted on steeds more content to stand idle and munch the grass, they were headed back to Burton. As they crested the gentle rise towards the manor, the white mill came into view and Jack's face darkened at the sight of it.

Richard, seeing his brother's expression change, moved his horse closed to his brother's. "So what is it about a mill that sours your temper, or have you still not forgiven me?"

Jack was about to snap back a curt answer, but then swallowed it, and said instead, "I have some business with the miller, Knoll, and it's past time that I paid him a visit."

"Well then," Richard said smiling, "let's go together. I've not seen the mill before, it'll be intriguing to see how it works."

"I knew you'd find it interesting," Jack said under his breath.

Knoll was there when they arrived. He must have seen them riding side by side along the road towards the mill and he met them on the bank of the millpond.

"Master Fitzwarren," Knoll said, bowing slightly in Jack's direction. Richard smiled with delight, and Jack gave him a dark look.

"A brief word, if I may," Jack said, striding towards the miller. Richard followed and stood at Jack's shoulder, listening to the exchange.

"It seems, Knoll, that the tenants are equally afraid of us both. None seem to want to talk to me about paying to use the mill. Shall I assume that this was a practice of Guy's and that it no longer takes place?" Jack was handing the miller an opportunity to exonerate himself, and one he had no choice but to accept.

"I'm sure you are right sir, this was probably a practice of Guy's, and I can see no reason why you would hear of it happening again," Knoll said evenly.

"Good, let me introduce you to my brother," Jack said. "He would very much like to see how the mill works."

Jack waited, sitting out of the wind, his back to the mill wall while his brother was taken on a tour. When Richard emerged an hour later, his hands dusty with flour, Jack was nearly asleep.

Richard's man sat, legs outstretched and feet crossed, his back against the giant trunk of the tree, in the same lookout that the brothers had visited a few days before. From his vantage point, he had seen only farm wagons, a peddler accompanying a lame horse and field workers using the road briefly on their way home.

Suddenly, his body stiffened, and his eyes narrowed to focus on the distant sight. Leaving his leafy perch, he mounted the saddled horse tethered at the base and spurred her homeward.

Richard saw the rider speed past the posting house and discarded his hand of cards onto the table. Jack, rising, flipped them over; aces smiled up. "That was good timing. I have been saved from poverty again," Jack said as he rapidly collected his cloak and sword.

They headed in the opposite direction to the messenger and shortly after, their horses stood side by side, blocking the road.

"You think this will work?" Jack asked uneasily.

"I have no idea," replied Richard pleasantly.

"Well, I suppose there are only two outcomes: either they stop, which would be a good thing, or..." he shifted nervously in the saddle, "they ride right over us, which would most certainly be bad."

The carriage and escort of six riders neared them. When they were at a distance where they could clearly be seen, Richard raised his hand in a signal for them to stop.

The entourage came to a halt, and the captain turned his horse back towards the carriage.

"My Lord, two riders stand in our way," Captain Davis said through the carriage window.

"Do they look like robbers, do you think?" Henry Walgrave, Renard's man, and not a Lord, leant from the window.

"I would doubt it. We vastly outnumber them and we are in the open. There is nowhere for others to be hiding," the captain replied.

"We will wait here. Ride ahead and see what they want," Walgrave ordered nervously.

The captain gave the command and his men took up a defensive position around the carriage. He rode towards the two riders, his eyes scanning the landscape to ensure that his original assessment that there were no others was correct.

"What business are you about?" Captain Davis demanded.

"My name is Richard Fitzwarren, and I must speak with Walgrave." He rode towards the captain. "This letter proves my identity. Take it to Walgrave and inform him I wish only a few minutes of his most valuable time." Richard passed the parchment to the captain, who wheeled his horse round and returned to the carriage.

The captain gestured for Richard to approach the carriage and he left Jack standing in the middle of the road. Jack watched the brief exchange and wondered idly what lies Richard was using.

"Is he deceived?" Jack enquired quietly as Richard arrived back.

"Most assuredly. He believes I am Renard's man," Richard replied. "Come, we have to be part of an ambush party shortly."

They turned their horses and headed cross-country, following in the steps of the messenger.

When they arrived at Burton Manor, the courtyard was the scene of smooth, controlled activity, filled with Gardiner's men who had ridden from London to join Fitzwarren. Their leader, a man Jack had no liking for, Edward de Lacon, was there now as they prepared to leave.

"Sir, you are just in time. Your man reports that Walgrave approaches and we are off to spring the trap," he announced.

"Excellent," announced Richard exuberantly. "Come, Jack, let us fall on the bishop like the hounds on the fox."

Twelve men waited in the sanctuary afforded by the trees. The carriage took longer to arrive than it should have, as Henry Walgrave had made an unscheduled stop. For his safety, he had changed places with Captain Davis. The riders fell on the band, hoods pulled up, kerchiefs hiding their faces.

Richard led his men in on one side of the coach whilst Edward brought his companions swooping down, yelling and screaming on the other.

Richard uncharacteristically did not play a leading part in the highway robbery, taking up a stance to the rear of the coach, his sword point bidding two of Captain Davis's men to remain where they were. Edward, whooping, held aloft a leather bag, the signal that the deed was done, and as quickly as they had descended, they disappeared into the veiled shelter of the forest, leaving the men to regroup and speed the carriage from the ambush.

Back at Burton, Edward tipped the contents of the leather pouch onto the table. Three documents of rectangular folded parchment fell from within, all sealed.

"It appears that you have been successful, Sir," Richard idly reaching for one of the documents.

"No Sir. These are sealed and will remain so, so there is no chance of the villainy they contain escaping." Edward scooped the papers from the table.

"Surely you have some curiosity as to what they may tell us," Richard replied slyly.

"None whatsoever. They contain only slanderous lies and tales of deceit," Edward de Lacon replied indignantly.

"Well the answer is simple then," Richard declared. "Burn them. I lay my own fire at your disposal."

"You have no appreciation of what we have done here tonight, have you? I will not be goaded into opening these letters for you to slaver over," Edward's tone told everyone present he had no respect for Richard Fitzwarren.

"Come on, man, we'd all enjoy a bit of entertainment." Richard received an affirmative murmur from his men in the hall. He turned back to Edward. "Come now, man, we have worked with you. Share the spoils."

"You, Sir, are a dangerous and most treacherous wretch. Lord knows what use you would put these papers to. I can see now why you were not most wholly trusted, and I care no longer for your company," Edward replied, signalling his men to leave.

"You do not trust my company now that you have your precious letters! I am most deeply hurt," Richard proclaimed, a wounded note in his voice. "I craved a little scandal and some entertainment, the same as any other poor soul. Come now, humour us before you leave. Can I be the only curious cat?"

Edward sensed the challenge in Richard's words, as he was supposed to, and detected the slight slur in his speech. "Sir, you are drunk. I will not continue this conversation." Walgrave's cargo protectively held under his arm, Edward left. He wished very much to be on the road now he had his prize. He might not have been so hasty if he had known that his departure was also in the mind of the man who had goaded him.

Jack sidled up to Richard. "Do you think he will open those letters and we will be soon undone?"

Richard seated himself on the end of the table, one foot idly swinging as he considered the question. "No, I rely on the fact that when the discovery is made, they cannot complain too loudly as they risk implication as traitors. Gardiner knows he implicates himself and Renard will still receive from me what he will hopefully believe are the originals that the Bishop of York held."

"I do hope you are right," Jack said over-cheerfully.

Richard broke the seal with his knife. He sat cross-legged in front of the fire in the silent privacy of his own room; the door locked against unwanted intrusions. The first packet revealed a single sheet of parchment. Holding it to the flame's light, he scanned the contents. It was a neatly penned confession in a clerk's hand, detailing the lewd acts committed between this tortured lover and Anne Boleyn. There was nothing in the text of any significance. It was a standard extracted confession statement prepared without the confessor's participation and with the sole purpose of having him sign it.

He turned the page over. The neat text continued to fill the reverse, at the bottom was the signature. The blotted, scraped pen strokes clashed wildly with the clerk's tidy and calmly prepared sentences. He stared at the signature. It was a long dead agony now that stared at him from the page and he felt nothing for that tormented soul. He discarded the paper on the floor and turned to the next. He had to admit mild surprise at the second confession; he had certainly never heard of its existence. It was written in the hand of Anne Boleyn. He read the document thoughtfully.

On the 11th day of the month of September, I did lie with him again in mine own bed. Between this time and finding myself with child, I did not lie with my husband nor any other man.

The document rambled through dates and events, but it seemed to lack passion and rage, both of which were Mistress Boleyn's most defining characteristics, and yet there was something about it that would not allow him to dismiss it as a fake. Its existence had surprised him. He knew the lady had hoped for mercy from Henry right up until the moment she was led to the block. He wondered at her motivation for writing it, if, in fact, she had penned it. Possibly she had written it in return for a promise to keep her daughter safe.

The next letter was from Renard to the Archbishop of York, outlining the repeal of the act of parliament that contained Henry's will. Richard discarded this straight into the flames.

The next document was older than the rest, the penmanship archaic, the paper yellowed.

Richard read it a second time, carefully, not believing what he held in his hands. He had certainly never heard of this rumour before, and scandal, like smoke, had a talent for escaping.

Richard closed his eyes for a moment, making a physical effort to still his breathing. What he held in his hands now could strike at the very heart of the succession. His hands still shaking, he folded the document carefully back into its original square.

It seemed it had not been the documents relating to Elizabeth that had been of interest to Renard at all. What he held in his hand had been the precious cargo, but the question was, who knew about it?

Richard sat for a long time before he reached a decision.

Chapter Twenty-One
London – March 1553

Richard was briefly back in London and bent to light the flame in the lamp holder in the attic room. He had duly delivered the papers to Renard's keeping as he had promised to do, receiving thanks for countering Gardiner's plot. Now, he had news for Elizabeth that she should hold her ground. It looked like Gardiner had continued to beg the Queen for clemency with Courtenay, and that he still persisted with his plans for Elizabeth's marriage with the Earl.

"The line is a fine one," Elizabeth was not smiling, "and it is I who am treading it not you."

"I have given you all I have. There is no more news, if there were, I hope you would trust that I would bring it to you." Richard replied.

"Elizabeth, please. I know this is not easy," Kate took a step towards her mistress.

Elizabeth shifted her gaze from Richard to Kate, and her expression immediately softened. "Kate, you are right." Then to Richard she said, "I am assailed from all sides. Effingham was here this morning again. They are all convinced that I have some backing that they are not aware of."

"I wish you did have," Kate sighed.

"I am afraid they believe that you have coherent support and that you are in contact with them. This is partly what keeps you safe, lady. Derby cannot prove or disprove the extent of your support, and while they feel that alienating your faction poses a significant political risk, they cannot move against you," Richard explained.

"But I don't have this, and they are tying me and themselves in knots trying to find it." Elizabeth was exasperated. "I am asked the same question a dozen times over, and the slightest variation is pounced upon."

"I know you can play your part well, so please trust me... You are safer while they believe you are a threat to the political stability," Richard said. "The greater danger will come when they can see behind the smoke and gauge the full extent of the support you have."

"This is your doing, isn't it?" Elizabeth demanded.

"It is always harder to fight an enemy you cannot see," Richard replied simply.

"I think perhaps you should share your plans before you action them," Elizabeth's voice held a note of rebuke.

"I am afraid I cannot do that, and even you have to agree with me that what you do not know, you cannot unintentionally impart," Richard said.

There was a silence between them for a moment.

"Every day, I stand on the gallows platform and wait for the door to open. It does little for either my patience or my sense of humour," Elizabeth said. Her arms were wrapped around her body and she turned her back on both Richard and Kate and paced across the room.

Kate smiled apologetically at Richard. "It is not easy. She is living on her nerves."

Richard smiled. "I know, you both are. I hope that it will change soon."

Richard was not the only one to have found himself in close communication with the Spanish ambassador. His brother also had been awaiting news from the same quarter.

"It seems my brother is untouchable," Robert snarled, pulling riding gloves roughly from his hands. He was at Harry's London house, where he had freshly returned from a meeting with Renard.

"That I don't believe!" Harry exclaimed, wiping dribbled wine from his flabby face with the back of his hand.

"Well, he seems to be, and I don't know why. I met with Renard weeks ago; he was most interested in a man proclaiming himself loyal to the crown who is visiting Elizabeth in secret. I contact him again and what do I get? A curt note that he has made enquiries and what I allege is of no matter. He wouldn't even see me," Robert's eyes blazed. "The bloody bastard must have Renard round his finger as well, or else he's blackmailed the Spanish runt."

"That wouldn't surprise me, not after what he did to me," Harry said, not heeding the implication of his words.

The taller man turned narrow eyes on Harry. "What did you just say?"

Harry's face fell as he realised that he had betrayed himself. Through a snivelled apology and a cut lip, Harry told Robert what he wanted to know: that his brother was both a thief and a murderer. Shortly Robert knew of the death of Peter Hardwood, and of the blackmail Richard had used to extort money from Harry.

Jack wandered in the direction of the stables. Corracha was staring at him over the stable door, evidence that his brother was indeed back at Burton.

Richard had arrived late in the night, and as yet Jack had not seen him, he'd received the news of his brother's return when he had come down from his room to the hall in the morning.

Jack wondered how long it would be before Richard managed to destroy what little they had. If he kept going at this pace, it would be soon. Already, in the brief time since Mary declared herself Queen, he had managed to place himself in between those two most wholly opposed sisters.

Most men would have taken Mary's kindness and generosity and been happy, but not Richard. Out of some archaic sense of duty, perhaps, he supported Elizabeth. Was it duty, Jack wondered, or was it more simply trying to make sure that they were on the winning side? If Mary was succeeded by Elizabeth, then Richard would stand to be rewarded a hundredfold in comparison to what Mary had given him. However, Elizabeth taking the throne was not something that Jack would place a bet on. If Northumberland had failed, then Anne Boleyn's daughter didn't stand much of a chance.

It was probably money, Jack concluded. There was no other reason why Richard would remain loyal to a girl who had allowed him to take the initial blame for Seymour's acts and done nothing to stop it. Why Richard was back, he didn't know; after he had returned to London, he had not expected to see him for months. Well, Jack thought, he was sure he would find out when Richard chose to tell him.

Jack was smoothing a hand down the neck of his brother's horse when the sound of footsteps made him turn. It was Dan, returned with his brother, and Jack smiled a greeting.

"Is my brother still in bed then?" Jack asked.

"It was late when we arrived," Dan replied defensively.

"Well, you are up?" Jack retorted. If he had been about to say more he was stopped when there was a shout from Froggy Tate near the closed gate.

Moments later, a rider arrived, his horse wheeling in front of the closed gates, breath billowing around them in the cold air. A shout from the mounted man ensured his admittance and a moment later there came the rumble and thump of the wooden bars being removed to open the gates. The man dropped from his horse. Jack set his feet towards him, but at the same time Richard appeared, dropping quickly down the few steps from the hall to the rider and Jack stood back and watched as a message was handed to his brother.

Richard opened and read it while Jack watched. The messenger Richard had despatched in the direction of the kitchen, but Jack's blue gaze was on the paper in Richard's hand that he had twisted and creased as he turned to walk back up the steps.

When Jack found Richard in the hall, he was standing near the fire. As Jack approached he could see his brother reading the paper thoughtfully.

"Who was the messenger from?" Jack asked, walking slowly towards Richard, his boots rustling the rushes on the floor.

Richard did not look around, he stowed the parchment inside his doublet. "A message from London, nothing you need concern yourself about, brother."

Jack matched his brother's stance and leant against the opposite side of the fire surround, regarding him with open blue enquiring eyes. "Are you sure?"

Richard met his gaze. Something seemed to change in his attitude. "It was a summons back to London."

"But you've only just got here!" Jack blurted. "The messenger must have been dispatched only hours after you left."

"I know," Richard rubbed a hand over his face, his voice tired. "And I will, of course, obey."

"Why do they want you back so soon?" Jack sounded confused. "For God's sake, you've just arrived. Surely you can stay for a day?"

Richard smiled. "What difference will a day make?"

"Or two?" Suggested Jack.

The winds had dropped later that day and the master had decided not to return directly to London but to hunt. The group of five left in the early morning, heading for the trees that surrounded Burton. Jack was riding close at his brother's side, Mat behind, and Dan, with Catherine, was bringing up the rear. She had taken plenty of taunts before they had ridden out, but seemed determined to keep up and ride well. They reached the trees and Mat held up his hand, signalling Dan and Catherine to wait. Richard and Jack had disappeared from sight into the darkness of the forest.

"Why have we stopped here?" Catherine said to Dan, her horse stamping at the mud beneath its hooves.

"They must have spied a beast. Probably they'll split and try and force it from cover into the open." Dan pulled his horse close to Catherine's. "Keep your eyes on the trees. I think I saw something over there."

Catherine shifted uncomfortably in the saddle. "We've been waiting for ages, it's freezing out here. Are you sure they have not forgotten us?" Catherine complained loudly.

"You wanted to come so less of your complaining, lass," Dan replied tersely. "They'll be out of there in good time."

"Couldn't we go in and have a look?" Catherine queried hopefully. Seeing Dan's face, she modified the suggestion. "Maybe just to the edge to see if we can see them?"

"You've less patience than Jack, if that's possible," Dan sounded exasperated.

Catherine considered this. "Jack's not impatient; he doesn't strike me as such."

"Oh you think so, do...? There!" Dan tightened his grip on the reins.

"Where?" Catherine said, alerting her horse, likewise, to the possibility of action. Dan pointed, and Catherine looked hard into the dim confines of the forest.

The hind burst from the woodland and paused for an instant, then, realising the folly of its move, it raced across the open meadow. Two riders, parted by some distance, appeared and turned to converge on the deer as it sped off into the slight valley, trying to make it to the sanctuary of the trees on the opposite slope. Dan had already turned his horse and began to spur it for the chase. Catherine was some way behind him. In front, she saw the lead riders beginning to gain on the hind as they neared the bottom of the gentle valley. There was a small stream, an easy jump for the hind, which made it to the other side. The two riders crossed the water-filled gap in the meadow with equal ease and continued hard on the trail of their quarry.

Dan was close to the stream, but Catherine was well behind still, cursing her tardiness and the horse beneath her. Ahead of her, she saw Mat and wondered briefly where he had come from. As the hind made her way towards the trees, Mat came down to meet her, having circled round for this very purpose. The hind, wide-eyed with fear and racing for her life, saw him and in her terror, turned back to face her pursuers. Seeing the trap, she veered to the left and headed back towards the stream, directly to where Catherine would make her crossing. Richard and Jack turned and rode across the field with Mat still riding down the slope towards them.

Catherine saw the hind too late. The horse reared, preparing to jump the gap in which the stream lay and the hind darted past her saddle. Catherine's foot slipped from one stirrup, and before she could scramble for her balance, she had slithered gracelessly from the side of the horse into the water. As her back hit the stream, the narrow gap in the field was crossed by Jack and Richard hard on the trail of the deer, and shortly after, by Mat.

Suffering no injury in the fall except a good soaking, Catherine retrieved her horse, which stood hock deep in the water next to its drenched rider. A wet hand pushed dripping hair from her face as she gathered the reins and climbed back into the saddle. Water ran from a nearly full right boot and trickled from the left, while her clothes clung uncomfortably to her body. Uncaring, she turned the horse back towards the spot where she had originally waited with Dan and urged it up the bank. In the distance, she spied the hunt; the desperate hind had almost made it back to the sanctuary of the woods. Catherine dug her heels in, attempting to catch them before they disappeared from view for a second time. She kept her eyes on the tree line as she rode up the bank.

Catherine had only a mental note of where the trio had entered the woods, and she rode straight for a gap between two pine trees with less care than she should have used. A low-hanging fronded branch slapped hard across her right cheek and then continued to drag bark against her skin, a reminder from nature to lessen her speed. Drawing back on the reins, she slowed the pace, aware of the imminent danger of losing an eye, or worse. Ahead, the noise of horses crashing through dried wood and rotting vegetation came to her ears, but the sound seemed to echo from the solid wood around her and it was no easy task to locate the hunt.

Slowing the horse further, she crossed the point where the forest took over completely from the meadowland. She continued in, with no thought for a way out if she should not find her companions. After half an hour of riding in what she believed was a straight line, Catherine admitted to being lost. There was no longer any noise save the sound of treetop birds in the dark green canopy above. Turning, she made to retrace her steps and return to the meadow, half expecting to be able to see her way back, not realising how far she had penetrated the deer's world. She was surprised to find that the way back was no clearer than the way in had been. Soon, doubt pierced her confidence, and the realisation dawned fully that she didn't know what direction she was going in. The cold of the cloth began to penetrate her body and the lack of sun meant it lay almost as wet as the moment she had emerged from the water. Anger at her foolishness and the humiliation she had brought on herself made her spur the horse on. If she did not get out of here soon, they would come and look, maybe, and that she would not be able to forget.

"Come on," she said to the horse. The sound of her own voice in the silence shocked her, but gritting her teeth, she began to concentrate on the path she would take. Not wanting to add further injury to herself, she kept her head low over the horse, relying heavily on the fact that her mount would not ride directly into the unyielding trees.

The horse stopped, refusing to go any further, its path blocked by bramble. The debris of nature was now waist high: fallen branches, sleeping bracken and barbed brier were all around. Catherine knew she had not passed this way before; the forest-skirts were not this overgrown. Forced to drop from the saddle, she led the horse behind her. The way forward was no longer an option; looking about, she chose the easiest route and set out, wondering if they were looking for her.

The deer was slumped over the hindquarters of Dan's horse, tongue extended, a broken arrow protruding from its chest, the steel bolt lodged deep in its heart. Jack was retelling for the fourth time how he had made the shot, how the arrow had arched, missing a branch, and made it true to the target. Mat leant over in his saddle and grimly exchanged a look with Dan. In the silent exchange, both acknowledged the other's fear that Jack would be nothing short of unbearable for the remainder of the day.

"It was a fine shot, Jack, but," Dan paused to allow Jack to acknowledge his praise, for it would be the last he got this day, "where's Catherine?"

"Last I saw, she was picking herself out of the water," Mat said, pointing back to where the hind had fled across the stream.

Jack chuckled. "Back at Burton then, in front of the fire." He set his horse homeward, eager to return. "Come, we'll have that tonight," he gestured at the carcass on Dan's horse. "Richard, you'll not join us?" Jack called over his shoulder, seeing his brother turn his horse away.

"I don't think she went back to Burton. She was foolish enough to have followed us into the forest," Richard gestured behind him. "Go back to Burton. If she's there, come back and let me know. I'll go and see if I can find her."

"She'll be in front of the fire drying out," Jack laughed as Richard spurred his horse back towards the trees.

Richard dismounted when he heard the noise of the horse and rider trudging through the woods. Tying his horse to a tree, he cast his eyes about until he located the source of the sound. It had been an easy trail to follow, crossing itself twice as Catherine had navigated in two circles back to the same clearing. Richard wondered if she knew of her folly. Leaning with his back to one of the massive oaks that dominated the forest, he watched the dim form of a rider leading a horse approach. If she did not look up, she would walk on and never see him. He said nothing and waited.

Shoulders slumped, she marched doggedly on, stopping to circumnavigate a fallen branch, and then continued leading the horse behind her. Still, she did not see the watcher. A thicket of knotted bramble and dried brown bracken blocked her advance and she turned left to avoid it, passing within feet of him.

The early March dusk was falling, but where they were, deep in the forest, he was sure Catherine was not aware of the imminence of the night. The horse was still plodding carefully behind her as she led it through the tangle of undergrowth. There was a clearing in the trees to her left and she headed towards the false hope of escape. On reaching it she found the thinning of the trees had been caused by the crash to earth by one of the mighty giants, and the younger trees, which had lived weakly in its shadow, had not yet had the chance to fully take its place.

As he watched, the girl cast her eyes around, still not seeing him, and set off in another direction.

Richard, folding his arms, recited to the trees.

"And wilt thou leave me thus?
Say nay, say nay, for shame
To save thee from the blame.
Of all my grief and grame.
And wilt thou leave me thus?"

Catherine stopped abruptly. The horse took two more steps, bumping into her back and forcing her to stumble forwards.

The poet continued, hiding a grin.

"And wilt thou leave me thus?
That hath loved thee so long.
In wealth and woe among?
And is thy heart so strong,
As for to leave me thus? Say nay."

Catherine tied the horse to an outstretched mossy branch and began to pick her way back towards him.

"And wilt thou leave me thus?
That hath given thee my heart.
Never for to depart,
Neither for pain nor smart?
And wilt thou leave me thus? Say nay,"

Richard continued, eyes still lifted to the green gilded canopy above. Catherine stopped, a hand on a rotting branch as she climbed over the final obstacle between them.

> *"And wilt thou leave me thus*
> *And have no more pity*
> *Of him that loveth thee?*
> *Hélas, thy cruelty!*
> *And wilt thou leave me thus? Say nay."*

Richard watched Catherine's clumsy approach. Finally she stood before him. The noise of twigs bending and snapping had stopped, and the pair observed each other in silence.

"Ah, apparently you'll not leave," Richard said, observing the dirty, damp girl with bright eyes that burnt with hate from behind lank hair.

"Spare me your words. I know them already," Catherine's voice was filled with anger.

"Do you indeed? Well, that's a trick if you can manage it. Tell me, lady fortune, what will I say next?" Richard enquired as he regarded her seriously.

"Don't," was the only reply he got.

"Please, come on, what exactly do you think I will say?" Richard insisted. "I've never met an oracle before."

Catherine sighed deeply. "That I have been a fool, that I have no right to be here, that I have caused trouble to no end... That I was probably lucky not to have killed myself."

"Undeniably a fair assessment," Richard agreed, nodding. "However, I was going to leave that to Jack. You have disappointed me."

"What then?" Catherine, pushing the damp hair away from her eyes, looked at him with confusion on her face.

"I thought perhaps to tell you that your skills on a horse had improved. Perhaps you should address your directional talents next. Moss," Richard paused, "only grows on one side of a tree, the north side. A point which should obviously be included in all young ladies' education in the future, do you not agree?"

Catherine's head hung from her shoulders. "I didn't know."

"But it's a lesson well learnt, would you not say?" Richard replied, unfolding his arms and moving towards her.

"Can we leave, please? I am sorry for what I have done. Believe me, I did not want to have this conversation with you," Catherine said, her voice still bearing an edge of anger.

"Ah, maybe I should leave again, if my presence is so unwelcome," Richard said sadly.

"Stop it, Richard!" Catherine shouted. "Let me be. The price of salvation is too high."

"What price is that?" he asked, watching as she turned to leave.

"That you mock me at every meeting, without need, without reason." Catherine turned back to face him, her arms thrown wide, tears running from her eyes. "Without provocation, and without mercy." Catherine pointed at the tree to her left. "North, I know now, thank you."

Richard watched her make her way back towards her horse. "Only one problem with that," he called when she was nearly there.

"What's that?" she said through clenched teeth. When no reply came, she wheeled back again. "What? Tell me." Catherine stormed back across the forest, snaring her boot in the brier and nearly pitching herself on the floor. Furious now, she shouted, "Tell me!"

"You want to go east," Richard confessed, grinning.

"East!" Catherine yelled at him, exasperation and anger warming her cold blood. "You just said north."

"No, I said that way," Richard pointed, "is north. I didn't say to go north, did I?"

The blow she aimed would never have connected. Richard intercepted it easily and held her wrist in a steel grip. Close together for a second, he held her immobile before wrenching her arm up her back and bringing Catherine to her knees in front of him. Crouching down behind her, he spoke quietly in her ear, "And that way – where your horse is standing, good lady – is east."

Catherine's head hung in front of her; damp tendrils of hair obscuring her face. Richard felt the fight leave her body. She had stopped pulling against his grip. He released the pressure on her shoulder and loosened his hold, but did not let go.

Still holding her wrist, he brought her arm around her waist and lifted her back to her feet. As she stood he could feel her legs trembling and she was forced to stand with her weight against him.

"Can you stand?" His voice was no longer mocking, there was serious concern in his tone.

Catherine did not reply in words but nodded; he was sure she would have made that response even if both her legs had been severed beneath her. Knowing her lie, he released her wrist but stood close as she swayed slightly when the prop of his body was removed.

Taking a firm hold on her shoulders, he reversed her to rest against the tree while he went to collect their mounts. The expression on her face told him just how miserable she was feeling.

Leading the horses back towards her, he resolved that he was going to have to do something about Catherine's situation. She was filthy, wearing outsized clothes, and covered in a good layer of grime. Jack might have ensured her physical welfare, but that was all. The girl needed to be removed from Burton, and he would try again to contact her family. De Bernay had been Mary's man, and it may be that he could press Derby to intervene on her behalf. He owed her that much.

Handing her the reins to her horse, Richard pulled himself easily into his own saddle. He watched her as she wrapped both hands around the pommel and tried, and failed, to pull herself onto the horse's back, her arms shaking with the effort. "I can't..." Catherine sobbed, the humiliation producing more tears.

Richard pulled his horse next to hers, extended an arm for her to take, and pulled her easily up to sit in front of him.

"Lass, you are freezing. Have this." The girl in front of him was shivering. He hadn't realised just how wet she was. Pulling his riding cloak from around his neck, he draped it over her shoulders.

Catherine tucked herself within the folds of the fabric and slowly they set off, Richard leading her horse behind his.

"I don't believe it!" the girl exclaimed in disgust soon after they had set off when his horse stepped from the wooded forest and onto the Lincoln Road.

"I didn't think you'd be very pleased either when you found out just how close you were," Richard turned Corracha towards the village, pressing his heels into its flanks as the horse quickened his pace. Shortly afterwards, in the dim evening light, they saw the darkened outline of the village, and beyond that, the towering structure of the mill.

Froggy Tate was in the courtyard when he arrived and caught hold of Corracha's bridle.

"Catherine, come on, get down and we'll get you warmed up." Richard didn't receive a reply. The girl wrapped in the cloak was wholly unresponsive.

"Froggy, help her down," Richard instructed, lowering the dead weight towards the man's waiting arms. Dropping from the saddle himself, he relieved Froggy of his burden and headed in the direction of the kitchen.

Catherine, cold and barely conscious, missed the argument between Richard and Tilly. The woman was halfway through butchering the hind with the help of her niece and had told Richard if he wanted water boiling, then he could fetch the firewood himself. There followed a heated and short exchange, after which Tilly left Ada to guard the carcass against the manor's dogs and went off to bring in the firewood and water.

The girl was still wrapped in his cloak when he carried her up the main stone stairs to her room. The cloak was wet, and he replaced it with a blanket from the bed, laying her on the floor, her head on a cushion, in front of the freshly lit fire.

"Oh, no, my pretty, don't you go to sleep," Richard said in a stern voice, his hands on her shoulders as he tried to rouse her. "Catherine, listen to me. Can you hear me?"

He didn't receive a reply. Her eyelids opened for a moment only, before closing again.

"Catherine, wake up," Richard looked around the room. Finding a pitcher of cold water, he slopped a good measure over her face.

"Ahhh!" Catherine exclaimed, the slap of the icy water jolting her back awake. "No, please, I want to go..." Her words trailed off.

Richard pulled her to a sitting position. "Listen, Catherine, carefully. You fell in the stream, spent half the day soaking wet in the wind and you are half frozen. You must stay awake. If you sleep, you'll not wake up again. Answer me," he demanded again, giving her shoulder a good shake.

"I hear you," Catherine replied quietly.

Satisfied, he let her go. Rising, he answered the knock on the door and let in Tilly as she dragged in one of the washtubs with the help of Marc. After Tilly had made a dozen trips back to the kitchen, the tub was full.

Catherine's eyes had closed against the world again when Richard picked her up. Her hand tried to ineffectually grasp at the blanket that slithered to the floor.

A moment later, Richard stood back, his arms dripping from the elbows, his shirt soaked.

Catherine, still dressed, was submerged almost fully in the hot water he had kicked the kitchen staff bodily to provide. He knelt, his arms resting on the rim of the tub, and looked at her. "Nice?" he enquired.

Catherine did not look at him, but moved down into the hot depths of the tub. "Did you feel it necessary to leave my boots on?" she asked, a half smile tentatively on her face.

"Foot," Richard commanded, moving to stand at the end of the tub. The surface of the water erupted as a boot emerged. "Next." The second was thrown to land, discarded by the first, water running to pool on the floor.

"Thank you," Catherine said.

"Shout before you dissolve and I shall get you out of there," Richard said. "I hope we can call a truce, you and I."

"A truce?" Catherine repeated.

"Can you not see that you and I are both on the same side?" Richard asked.

Catherine looked away, ashamed. "I suppose I can... a truce, then."

Chapter Twenty-Two
London – May 1554

On May 19, 1554, Elizabeth finally left the confines of the Tower. Renard had ceased to press for a case of treason to be laid against her and the Privy Council admitted to Mary that there was indeed only insubstantial evidence against her. The Council was also swayed by fears for the succession. Mary remained unmarried and doubts continued about her ability, due to her age, to bear a child for England. Instead, marriage plans for Elizabeth were the subject of council conversations as a possible route to securing an heir.

That same month, the Court moved to Richmond, and Elizabeth to Woodstock in Oxfordshire. It was an improvement on the Tower, but still she remained as she had done at Whitehall: under close guard. There was to be no doubt in her mind that she remained Mary's prisoner, her household comprised of six servants only, including Kate. She was not allowed visitors, and Bedingfield, her gaoler, had instructions to keep from her the means to write letters. Elizabeth's communications with Mary were not welcomed. They wished to silence the thorn and leave England's rose quietly in the wings while the country's main players watched to see if the pending marriage could solve the question of the succession.

Elizabeth and Mary were not the only ones to have been moving. Catherine too moved that May from the draughty rooms at Burton to slightly more comfortable rooms in Lincoln. Richard decreed that it was not suitable or safe for her to remain at the manor. Catherine did not argue. Although no longer afraid of Richard, she was still uncomfortable in his presence and life at Burton was, to say the least, not easy.

How they made the connection he was never sure, but nevertheless Richard found himself linked to the conspirators, Wyatt and Courtenay.

The night he visited Kate in the garden after Elizabeth had left for the Tower, he had been watched over by a man who followed him back to his house and had then reported the incident to Renard. From that moment, a watch was set on his house, and although for many months nothing damning was revealed, eventually a messenger leaving Richard's house was traced to Thomas Parry, part of the Lady Elizabeth's household, and the connection was made. The allegations that Robert had made were now painfully confirmed.

Renard had contacted Robert after closer scrutiny had revealed that certain papers he knew had been through Richard's hands were not what they should have been. Now Robert found himself meeting with Thomas Pierce, Renard's man.

"It has been asked that I should come and talk about a matter you raised with Ambassador Renard some time ago," Thomas Pierce said shortly. He was elderly, single-minded and a cleric by trade and nature. Dourly dressed he was in sharp contrast with Robert's lavish ostentation.

"That's right. Seen sense, has he?" Robert sneered, not offering the man a seat.

Thomas Pierce chose to ignore the remark. "I wish only to know if you can tell me where we may find your brother."

"I don't know," Robert admitted. "Do you believe now what I told you?"

"It has come to light that there may be something in what you alleged, yes," Pierce conceded.

"Well, it's treason, issue a warrant for his arrest. A day in the Tower and you'll know for sure that I was right," Robert said hotly.

"Unfortunately, no," Thomas Pierce said, folding his hands in front of him. "So you have no idea as to his whereabouts?"

"What do you mean, 'unfortunately no'? You can't leave him to his own devices any longer, surely?" Robert exclaimed.

Thomas Pierce sighed. "We wish to trace your brother, but a public execution is not our intent. Maybe some other charge..." He left the words to hang in the air between them.

Robert smiled. "Would murder be a valid reason to issue a warrant for his arrest?"

Thomas Pierce was smiling now. "Some such charge would allow him to be pursued as a common criminal, that's true, it would be very helpful."

Robert supplied him with such details as he had about Richard's killing of Harry's men. The bargain was plain. Should they move to arrest his brother then he, Robert, would be informed? Pierce told him they knew of the house in Chapel Street and confirmed their quarry had slipped from there and that he awaited word on whether he was at Burton. If he was, then, of course, Pierce would inform Robert.

Dan left Chapel Street when men came in search of Richard, stole a horse from the stables of the Fox and spurred the beast from London to Burton to warn the master.

Richard's mistake was that he was too sure that the charge he was to be arrested on was treason; that it would be couched in terms of blackmail and murder, he missed.

Richard grabbed his brother's arm and steered him quickly along the corridor to his own room. Pushing Jack inside, he slammed the door.

"What the hell..." Jack protested, turning to face his brother.

"For once listen," Richard's voice was hard and serious.

"All I..." Jack tried again.

Richard raised his voice a fraction. "For once, listen. I will tell you all the bloody facts and then I will ask you, beg you if need be, to do something for me. I am to be arrested... Silence, Jack!" Richard raised his hand. "... very soon. The constable's men are in Lincoln now. The charge, I believe, is treason. I want you to go and strike a deal with the constable for your life, the men's lives and Burton, if you can manage it, in exchange for me. There's plenty will believe your actions. I want you to do this now." He raised his hand again. Jack's eyes were wide. "Your conscience will be clear." Richard produced a wry smile. "Don't make me beg. It will make no difference. They will have me one way or the other, so take what you can from it. Now, go to Lincoln. There is a price on my head. Claim it. Take Dan with you. He knows already. Go."

Richard had to physically propel Jack back towards the door, his brother was not for leaving. Dan appearing then, took a strong hold on the protesting Jack and managed to drag him from Richard's presence. Jack, confused and with questions pouring from him, allowed himself eventually to be taken by Dan to the yard and the waiting horses.

Richard watched them leave Burton, the horse's hooves clattering on the cobbles at the gateway and then beating loudly on the wooden bridge before they took the road to Lincoln. The manor suddenly seemed silent, Richard was sure the only noise now was coming from inside his head. Rubbing a hand hard across his face and closing his eyes on the world for a moment he readied himself for what was about to happen.

Catherine was in Lincoln, it was market day and she had been perusing the stalls when she saw Dan loitering near a group of tethered horses. Crossing to him she found the big man agitated, and he soon told her what he knew.

"Master is just going to sit and wait for them. I cannot..." Dan was lost for words, his voice full of pain.

"Maybe he doesn't believe they are really coming for him?" Catherine said, sounding confused.

"He knows alright, and just to make sure he's sent Jack here to strike a deal for him," Dan said shaking his head. "I was wrong, I was so wrong. Richard was right. He knew this would happen."

"I don't understand. Jack wouldn't betray Richard, would he?" Catherine said, disbelief on her face.

"No. Unfortunately the master has set him to do it, and Jack didn't stop to think. I rode over with him just now, and he's with the sheriff working out what he can get for himself. Look, over there." Dan pointed and Catherine recognised Jack's horse tethered where some uniformed soldiers waited. "Master made me swear to stand by Jack and carry out his wishes, but it is not something I do happily."

"You're right! We can't just let them take him, we've got to warn him." Catherine's eyes had widened as she realised what was about to happen.

"Listen, lass, he knows well enough that they are coming, but if you want to try and shift him, you're welcome to try," Dan said. "I can do nothing, I have sworn to stand by Jack and I will not let the Master down."

Richard saw the horse approaching from where he watched through one of the narrow stone windows on Burton's top floor. From here he had the best view of the Lincoln Road and he been watching and waiting for the constable's men. Instead, he saw a lone rider making their way directly to the manor.

Richard swore as he recognised who it was, hands pushing away from the wall he headed quickly down the main stairs. As he crossed the yard, he could hear the horse approaching on the other side, the sound of the hoofbeats told him the horse had not slowed from a canter when it had started to cross the wooden bridge leading to the closed manor gates.

Running, he tried to cross the yard before the horse arrived. Before he got there, he heard the horse neigh, the sound of a falling rider met his ears along with a loud cry of exclamation.

Richard ripped the locking bar from the back of the gate and let it tumble to the ground, both hands on the gate he hauled it open.

Fallen from her horse, Catherine was in the process of pushing herself back up.

"If you have something to tell me I hope you have not just knocked it from your brains." Richard took hold of her arm and pulled her quickly to her feet.

"The Queen's men are bound this way now, leave quickly before they get here, there's still time," Catherine blurted, swaying on unsteady feet.

"That is most unfortunately true and, alas, not a product of the knock on the head you just gave yourself," Richard moved past her and took hold of the horse's trailing reins.

"They won't be far behind me. I saw them in Lincoln," Catherine said, and then added helpfully, "there were eight of them."

"There'll be more than eight of them by the time they get here. The constable's not stupid enough to try and take Burton with eight. He'll pick up a force from the Bishop of Lincoln," Richard said, pulling Catherine and the horse through the opening. Froggy Tate had arrived and, after a word from the master, secured the gate and then led the panting horse away.

Richard said nothing. He propped her against the wall, and when she did not seem in fear of falling, left her.

"What will you do?" Catherine said stepping quickly after Richard on unsteady feet as he headed towards the hall.

"Master says you are to come with me," Froggy had reappeared.

"What?" snapped Catherine.

"The master said I'm to take you out of here now. Come on," Froggy moved to catch hold of her arm.

"No, I stay. I didn't come here to be ignored," Catherine hissed at him. "Where's he gone?"

"He's in the hall. Now come on." Froggy made a grab for her arm. Catherine ducked and ran for the hall, her knees still trembling from the fall. Richard was seated on a chair on the dais, a cup of wine in his hand.

"Didn't you listen to me?" Catherine yelled as she ran through the door into the empty hall towards him.

"What would you have me do?" There was anger in Richard's voice.

"Leave before they get here would seem the sensible course," Catherine said, arms apart, leaning across the table towards him. "Do you intend to sit here and let them take you?"

"A perfect observation," Richard replied coolly.

"Why?" she yelled at him. "Go! You can get away still. I cannot believe you are going to sit there."

"The lamb to the slaughter," he said quietly, swilling the wine around the cup.

Catherine pushed his shoulder back, so he was forced to face her.

"Unhand me, lady. Believe me, this will be difficult enough. It is not, I hope you realise, an act I do with pleasure. Now get out of here, this is not a child's game," Richard voice was angry.

Outside the hall, both of them heard a number of horses entering the yard.

"They've opened the gates and let them in!" Catherine gasped.

Richard took her arm in a frightening grip. "Get you from my hall." He pushed her away from him. Catherine stumbled backwards.

In the corner was the narrow wooden door leading to the rooms above and to the wooden gallery that overlooked the hall. Catherine, her eyes never leaving Richard's made it to the door in half a dozen quick paces, closing it a moment before the constable's men burst into the hall.

Catherine arrived on the balcony over the dais in time to see Mat leading the men towards Richard seated at the table. One officer advanced towards the Master and she saw him take from his doublet a document and bang it down in front of the seated man. Richard raised his cup in what looked like a toast to the officer. Catherine watched open-mouthed as the officer slapped it from his hand, wine spilling the length of the table, glistening like blood on the surface.

More men entered. Catherine's eyes widened as she recognised the figure of Alan striding in amongst them, laughing confidently. Mat, she saw, was still deep in conversation with the uniformed officer he had entered with.

Richard was hauled to his feet. The men in the hall watched as his doublet was ripped from him until he stood in his shirt. He wasn't resisting, but two men held him tightly and pressed his hands together where they were bound securely.

As he began to walk across the hall, one of the men who had held him placed a hand in the small of his back making him stumble forward. Alan suddenly stepped in close to him. Catherine could not hear the words, but the final comment was a punch to the head from Alan which knocked Richard to the floor. Awkwardly, and slowly, he got back to his feet, watched by his own men who stood around the hall. They led him out through the kitchens so she deduced they were not leaving but must be using the storerooms as a temporary gaol.

Catherine continued to look on. None of Richard's men were being rounded up. They were still armed, drink had been broken out and the scene in the hall was nothing short of one of revelry and celebration. Had they sold their master? She could think of nothing else but this to account for what had happened. What to do? Where to go now? And where was Jack?

The balcony was dark, and she knew she couldn't be seen from below, but even so she crawled to the furthest end and curled up. Knees pulled tightly to her chest and her arms wrapped around her body she shut out the world.

Catherine was startled awake by the noise of the hall door slamming shut. It was dark now, and the hall was lit by tapers and a few candles in the wall sconces. Peering between the rotting wooden balustrades she could see that two men had entered the hall and were greeted by the officer who had banged the document down in front of Richard earlier.

As soon as the taller of the two discarded his riding cloak, she recognised him as Jack. Pressing her face hard against the carved oak, she tried but failed to hear the words they exchanged. What did meet her ears though after some minutes was the unmistakable sound of laughter. The officer clapped Jack on the back and handed him wine from an opened bottle on the table, and the small group sat down to share a drink and conversation by the fire.

Catherine crawled the length of the gallery and peered down the narrow stairs that led to the hall below; there was no one in sight. Keeping low she made a quick descent. The old wood creaked loudly despite her careful tread, but the noise brought no one to investigate. The gallery stairs led to a corridor at the back of the hall, taking you either to the kitchens or out to the courtyard; she took the kitchen route. Rounding a corner Catherine heard the sound of voices and, dropping to her knees, she peered round the wall.

Two men sat playing cards in the corridor: Richard's temporary gaolers, she guessed, and the gaol was one of the storerooms.

Jack's room was thankfully unlocked. She breathed deeply as she slid the door open and entered. The shutters were not drawn, and some light spilt in from the moon. Catherine knew exactly what she wanted. On a shelf she found a knife and collected a doublet from the back of a chair. Carefully descending the stairs, she made her way through the deserted kitchen, pausing at the table to retrieve a bottle of wine which stood open, forgotten by the revellers.

The storerooms, of which there were three, were below the level of the ground at the back of the Manor, keeping them cool all year round. Slatted iron grills, however, did admit some light, and these were at grass level. He could be in any one of the three, she thought, crawling along the grass she peered through the grills trying to determine which one.

"If you make any more noise, you will most certainly rouse the constable's men." It was Richard's voice that met her grateful ears.

"Where are you?" Catherine whispered into the dark.

"Down here and not likely to be going anywhere." Laid flat on the grass she peered into the storeroom. Her eyes, growing accustomed to the gloom, found themselves staring into Richard's, his face lit by the moonlight. "So, fair damsel, have you come to rescue me? I do hope not," Richard's voice was light and careless.

"I don't understand. What's going on? Jack's with them as well, he is in the hall with those men," Catherine said, and then added, "they're laughing."

"Ah well, I am a comic figure am I not?" Richard didn't sound overly concerned by his situation.

Catherine suddenly remembered her acquisitions. "Here, I have a doublet for you. It must be freezing in there."

"The rats and I are not particularly warm, it's true. However?" He raised his tied hands so she could see them.

Catherine received a genuine smile from the captive as she slid the knife through the bars to cut his bonds. Touching his skin as she removed the rope, she got a good measure of how cold he was.

"I got this as well," Catherine handed the bottle of wine along with the doublet through the bars.

"Ah Catherine," Richard smiled, "to what shall we drink?"

"To you getting out of here," she said quickly.

"That, I am afraid, is not possible," his voice said in the darkness.

"Why?" Catherine said receiving the bottle back.

"I will give you the simple version. Jack's dislike of me is well known. On hearing of my pending arrest, he contacted the constable, told him my whereabouts, and struck a bargain. The results of which are that, if the men fall under Jack's leadership and he hands me over to the Queen, then he takes control of the manor and men, and everyone, obviously with the exception of me, is happy."

"But..."

"Before you confront him he does it with my blessing," Richard said firmly.

"Why?" Catherine was exasperated.

"That I cannot say," Richard said receiving the bottle back.

"Is it something to do with Elizabeth?" Catherine used the scrap of information that Dan had given her.

"Who told you that?" Richard's answer was confirmation enough.

"That I cannot say," she mocked him, "but they will take you to the gallows."

"I do not think they intend for me to live long enough to swing from a rope," Richard said bluntly. "We will have to see."

She took the bottle back again and drank.

"Did I hurt you?" asked the voice quietly from the dark.

"Which time?" Catherine answered quickly.

"I am a wretch in a cell. Forgive me if you can," Richard replied.

"I was hoping to have the opportunity to get even," Catherine's voice was bitter.

He appeared not to have heard her. "Go to my room when you can. Lift the stone in the grate, you'll see a hole in it, use the poker to move it, take what you find there and give them to Jack," he said. "I hope he will have some use for them. There wasn't time earlier."

Chapter Twenty-Three
Lincolnshire – June 1554

Catherine entered Richard's room nervously. Closing the door quietly behind her, she set the latch back into place quietly and hoped no one had seen her enter. She turned to view, for the first time, the interior. Scantily furnished, for Richard had hardly ever been at Burton, it contained a bed, desk, and two sets of shelves. Everything was in disarray; the room had been searched; it seemed.

A book lay on the floor next to the bed, discarded there as the thieves had looked for better loot. Catherine leant over and retrieved the volume, though she was unable to discern its contents, as the language within was French. The pages were laid out in the fashion of poetry, and with more care than had been used to put it on the floor, she placed the book back on the table.

There hadn't been a fire in the grate for some while, but it was still filled with ash and part burnt wood. Catherine used her hands to push the debris out of the grate and onto the hearth. The cracks in the stone flagging beneath were visible, as was the hole he had told her about. The edge of the poker fitted neatly and provided the tool to lift the stone.

Anything beneath would surely be burnt, she thought. The heat would easily penetrate the slab. But no, the stone fitted well and below was a deep shaft, probably originally leading to the floor below. At full arm's stretch, she felt in the darkness. On a ledge in the shaft her fingers ran over something that felt like leather, and next to it her fingers touched something icy cold, her inquisitive hands pressed over its sharpened surface. Wrapping her hands around the palm-sized object, and moving carefully so not to drop it to the bottom of the shaft, she lifted it out into the light.

Despite the cover of dust, Catherine stared wide-eyed at the jewelled cross she held, the chain still hanging beneath in the darkness. Without hesitation, she pulled it over her head before reaching back again for the other object she had felt on the stone shelf in the blackness.

Jack heard the noise as he passed the door to Richard's room. Who was in there? Squaring his shoulders, he lifted the latch silently and let the door swung quietly open.

Catherine!

The filthy figure kneeling near the hearth could be no other. He watched as soot-blackened hands dropped a stone back into place and began to shovel the debris back into the fire. What the hell was she doing here? The question was the herald of the answer, which exploded on its heels. She had done this! She had finally succeeded and taken her revenge against his brother. Richard had been right.

His hand behind him, Jack quietly closed the door. The latch clicked loudly, metal on metal as it dropped back into place.

"Jack! You gave me a fright." The dirty face smiled up at him from where she was still kneeling near the grate.

"What were you doing?" Jack asked, his face set hard, blue eyes blazing with anger.

"Richard told me to get—"

You bitch.

Catherine hesitated. She seemed suddenly unsure, and the smile had dropped from her face. "I was..."

Roughly, he took hold of her arm, hauling her to her feet. "What have you done?"

Catherine stood in front of him, her hands holding something out.

"Here, Jack. Please take it. What's wrong? What's happened?" Catherine was holding something out towards him, her voice pleading with him.

"And this?" A fist grabbed the cross, gouging the chain into her skin. He jerked it so hard that she stumbled to her knees before him.

"I found it with the papers," Catherine's voice was almost a scream as her hands fought to pull the chain from her neck. "Please, Jack. Please..."

Suddenly, Jack let her go. Catherine dropped to the floor. As she did, he flipped the chain over her head, retrieving the cross.

"Jack... what are you doing?" Catherine cried, tears cutting streaks through the soot on her face.

"Why?" His words were agonisingly hoarse. "Why did you set the dogs on him?"

"I didn't! I came to warn him." Catherine told him quickly how she had met Dan in Lincoln. "Why don't you believe me, or is it that you have truly deserted him? You were in Lincoln and I saw you in the hall, Jack, with those men, and Alan is here as well. It was you, wasn't it? I wouldn't have cast you in the role of Judas."

"I saw this. I don't know who to trust," Jack stepped back and sat on the edge of the bed, his head in his hands, "and that comes from one who is himself the traitor."

"No, Jack, no." Catherine got from her knees and went to sit on the edge of the bed near him. "Richard told me you are not a traitor and that you do this at his bidding."

Jack looked up, half a dark smile on his face. "Did I?" He held the cross up before sliding the chain over his head and dropping the cold metal beneath his shirt. "I saw this and... God, what have I done?"

Jack rose from his seat and the cross swung back to lightly pat his chest as he stood. He had given it to Richard during their time in France when their funds were gone. Richard had told him plainly that he would redeem it, to trust him. Jack's temper had been ignited as his rich and noble brother attempted to deprive his bastard sibling of one of the two items of value he possessed. He had told him as much and the argument had ended when he flung the cross in Richard's face. But here it was. Jack ran his hands through his already untidy hair.

"I don't understand why he sat there and waited for them to take him," Catherine said, reviving his attention.

"Don't you?" Jack said bitterly. "They have connected him with Elizabeth and he thought they came to arrest him as a traitor. Richard thought he would go to London, be tried and condemned as such. If he left and ran, he would have still been branded a traitor and Elizabeth would have been tainted by his deeds. If he was tried and managed to resist confession, he could have done as Wyatt did and, with his words from the scaffold making it clear his actions were his own, try to keep the lady safe." Jack lifted his eyes to consider her. "You don't look like you believe me. Why?"

"Oh, I believe you. I am just surprised. I cannot comprehend why a man like Richard would sacrifice himself like that," Catherine said.

"What do you mean by 'a man like Richard', exactly?" Jack asked, although he knew fairly well what she would say.

"I saw him in the hall, the way he looked, what they did, and I felt sorry for him. But Jack, you know what he is like better than anyone. In whatever he does, he is acting for himself." In a rush, the floodgates holding back all the resentment she had felt for this man, and bottled up, came rushing forth. "What you tell me he is doing is so at odds with all else he has done. I would have attributed to him with many things, but a conscience? To die a martyr? No, I can't believe this. There has to be more to it, Jack. He rarely speaks the truth. Are you sure this time you are right? Richard is more apt to watch others suffer than to suffer himself." Catherine had moved to sit opposite him in the only chair in the room.

Jack shook his head.

"You don't agree with me, do you?" Catherine asked, looking at Jack's saddened face in the firelight. "What about when he sided with Northumberland, a paid mercenary, and everyone at Assingham was murdered?"

"It was not Richard; it was Geoffrey, Byrne's son. He was bored from waiting, so took some of his men and attacked. Richard beat him half to death. Geoffrey's father thought Richard was set to kill his son. He has tried to tell you this," Jack supplied.

"And my father? He was killed as well, don't forget that," Catherine retorted.

Jack shook his head. "But not by Richard, not by us. He rode into a group of armed men as Northumberland tried to take Mary. You can hardly blame Richard for that, can you?" Jack reasoned.

"It could have been his men who killed my father. He's never denied it. He was on Northumberland's side then," Catherine said hotly.

"Stop! Believe me, it wasn't us. Richard and his men all left Assingham and went straight to Framlingham without incident, while I took you to the Abbey," Jack said, his voice weary.

"But I can't... he's..." Catherine trailed off, trying to think of more evidence to support her argument.

"Stop, Catherine, please. I know how you feel. I told you a long time ago that he acts; that you shouldn't believe what you see. He does nothing himself to make you feel any different. He's told me before that you needed someone to blame, and he was happy to take that blame. He thought it might have helped you." Jack looked up and his blue eyes met hers. "I think you should forgive him."

"I believe you, but..." her words trailed off. "How long do you think they will keep him here before he goes to London?"

"I'm not sure, and there is a chance that they intend to take him south," Jack's voice was serious.

"But you said he would be tried for treason," Catherine sounded confused.

"No, I said Richard believed they would try him as a traitor. If he did not believe that, he wouldn't have let them imprison him below. He's got connections, lots of them. I can't even begin to guess at who they are and he never talks about it. Perhaps he believes that if they take him to London, they will save him. God's bones, I don't know what's happening, and I can't think!" Jack's voice was filled with anguish and he spoke from behind, hands that covered his face.

"So, what will happen?" Catherine stood, her tone desperate.

"I don't know. I think maybe they will kill him here," Jack said in monotone. "Soon, probably. I suspect the constable awaits confirmation of this order. When I spoke to him in the hall, he hinted that Richard would be lucky to leave here alive."

"No! It didn't seem so bad if they were to take him to London. There would have been time, but now..." Catherine sounded horrified.

"Mat is watching for a rider from the south. If I get advance warning, perhaps I can do something." there was agony in Jack's voice.

"Does he know?" Catherine asked, her eyes wide.

"Richard is no fool. I suspect he knew it was always a risk, but he was willing to take it." Jack's voice was quiet.

"What are we going to do?" Catherine asked.

"I wish I knew the answer to that question. While there is the possibility that there could be a trial or that he will be taken to London, I do not think he will wish to escape. Time is not on my side. That's why I have Mat posted to give me some warning." He could feel the unaccustomed weight of the cross against his chest, and he swallowed hard.

"And you, what do they think you are doing?" Catherine asked.

"They think," Jack paused, and the pain returned to his face again, "that I wish him dead. Perhaps I did; once, but not now. The deal is they leave me Burton in exchange for my help, but I feel that there is more than a good chance that they will renege on it fairly easily."

"They don't trust you?" Catherine asked.

"Oh, I think they fairly believe I want rid of Richard and that I wish to succeed him here, and at the moment they will argue no different–the men here outnumber the constables. But they'll not leave a troop of mercenaries with no fixed allegiance for long unchained. I am sure the Bishop of Lincoln perceives me a threat to the peace of the area. Time will tell," Jack said.

"Alan, I saw him... What's he doing here?" Catherine said, "I almost forgot about him. He was in the hall and he hit Richard."

"Now that is a question I can't answer. He was with the constable's men when I arrived at Lincoln. There was little I could say to him in their company. I am fairly sure he's here with the intention of taking Richard's place, but how he's involved in all of this, I don't know." Jack's head hurt. "Richard would know."

"There were these as well, you've not looked at them," Catherine crossed the room and tentatively held out the leather roll towards Jack, then when he didn't take it, she pulled away the securing strings and revealed the papers folded inside. "Here look, he told me to give you these."

"Let us see what Richard had," Jack reached out and took them from her. Catherine returned to the chair and watched him in the firelight as he began to study the papers.

"These will not help," he said, sighing deeply. The paper slipped from his hand and dropped onto the floor.

"Jack?" Getting no reply, she picked up the paper and read for herself William Fitzwarren's confession. "Jack, is this you? Jack?"

Recovering, he met her eyes, his face pale. "Aye. Let us bury this for the moment." Jack took the page from her hand and put it inside his doublet. "I must start to act like a brother. You said you spoke to Richard?"

"Yes, through the window at the back near the kitchens, they are keeping him in one of the storerooms." Catherine sounded eager now, hoping he had some ideas on a course of action.

"Do you think you can speak to him again?" Jack asked, "without being seen?"

"Yes, it's dark, it should be easy," Catherine agreed quickly.

"Go, speak to him. Tell him that you've spoken to me. Tell him that I believe that they will not let him leave here alive."

Catherine nodded.

"Ask him why he thinks Alan is at Burton? Gauge his reaction, see if he welcomes help and then come back here," Jack said. Catherine hesitated. "Go now, off with you," Jack said, and then, seeing her disappointment at his own lack of actions, added, "I think better when I am alone."

Catherine took more wine with her and silently made her way to the back of the manor. For the second time, she lay on the grass and stared into the darkness.

"Well, if it isn't Catherine, come again to enjoy my misery," Richard said from the blackness below her.

"Are you all right?" Catherine replied.

"Save your platitudes for those who welcome them. Speaking of such, how is that brother of mine?" Richard sounded annoyed.

"Jack sent me," Catherine whispered, ignoring his tone.

"Did he?" Richard replied bluntly.

"Yes, he's trying to help. He doesn't know why Alan is here, but he suspects he has something to do with this," Catherine explained quietly.

Richard moved nearer to the grilled window and stared up at her. "I am sure he does."

"Why? Tell me?" Catherine said, concern in her voice, and one of her hands tightening around the bar at the window.

"It means, mistress, that my brother had better have his wits about him. That Alan is here can mean only one thing, that he is looking to take my place."

"But why is he with those men?" Catherine persisted.

"I don't know," Richard replied.

"I talked to Jack; he doesn't believe they'll let you leave here." Catherine inched forward on her stomach to better see into the storeroom.

"So I shall be martyred and none shall know my cause." Richard sounded bored. "I accept; it matters little."

"If there is no purpose, get out," Catherine's voice was insistent, the pitch raised.

He reappeared before her suddenly and she stopped, surprised by the intensity of the eyes that met hers. "Who will help me? You, Catherine? Please, I shall not dwell on the hope you offer. To hold out a hand to mine enemy is divine, but please, girl, don't overdo it," Richard's voice was heavy with sarcasm.

"No, you misunderstand. Please, there is hope. You must believe me," Catherine continued.

"I believe nothing anymore, Catherine. Please go," was all he said.

"I can't believe you can just give up," Catherine was angry now.

She heard the laugh from below. "Now you attack my courage and liken me to a witless idiot."

Catherine tried again. "Whatever you seem to think, you're worth more alive than dead."

"To whom? To myself, no, I think not. To you, I doubt it. To Jack, I hope not."

"Here." She passed the bottle through the bars. "If I had seen you like this before I came, I would have unstopped it and filled it with poison."

"I am sorry you did not think to put an end to your sufferings in such a fashion. It would be a fitting end to have my demise at your hand, wouldn't it?" he replied, taking the bottle. "I will not dance for the comfort of your soul, lady."

"Go to Hell, Richard," Catherine shouted into the dark tears of fury springing to her eyes.

"Undoubtedly. Tell Jack I will wait for him," he said, laughing.

Jack paced across the room. At the moment, the men here outnumbered the constables. If he took control quickly, could he turn the tables? Would they follow his orders? There were many he knew who favoured Alan, and why that man was back here now he had no idea.

His train of thought was stopped when the door to his room opened abruptly, and Dan stepped inside.

Jack looked into his face and knew immediately that whatever news Dan carried, it was not good.

"What's happened?" Jack questioned.

Dan closed the door behind him. "Robert's here!"

Jack just stared at him in confusion.

"Robert. Richard's brother, your brother. Damn it, Jack! He's here, and he wants to talk to you," Dan said, his voice worried.

"Robert? Why is he here?" Jack dropped back down to sit on the edge of the bed.

"Up now!" Dan commanded, "I don't know what he's here for, or why, but he's coming to talk to you."

"I don't know what to say to him," Jack's face clouded with uncertainty.

Dan dug his hands into Jack's arms and hauled him back to stand before him, his face close. His words were quietly spoken. "And neither do I. Jack, for once, prove to me that you've got some Fitzwarren blood in your veins and give a good account of yourself."

Jack was about to say something, but he read the plea clearly in the other man's face and remained silent.

A moment later, they both heard the sound of boots on the wood floor outside the room. Dan released Jack as the door was flung open with enough force to make it rebound off the wall, and Robert stood framed in the doorway.

"Come in," said Jack, facing his brother for the first time.

Robert motioned to those behind him to stay outside. He glowered at Dan, who retreated, closing the door as he left.

"I'm Robert, Richard's brother, damn the man. I had to come and see you. My thanks are yours," Robert said, smiling broadly at the man in front of him.

Jack was careful. "Why is that?"

"The man broke my father's health, dragged our name, my name, through all the filth of England, conspired against the crown, and tarred my family with treason. You wonder what for?" Robert sounded incredulous, and then added, "Whatever your reasons were, those were mine and I am thankful that this is all at an end."

Jack nodded in acceptance of his words, but remained silent. Robert wandered idly to the fire. "So you're the man who poor Harry blames for his failure on Harlsey Moor. Was it as he says and you hit him from behind just as he was about to kill Richard, who was begging for mercy at his feet?"

"Not quite." Jack moved to seat himself near where Robert stood.

"I thought so," Robert said slowly. Dropping to his haunches, he picked the poker up from the where Catherine had left it and hefted it threateningly in his hand.

Jack could not see Robert's face. "So why did you leave Harry then?" the lazy voice asked him, turning the poker over.

"Would you have stayed with him? I was a free man. Why not leave?" Jack stated simply.

"And take up with your brother, Richard. Yes indeed, why not," Robert agreed, nodding.

"Half brother," Jack corrected. He had learnt well from Richard.

"Aye, whatever," Robert said. "My father was always raising bastards. Said he wanted a daughter, and can you believe it, the only girl he ever sired died in infancy. But boys! There's a dozen bastards from his loins, at least," Robert said, his voice still lazy.

Jack ignored his words; he knew the lie and the intent behind them.

"So, what will you do now?" Robert asked.

"I think, after today, I have more than I could want, don't you?" Jack replied carefully.

Robert turned and looked squarely at Jack. "What I can't understand is why leave Harry, take up with Richard, and then turn sides again?"

Jack's face hardened. "Treachery must be a family trait. I have no liking for the master. He has done me no favours, and now I have what was his. It's enough for me. As for him, I care not what happens."

Robert smiled and returned his eyes to the poker. "One of your men tells me that this is a house of unfortunates. There is another in Richard's keeping, a woman, Catherine de Bernay. Is this true?"

"Yes, she's here somewhere. Why?" Jack asked, trying desperately to think. How could he keep her safe?

"I was just thinking that as you have served yourself so well today, the safety of the woman may be of some value to her family, and I have decided to undertake that task," Robert replied, rising to stand and stare down at Jack.

Ah, thought Jack, *here was part of what Robert wanted.* He believed Catherine was heir to a manor and land, and obviously thought he could use her to control this. The irony of it was that had he known the size of Assingham, he probably wouldn't have bothered. Jack knew he had no choice. "Seems fair. Where she is now I can't say, but I will find her for you tomorrow. The woman has a sizeable estate. I'm sure she'll be delighted to be returned there." It was a lie, but it was what Robert wanted to hear, and it made Catherine valuable, which meant she'd be safe, at least for the moment.

Robert seemed happy with Jack's acquiescence. He dropped the poker, and it rattled noisily on the hearthstone. "Well, my thanks again." His eyes were hard on Jack's relaxed face. Jack's impulse was to stand, but he suppressed it, ignoring formality and deferment.

"There is no need, but if in serving myself I have done you a service also, I am grateful." Jack replied.

"Just one last thing," Robert said.

Here it comes!

"Did you know Richard is a cuckoo?" A slight sneer appeared on Robert's face.

Jack adopted a puzzled expression.

Robert continued. "My father, Lord knows why, swapped his wife's child for one of his bastard sons born from one of his whores. The bastard was Richard. The child of his wife died, I am told, so the case could never be set to rights. I am as surprised as you. Poor father cleared his conscience of his sin when he died. Didn't you know he was dead? Ah yes, some three weeks ago. Signed his name to the confession before he died," Robert concluded.

"That makes little difference to me. Although I'm not surprised." Jack shrugged, his voice indifferent.

Robert didn't reply. His eyes roved over Jack seated before him, a look of distaste on his face. Then, turning abruptly, he left. The door remained open, and Jack let out a long breath as he watched him depart along the corridor.

Jack knew that Robert had neatly solved his problems; making Richard the bastard who was about to be disposed of, left him with no contender for his place.

Jack looked up as Catherine slid back quietly into his room. "Well?" he asked. Catherine didn't answer, but he could see from the expression on her face that her meeting with his brother had not been a positive one. "Ah, it went that well, did it?"

Catherine nodded.

"Robert is here, Richard's brother. I don't know why. He might be connected with Alan. God, everything is so tangled I don't know what to think, let alone do." Jack told Catherine of Robert's visit and of Robert's plans to take Catherine into his own care. "I don't believe what Robert said any more than he does," Jack finished.

"Why then?" Catherine asked.

"It was to stop me in any plans I may have to lay claim to Robert's place. He isn't sure whether I know the truth, but that was intended to dissuade me if I did," Jack supplied.

"So that makes Richard a bastard and you..." Catherine stopped.

"It was a brief journey was it not from bastardy to legitimacy and back again?" Jack was smiling. "It makes no difference, Catherine. Anyway, how do we know what he said is true?" Jack continued smiling. "Have we seen all the cards he holds? No, we have most certainly not."

Chapter Twenty-Four

Lincolnshire – June 1554

Robert was in the middle of a meeting with the Sheriff in one of the rooms off the main hall at Burton.

"My brother is a common criminal, a murderer, and he should be tried as such," Robert concluded. "Surely I've shown you enough evidence to prove that to you."

"Indeed, but the crown still has an interest in him," Ayscough replied coolly. "I have a duty to comply with the demand to take him to London to be questioned over these charges of murder."

Robert scowled at Ayscough, then he gestured to Alan who was standing silently near the door. "This man here has testified to the murders he committed in London, and you have further evidence here that he is a murderer." Robert's forefinger stabbed the paper on the desk in front of Ayscough. "He should be tried immediately for these crimes, and not dragged to London and be allowed further chance to escape justice."

"My duty, Sir..." Ayscough tried again.

The purse Robert dropped on the table in front of the constable landed with a dull thud that told of the coins within the tied leather bag. The man could not help letting his eyes gaze on the purse, involuntarily he licked his lips, and Robert smiled.

"That's yours," Robert said, his gaze catching the constable's. "It would suit me if my brother did not make it to London and if you would try him here and now for murder."

Ayscough's eyes flicked from Robert's face back to the money, the agony of indecision plain on his face. "Sir, if it were my decision I would, but these orders are from London, they have the seal of the crown on them, they take precedence over any other jurisdiction and I have to comply."

"I understand. Let me help make this decision a little easier for you," Robert said, his eyes narrowing.

The constable didn't reply, but he inclined his head holding Robert's eyes.

Robert continued, making his proposal quite clear. "A man like my brother is likely to try and escape, I hope this purse would ensure that he would die in the attempt."

A wide grin settled on constable's face and a moment later he swiped the purse up from the table. "You can rely on me, Sir. Should he try to escape he will not leave Burton alive."

"Do we understand each other?" Robert demanded, leaning towards the man, "not 'if' he tries to escape, damn it man how clear do I have to be?"

Ayscough's hand tightened on the purse. "I understand you. When he tries to escape, he will be apprehended and die in the fight."

Robert held the man's eyes for a moment longer. "I am counting on it."

Mat didn't wait for an answer to his hurried knock and burst into the room, Catherine close behind him. "Riders, they're at the village. They took a different route, and I missed them. I was at Lincoln. I was told the Queen's men had passed north. Jack, I'm sorry," Mat gasped.

"Jesus! Help me," Jack was on his feet in a moment reaching for his sword.

Mat grabbed Jack's arm that reached for the blade. "What are you doing? You'll not help like this."

Jack shook off Mat's hold. "I have to do something."

"You'll be dead before you draw your blade, Jack," Mat said urgently.

"Well, let it be so then," Jack said, buckling on the belt and reaching for his doublet. It was creased and stained. Sad attire to meet his death in. He discarded it; a shirt would do.

Mat moved to stand in his way as he made to leave the room. "I'll not let you do it. Don't let them take you both in one day, Jack. You can't stop them."

"Listen to Mat. He is right. This is misplaced, please," Catherine pleaded.

"What would you have me do? I'll not stand by and watch?" There was agony in Jack's voice.

"If it is to be, yes," Mat said harshly.

Richard stood between two men in the hall, his hands bound again in front of him, his back to the fireplace, and his heels against the stone fire surround. He was flanked on either side by two of the constable's men, both of them having a tight, and unnecessary, hold on his arms.

Jack entered the hall from the small spiral staircase in the corner with Mat hard on his heels, he pushed to the front of the ring of men surrounding his brother. It was clear that whatever was about to take place had been planned, and his presence was not needed.

Many of Richard's men were already present, more entered quietly, some appeared from the head of the tight stone stairs that led to the rooms below the hall, and some filed through the main door that stood open. Robert, flanked by several of his men, stood with his arms folded and face impassive, watching Richard closely.

Catherine had followed Jack and Mat and peered round the narrow door into the hall, all the eyes were turned towards Richard and his captors and none saw her press forwards until she stood behind Jack and Mat.

Robert spoke a few words quietly in the constable's ear before walking forward to face his brother. Richard never let his eyes leave Robert's face.

"So how fares our father?" Richard said in greeting when Robert stood in front of him.

"Duplicitous to the last," Richard said sadly.

"You even admit it? Now, when called to account for your crimes?" Robert sounded incredulous.

"I wasn't talking about myself," Richard replied evenly.

The back of Robert's hand smacked hard into Richard's face and when he turned back, there was blood on his lips.

"You are about to get the justice you deserve, just like that bitch you support who is in the Tower now," Robert spat the words at his brother.

Richard didn't reply but his whole body stiffened.

A malicious smile spread across Robert's face. "You didn't know that did you? She'll be sharing her mother's fate before the week is out." Robert, laughing, turned away and stood again at the constable's side bidding the man to continue.

"Richard Fitzwarren, you have been brought before us now to answer for your crimes," the constable announced, his thumbs tucked into his belt.

"Will that be one at time or altogether?" Richard enquired conversationally.

"Untie him," the constable commanded and took a step back.

The man to Richard's right produced a knife and in three rough strokes he'd severed the bindings holding his wrists together.

Richard, his eyes never leaving those of the constable, rubbed his wrists and pulled away the remaining brown cord still surrounding them.

"Give me a blade," the constable commanded. The man to his left, handed him the hilt of his own weapon. Taking it the constable cast it down on the flags at Richard's feet. The metallic clang of the hilt hitting the stone and the scrape of the blade reverberated around the hall.

Richard ignored the sword, his words were loud enough for everyone in the hall to hear. "Altogether then."

"Pick it up," the constable growled.

Richard did not move to obey but stood motionless, his eyes locked with those of the constable's.

"Edmund, persuade him to take it up," the constable spoke to one of his own men, an ugly sneer on his face.

Edmund moved his hand to draw the steel from the scabbard and the surrounding men dropped back immediately, their backs against the stone walls.

"Either pick it up, or die where you stand," the constable stated bluntly.

Richard did not reply, but crouching slowly, his eyes never leaving the armed man who was levelling a blade towards him, he reached for and found the hilt on the floor.

"Jesus no!" Jack said under his breath.

Catherine hearing Jack's words said quietly, "That man will be no match for Richard."

"I don't think that this will be a fair fight," Jack hissed as he fastened a hand around her arm and drew her close to him, "what the hell are you doing here?"

If Catherine replied Jack didn't hear her. A moment later steel clashed with steel and the first sparks flew from the conflict. Every one of the men in the hall retreated as far as they could giving the combatants the maximum amount of space.

Edmund's first thrust was easily deflected up when Richard raised the blade quickly from the floor, engaging with his attacker. For several minutes, he parried the blows aimed at his body. Edmund's swordplay was simple, but Richard remained on the defensive, easily evading the steel of his blade.

"Go on, Edmund, you have him," one of the men yelled encouragingly.

Edmund though didn't press his attack, and a moment later stepped backwards to join the ring of observers as another man entered to challenge Richard. It was another of the constable's men, the look on his face told of his eagerness to test himself against the captive. Richard's movements remained as conservative as possible, not forcing an attack onto the newcomer, his blade acting only to deflect the strokes aimed towards his body. The minutes passed and another man, his sword drawn stepped forward. It was Alan. A ripple of quiet comment surged around the hall.

The constable's man chose his moment carefully, stepping back into the ring of observers and letting Alan advance on his commander.

Jack's hand closed involuntarily tighter on Catherine's arm. He knew what they meant to do, wear his brother down and then kill him. Casting his eyes around the room, he realised that there was more to this humiliation; utter and complete humiliation was their game. However, Alan's challenge was even more than that. If he won, then it was an assertion of his right of leadership. His appearance had created division amongst the men. There were those who would readily side with him, given the choice. Jack prayed that Richard wouldn't let Alan's blade break through his defence.

"You've had this coming for a long time," Alan hefted the hilt in his hand.

Richard did not reply. His breathing was now coming a little faster, and the linen on the back of his shirt was beginning to cling to his dampened skin. Jack knew that in a fair fight Alan was no match for Richard, but this was no fair fight.

Alan's heavy attacking strokes were aimed at driving Richard back. The hall was small, and the round raised hearth surround protruded into the hall from the fireplace. Another two paces backwards and Richard would be on it. Jack wanted to shout a warning. One more pace and he would trip over it.

Releasing Catherine's arm, Jack ripped his sword from the scabbard.

"What are you doing?" Catherine tried to grab his sleeve, but the material was wrenched from her grasp.

Jack entered the ring next to Alan. "My turn now," was all Jack said. Alan, his face furious having sensed victory, was forced to lower his blade and step back.

Richard stood waiting for Jack's first move, his breath ragged now from the exertion. Jack laughed. "I have waited a long time for this." His blade engaged lightly, his swordplay meant to provoke, not injure, and he continued to verbally goad his brother.

"Have you nothing to say?" Another blow.

"Do you want to ask me for mercy, as you have made me beg to you on so many occasions?" Steel scraped together. The attack was one easily parried by Richard.

"Come on, you bastard, talk to me." Jack stood ready for his brother's attack, but made none of his own. The tirade of verbal abuse and limited action was allowing Richard time to regain his strength. The charade continued until Gavin, one of Richard's men, stepped up behind Jack.

Richard locked his sword in the hilt of Jack's and dragged him close. Both feigned the struggle. "Thanks," Richard's head was close to Jack's for a moment, then suddenly he let Jack go, kicking him in the stomach. Jack fell backwards obligingly, landing heavily against Gavin, sending Richard's newest opponent sprawling to the floor.

Jack's actions had the unfortunate ramification that now no one in the hall remained loyal to the Master, and John, another of Richard's men, stepped in taking Gavin's place. Jack knew in a moment that the game he played with the Master was a fatal one. There was malice in the sword strokes he sent in Richard's direction.

Jack had stepped back and taken his place again in front of Catherine.

"Your knife," Catherine hissed in his ear, tugging on his arm. "Give it to me."

Jack turned and looked at her.

"Just do it," she prodded him hard in the back with a finger to make her point. A second later, a hilt appeared in his right hand behind his back. Catherine took the weapon.

John had stepped back and Gavin had made a second entry into the ring. The effort of fending off the continuous blows was starting to tell on Richard. His hair was stuck to his forehead and the shirt clung to his body with sweat, his chest heaving with exertion, knuckles white on the hilt of the sword. It was obvious to Jack that very soon someone was going to break through his guard.

Catherine moved to stand in front of Jack. He had no idea what she was thinking, but if it might buy his brother some time then so be it.

Richard stumbled, dropping to a knee. Gavin's eye's widened in delight and he moved in with the clear intention of making the kill. He had both hands on the hilt of the blade that raced through the air towards Richard's neck with as much strength as he had. Richard spun to block the blade but failed to deflect the sword, its speed not fully deadened, it made it through his defence and sliced into his left shoulder.

There was a cheer from some of the men in the room. Gavin backed from Richard for a moment, preparing to deliver the last killing blow. Richard, his blade lowered in his right hand, was bent forward, breathing raggedly, his other hand resting on his thigh, taking his weight.

Jack swallowed hard as he watched, helpless, as Richard began to lose the last of his strength, blood running from the wound. Richard looked up and met Gavin's eyes as he prepared to attack, staggering backwards as if off balance.

"Finish him," Jack hissed to himself under his breath, recognising the tactic.

Gavin's eyes widened in delight as he saw his opening. He raised his sword high, hoping to bring it down on his victim so hard that it would bury itself up to the hilt in bone and flesh. Jack watched, his body rigid, hoping Richard could still take full advantage of the opportunity he had been given. He did. Dropping to his right knee, he avoided the blow and his sword entered between the ribs of his surprised opponent, who hung on the sword for an age before Richard sharply pulled it back. The dying man collapsed to the floor in a pond of spreading blood.

Richard stepped back from the body. The man's death had bought him a few moments. New entrants were not so willing now. David stepped aside to allow one of the constable's men to enter again, and then Catherine made her move. As she pushed past Jack, she hissed, "St Marie's."

"No," Catherine shouted, the knife in her hand. "Turn and face me, Richard. Give me that satisfaction."

There was a murmur of voices accompanied by grins, and some shallow laughter. "This will be humiliation indeed," David said, pulling the constable's man back from the fight.

"She has more than enough reason to want revenge," Alan called from where he stood on the sidelines.

Richard watched her approach, his hands on his knees, his breath filling his lungs in harsh gasps. The blood staining the sword blade was Gavin's, but that dripping from his left arm to the floor was his own.

"Ah, Catherine, there is some justice in this, I suppose," Richard said, smiling, his eyes meeting hers.

Jack heard his words. *Jesus!* Jack thought, *he still thinks she is going to try and kill him.*

Suddenly, the danger she was in dawned on him. Richard did not see her as his rescuer, but as a final foe. Jack was about to step forward, but in that moment Catherine swung the dagger at his brother's head. Richard grabbed her arm, twisting it cruelly. Catherine howled in pain and dropped the knife.

For a moment, their heads were together. "Take me hostage." Richard heard the gasped words.

Richard took the opportunity offered.

Retrieving the knife from the floor, he spun Catherine round, pulling the blade to her throat. "Back away. I think the odds have just changed." Richard's voice was hoarse.

Two men moved forward.

"No!" yelled Jack, spreading his arms wide to stop them. "He's got de Bernay's daughter." There was a murmur, and they duly fell back and allowed Richard to make his way to the door in the corner of the hall.

"For God's sake, man, stop him!" Robert pressed forward, a hand grasping the constable's arm.

Richard, now only four paces from the door, tightened his hold on Catherine, the knife angled menacingly at her neck, the threat clear. "Stay where you are."

Without orders, the men in the hall didn't move; they glanced between Jack and Ayscough, but none moved to intervene.

Reaching behind him, he pulled it open and dragged Catherine through it, slamming it immediately shut and dropping the bar in place.

"Come on, that'll not hold them." The pair fled down the steps from the hall and spilled into the yard.

"Here," yelled a voice, hauling a saddled horse towards them. "I'm way ahead of you, Catherine," grinned Dan.

"Look after her," Richard was in the saddle in a moment and pressed the horse towards the opened gate. Catherine's feet barely touched the ground as Dan dragged her from the yard before both the constable's and the Master's men found them.

Jack was first at the barred door, ineffectually beating it and cursing like the soldier he was. "He'll go north to the port! I know the bastard too well." Jack continued to be in the way as the men tried to use a table to batter through the door.

The ruse of sending the pursuers to the port quickly failed. The riders questioned those at the roadside. No horse had been seen speeding that way, and the group soon saw their folly and headed back. Jack judged his timing wrongly and found himself forced at sword point to dismount in the Manor's courtyard on his return.

"Inside, damn you," one of the constable's men growled.

"Who's the woman then, eh?" the constable barked across the hall at him.

Jack's eyes narrowed as he looked at Alan. Traitor, he thought. "You are right, she's a valuable asset," Jack said simply, moving to seat himself in one of the chairs in the hall, forcing himself to remain at ease as he surveyed the constable. "She is Catherine de Bernay, a wealthy heiress with lands and a manor at Assingham. How she fell in with Richard, I don't know. I had intended to trade her back to her family in return for..." Jack left the sentence unfinished. His brain hurt. He was trying to think so fast. "As you can see, she is not worth much dead, but alive and kicking..."

"Aye, she was kicking all right when your man brought her here." The constable grinned.

Jack wondered where she was.

"You can prove your words?" the constable said.

Jack thought for a minute. "I believe I can confirm her identity to your satisfaction, yes. I was to hand over her care to Robert Fitzwarren. He has undertaken the mission to return her back to her family. So what do you intend to do, Constable? I am in your debt, as you can see," Jack waved his arm around the hall. "I have triumphed this day even if you, unfortunately, do not have your charge anymore, and I am grateful to you. The deal still stands, I assume."

"I've got men searching. He can't be far from here, not with a good wound like that," the constable replied bluntly.

You may be right, thought Jack, wondering where his brother was.

Richard stumbled on the step to the mill, his boot catching on the raised stone. An outstretched arm caught the door frame and saved him from falling, but the impact caused him to gasp in pain. His eyes cast down for a moment. He saw the telltale drops of blood on the white dusty stone and cursed. The cloth he'd wrapped round the cut had failed to stop the blood, and he knew he had left a trail his pursuers could not fail to follow. Stepping over the threshold and into the reverberating mill interior, he swung the door shut and slid the wooden bar through the iron loops to secure it. It wouldn't slow them for long.

The grey mill stones were still, the mechanism disengaged and the axle that went through the ceiling was stationary. Outside, the paddled wheel still turned and the room still thrummed with the sound of the wooden structure being propelled by the cascading water. Richard crossed to the steep stairs and began a rapid ascent.

Then he stopped.

Above him, he could hear the clear sound of voices engaged in a heated argument. Taking three more steps up, he could hear the words.

"It was twenty sacks, and we agreed on a price per sack," Guy's voice stated.

"That was when you were steward at the manor, Guy, but that's changed, hasn't it? You're not bringing me half the work you promised, and I'm not paying top prices for what little you do bring through my door," John Knoll stated bluntly.

"I can take them to the Lincoln mill, and then you'll make nothing," Guy countered, his voice raised.

Richard peered up from the floor level. Both men had their backs to him and were too concerned with each other to notice him.

"You damn well take it to Lincoln then, and see if I care. You'll have to pay for it to be taken and then brought back and by the time you have parted with money for that you would have been as well to take what I am offering," Knoll said, his arms folded and his eyes fixed on the fat face of Burton's former steward.

Guy's colour rose. "I'll be steward again. You mark my words. And when I am, John Knoll, you'll be looking for another mill to work in."

Knoll laughed at that. "Guy, take what I am offering per sack or take it to Lincoln, that's the only bargain you'll get out of me."

"We agreed to a rate, you can't cheat..." Guy broke off, his eyes widening as he saw the man who had emerged from the stairs and was now standing behind Knoll. Guy shrieked.

Knoll whirled around and found Fitzwarren's poniard levelled at his chest.

"Not in my mill, you don't." Knoll, with the corded arms of a wrestler and wearing a pigskin leather apron, lunged, his body impacting with Richard's wounded shoulder, the blade rattling uselessly on the wooden floor. Richard staggered back, hitting the wall behind him hard.

Guy stepped forward and trapped the blade beneath his boot, shouting in triumph. "I've got his knife."

"I don't need a knife," Knoll growled and sank his fist into Richard's stomach, a grin spreading across his face as his assault caused the man before him to double and gasp at the pain.

The miller pulled back his fist, clenching it tightly, aiming a blow that was meant to smash the other man's skull against the wall behind his head. Richard, the knife from his boot now in his right hand, straightened and slashed the blade across Knoll's body. The short blade scored the leather apron but went on to cut a searing red gash in the flesh of his shoulder, blood spilling from the wound to patter on the dusty floor.

The miller stared in surprise at his injured shoulder, and in that moment, Richard pushed him backwards. Knoll staggered two paces back, then the back of his legs caught on Guy's stooped body, where he was straightening from picking up the fallen knife.

The miller exclaimed as he started to fall and Richard, quickly moving forward, again pushed him a second time. Knoll, his balance lost, arms flailing, fell backwards. At the very last moment a look of pure horror darkened his face as he realised what was happening. His back impacted with the flat ledge of the opening in the wall, beyond which was the spinning water wheel. His weight was already on the wrong side of the wall. An additional shove from Richard pitched him out of the opening to land on the top of the wooden paddles of the wheel.

Knoll screamed, held out his hands for help, and fought to remain at the top of the wheel. Unable to gain purchase on the slippery wood, he fell down the side of the wheel into the bottom of the pond, screaming as the wheel covered him in a shower of icy water.

Richard turned on Guy before Knoll had landed in the millpond.

Guy still held in his hand the blade he had retrieved from the floor. At the sight of the man advancing upon him, he dropped the knife, his hands raised defensively in front of him. "It was Knoll. It wasn't me," wailed Guy.

Richard stooped and retrieved the fallen knife. He could already hear below him the sounds of the hammering on the closed door–it would not be long before it gave way. Richard gestured with the knife for Guy to move sideways. When the fat man was far enough away he stepped past him and pulled open the door leading to the sluice gates. Richard stepped through the door and onto the top step. "When they come up those stairs, you tell them I jumped from the room onto to the wheel."

Guy, pale, nodded.

"And remember, I will be right behind you," Richard threatened and yanked Guy back to stand in front of the doorway before he pulled the door partly closed again. Guy let out a nervous groan of fear, and Richard applied the sharpened steel tip of his blade to Guy's back, hissing in his ear, "Don't get this wrong, Guy."

The hammering went on below them until Richard thought they were going to give up when suddenly he heard the sound of the wooden bar splinter and break.

The heavy sound of boots on the stairs was followed by a cry from Guy, the steel in his back underlining Richard's intention. Flinging his arms up in the air, Guy yelled, "The wheel! He escaped onto the wheel."

The three men crowded into the opening over the wheel for a moment. "He could have got down from the top of that onto the bank over there," one of the men said, pointing.

"It's a hell of a jump. Come on."

Wherever Knoll was, it was obvious he couldn't be seen. A moment later, all three had gone back down the stairs and were leaving the mill to round the side where the wooden wheel continued to turn.

Richard moved back into the room, the knife still in his hand, and the look he cast in Guy's direction told him to remain quiet.

Below the window, they could hear the noise of the three men rounding the side of the mill on the stone path that led to the pond and the water wheel.

"He's under the wheel! Look!" One of the men shouted as he arrived.

A smiled twitched the corner of Richard's mouth. Knoll was going to buy him some time. But he couldn't leave Guy in the mill. Under his breath, and gesturing with the knife towards the steep steps to the sluice gates, he said, "Down those steps now."

Guy's eye's widened, "No, no, I won't tell anyone."

"Get down those steps," Richard commanded.

"No, please," there was terror on Guy's face. He clearly didn't want to turn his back on Richard.

"Now, go." Richard pushed him towards the narrow wooden door.

"Please, don't, I'll not say a word!" Guy's voice was high pitched and shrill, cutting above the thrum of the water wheel.

"Guy, now."

Guy didn't turn, but stepped back. The door was open behind him and his right foot stepped into the void of the stairwell. Losing his balance and falling backward, he let out a horrified scream. Richard automatically extended his hand, but Guy's fingers failed to close around it and he fell, his head impacting against the stone wall to land in a crumpled heap at the bottom of the steps. The space was small, his legs were raised up the wall, his back against the other and like some untidy sack of spilled grain, he had landed to sag onto the floor, partly blocking the door.

Richard dropped down the steps and tried to prise the door open. Guy's body was acting as an effective block and the door wouldn't open enough for him to escape. Richard abandoned the door and shifted his focus instead to hefting Guy's inert form away from it so he could open it. An arm grasped in both his hands as he heaved, but Guy's bulk remained on the floor. Suddenly, above him, he heard the sound of boots on the stairs as the men returned to the mill. A foot braced against the wall, his teeth clenched tight against the pain from the sword cut. He heaved on Guy's arm, rolling the body sufficiently for him to open the door enough to get his good shoulder behind it. With the weight of his body behind the resisting wood, he managed to force it open enough to allow him to slide through.

The door banged shut at the exact moment one of the men peered down the stairwell to find Guy dead at the bottom.

"What happened?" Jack stood with the rest of the men at the side of the mill, where the wheel still turned.

"He tried to escape from the window, then fell under the wheel, when we got here the water was red with blood, we think the body is still trapped down there, if it wasn't it would have fetched up over there by the weir by now," one of the constables men said, pointing to further down the mill course where the water indeed did run over a stone banked weir.

"Stop the wheel," it was all Jack could think to say, horror on his face.

"We can't. The mechanism to the sluice gates is jammed, one of the men has gone to the village to summon the miller. If he's under there still, there'll not be much left of him."

The miller could not be found, and so the village blacksmith was escorted to the mill site. After he inspected the gate mechanism, he returned to his workshop for tools and it was another hour before the pegs securing the chains to the gates were back in place and they could be lowered to alter the course of the water.

The men still standing expectantly around the wheel saw the water slow and then reduce to a trickle. The wheel, turning on momentum, only came to rest after half a turn, rotating backwards a little before it came to a final stop. They had found John Knoll's assistant in the village, and white-faced, he'd supervised the securing of the wheel. Inside the mill was a hole through the wall and a massive post could be slid through this to anchor the wheel so it would not turn when repairs were being carried out. There was, however, no sign of a body.

When a sum of money was offered by Ayscough to explore the now still pond, it was the blacksmith who stripped to his breeches and waded in. The pond was no more than waist deep, for an efficient wheel the less of it that was submerged, the easier it was to turn, and only the bottom two feet were under the water level.

The blacksmith's explorations pulled free first a handful of once white linen which he slung on the bank before his hand had closed around soft, mutilated flesh. The body, what there was of it, turned the stomachs of the men on the bank. Jammed beneath the wheel by the force of the water, it had been torn apart by the paddles. Stripped of flesh, ragged and smashed, it was recognisable only as being human.

A large hand grabbed Jack's arm and fastened non-to-gently into his flesh, and Dan dragged him from the bank near the mill pond and propelled him back to Burton.

Jack did not see Catherine again. When Dan had dragged him back to Burton, they'd found Robert and his men gone, and they had taken her with them. He was uncomfortably aware of Alan's presence amongst the men in the hall, but while some of the constable's men still remained at Burton, there was little he could do about it.

Jack took a seat at the dais, and this time he did drink heavily. His mind was numb. Richard should have returned to London and stood trial and denied Elizabeth's involvement in his schemes, but that had been undone. They had tried to kill him here instead, and prevent a trial, and he had died trying to escape. Perhaps it had been done on the Queen's orders? Richard had received royal favours; such a trial would have been humiliating for the crown. Yes, there were more reasons to have him dead than to allow him to stand trial. He could implicate too many people. Then there was Robert. He too had plenty of reasons to want his brother dead. Whatever had been the cause, it didn't matter anymore. Richard was dead.

God, Richard, you lost this time.

The stakes were far, far too high, and he had paid with his life.

Jack put his head back in his hands. He wanted to weep for the utter destruction of it. In the sword ring, he was sure he had seen in Richard's eyes the request to end it there, but he had pushed that aside.

The table on which his eyes were locked bore no message of advice. He did not hear the door to the hall open, but he felt the coldness of the air it admitted on his face. His mind elsewhere, he paid no attention until he heard the light and uneven footfalls of a man limping towards the dais. Jamie moved forward until he was close enough for his words to be heard by Jack only.

"Get yourself up, lad," Jamie said quietly. "Come on out of his room now before they see. Come on, follow me."

Jack allowed Jamie's bony fingers to prod him into mobility, and he followed the priest blindly from the hall.

"Where's your room?" Jamie said quickly.

Jack pointed and Jamie continued to push his charge down the corridor, up the stairs, and finally through the door. Only when they were inside did he stop.

Jack stood in the room, arms wrapped around his body, shivering uncontrollably. Jamie moved and dragged a chair over until it was behind Jack.

"Sit down lad, come on."

Jack didn't move, and Jamie was forced to push him into it. Jack fell forwards in the chair, elbows on his knees, head in his hands. Soundlessly, he sat there. Jamie sighed, shaking his head. He placed his hand gently under Jack's chin and lifted his head. Jack looked blindly at him. Jamie's fingers caught the chain around his neck and he pulled the cross from over his head. Turning Jack's right hand over, he placed it in his palm and closed his fingers around it. The priest looked at him for a long time, then sighing, he busied himself building a fire in the darkened, cold grate.

The day was freshly born when Jamie moved from in front of the fire and looked again at Jack. He had slept at last, slouched uncomfortably in the chair, the chain of the cross wound round his fingers. Jamie left the room and went in search of Dan. Unashamed, he kicked several of the sleepers until he found the one he was looking for.

"Dan?" Jamie said quietly.

"What do you want?" Dan's voice was thick with sleep and heavy with grief.

"Up with you. I've got to talk to you." The man before him made no move to leave his cocoon of blankets.

Jamie stooped lower. "Now. I have a message from your master." The words were enough. "Come on, follow me." Jamie led Dan from the hall, up the stairs he had pushed Jack up the night before until they were outside the room Jack slept in.

"What message have you? Tell me," Dan said desperately, "did he escape?"

Jamie shook his head and Dan turned from him, both of his fists pounding into the wall behind him, a gasp of agony escaping his lips, his forehead against the stone. Jamie, although impatient, let him alone with his thoughts and mumbled through one of his longer prayers as he waited.

Finally, he placed a hand on Dan's shoulder. "The message," he said. He saw Dan with an effort to gather himself and turn to face him.

"Go on, old man," Dan said almost silently.

"He gave me this days ago, so you'd mark his words, if the time came," Jamie produced a ring from one of his sleeves and handed it to Dan, who received it wordlessly. "It's for Jack. He said you are to help him, and these are my words, not his. He needs help."

Dan turned the ring over in his hand. "Where is he?"

Jamie gestured to the door. Dan took a step towards it, but Jamie stopped him. "He's your master now. You know that, don't you?" Dan gave him a grim look.

Dan paused when he closed the door behind him, looking at the broken form in the chair. "Jack, I'm here to help you. If you don't let me, you'll be joining him soon. Now get out of there." Dan's words were brutal, and Jack sat there staring at him, the feeling of coldness still on him.

"Up, Jack, now. I served that man most of me life, knew him longer than you ever did. Now he wants you to take his place. Why, I don't know, and I'll not question him, but I'll be damned if I'll let you sit and feel sorry for yourself. You will get up and take his place, and if you do it badly, or not at all, I'll kill you myself. Up!" Dan's temper flooded his words, and Jack moved to comply, as he was meant to.

"He sent this for you." Dan opened his palm and held out the ring. Jack carefully took it and held it up to the light. He made to slide it on his right hand, but Dan's hand went out and snatched it back. "You'll not put that on looking like the gutter whelp you do now."

Jamie, satisfied, took his ear from the door and shuffled off.

By mid-morning, Dan, with a combination of verbal abuse, bullying, and physical blows, had managed to coax Jack back into the land of the living, giving him no time for his grief. Clothes were bundled up in his arms, and when Jack protested as he tried to leave the room with them, Dan threw them on the fire.

"You know you've got to make your mark with them today or you're going to lose your place," Dan said, still moving around the room, picking things up, discarding them again and moving on. "That cur Alan is here. You need to put down his challenge quickly."

"Yes, I know that," Jack sighed. He was fingering the single piece of parchment taken from Richard's room that he had not burned. Dan's eyes rested on it.

"Mat's with you and me, which is a good start. I think you could have trouble with Gavin and John," Dan said. "They both tried to take the Master's life."

Jack's blue eyes were lit with a cold light at the mention of the names. They were a focus for the fury and temper burning in his chest.

The sun was low, the early darkness of autumn descending soon over Burton. Jack moved to a table where ale stood and reached for a cup. Dan intercepted his arm. "No, not tonight. You'll need your mind clear to face them if you're to make your mark."

Jack turned his icy blue eyes on Dan. "I hear you."

Dan watched him as he stared from the window. Finely dressed now, Jack looked much like Richard, apart from the stark contrast between black cloth and blond hair.

Evening came and the remaining group of Richard's men were silent in the hall. Jack sat at the dais, where Richard had sat only days before, alone, shunning company. A large quantity of beer stood on the table and Jack, who appeared drunk, did not move. The mood in the hall was expectant. The message had been passed of his brother's death, and they knew Jack meant to take his place. The reactions had varied when he had appeared in the hall. Friend had become foe when they judged he tried to emulate the Master. Some pitied him; others saw a new light in his eyes and weighed the danger that lay there. Many decided to delay their judgement until they could view his acts.

Jack raised his head. Blond hair fell over his eyes. He found his first quarry seated by the fire playing cards, laughing, and drinking. Jack watched Alan, and his blue eyes darkened. The man had just won and was raking coins across the boards towards him. Blue changed to black. The cards were dealt again. Alan reached for his beer and drank a lengthy draft. Black eyes reflected the yellow dance of the fire. Jack raised himself from the dais and stood above them, pushing the table from in front of him. The scrape of wood on wood drew the attention of some of the men in the hall, who turned to see Jack standing alone. Drawing his sword, the sound of steel rasping from the scabbard gained the attention of the rest.

"Alan, stand. Our business is unfinished," Jack said loudly over the silence that had settled in the hall.

Alan stood immediately. His sword was leant against the bare stone of the wall, ready, and he ripped the scabbard from the blade, discarding it. "You are right, you brought this on the Master," Alan pronounced loudly enough for everyone in the hall to hear, "we all saw you bring Ayscough's men here. I'll not follow you, Jack, and neither will the men."

Jack jumped lightly from the dais. He stood some paces from Alan, prepared, sober and resolved to carry out this justice.

Alan stood, his blade ready, in the middle of the hall. Jack strode towards him with a purpose and speed that made Alan waver for a moment. It was not a fight; it was an execution. Alan's sword touched Jack's only once, then the steel was forced from his hand with a brutal blow that made the blade shiver. Before the weapon had finished rattling on the floor, Alan was dead, a steel point protruding from his back, his final expression one of horrified surprise.

The hall remained silent while Jack taught his remaining followers a lesson in loyalty. Jack stood silently and looked down the length of his blooded sword at the body of the man who would not betray him further. He returned alone to the dais, laid his sword on the boards, and poured ale into a cup.

The silence in the hall was broken by small degrees until the noise was back to its previous level as they considered what they had witnessed. Jack cared not if they sought to further challenge him, cared less what they thought of him, and worried not about the words they now exchanged.

Dan, sitting at the end of one of the tables, called down to Froggy, who was partway along, his words clear and loud enough to be heard by all. "Pass me that jug for the Master."

Froggy looked up, met his eye, and moved swiftly to comply. Jack heard his declaration, but his face registered nothing. Dan, rising, crossed to Jack and placed the jug carefully and quietly in front of him.

"Here." Dan placed the ring he had snatched from Jack earlier beside it.

Jack's eyes looked down at the ornament and then back up to meet Dan's gaze. Dan was not smiling, but there was a satisfied look on his face.

Chapter Twenty-Five
London – July 1554

It had taken Richard three days to get to London. On the first day, he'd left the mill at Burton and made his way through the woodland, unseen, to Jamie's. There, he had left instructions for the priest to deliver to Dan and his brother. There was too much at stake, and the fewer people who knew of his survival, the better. It was preferable for Jack to remain in ignorance, he reasoned, than to trust in his ability to dissemble.

The following day, when he was sure they were no longer looking for him, he had set out for London. The horse he had borrowed from Jamie was an aged and ponderous animal and the journey was a painfully slow one. Without funds, he could not buy another mount and he had no money for inns, spending two nights wrapped in Jamie's thickest winter cloak sleeping rough near the road.

Richard had lit the lamp in the attic room and when he dropped silently into the walled garden, Kate was already there waiting for him. The pain in his shoulder was acute, and he drew a shuddering breath, forcing himself to ignore it.

It had rained all day; the grass and leaves were wet and her skirt hem was dark with water from where she had walked around the small box-hedged garden, the spaniel trailing sullenly behind her. Kate had been in the garden for a while, waiting for him.

The look on her face told him something was wrong. Very wrong. Had Robert told the truth?

Kate came towards him as soon as she saw him. "Richard," Kate's voice shook, "we have no need to fear discovery tonight."

"It's true then?" Richard stepped forward.

"They took her to the Tower. I was not allowed to accompany her. The Queen provided ladies of her own to look after her. She was scared to death. The guards laughed, said if she behaved herself they'd allow her to pay her respects to her lady mother. Oh God, and there was nothing I could do, nothing..." Kate sobbed, tears flooded from her eyes. "Do you think they'll...?" Kate was unable to finish the sentence.

"I don't think so," Richard said thoughtfully. "I had thought I would bring good news tonight. Are there any guards here?"

"No, they all left the house when Elizabeth was taken," Kate sniffed. "There is just myself and some of her ladies here now."

"Well, what say we retrieve your errant hound and I shall escort you back to the house," Richard smiled.

The dog, roused from the hedge by their approach, sensed a game afoot and led them a merry dance around the garden until Kate managed to stamp on his trailing lead. She found herself laughing and was grateful for it.

Once inside and seated at a table, the Spaniel sniffing at Richard's boots, Kate could see him clearly in the light. "What happened to you?"

"I do look a sorrowful sight. I'm sorry. I had to evade pursuit," he supplied the excuse quickly.

"Well, it's a thorough disguise, in both appearance and smell." Then Kate, gnawing her lip, asked, "Do you think they will release her?"

Richard took her hands in his, squeezing them tightly. "I believe she is being held as a device to ensure Parliament ratifies the wedding. I think Derby has made a move I didn't anticipate. However, I am sure she will be safe. Kate, there are too many of the nobles opposed to the wedding with Philip and Elizabeth's survival is a key to ensuring their cooperation. She has fallen pray to politics, the deal is almost completed, and it is probably felt that it would be safer to have Elizabeth under lock and key. I am sure she will be safe. If they made any move against her now, they would jeopardise Mary's wedding." Richard finished.

"Are you sure?" Kate asked, sounding reassured by his words.

"I am, Kate, and I have many reasons that I cannot share with you why I believe this will be the case," Richard smiled and released her hands.

Shortly after Richard left the house the way he had arrived, and in the dark shadows of the London night, he made his way back across the City. The assurances he had given Kate were not ones he truly believed in, and he needed to find out why Elizabeth was now in the Tower. What had changed?

Elizabeth laid down the pen next to the completed page and reviewed her work. Sighing, she folded and sealed the letter. It was possible that this would be her final plea to Mary for her life, asserting that she had played no part in the plot against the Queen and remained a faithful servant. She again requested that she be allowed an audience with Mary, to answer for herself the charges and accusations levelled at her by the Privy Council. Wyatt had, it appeared, remained faithful, and she felt such pity for the man after hearing that on the scaffold his final words had been to further state publicly that she had played no part in his plotting,

...neither they nor any other now yonder endurance was privy to any rising before I began, as I have declared to the Queen's Council...

She wondered at what cost those words had been bought.

The gaolers had a stark sense of humour and placed her in the rooms occupied by her mother before her lethal appointment with the blade. When she had landed from the boat, her hand had instinctively sought Kate's, and it was only when she realised that she was finally alone that her resolve had almost left her. How she had managed to remain upright, walking to what she felt was her death, she didn't know.

Elizabeth's pleas from the Tower lay on a table, discarded by Mary after she had briefly read the content. Bishop Gardiner stood fidgeting in front of the Queen.

"We understand well the thrust of your accusations against Elizabeth, my lord bishop, but we wonder if she does have a good reason for complaint. So far, I have heard little in the way of substantial evidence against her. Despite assurances, Wyatt went, did he not, to his death, denying her involvement?" Mary said curtly.

"He did indeed. But, Your Majesty, we did have good reason..." Mary's raised hand stopped his words.

"Yes, we do understand your reasons, but it does not deny that you cannot give us a case against her, can you?" Mary paused, and the Bishop opened his palms, accepting the truth of her words. "Are we to assume, then, that there is a possibility that in this instance Elizabeth may have no case to answer?"

"Your Majesty, the Privy Council wishes to question Elizabeth again. Maybe then..."

"My lord bishop," she interrupted, "have you not already questioned her and gained nothing? Why again? We will not be made to look a fool in this matter. Renard indicates that you prolong this because you wish to keep her heir to the throne, and we do most fervently hope that is not the Council's intention. We want a final answer. What are we to think," Mary's withered hand snaked out and retrieved Elizabeth's letter, "when we receive communications like this? You are making fools of yourselves. You may have one more interview with the lady, and then we will know your case if there is one to answer."

His appearance was a poor one, and it was with some difficulty that he persuaded John Somer's steward to inform his master that he wished to see him. It was only his insistent manner and accented speech that finally persuaded the man to take the message to his master that there was a visitor by the name of Fitzwarren begging for an audience.

Richard did not have long to wait, and found himself being led to Somer's study soon after he had arrived.

"Good God, man! What happened to you?" Somer said, taking in the dishevelled image of the man before him.

Richard, filthy, wrapped in a coarse homespun cloak lined with a malodorous sheepskin, stared back evenly at Somer. "Quite a lot," he replied as his eyes wandered to the chair at the end of the desk.

"Of course, sit. You look terrible." Somer dragged the chair forward and watched as Richard dropped heavily into it. "There must be a matter of some urgency you wish to talk about if you have arrived like this?"

Richard nodded and swallowed hard before he began. "There is," he reached inside the cloak for a small bag slung over his shoulder, wincing at the pain the movement caused.

Somer, confused, came forward. "Please let me help you."

Richard nodded and dropped back in the chair. Somer opened the cloak and then the leather bag that he found there. He pulled out the folded sheet, but rather than opening it, he held it out for Richard to take. "Is this what you wanted?"

"Yes, thank you," Richard's voice was hoarse and strained.

Somer cast his eyes around the room. Finding what he wanted, he rapidly filled a glass with wine and held it out. "Here, drink this."

Richard accepted the glass, raising it to his lips, his hand shaking. Somer waited patiently for him to speak. The glass empty Richard leant forward to place it on the desk, his judgement wrong, the glass tipped off the edge of the wood when his fumbling hand released it. Somer caught the glass and pushed it onto the safety of the table.

Richard swallowed and dropped back again in the chair. "Is Elizabeth still in the Tower?"

"Yes, yes, she is. She has been questioned by the Privy Council about her complicity in Wyatt's rebellion," Somer supplied quickly.

"Will they release her?" Richard asked.

Somer looked thoughtful. "There is limited evidence against her. Everythin is circumstantial, however there is a lot of it and, of course, the lady had a lot to gain if Wyatt was successful."

"That didn't answer my question," Richard said quietly.

Somer held Richard's eyes as he replied. "No, I do not believe they will release her."

Richard let out a long breath, and his eyes closed.

"Richard!" Somer sounded alarmed. "Are you unwell?"

Suddenly, the dark eyes snapped back open. "Do you believe they will hold her in the Tower, or press for an execution?"

Somer didn't lie. "There are many on the Privy Council who will press for a permanent solution, and Elizabeth's execution would secure Mary's throne."

Richard nodded, his eyes dropped to the paper in his hand. His voice shaking, he said, "Then read this."

Richard's hand did not move. It remained in his lap; the paper held between thumb and forefinger. Somer reached down and slid it from his hold. Fishing about on his desk, he produced a pair of spectacles and, moving an oil lamp closer, he read the script on the sheet. When he had finished, his mouth open in shock, he looked up and met Richard's dark grey eyes, watching him intently.

"If the lady is not released, then that will be made public," was all Richard said.

Somer looked from the paper to Richard and back again. "Who would do this? Who? And where did this come from?"

"I have nearly died to bring you that, and news of the threat," Richard's voice was quiet.

"What is to say that if the Privy Council release Elizabeth that this will not be made public anyway?" Somer asked.

"You have my word,"

Somer looked at him, his expression hard. "Is this your doing?"

Richard remained silent, matching Somer's stare.

"I think you have shown me your hand," Somer said. "If I burn this and call for my steward I think I could be fairly sure that there will be no revelation. Am I right?"

Richard still did not reply.

Somer let out a long breath. Taking his spectacles from his nose he discarded them on his desk. "Is this the only copy?"

Then, when he still did not receive a response, Somer asked again, "Is it?"

Richard's attention was revived, and he seemed to arrive at a decision. "Yes."

"Very well," Somer replied, his voice serious. "I understand what you have entrusted me with."

"I need to go. If I could borrow a horse, I would be in your debt," Richard said, moving his hands to the arms of the chair and preparing to rise.

"Good Lord man, you're in no fit state to go anywhere," Somer said, shock in his voice.

"A horse please, I will return it. I need to get back to my brother," Richard continued as he rose from the chair.

"Your brother can wait," Somer said, moving towards Richard, who swayed on unsteady legs.

"No, no he won't. I need to get back to him," Richard wondered for a moment if Somer had closed the shutters on the window. Why else had the room grown so suddenly dark?

Somer let out an alarmed exclamation as the man before him collapsed in a heap on the carpet in his study.

It took an hour for Somer to supervise the removal of the unconscious man to one of the vacant rooms in his house and send a servant to summon his physician. After this, he returned to his study and smoothed flat the paper Richard had given him. Marked with age, creased and now somewhat stained with the blood of the messenger, it was a deposition that he knew could never be made public. Signed by one of Katherine of Aragon's ladies-in-waiting, it confirmed that Katherine had suffered an early miscarriage. The unfortunate event, however, had not occurred whilst she had been wed to Henry, it was dated to the time when she had been married to Henry's brother, Arthur. Henry had married his dead brother's wife, claiming that Arthur had never consummated the marriage. What Somer held in his hands showed that it certainly had been, and Henry's marriage to Katherine should never had taken place. Quite simply, it made Mary Tudor illegitimate.

Where Richard had got it from, he did not know. After his physician had left, Somer had entered the room where the injured man slept. His questions were not going to be answered anytime soon. The inert form in the bed was deep in a laudanum induced sleep.

The servant heard the movement from the truckle bed in the corner as the man rolled over and he knew he was awake then. He'd been given instructions by his master and hastily went in search of him.

"What day is it?" Richard's voice was weak and broke as he tried to form the words.

"It's a Tuesday... not that that will be much good to you." Somer chuckled.

"Tuesday... that means I've been here for nearly a week." Richard said in a hoarse rasp.

"Like I said, that fact of a Tuesday would be no good to you, lad; you've been there for nearly three. And as likely to stop there, another couple I would guess," Somer said. "God has saved you. He didn't have to, but he most assuredly did."

"So long... but it can't..."

"It was, and it is. You'd a bad wound, and you bled a lot. I thought we'd be digging a grave for you the next morning I surely did, or at least the morning after. I prayed for your soul when I saw that there was nothing else that could be done."

"A drink..." Richard's voice managed.

Somer poured one from the pitcher on the table and handed it to Richard. A hand behind his head, he helped him raise himself so he could sip from the cup. Sweat beaded on his forehead and he fell back, spent by the effort of sitting up.

Richard's eye's focused finally on Somer's face, and he became aware of who he was talking to. He spoke only one word, but it was filled with foreboding. "Elizabeth?"

Somer smiled and lay a hand on his arm. "She has been released from the Tower."

Richard closed his eyes and let out a long sigh of relief. "Is she safe?"

"She is. Mary released her from The Tower and she has returned to Durham Place," Somer reassured, then added. "You have served the lady well. I am sure you have her gratitude."

"I need to return North, my brother. He needs me," Richard said.

"I'm sure he does. He is at Burton. I took the liberty of making enquiries on your behalf. It seems he benefited from a deal with the Sheriff and has control of the manor and men. From what I have been told, he is an able commander and both he and the manor are secure. You have no need to worry on that account at the moment. When you are well enough, I will help you leave London, but for the moment it seems I have the pleasure of your company as my guest."

Richard smiled. "I am indebted to you, sir." It was more than he could have hoped for.

Both Jack and Elizabeth were safe.

Jack had held onto Burton, and with Dan at his side, Richard was sure he would have all the help and guidance he needed. Richard could not return there just yet. There was still a charge of treason hanging over his head. But treason was a charge that very much depended upon your point of view, and if his luck continued, then the next monarch might just forgive him. He would send word to Jack and take himself to Holland or Ireland, it mattered little where. Richard had every faith that Jack would be able to hold Burton for him until he returned.

Catherine, bless the lass, was with Jack. The girl had more courage than a lion, and he knew he owed her his life. He could trust Jack with her safety. He knew he could rely on his brother to make sure she came to no harm. Then, when times were more favourable, he could make amends and help to restore her to her home.

Elizabeth, thankfully, back at Durham Place, would be with her own household and have the comfort and support of Kate. The journey had been a difficult one, but the outcome had been worth it. It was almost beyond belief that all those he cared about still had both their lives and liberty. Elizabeth was safe and Catherine, the men, and Burton were now in his brother's more than capable hands.

Richard closed his eyes. For once there was no reason to worry, and sleep came easily.

Extract from the next book in the series

A Queen's Traitor

'Jack is leaving.'

It was known by a few, but rumour soon courted everyone's ears, until they all were aware that they were about to be abandoned, leaderless. Some cared, some sneered, some worried about the future, but most were indifferent.

Since Richard's death, Jack had existed in a state of melancholy. His nerves were raw; a passionate and pleasant nature had now twisted into a temper fuelled with incoherent rage. His was a palpable grief, worsened by the feeling of utter dejection that had been his brother's final gift. That he had left Jack, and the world, for another, was too abhorrent for him to consider. Whilst the men at Burton felt leaderless and looked to the future with concern, Jack was adrift. The only person who could have reached out to still his destructive passage was dead. Jack listened to no-one.

'Jack is going today.'

It was said amongst the men, quietly, and they considered the news. Would he pay them? Would he come back? Would he say anything at all? They pressed the only person who had any link at all with Jack, and they hoped for some answers. Dan, however, was reluctant to face him again. He was only too well aware of his state of mind and didn't at all relish yet another confrontation. He'd tried; there was little more he could do. But they pressed him further, and eventually he gave in and went in search of Jack.

He knocked, opened the door, and received the reply he expected. "Get out."

Breathing deeply, Dan squared his shoulders and strode into the room with purpose.

"Not this time, Jack. The men have sent me. They have a right to know what is going to happen," he said bluntly.

Jack sat in the window embrasure in his room, ignoring him, his eyes unfocussed, lost in the distance. He didn't want to talk to Dan or to anyone.

"You need to let them know what we are going to do. You can't sit in here forever." Dan crossed the room and placed a hard, sinewy grip on Jack's shoulder, forcing him to look at him. This time, he'd get an answer.

Jack twisted away. Springing to his feet, he faced Dan; his eyes cold and mouth set in a hard line. "Get out."

"You owe them an answer Jack, you know you do." Dan was prepared for a fight now and watched the other man carefully.

"I don't have the contacts Richard had. What do you want me to do?" Jack was breathing deeply. "Just get out."

"Not this time. There must be something you can do? You can't just throw it all away for nothing!" Dan argued, keeping his eyes firmly on Jack. He could sense that the man's temper was about to break.

"If we stay, they will drag us before the next Assize as sure as anything: we were Richard's men. He was a bloody traitor Dan, a traitor to the Crown! Like it or not, he was, and we are tarred with it as well. Do you really think they are going to leave a little nest of treasonous sinners to their own devices? Really?" Jack was shouting now.

"Well, you'll just have to think of something," Dan was not having any of it, his next words adding to Jack's misery, "The Master would have."

They were merely words, but the blow they delivered was a physical one. "Christ Dan," Jack had gone pale, "I'm not him, am I? As you keep reminding me. I don't have his connections, I was not privy to his thoughts and I don't know what he would have done any more than you do. I am going to get my backside out of here before it gets dragged out for me and I get my neck stretched. And if you don't want to end up swinging from a rope, you'll do the bloody same."

"He left you all this," Dan flung his arms wide, "you can't just throw it all away for nothing."

Jack's temper snapped. A moment later he had a poniard in his hand, "He threw it away. He didn't care what happened to any of this, or any of us."

Dan's eyes moved between the blade and Jack's face, and he took a precautionary step back before he deliberately delivered the words he knew Jack didn't want to hear. "He didn't care about you? Is that what you think?"

The blade was still, July sun sparking from the tempered steel.

"He cared for her more than any of us. More even, than he cared for himself," Jack swallowed hard. He'd not meant to vocalise that thought.

"He cared more for her than for you, that's the crux of it isn't it?" Dan accused.

Jack didn't reply: faced with the truth he couldn't.

"Put that away Jack, for God's sake, there's been enough bloodshed already. You need to decide what we are going to do next," Dan advised. He watched Jack's face and saw the anger turning to pain. A moment later, Jack slammed the knife back into its sheath.

"Damn you, I'm leaving here. I'll not stay for more of this. Get out of my way," raged Jack, his voice hoarse.

"You can't just leave!" Dan continued to argue, bringing the argument right back to the start again.

"Just watch me, you can stop here and do what the hell you like." Blood was pounding in his head, his throat was tight, he knew he couldn't take any more of this, and, as it was, his decision had been made for him when Mat suddenly burst through the door.

"There are three men here from Lincoln," Mat glanced between the two men. He could sense the tension in the room, "they want you, Jack."

"Are they at the gates?" Dan questioned, his attention drawn by necessity to the newcomer.

"No, they are in the hall," Mat blurted, still holding the door open behind him.

"What!" Jack exclaimed in disbelief, pausing in the act of reaching for his sword belt. "When did we stop bothering with closed gates?"

"Sorry, the men didn't think," Mat apologised.

Jack swore this was his fault. The gates would never have been left to stand open while Richard was alive. The leather belt was tight, he rammed a short blade into a wrist guard and pulled his sleeve back down to conceal it.

It seemed an end had come, and Jack welcomed it. "Right then, shall we greet our guests?" Jack squared his shoulders and pushed brutally past Mat and Dan, leaving them to catch up with him. It was a short corridor that led onto the open stairs to the hall. He dropped down the steps easily, and as Mat had said, there were indeed three of them watching his approach carefully.

Jack smiled broadly. "Gentlemen, how can I help?"

"I'm Nicholas Norton. We've come from the Sheriff, he'd like for you to come with us," it was the tallest man who spoke. His face was impassive and his voice calm, which was at odds with the nervous faces of his companions.

"That's good," Jack replied quickly, still smiling. "I had a mind to see Sir Ayscough as it happens." Then, calling over his shoulder, "Dan, get my horse ready."

"We can ride to Lincoln together," Norton suggested. He had been told that he'd know Jack Fitzwarren when he found him, and they had not been wrong. The man's hair marked him out. Bright burnished yellow, falling to his shoulders, it framed a fair-skinned face with ice cold blue eyes. Ayscough had branded the man a fool. Norton, looking at Jack Fitzwarren, doubted very much that this was the case. Confident, well built, and wearing a sword-belt that spoke of use; Norton knew he should not underestimate the man.

The incumbent Sheriff of Lincoln was one Sir Francis Ayscough. Jack had already met him when he had negotiated the deal to trade his brother for the manor and the liberty of himself and the men. Ayscough had made promises that Jack could retain Burton, but he knew perfectly well that this was likely to be reneged upon.

Had he known it, Ayscough actually owned land that bordered onto the woodland surrounding the small manor at Burton, and he had every intention of extending his Lincolnshire landholding. With Jack gone, he could easily, and legally, disperse his men to procure the place for himself. What information he had about Jack came mainly from Robert, and he cast the man as a simpleton who had inherited Burton upon the death of Richard: he seemed to think the man had neither wit nor sense. So it had been with little worry that Ayscough had sent three of his men to summon Jack to his office in Lincoln.

'Think! Damn you'. Jack silently cursed himself. It was only half an hour's ride to Lincoln and once there, he knew he'd lose his liberty or worse. If he had acted against Ayscough's men at Burton, every one of his men there would have been branded with the crime. At least this way there would only be himself, and Jack cared little anymore. Analysing it, he supposed he would prefer a quicker end, rather than a filthy one entombed in Lincoln's gaol until the day arrived to have his death delivered at the end of a choking rope.

There were three of them, and all looked more than capable. These were poor odds, but Jack was going to take them. He drew his horse a pace or so back, so she neared the back of the pack: he knew there was a meadow on the left soon and a break in the trees. There was little chance he could outrun Ayscough's men, but if he could put a little space between them, he could turn back and bring the fight to them on his own terms. At the moment, he was too close: if he drew his sword now, he would easily be hacked from his mount.

At this point, the road to Lincoln was still enclosed on both sides by trees, and the three riders waiting impatiently on the road ahead were obscured from view until Jack rode around the bend. One of Ayscough's men riding on the outside saw them first and stiffened in the saddle, shouting, "This looks like trouble."

Trouble it was. Dan, Mat and Froggy Tate sat astride sweating horses blocking the road. Jack could not hide his smile. The officer who had spoken wheeled his horse round to cut Jack off from his men. The other two closed ranks as well. There was a resonating hiss as the men drew their swords. Jack also had steel in his hand, but his route was blocked.

"What do we do?" Mat asked, holding his horse next to Dan's. "If we ride in, they'll kill him."

"And if we don't, they will anyway," Dan shot back. "Jack can look after himself. He'll have to, come on." He pressed his heels into the horse's side and asked the panting mare for one last short gallop.

They saw them coming, and it split the group. Nicholas Norton, the nearest to Jack, hauled on his reins, pulling his mount next to Jack. Jack heeled the mare round. The reaction was instinctive. She spun and her hindquarters crashed into the side of the other horse, momentarily pinning Norton's leg between the two horses. It was long enough for Jack to grab a handful of the man's jacket.

Pushing his horse further back, he sought to pull him from his saddle. If the other rider's horse had not at that moment reared, he would have succeeded. Unseated from the vertical horse, and dragged as well by the man behind him, Norton cannoned into Jack, dismounting them both. Training kept both men's blades in their hands as they fell.

"Jesus." Jack swore. As he landed heavily on his left shoulder, his right leg took a glancing blow from one of his mare's rear hooves as she swung to bite the rearing horse. In the moment of the fight, his mind ignored the pain. Before he had stopped falling, he was already trying to get to his feet. His assailant fared little better and rolled over twice from the force of the fall. Jack was righted and on his feet a second before him.

Jack offered Norton no quarter, his blade aimed to kill, the leading edge set on a path for the other's head. A defensive up thrust forced it away, the lethal blade only inches above the exposed head. Breathing hard, and using his body's weight to add speed to the sword, the point of the other's weapon made for Jack's exposed chest. Jack easily forced the blade away, but as he stepped back, his right foot found a hole in the road. His balance was hopelessly lost.

Nicholas Norton sneered and took the opportunity he had been given, all of his strength behind a killing blow aimed at Jack's exposed left side. To stop the blade, Jack was forced to hold his sword level, using it two-handed to block the attack. The impact forced his own blade to slice into his left hand, where it held the edge.

But it gave him an opening. For a moment his Norton's sword was stopped dead, all the man's weight held on Jack's blade. Removing the support meant it was Norton's turn to stagger.

Printed in Great Britain
by Amazon

53945877R00258